The Valley of the Shadow

Robert Burslem

COPYRIGHT

Robert Burslem
rburslem@fsmail.net
2 Castle Park Road
Sandycove
County Dublin
Republic of Ireland

Dedication

To

Maureen

This book could not have been completed without her constant help

and encouragement.

And

To all good people of Africa.

Preface

This is a novel, a fictional story, but it is as close to fact as I dare make it. Just about all the events described really happened in one way or another. Historical characters appear from time to time in their correct context although their 'conversations' and 'actions' are obviously created by me on the basis that this is what they might have said and done given the eventual outcome of events. The political background is correct, at least from my perspective. My fictional characters are based on the personalities of people I have known, some of whom I would like to consider as friends (the nice ones). The names of certain places and individuals have been changed. Notwithstanding any of the above I do not want to undersell the contribution of my imagination to this tale.

There is no single facet to conflict. War is multi dimensional, as well as the political and economic aspects, personality, ambition, emotion and even love, have their contributions to make to the whole. To understand all it is necessary to consider all.

Firstly I hope this is a good story that you enjoy but I also sincerely hope you get more than that from the words. The story of Africa is a dark one yet I remain optimistic.

Robert Burslem
Portugal
March 2012

TABLE OF CONTENTS

Prologue

Stornoway, Western Isles 1955

The sheltered lee of the craggy outcrop was his secret sanctuary. Sometimes it seemed to the child that Nature rationed his time there. Too often rolling mists shrouded the slopes. Only when there was wind could he huddle, protected by the rock and look down the hillside to the grey sea. For hours he would stare into the distance, taking his mood from the waters. He would unleash his imagination and explore lands far beyond the Western Isles. But the ancient rock and pounding waters also taught the unwitting child a subliminal lesson. The hours of solitude, staring and thinking gradually gave him the ability to enjoy his own company and gave him the inward strength to be alone.

The child would never know the full story; that his parents had moved to Stornoway in 1937, exiled from their Highland community, victims of Clan rivalries and an unyielding Presbyterian Church that imposed an impossible moral burden. He would not know that his father, Angus Murdoch endowed Janet McDonald with child outside the bonds of matrimony and that both Murdoch and McDonald families were shamed. Marriage could not rectify the sin or earn forgiveness. Ostracised in their own communities they had moved to the Western Isles. They'd rented a Croft that could hardly support a family. Angus had supplemented his income by working at the fishery in Stornoway and settled into a life of penance. Some said it was God's revenge that the child was stillborn, others attributed it to the fact that the young couple could not afford a doctor.

The moral fibre of the tight knit community in Stornoway was no less strong than that of the Highlands. Angus and Janet would never belong and would always be considered as outsiders.

For years that followed their marriage was as barren as the hillside they farmed. It was not until 1948 that Janet produced her second and last child, a healthy boy. Even in his formative years he bore the physical characteristics that would dominate his adulthood. There was a rugged handsomeness in his features, a proud chiselled face with high intelligent brow, topped with a shock of wiry blond hair that might have appeared amusing if it were not for the almost permanent serious expression he wore. His tall body carried no excess. One might have been excused for thinking that this was due to the poor diet of a 50's child. But even when better fare was plentiful he never gained. His lanky proportions were preordained at birth.

Austerity was normal to the child, surplus a rarity. This was also true of the relationship with his father. Angus was dutiful to his son. In return the child respected his father but they remained strangers. The relationship was utilitarian. No pretence was made that son should follow father. It was clear that the child would have to make his own way in the world. The Croft would never support a family. When Angus and Janet were finished the Croft would become another anonymous group of cold abandoned buildings on a remote Scottish hillside. Such was the beginning of Duncan Murdoch.

Moscow 1966

"I'm twice as productive as Winston Churchill!" Comrade Molenski slapped the conference table with his fat hand. "Do you know why I'm twice as good as that pig?"

Sergi smiled. Feigning thought he shook his head. Even if he knew the answer he was smart enough to realise it would not be good to spoil his boss's punch line.

"No Comrade, I don't."

"Well," said Molenski puffing out his chest, "Mr Churchill was a busy man during the war. Because of this he only ever let his subordinates give written reports on one side of paper. Myself however, although just as busy, allow you to give me reports on two sides of paper. So I'm twice as productive. Eh!"

Comrade Molenski leaned back in his giant padded swivel chair and laughed at his own joke. Sergi joined in the laughter doing his best to make his mirth look unforced. He sensed Comrade Molenski was testing him.

There was just the two of them in the overheated, oversized and over furnished Kremlin office. For Sergi it was a risky gamble. If he succeeded at this meeting it would be a boost for his career, if he failed the opposite. He waited nervously.

Comrade Alexia Molenski had two jobs. First he was a general of the Red Army. This was his power base. The unification of that power with total loyalty to his mentor secured his second and more important position as a permanent Member of the Politburo of the Union of Soviet Socialist Republics. His route to the Supreme Soviet had been unusual. He did not have the normal political background. In 1942 he was a young officer in the rifle corps of the First Ukrainian Army. His peasant upbringing had made him more cynical than ambitious and he possessed the ability to overcome adversity with coarse humour. But he was not overtly ambitious. It was because Alexia Molenski apparently lacked political ambition that he came to the notice of an ascending Party member, Nikita Khrushchev. Khrushchev picked Molenski as his personal adjutant because he was not going to be a threat. In the winter of 1942/3 Molenski served Nikita Khrushchev when he was the Political Commissar for the besieged city of Stalingrad. The two were confined together. For months they fought their war from a bunker on the banks of the freezing River Volga. Their lives were constantly threatened from a rain of German shells. In such life threatening depravation men come to form a bond and learn to recognise those they can rely on.

Khrushchev was possessed and ruthless. He received the credit for maintaining the patriotic fervour that made men fight like demons. In turn Khrushchev recognised the loyalty and strength of men like Alexia Molenski. After the War Khrushchev needed loyal supporters high up in the Red Army. For this reason he used his influence to ensure that Alexia Molenski progressed through the military ranks as fast as he himself climbed the slippery slope of politics. When Stalin died in 1953 Khrushchev was ready. A deft political player he had garnered sufficient support. He was elected Party Chairman and successor to Uncle Joe Stalin. Quickly he needed to consolidate his position by packing the Politburo with trusted followers. Comrade Molenski's time had come.

To many he appeared a dimwit. Molenski would do nothing to dispel that belief. But in reality he possessed a natural political intuition and a sense of mischief. He became a constant thorn in the side of the US during the Cold War. He had an eye for an opportunity and the astuteness to side step an issue when it became threatening. Above all he had a well developed sense of self-preservation. In this respect he was a dangerous man to deal with.

"Enough of the fun, to business, your report. Read it to me, slowly." Molenski had already read the report but he wanted to study the man in front of him. He had to decide was he very smart or very stupid. For sure he did not occupy any of the middle ground.

Sergi Andropov looked younger than his 30 years. He appeared more like a student than a KGB Agent. He flouted swept back blond hair and blue eyes behind steel rimmed glasses. He stood out. This itself was unusual in a system where most people sought security in mediocrity. His work was good and he had confidence. Most young people kept their head down and hoped to progress by small increments but not Sergi. He did not hide his ambition.

Comrade Molenski mused to himself, "He's a risk taker all right. If he has good judgement he will climb the hierarchy, if his judgement is bad he will end up in Siberia. Either way he is going far." Molenski chuckled at his second joke of the day.

Sergi, unaware of Comrade Molenski's thoughts straightened his back and began to read aloud.

"Abstract of Memorandum, To: Comrade Molenski, Chairman,

*Committee for International Policy, From: Lubianka International Research
Unit. Area: Southern Africa, Subject: Strategic Opportunity, Date 23rd
March 1966, Sources.........."*
> *Molenski broke in, "Just read the substance, leave the rest."*
> *"Yes Comrade.*

*Our long-term policy for the region of southern Africa has been to
encourage independence movements wherever they occur with the aim of
isolating South Africa and ultimately securing that country's independence
but within the Soviet sphere of influence. We are currently supporting
independence movements in Angola, Namibia and Mozambique. We expect
success in these countries within ten years. Countries already independent
in the region are Botswana, Zambia and Tanzania.*

*Until recently there has been no radical opposition in Rhodesia.
However on the 11th November 1965 the Colonial Government of Rhodesia
declared itself independent from Great Britain. Great Britain does not
possess the political will to suppress the rebels militarily. Instead they want
the United Nations to impose sanctions on the country.*

*Our sources in the United States indicate that The White House
whilst outwardly supporting their British allies are really opposed to the
imposition of sanctions. The grounds for their objection are the dependency
of US industry on certain minerals from Rhodesia, primarily chromium. The
situation is compounded for the Americans in that their own supplies are
failing not only in quantity but also quality. Chromium is an important
strategic material. As we in The USSR have ample supplies of our own it
would appear that the United States and its allies could become exposed.*

*We can conclude that Rhodesia has become a strategically important
country that could present us with an opportunity to threaten the economies
of our enemies. If we can gain control of Rhodesia we could expect to cause
major problems for western industry or at a minimum be able to influence
the world price for commodities to our own benefit.*

*Furthermore the political situation has moved in our favour. The
Rhodesian government has banned the only notable black African political
party, ZAPU. Tentative contacts have been made and they are receptive to
our overtures. My recommendation is that we develop and secure our
relationship with the leader of ZAPU, Joshua Nkomo who is bound to
become the first black leader of Rhodesia.*

That concludes the report Comrade."
*Sergi looked up for the first time and saw Molenski reclining in his
chair, arms folded across his ample stomach, eyes closed. For a moment he
thought the Chief might be asleep. But without opening his eyes he spoke.*

"What hard evidence do you have that the Americans are really concerned?"

"In the United Nations the Americans agreed to implement sanctions against Rhodesia but the Bill they put before their Congress for ratification had been changed. It contained the so-called Byrd Amendment, which excludes chrome and other minerals from the sanctions. This is clear evidence of their concern. They also refused to join the British in a sea blockade of Southern African ports in support of sanctions."

"Good," said Molenski. "Now what about this Nkomo? Is he reliable?"

"He has the universal following of his people and is known throughout the country as 'Father'. He is an intelligent man, a leader and organiser. The whites are scared of him. The Party leadership is already in exile in neighbouring Zambia. They accept that the route to power will be an armed struggle. But they need a sponsor."

"The only concern is a minor one," Sergi continued, "Nkomo has grown literally fat in his position. He shows signs of decadency and may be unwilling to make personal sacrifices. But this is not unusual in African leaders."

"You sound confident. Do you have no worries?"

Sergi thought for a moment. Should he mention the latest intelligence that had come in after he had written his report, the news that there had been a split in Nkomo's Party? The reports were disconcerting but unconfirmed. "No Comrade, I have no worries."

"So you are telling me that Rhodesia will eventually fall to black power and that the new leader will be Nkomo. You also say we can influence him if we support his war. Also the Americans have, what you say, an Achilles Foot with chromium?"

Sergi wondered if he should correct his superior. He decided against it.

"I would use almost the same words myself," he replied. "We even know the name that Nkomo will give to his new country. It will be Zimbabwe."

Molenski smiled. "I hope you have chosen well Andropov. You may proceed. This project will be your responsibility. Take the situation to the next stage. Keep me informed."

Sergi fought to suppress his joy. "Thank you Comrade Molenski."

"Tell Olga to make sure I am not disturbed." He swivelled his chair towards the window, dismissing his junior.

Sergi thought Molenski was most probably asleep before he had finished passing the message to Olga. That didn't bother him. He had what he wanted: his own war.

The Ottrel

Aden, July 1967

Duncan looked through the open window. The sky was cloudless and the sun at its zenith. Over the rooftops he watched an Arab dhow in the bay as it tacked towards the harbour, its lateen sail gasping for a whiff of hot desert air. Along the shore a string of pelicans effortlessly glided, skimming the water's surface. Four crisp shots somewhere in the distance broke the serenity of the scene.

"Move away from the window you dimshit," barked the Corporal.

Without a word Duncan dropped to the floor and leaned against a kitbag, cradling his FN rifle. Minutes passed. None of the eight-man squad said anything as tension built on the top floor of the commandeered building that served as Company HQ. In the next room a radio operator spoke unintelligible words into his mouthpiece.

Duncan closed his eyes, remembering seven days ago when they'd boarded the chartered Tri-Star planes at Gatwick. He was in the lead plane with 'B' Company. They'd joked about going on holiday, laughing about forgetting their buckets and spades. They'd been in the air for an hour when the CO came on the PA. Lt Col Mitchell's reputation for directness was well established in the regiment.

"Men," he started in an accent that had been part anglicised at Sandhurst but which retained its Scottish grittiness. "As you know our task was to take over from the Cheshire's for a spot of garrison duty. Unfortunately there has been a change of plan. It appears the native police have seen fit to exploit the confusion of regimental changeover and decided to create some mayhem. They have mutinied and taken over the Crater District. The result is the Cheshire's have lost our billets for us. This is of course unacceptable.

So on reaching Aden we will have a short rest before advancing from the airport to our accommodation in the Crater District on foot with fixed bayonets. We will start as we mean to go on."

The change in mood was instant. Duncan felt a shiver of

nervousness deep inside but drew courage from Sergeant Scobie and the other seasoned soldiers, veterans of the Malaya campaign.

"Finally, men," continued Lt Col Mitchell, "remember if you're soft in the beginning they will sense weakness and you will lose the initiative. Hard and quick is the motto. It will make it easier in the long run. Let them know who's boss."

When Mitchell finished a buzz of anticipation grew within the cabin. Sergeant Jim Scobie, sitting next to Duncan, remained calm. He leaned towards Duncan.

"Looks like you'll see your first action a bit sooner than expected. Nervous?"

"A little, Sarge," was Duncan Murdoch's honest reply to his mentor and protector.

"I've always looked after you haven't I?" said Scobie.

"Yes Sergeant."

"Well nothing has changed. Don't worry. You'll be fine".

Duncan relaxed. He trusted Jim Scobie.

Lt Col Mitchell was true to his word. Within an hour of landing Duncan watched the first reconnaissance patrol leave the airport. Two hours later "A" Company began its probe in force. First reports were that the native police disappeared into the ether as soon as bullets started flying. Duncan heard that by dusk 'A' Company had penetrated the walled citadel and was bedding down for the night in the streets. Before dawn 'B' Company had received orders. Duncan advanced with his troop and passed through 'A' Company to take the lead.

Remnants of the native police barricaded themselves in the police compound. Duncan watched as two grenades were thrown over the wall. It was enough. A white flag appeared at the gate. Out came the renegades, two abreast, hands raised, hungry, having made the unfortunate mistake of locking themselves in the compound without supplies.

But the police mutiny had set off others. News of the first action came mid-morning. This time it was communist insurgents, embedded in the population, beginning to put up resistance, ambushing and sniping at isolated patrols. Word came through that Lt Col Mitchell was making 'routing them out' a priority. Nobody stood on etiquette. Duncan's squad didn't knock at doors or wait for an invitation before entering buildings. Duncan learnt firsthand about shock tactics and the effect that facing the wrong end of a

British Army Service Revolver had on people's tongues. The Regiment ran riot. Everybody knew the press were around but nobody cared. Neither Duncan nor his unit were aware that by day three of the operation the Daily Mirror had coined the name the whole media was to adopt. Everybody in the UK soon knew that 'Mad Mitch' of the Argyle and Sutherland Highlanders had arrived in Aden.

The crackle of static from the radio room increased and urgent voices roused Duncan from his thoughts. Instinct made the rest of the men stir. They began pulling on their webbing and checking weapons. Suddenly the Lieutenant appeared in the doorway shouting.

"Move your arses. Western Patrol ambushed and split. Man down. Get over to the Mosque Square. Return fire. Extradite the patrol if possible. If not form a defensive position till relieved by Lieutenant Cameron from Battalion HQ. Go!"

Boots clattered on wooden stairs. Duncan pulled himself on to the back of the first open Land Rover in the courtyard. The engine barked into life. The vehicle jerked forward. He jarred his back on the metal seat. Duncan watched the others as they pulled back the bolts on their FN's and pushed a round into the chamber. He followed suit. The streets were quiet. They always were at the hottest part of the day. The hard suspension of the vehicle gave no comfort as the Land Rover wove through the narrow cobbled streets. It would be impossible to take an accurate shot on the move so Duncan flicked the lever on his rifle to automatic. If he saw anybody suspicious he would let the whole magazine go in the general direction. He knew the labyrinth of streets was a bad place to get ambushed. The terrain favoured the enemy.

The Land Rovers burst into the square. In front was the grandiose dome of the mosque, a building of opulence that was in stark contrast to the rest of the buildings in the Crater. To the right stood the pencil thin minaret, the tower from which the faithful were called to pray five times a day. Rumour had it that Mitchell had warned the Mullah. "One sniper uses the minaret and the minaret becomes horizontal". No sniper had used the minaret from then on, confirmation that the Mullah had lied when he said he had no influence over the insurgents.

In the middle of the square was the fountain, intricate and ornate. Water bubbled from the centrepiece and ran down channels to the circular trough where the faithful ceremonially washed in running water before praying.

The Corporal pointed at the fountain. Cowering under its protecting overhang were two khaki clad British soldiers.

Born in another place Ahmed Kahn might have been studying to be a doctor or lawyer. Unfortunately the harsh desert interior of Yemen offered limited opportunities for the intelligent and quick witted. He could have taken the way of Allah and would have made a good Mullah. But the relentless rote learning of the verses of the Koran was not stimulating enough for him. Instead his mind became fertile ground for those that preached that all ills were the fault of the colonial oppressors. But like most members of the Yemen Socialist Liberation Army he was attracted to communism not for the people but for himself. He wanted to be a leader in his country once the Colonialists had been expelled. Now they were on the cusp of success. The old guard was tottering and just needed a final push.

He peered over the low parapet on the roof. Across the square he could see the two soldiers still hiding behind the fountain. He worked his way across the roof looking into the side street below. He saw the upturned cart and behind it the tell-tale whip aerial of the soldier's radio.

Ahmed turned and sat with his back to the parapet. He spoke quietly.

"Mohamed, Yousif. You two stay here as long as you can. If the soldiers at the fountain move shoot at them. You must also watch the ones behind the cart. If they try to break out throw a grenade. I will go back for the one who is alone, the wounded one. When you hear my shots you can make your escape, God willing."

"Allah Akbar", both men replied in unison.

Ahmed moved off in search of his quarry.

A few moments later Mohamed looked over the square and saw the Land Rovers drive over to the fountain. He looked to Yousif. Without word they gathered their weapons and slipped away.

The two Land Rovers made an imperfect triangle with the fountain. The troop dismounted and took covering positions behind

---

4

their vehicles. The Corporal shouted at the two cowering soldiers.

"You can come out now, the cavalry's here. Tell me what happened."

The younger one spoke. "We was in single file coming to the square from that tiny alley over there."

The soldier pointed to a narrow entry midway along the side of the square facing the mosque. "The Sarge was bringing up the rear. We was in front of him. The rest of the patrol was a few yards ahead again, just coming into the square. Then somebody lobbed a grenade at us, out of nowhere. It landed between us and the Sarge. We ran forward and ducked into a doorway before it went off. We didn't see much then. Somebody started shooting and the Sarge shouted for us to fuck off or something like that. We ran after the rest of the patrol but couldn't see them when we got to the square so we ran to this fountain. Then we heard shots from that big entry next to the alley." He pointed to another entry a few yards further along from the alley.

"We reckon the rest of the patrol went down there for cover."

"And what's happened to Sergeant Scobie?" asked the Corporal.

The soldier shrugged his shoulders. "He might be with the rest of the patrol. We was cut off and just waiting for you lot. Not much we could do."

"You're a pair of bloody heroes you two."

"Thanks Corp," they replied in unison, the sarcasm going over their heads.

The Corporal called his men together. "Right we'll go on foot to the big alley where we think the patrol is. If they're all together and it's clear of snipers we'll signal for the Land Rovers to collect us and we'll piss off out of here. If Sergeant Scobie is not with the rest of the patrol we'll have to form on the square and start a search. Okay?"

The Corporal turned to Murdoch. "You stay here with those," he said pointing at the two heroes. "Give us cover and watch out for my signal. If I call you come with one Land Rover and they can bring the other."

Jim Scobie was alone in a doorway in the narrow alleyway. He hadn't felt the shrapnel at first. He mistook the wetness for sweat. Then it started to ache, like he'd banged his thigh. He looked down and saw the pool of blood forming around his foot. The numbness began and his leg wouldn't support him anymore. He knew he'd have to stay put.

Ahmed worked his way into position below the parapet. Every second he was exposed Ahmed risked a premature meeting with his maker but he needed to look. He saw the soldier sitting in the doorway and the scorch marks from the grenade on the whitewashed wall. He saw the trickle of blood that ran towards the centre of the alley. Silently he worked his way from rooftop to rooftop to reduce the angle for his shot. He needed to look once more. He edged his head upwards and spotted his target, just as his target saw him. He ducked as the rifle cracked. A chip of mortar flew from the edge of the parapet. Ahmed thanked Allah for sparing him.

The single shot didn't echo. Duncan was sure of the direction.
"That came from the little alley," he said, "we should go over and take a look. Sergeant Scobie needs our help."
"Our orders were to stay here," said the little one.
Duncan was agitated.
"You go if you want," said the other soldier, "we'll cover you and keep an eye on the Land Rovers. Keep weaving. You should be all right."
"Arseholes," said Duncan. He knew it was pointless arguing with the heroes. He got up and ran, zigzagging across the square.

Scobie saw Duncan edging up the opposite side of the alley pressed tight against the wall. He motioned a warning, touching his eye and pointing to the rooftops. Duncan read the signal. They didn't need to speak. He crept forward, eyes scanning. He drew level with the Sergeant.
"You okay Jim," he whispered.
"Yeah, I'll do. But watch out there's one around here somewhere."

Ahmed knew the wounded soldier was looking at the roofline so he made his way to the back of the flat roof and dropped the six feet to an external half landing. The shutters on the first floor window were open. He climbed into the building and worked his way to the front room. It was in semi-darkness, the louvered shutters were closed. He peered downward through the slats at the wounded soldier. He could see the legs outstretched. The soldier was sitting, leaning against the door. Ahmed kissed his weapon and silently prayed. He would trust in Allah and surprise. He steadied himself in front of the window and raised his gun, pushing the louvers with the barrel of his gun, they swung open freely.

The shot was crisp. It was close, so close it rang in Duncan's ears. He saw Scobie's legs kick involuntarily, a reflex action. He saw the body stiffen for an instant before slumping forward.

Duncan was frozen still but his senses were razor sharp. For the first time in his life he felt the acute awareness produced by a real adrenaline rush. A few grains of sand fell past his face. He instantly knew and stepped out, raising his gun. Too late, he caught only a glimpse of the barrel as it disappeared back into the room. In two steps he was at the double front doors of the building. In a single movement he threw his weight against them. They gave easily and revealed the dusty wooden stairway. He took the treads two at a time. One of the doors on the landing was ajar. He pushed and entered with levelled gun. The pungent whiff of cordite lingered. A shell casing lay on the bare boards by the window. From the window opening he saw Jim Scobie's motionless body. There were shouts. Duncan saw Lt Cameron running up the alley at the head of the HQ support squad.

Somewhere behind a floorboard creaked. Duncan turned and went back to the landing. The second door on the landing was shut. He applied pressure. It was firm. From inside came muffled sounds. With the flat of his foot he kicked the door. It yielded. A window shutter swung. He stepped forward to the opening. Below, in the alley, a white robed figure raced, panic in his stride. He clung to an AK.

The Arab glanced back over his shoulder. For a second the eyes of both men locked together. There was no time to take proper aim. Duncan squeezed the trigger too soon. A puff of dirt erupted ahead of the Arab which gave him added impetus. Duncan squeezed again but didn't see where the second round struck. He cursed. There was no time for a third shot. The figure suddenly swerved and disappeared into an opening.

"Any luck Murdoch?" Lt. Cameron was at the doorway.

"No sir, missed. Can we go after him?"

"No point he will be in the Mosque in a few seconds and that's out of bounds," the Lieutenant said.

"Jim Scobie?" asked Duncan.

The Lieutenant shook his head. "Come on, you did well."

Daylight was fading as Ahmed made his way through the narrow passage ways of the bazaar that was coming to life as the sun's heat dissipated. He passed a hundred shops and stalls before coming to the coffee house. White robed Arabs in identical keffiyeh headdress and rope agal occupied the tables and chairs. His four Comrades were already huddled in conversation.

"Mohammed blessed our mission today", said Ahmed as he joined them.

"Allah Akbar," was the response.

Ahmed continued. "Allah blessed the mission but Comrade Khrushchev provided the weapons. Long live the USSR."

"Long live the Revolution," the others replied in quiet unison.

Ahmed spoke. "Today will soon be over. Now we look toward tomorrow. In the morning we strike another blow for our liberation. "Insha Allah, God willing."

"Insha Allah," they replied. "We are ready."

The night was long and restless for Duncan. His camp bed offered little comfort. He'd received more from Jim Scobie than he had from any other man in his life. Duncan knew he would not weep for his father but he wept for Jim Scobie. His confused mind compared the men.

He'd only ever made one trip with his father. From his home on the Isle of Lewis to the army recruitment centre in Glasgow. It was a frugal journey, like his life on the Croft. His father would not have gone had it not been necessary. Duncan believed the thought of one less mouth to feed was the only pleasure derived from the trip for his father. Throughout the long bus journey the two had only spoken through necessity. It was as if words needed to be conserved. He recalled the dingy bed and breakfast, the shared bed and the long walk into town the next morning.

Duncan remembered how he'd flown through the battery of physical and mental tests while his father sat waiting, impassively. When presented with the consent papers he signed away his son without thought or question. Six weeks later Duncan left the tiny crofter's cottage that had been his home since birth. He never looked back. Janet, his mother, stoically concealed her tears. Angus, as a concession, came down from the high field and shook his son's hand. It was the only time Duncan remembered touching his father's flesh.

Basic training was easy, an improvement on his past life. He'd expected hardship. Instead he found hot showers, three meals a day and central heating. He was sent to Sterling Barracks after basic training. The unit was working up for Borneo. Duncan, in his mind was ready. He shared in the excitement and anticipation of the battalion. When individuals were given embarkation leave to say goodbye to family Duncan didn't apply. He just wanted the posting to start. The last days dragged. The unit's main kit had gone off by sea, inoculations were complete. They were ready and waiting. Then the message came.

From diagnosis to burial was only five weeks. She never asked for Duncan, not because she didn't love him, but because she didn't want to disturb the happiness he had found. But the Pastor insisted. By the time Duncan arrived there was nothing to be done. He sat at her bedside for the last twenty-four hours. It was a morbid scene. The cancer had taken her will to live. She slipped away holding the hand of her only child but drawing little comfort.

Duncan remembered his father, as emotionless in death as he was in life. It was a wintry, cloudy day when they buried her, father and son not even united in grief. He'd been given two weeks compassionate leave but Duncan went back to Sterling the day after the funeral, vowing never to return to his home.

He'd wandered the deserted barracks. The battalion had left the previous day. His sense of loneliness was complete. Everything that mattered to him was now gone. But he was not alone. Sergeant Jim Scobie had the job of sorting out the barracks and tiding up the unit's administration. He'd been chosen by lottery to stay. Only married men with kids were entered into the lottery.

"What are you doing in my nice clean barracks?" was Duncan's greeting when Scobie found him.

"You ain't supposed to be here son. You're supposed to be on compassionate leave."

"I came back early Sergeant. Thought I could stay here till I get orders," said Duncan.

"You can't stay here son. There are others moving in."

"I'll find somewhere else then Sarge," said Duncan.

"Where will that be then?"

"Don't know Sarge," he replied.

"Well seeing as you're here you can most probably earn your

keep for the next few days. You can get your head down in my place. My Missus will look after you. She likes waifs and strays. Get your kit."

"What you brought home this time?" said Mary Scobie. "Come in. Take your coat off."

He remembered her warm open face. Crows feet evidenced her almost permanent smile. But there was a no nonsense side to her. Managing three children made her quick and to the point, the practicalities of life dominated, by necessity. Duncan was immediately drawn into the family. That's the way it was in the Scobie home. For two weeks he worked with Jim during the day and returned to the family home in the evening. He recalled never knowing the meaning of family before.

Duncan was an attraction for the children. Their persistence eroded any reserve that might have lingered. He found himself rolling around on the floor, kicking footballs, playing games, wiping tears.

Oh God! His mind came back to reality, to Aden, as if somebody had stuck smelling salts under his nose. He could see the children. There would be rivers of tears to wipe away now. Dawn came slowly and, as the sun rose, so did his anger.

"Stand easy Private," Lt Cameron sat behind a trestle table that served as his desk.

"It's hard seeing your first casualty. Worse if you know the chap. I understand you were close to Sergeant Scobie?"

"Yes Sir," replied Duncan still at rigid attention.

"Duncan, isn't it? Listen relax, stand easy. You're a young lad. We can cut a bit of slack. I'll send you back to the airport for a few days and you can work with the Quartermaster. How would that suit?"

"No thank you Sir."

"No? Not many people get offered that," said the Lieutenant.

"I appreciate that Sir but I'd like to stay with the lads. I'm not a special case."

"All right, well done, I'll l see you get light duties for a couple of days, alright?"

"No Sir."

"I'm only trying to help you know." Exasperation tinged the Lieutenant's voice.

"I know sir. I just want to go out on patrol with the lads Sir. In the Crater," said Duncan.

"Not sure if that's a good thing just now. But tell you what; I'm taking a foot patrol to the harbour mid morning. You can go on that and we'll see how you get on."

"Thank you Sir." Duncan saluted and left the room.

"Mustafa, where did you learn to drive?" Ahmed was still in buoyant mood after yesterday's success.

"The British taught me. I worked in the Civil Administration Office," he replied.

"You should be good then. Their training is the best," said Ahmed.

All four men laughed.

Mustafa slapped his hand on the bonnet of the Austin Cambridge saloon. "Good British engineering too."

"Check your weapons," said Ahmed, "Remember we must be quick. When the call comes we move. We will have only minutes to complete our mission. Insha Allah." Ahmed looked towards the wall phone that hung on the garage wall and waited.

Lt Cameron organised the patrol. He took mid-point with the radio operator behind him and Duncan immediately in front. They set off in line quietly working their way towards the southern gate and then on to Marine Drive, the road that led down from the Crater to the harbour. The patrol was safest once past the gate, away from the narrow streets where there were less ambush points or cover for snipers.

Motorised traffic was rare in the narrow streets of the Crater but Marine Drive was a thoroughfare. Most days overloaded trucks lumbered up the incline, hauling supplies from the docks, around the walls of the Crater and into the high interior. But today was Saturday and there were no trucks, only occasional cars going to the yacht club that was the centre of Aden's elite social life.

The Patrol was well spaced. European occupants of cars waved as they passed, coming down from their protected area, high in the hills. The patrol passed the half way point.

"Halt!" shouted Lt. Cameron. "Two minutes rest and a radio check."

The men dropped to a crouch. Every direction was covered. There was no chatter, only observation. The radio operator unslung his backpack and pulled back the stiff canvas cover that protected his equipment. He donned headphones over his berry. He fiddled with the tuner. "BRAVO, NOVEMBER this is CHARLIE ALPHA MIKE. Radio Check, over." He repeated the message.

Tail End Charlie, the rear guard, watched as the Morris Oxford came towards him. He raised his hand ready to return the wave. When the vehicle was close he realised the occupants were Arabs. He turned to tell the Lieutenant but the officer was preoccupied with the radio operator. The car passed.

"Up, let's go!" Lt Cameron was on his feet.

The men rose. Tail End Charlie said nothing.

"Volunteer for the point?" asked Lt. Cameron.

"Me," Duncan put his hand in the air.

The Lieutenant hesitated for a second.

"You have to do it sometime I suppose. Okay. Take the point as far as the harbour."

Duncan moved up, twenty paces ahead of the next man. He raised his hand high and motioned the troop forward with an exaggerated wave to the front. Somebody at the back said, "He thinks he's on bloody Wagon Train". It was the first banter of the day.

Duncan concentrated; watching for mines, booby traps, shadows, anything. A couple of cars came up the hill. Duncan didn't return the waves, leaving it to those behind him.

Ahmed's heart was pounding. It happened fast and to plan. He climbed in beside the driver and slammed the door. He placed his pistol in the folds of his robe.

"Go Mustafa, quickly as Allah will allow."

Mustafa was sweating, gripping the steering wheel tightly. He over-revved the engine and the rear wheels spun on the dry gravel of the yacht club car park. A cloud of dust billowed from the rear of the vehicle. The tyres gained traction and the car moved forward.

Ahmed looked into the rear view mirror and saw the three strained faces on the back seat.

"Relax. We've done it. Cover your guns and be calm, just look ahead."

Duncan saw the Morris Oxford exit the Marina gates too quickly. He watched the car's progress as it came towards him. His instinct told him something was wrong. He pulled the FN closer to his chest and let his thumb slide the safety to off. He stopped walking and gave the halt signal to the patrol. The car drew close. He turned with it, keeping eye contact with the occupants. The Arabs ignored his gaze and stared ahead. As the vehicle came level everything went into slow motion and Duncan felt that sharpness once more.

The face was indelibly etched on his mind. He levelled his gun and fired. The patrol dropped and brought their guns to bear. Lieutenant Cameron raised his hand in restraint.

"It's the bastard that shot Scobie," Duncan shouted.

The occupants of the car suddenly sprang to life. The driver dropped a gear and drove at the patrol. Ahmed withdrew his gun and fired out of the window.

The Lieutenant's arm fell and no further orders were necessary. The patrol split and fired on the move. The first shot hit the driver of the car, a clear shot straight through the windscreen. The toughened glass deformed the lead point of the bullet as it passed so that it acted like a dumb dumb. The round entered absolute centre, between nose and lip. It was no clean wound. The Arab's face exploded splattering the occupants with bits of blood and tissue. In the mess an artery had been severed and blood pumped wildly. In his last seconds of consciousness Mustafa tried to scream but his mouth was gone and the remnants of his jaw hung limply. His throat flooded with blood and he emitted only a low-pitched gurgle. The car veered wildly to the left, coming to an abrupt halt as it crashed into a low wall. Ahmed took several rounds any one of which could have been his ticket to paradise. Bullets peppered the car body with a hollow metallic thud. The frenzy of fire from the patrol began to abate. The rear car door opened. A passenger fell onto the road. Duncan ran towards the vehicle.

Lt Cameron barked the order, "Cease fire. Make safe."

Duncan reached the car. He looked with contempt at Scobie's killer. There was no doubt. It was him. From inside came a moan. A body moved. A head lifted. The face half smiled at Duncan and a hand moved toward the pocket of his jeans.

Duncan didn't hesitate; he emptied the remainder of his magazine into the body then turned away. He had avenged Scobie with his first blood.

The first indication that something was amiss came at the debriefing.

"Yes Lieutenant it was the same car that came down the hill," said Tail End Charlie, "The only thing is I was sure there was only four people inside when it passed me."

"Well there are five bodies now," said the Lieutenant. "How do you account for that?"

Charles Henderson followed silently. His escort stopped and reached for the handles of the ornate double doors and glanced over his shoulder to see if the diplomat was ready. Henderson nodded. The escort opened the doors and stepped aside to give Henderson free passage.

"His Excellency, the British Ambassador."

Henderson strode into the office of the Egyptian Foreign Minister. "Minister, it's so good to see you again." Henderson offered his hand. The Minister shook it without enthusiasm.

"I do not wish to beat about the bush; it is a matter of extreme concern. I hope that you have come prepared with a satisfactory explanation," said the Minister.

The two men remained standing, facing each other, an indication of the seriousness of the situation.

Henderson spoke without notes. "I have the preliminary response from my Government in London. Two days ago a British Army foot patrol became suspicious of a car observed leaving the marina at the port of Aden. When they attempted to stop this car the occupants drew weapons and fired on the patrol. The patrol returned fire causing the vehicle to come to a halt. The exchange of fire continued. Unfortunately there were no survivors from the vehicle. On searching the bodies one was found to be in possession of an Egyptian diplomatic passport. Enquiries identified the carrier of the passport as the eldest son of the Egyptian Ambassador to Aden. It is understood that the other occupants of the car had just kidnapped the Ambassador's son from the marina. The other occupants of the car are believed to have been communist inspired insurgents."

The Foreign Minister nodded. "How many of the British Army patrol were killed?"

"None Foreign Minister," said Henderson.

"Wounded?"

"Also none."

"Very lucky people," said the Minister. "Can you tell me what unit the patrol came from?"

"The Argyle and Sutherland Highlanders, an historic and highly disciplined unit Minister."

"Really, I believe this unit is commanded by, eh, a Mad Mitch?"

"Lieutenant Colonel Mitchell to be precise, a very experienced Officer."

The Foreign Minister picked up a newspaper from his desk. "Daily Mirror Mr Ambassador, it is British isn't it?"

"It is Minister."

"I have a little difficulty Mr Ambassador. You see I did not give this Lt. Col. his name. It's actually what YOUR NEWSPAPERS call him. You do read your own newspapers don't you? It would appear that even people in Britain think he is out of control."

"I think this is a little unfair Minister. This patrol almost rescued your poor chap from a kidnap situation. It is only accidental he did not survive. You might have ended up being very grateful had the rescue attempt been successful."

"It's not accidental Mr Ambassador." The Minister's voice rose in anger. "You insult my intelligence. It is typical of British arrogance and colonialism. Do you honestly think that boy would have been shot if he was white? Don't answer that. You will only make me angrier. NO. He was only shot because he was the same colour as his kidnappers. As far as the British are concerned we all look the same."

Henderson spoke calmly. "Minister I do think you might be over reacting to the situation."

"Tell that to the parents of the dead boy Mr Ambassador. But there is more. I have information the Officer leading the patrol gave the order to cease fire and it was after this order was given that our national was murdered."

"Murder is a very strong word Minister," Henderson protested.

"If a soldier disobeys a direct order from his commanding officer and shoots a man what do you call that in the British Army? In the Egyptian Army we call it murder."

"I give you my unequivocal assurance that Her Majesty's Government will uphold the rule of law. If an offence has taken place the individual responsible will be punished."

"We will see about that Mr Ambassador. I expect your Government to inform me of the consequences of this formal protest. When you have done that the Government of the Republic of Egypt will decide what further action is necessary."

"If any?" added Henderson.

"That is all for now. You may go. Thank you."

"Why do they call it the Glass House?" asked Duncan.

The Red Cap looked at his prisoner. It's to do with the old military prison in Aldershot. They pulled it down just after the war and built a spanking new one in Colchester, that's where you are going. But the old one used to have a big glass atrium in the middle. It was the only daylight anybody saw when they went inside. They called it a glass house. The name just stuck. Any army prison is called the glass house now."

"Why is the prison...?"

The Red Cap cut Duncan short. "Listen bud, I didn't ask to be handcuffed to you; I'm just taking you back to England. Just give me a break. It's a long time before we get you to your cell. Then you can speak all day long, in fact for the rest of your life, if they don't hang you that is."

Salisbury, Rhodesia, May 1968

From the corner of her eye she saw the small hand shoot forward across the table. She moved quickly and grabbed the wrist before it had a chance to retreat. Clasped firmly between the child's fingers was the last piece of meat, snatched from her enamel plate.

"Joshua that is mine, it is bad to steal from your mother," she scolded.

"I want it," demanded the boy wriggling his hand to break free without lessening his grip on the prize. Her resistance melted and she allowed his hand to slip away. He pushed the chunk of meat into his mouth and chewed. Only when the last morsel had been swallowed and he'd sucked each finger clean did he look at his mother again.

"You can have my sadza. I don't want it," he said pushing his plate towards her across the boxwood table.

"You're a growing boy," she sighed, the excuse more for her own benefit rather than his. "You need food to study now you are going to secondary school. Soon enough you will be a man!"

The child drank from at a mug of sickly sweet tea whilst his mother silently cleared up around him.

"Mother," he spoke between gulps, "I was cold last night. I need another blanket."

"You already have the best blankets," she sighed. "Blankets are very expensive."

"I was cold," Joshua was persistent. "You must do it."

"I will do what I can."

Joshua smiled knowing his demands would be met. They always were because he was special. From the very beginning he'd felt different, better than others. At first he thought it was because he was an only child but later he knew it was something else, something about him that was unique.

Some things however were non-negotiable for the child. Bedtime was one of them. When darkness fell in the crowded African ghetto, the anonymous two-roomed cinderblock house took on a clandestine role. Each night Joshua would lie in his metal-framed bed, pushed tight up against the party wall and listen to the words of his father in the next room.

It always started in the same way. Quiet knocks on the door. His father would ask in a hushed voice, "Who comes?"

"Shamwari," was the invariable response, friend.

"Enter Shamwari." Joshua would hear the door open as someone entered. Then a few moments later would come another knock and the ritual would be repeated. Soon there would be seven or eight with his father, all speaking in hushed tones. But it was Silas, his father, who did most of the talking. Silas Sovimbo always spoke with excitement and enthusiasm, as if he had just discovered something fresh, something he wanted to share with his visitors. Each night Joshua listened till he fell asleep. He became familiar with the hallowed names; Karl Marx, Fredrick Engels, Trotsky, Lenin and most importantly of all, the great leader, Chairman Mao. Joshua knew Mao was the most important because his name was spoken with utmost reverence. He learnt unusual words too; colonialism, imperialism, the proletariat and the bourgeoisie. It was never said but Joshua knew the words he had learnt must never be repeated outside the house.

Joshua discovered the pattern too. After somebody had been coming to the house for some time his father would ask that person a series of questions to see if they had understood what had been taught. When his father was satisfied he would make the person swear an oath. Then they would be changed. No longer would they be a simple Shamwari or friend. After the oath was taken they would be called Comrade.

But this night was different, special. Only one man had come to speak with his father. The tone was urgent. It was a conversation not of teacher and student but of equals. The stranger was insistent.

"There is no choice. You must go before it is too late."

His father replied, "I should not desert my people. I should stay with them during difficult times."

"Whatever happens you will not be staying with your people. You go into exile or you go into prison. These are the options." The stranger was angry. "You can do good in exile. You are the ideological leader. You alone can convince the Chinese to help us. There is no point in arguing. The arrangements are made."

"The basic strength of communism is that all men stand together," said Silas. "In this way they become stronger than their oppressors. I should stay here," Silas persisted.

"Above all you should know that communism is the doctrine of pragmatism," responded the stranger. "Chairman Mao himself went on his long march into exile only to return when he was strong enough to overcome the agents of imperialism. Silas, you and your family must make your own long march. You must start in the morning." The stranger was unyielding.

Joshua slipped into an uneasy sleep with the unappealing prospect of a long march!

Silas Sovimbo was born on the citrus estates in the Mazowe valley, north of Salisbury, in 1922. His parents laboured in the orange groves and lived in the native compound. When Baptist missionaries taught Silas to read they unleashed an insatiable appetite for the written word. In the early years the written word was the Word of the Lord. The Baptist church became Silas's life. As a young man he stood outside beer halls extolling the virtues of abstinence. By the age of twenty he was a Baptist preacher. He attended any gathering in the hope of speaking. That is why he was at a meeting of the newly founded African Youth League in 1955.

The organisers would not let him speak. He had to listen, listen to another man of the Cloth, the Reverend Edson Sithole. Sithole was two years older than Silas and was concerned as much with the temporal as the pastoral. For him the present carried as much weight as the life hereafter. Sithole opened a door for Silas who willingly entered another domain. Silas met Joshua Nkomo and his side kick Robert Mugabe for the first time. The Communist manifesto became his bible of the present. Silas saw no contradiction with his faith, he saw Jesus as the first true socialist.

In the following years he dug deep into his intellect and grappled with concepts beyond the understanding of most of his peers. He became a purist and deplored the 'bastardisation' of communism that had occurred under Stalin. He stayed true to Marx and believed in the interpretation of socialism expounded by Mao. He became the intellectual and moral authority within the fledgling liberation movement.

In the 1960's he watched helplessly as fissures began to

appear in the movement, cracks along tribal lines. Nkomo the authoritarian Matable ran roughshod over his Shona deputies, including Mugabe. Eventually they split away. In his heart Silas had wanted to remain loyal to Nkomo but Nkomo's association with the Russians made Silas side with the breakaway Shona who leaned towards Mao.

As the fissures in the liberation movement grew, the Rhodesian whites moved to the right and elected Ian Smith as Prime Minister. Rhodesia unilaterally declared independence and there followed a crackdown on the liberation movement's leadership. Black political leaders were rounded up, Nkomo and Mugabe shared the same prison. Silas was missed in the first sweep.

Silas told his wife and child of his decision. "Today, in the next hours, we will leave our home. We are going away from this land now called Rhodesia. When we come back to this same place it will be called Zimbabwe and it will be a land liberated from oppression."

Silas's wife accepted without comment, only Joshua spoke.

"How far do we have to walk? Last night I heard you say we would go on a long march."

Silas laughed. "It is not that kind of march. We will actually travel mostly by bus, some by car and only a little walking. We will go to Zambia. Then later maybe we will move somewhere else."

"What are these places like?" Joshua asked.

"They are places that have already won their freedom. Places where black men are no longer dominated by white men. They are places where all men are equal. Even as guests we will enjoy freedom, equality and justice."

"Will I be the same as white boys? Will our families be equal?"

"Yes, you will be equal to the whites that still live in those places," said Silas.

"So we will have a car, servants and a swimming pool just like the white boys here?" asked Joshua with a glimmer of hope.

Silas shook his head. "Joshua, you do not understand. We will be rich in other ways. The things you talk about are unimportant. They are only the products of a material world. They will not make you happy."

The young mind of Joshua did not believe his father for half a moment.

Colchester Military Prison, UK 1972

"Major Cameron, come in. Sit down, tea or coffee?"

The desktop was clear except for a phone and a name plaque, *'Lieutenant-Colonel Black'*, inch high letters, white on black plastic.

"Coffee, white please," replied Cameron scanning the characterless room. Formica furniture, Marley floor tiles, plastic venetian blinds, abstract wallpaper. The office had a hollow sound. Lt Col. Black stood almost to attention behind his desk. Thin and pristine in appearance he achieved no great stature. He looked at the orderly that had shown Cameron into his office. An almost imperceptible nod by the officer sent the orderly scurrying off for the coffee.

"It's tight discipline here. I make sure everybody knows what is expected of them and I don't accept any deviation. It is the only way to restore discipline to those that have wavered," volunteered Black.

"I can see that," said Cameron sitting and placing his peaked cap and leather gloves on the desk in front of him.

"Jolly unusual to get one of you chaps from Army Intelligence taking any interest in this establishment. My customers are normally considered to be a little deficient in that department."

Major Cameron thought that Black was suited to his position. There was something about short men and authority. The Lieutenant-Colonel obviously relished governing HM Military Prison Colchester.

"I report directly to the Provost Marshall. He reports directly to the Queen," said Black volunteering more information.

"An anachronism?" said Cameron without thought.

"Not at all my good man," Black straightened his back. "Logical. Totally logical, logical and practical, totally practical, wouldn't work any other way."

"Sorry. I wasn't thinking." Cameron backed off smartly.

"Still, to the purpose of my visit."

"Yes, yes. Private Duncan Murdoch." The Lt Col pulled a thick buff file from a desk drawer.

"Came to us just over five years ago, subject of a General Court-Martial here in Colchester. Charged with murder, shot a local in Aden. Back here before you could blink an eyelid, caused quite a stir at the time. Bit disproportionate if you ask me. Guilty of course, was even talk of the death penalty for a while. Would have been my first you know. Not sure if we'd have used bullet or rope," Black mused wistfully to himself for a moment.

"Still we never got the opportunity in the end, life sentence with no minimum tariff. Chap himself? No problem, keeps himself to himself, does as he is told. Takes all the physical exercise he can. He studies all the rest of the time, mostly military manuals. No next of kin declared but gets occasional mail and parcels from a woman in Scotland, a Mary Scobie."

Cameron raised his eyebrows.

"Nothing more to add really," finished Black, "But why the interest from Army Intelligence?"

"Can't say at the moment," answered Cameron. "But I assume you have received the request for your co-operation from my CO?"

Black nodded.

"It would be good if I could see Pvt. Murdoch. Alone please."

The interview room had two plastic chairs and a table. The guard pointed to the red panic button on the wall.

"Press that and we'll be in like a dose of salts," he gave an affirming wink. "Shall I bring in the prisoner?"

Cameron was surprised at the sight. Duncan Murdoch had grown, physically grown. Incarceration had not weakened him.

Duncan immediately recognised Cameron and started to move his mouth but five years of prison discipline overrode his instinct. Prisoners did not speak unless spoken to.

"Hello Duncan," said Cameron. "Stand easy. Take a seat," he smiled.

Duncan sat uneasily. In prison any change from the routine was treated with suspicion.

"You do remember me don't you?" said Cameron. "It's been five years."

"Lieutenant Cameron Sir," said Duncan. "Aden."

"Well actually it's Major Cameron now. Things are a little less static on the outside. I've changed unit too. I'm with Army Intelligence at the present time."

Duncan masked his surprise. "What would you be doing in this place then?"

"Actually I've come to see you." The Officer hesitated whilst he choose his words. "Your predicament does not rest easy with me," said Cameron.

"Guilt Sir? It was your evidence that put me down."

Cameron was surprised at the caustic response. "Duncan, let's clear the air. I have no guilt. You shot that boy after I had given the order to cease-fire. You didn't shoot him once; you emptied a magazine into him. That's a fact. I had no option but to say that to the Court."

Duncan stared impassively.

The Major continued, "I do however feel bad about two things. Firstly, there was a lot of political pressure over the issue and we all know how far a soldier can trust a politician. The Foreign Office wanted the key thrown away as far as you were concerned, to pacify the Egyptians."

"Are you saying the Court was rigged?" asked Duncan.

"No. But I believe if you had shot an ordinary Arab in the same circumstances it would have been a Field Court Martial in Aden, most probably heard by people within the regiment. A General Court Martial in the UK, with all the publicity, was not necessarily in your best interests.

Secondly there were strong mitigating circumstances. You were only nineteen years old, a few days into your first action and had just seen a friend killed. The Court never properly took those circumstances into consideration as far as I am concerned. That was not fair. Indefinite detention, in those circumstances, was excessive in my view. That's all I've got to say on the matter. Take it or leave it. If you're unhappy with that I'll go."

Duncan nodded. "So what are you here for now?"

"I felt you had the makings of a good soldier in Aden. I thought your attitude was good. You made an impression that stuck in my mind. Now something totally unrelated has come up that might be of mutual benefit to us. But I want to take it one step at a time. If you give me your word of honour to behave I'm willing to stick my neck out and try and organise a second chance for you."

"Back to the Regiment?" Duncan asked.

"I'm sorry that's not possible. Your conviction will always stand," said Stuart, "but I may be able to get you out of here, on a temporary basis to start with, a few weeks. You'd have to report daily to your local police station of course. But it would be freedom of a sort."

"What's the catch?" asked Duncan.

"The only catch is you come back when I tell you to. No arguments or funny business. Otherwise you're on your own. If, and it's a big if, if things go right I might have something of a more permanent nature for you. But let me tell you straight, I can't afford to have somebody working for me with a chip on their shoulder. So I'll be watching closely. Do you want to give it a try?"

Duncan thought for a while. "Eh. No, I think I'd rather stay here for a while longer. I'm quite settled in my cell."

Cameron's mouth opened.

Duncan smiled. "Of course I'll bloody try it. What have I got to lose?"

Cameron smiled. "I suppose sarcasm is to be expected. You had me there for a second."

More than five years had passed since Duncan Murdoch had entered Colchester Military Prison. He'd believed he would never see the outside world again. Now he walked past the guardhouse, down the long drive to the main road.

Fields stretched either side into the distance. There had been a frost overnight, the grass was white and the morning air was crisp. The sun had yet to drive off the cold.

He walked briskly, shoes clattering on the tarmac. He came to the main road, there was no traffic. A lone gull winged green Ford Zodiac was parked in the lay-by across the way. The engine was running and white smoke came from the exhaust. A 'Private Hire' sign on the roof was unlit. Seeing Duncan the driver got out and walked over to him, "You Mr Murdoch?"

Duncan had not been called 'Mr' for a long time. It had been Private Murdoch or Prisoner Murdoch for as long as he could remember.

"Get in, the heater's on. Where do you want to go?"

Duncan thought. To his name he had a brown paper parcel containing some clothes and a shaving kit. In his pocket was a travel warrant for a train journey. He had been given a single £5 note. It would have to last. "I don't need a taxi. I'll walk, which way to town?"

"It's paid for," said the taxi driver. "Just tell me where you want to go."

He could think of only one place. "I want to go to Scotland."

"It'll be the station for you then. I don't go that far myself. They didn't give me enough."

Duncan was not used to choice, even if it was only yes or no.

At the train station the ticket inspector looked at the travel warrant. "Yeah, that's fine. Good for anywhere in the UK so long as the journey is completed within 48 hours. Best bet take the next train to London Liverpool Street, underground to Euston and then direct up the West Coast main line."

A blanket of snow covered the ground in front of the Old Priory at Chicksands in the Bedfordshire countryside. It was bitterly cold outside. The massive coke boiler in the cellar of the main building was almost throbbing as it pumped scalding water into the oversized central heating system. The corridors and offices were warm and stuffy.

Stuart Cameron sat on the leather chesterfield. His boss occupied the matching wing back chair. They faced the picture window and watched as an American Willis Jeep slipped along the unsalted drive, engine revving, as the wheels fought for traction on ice.

"Shame we have to share the facility with the Yanks. They spoil it, too loud. Still I suppose we had to let them in. Otherwise we might have ended up giving them access to GCHQ. Then they would have found out just how much time we spend looking at them." The boss smiled. There was an absence of formality; a casualness existed that is only found in intelligence circles.

The boss mused. "I came to Chicksands when it was the HQ of Army Intelligence. For years we existed quietly. Even the Germans never disturbed us for the duration of the war. Then came the bloody Cold War and some bright spark in the Ministry had the idea that the US Intelligence Corps could share the facility. I knew it was wrong as soon as they arrived. Masts and antenna sprouted all over the place. We might as well have placed an advert. Our tranquillity was shattered, never to return. It became apparent that the word 'clandestine' was missing from the vocabulary of the US Intelligence Corps.

Still that's enough about the past," said the boss. "How's your project getting along?"

"It's a devil of a job," said Stuart, "particularly when national sympathy is with the other side. I've tried recruiting internally of course. We do have excellent contacts but I just keep getting the old 'heave ho'. I'm resigned to the fact that we are going to have to place our own implants. That unfortunately takes time. But I've made a start and I have one promising candidate."

"Where did you pick him up from?"

"Colchester Prison. Problem is he was in Colchester for a long time and the Army was his only home before that. He might be too institutionalised, unable to operate alone. I'm testing him now. I'll know in a few weeks."

Duncan stretched and touched both walls of the room at the same time. The width of his cell at Colchester had been bigger. He looked around despairingly. It wasn't good. A single stained divan was pushed tight against the wall. A battered wooden chair acted as a bedside table and a flimsy wardrobe held his possessions, such as they were. A hook was provided on the back of the door to hang his jacket, only it was so cold at night he had to wear his jacket in bed. The scrap of carpet, with frayed edges, that lay alongside his bed offered scant protection from the cold concrete floor. The nauseating stench was of stale tobacco and piss, Glasgow perfume.

For a moment his thoughts were broken by the sound of the alcoholic in the next room heaving the contents of his stomach. The early hours were always the same; a mixture of drunken rowdiness, incapable fighting and vomiting. Peace only ensued as the tenants sunk into a drunken stupor. Many times Duncan wished for the security and comfort of his prison cell which was far superior to the decaying Victorian red brick building with decorative porticoes that was the Glasgow YMCA.

On the train journey to Scotland he'd been unsure of his final destination. The Isle of Lewis and Stornoway had never been a consideration. He didn't even know if his father was still alive. The train stopped in Glasgow, so he did as well.

Mary Scobie lived in Glasgow. He told himself he didn't want to see her, it would only resurrect past feelings, even if she was his only contact with the outside world. He spent the first two nights at the train station but was continuously moved on. Eventually he was drawn to her; perhaps he was going there all the time but couldn't admit it to himself. He'd stood in the yard of the grey tenement block. He'd looked at the slum buildings and piles of rotting rubbish that littered the derelict open spaces. They were the only visible sign of protest. Even before he arrived his heart was bleeding for the Scobie family. A few days were all he could manage. She'd made him welcome. He'd remembered the last time he had stayed with them and it made him aware of the transient nature of happiness.

"A war widow's pension doesn't go very far," she'd apologised.

The kids were not as Duncan remembered them. They'd adapted to the harshness of the street. Duncan knew it was not what Jim Scobie had wanted and he could not bear to watch so he moved on to the YMCA.

Tanzania 1972

For two days Silas Sovimbo sat next to the lone Zambian girl. As the bus made its way from Lusaka to Dar Es Salaam their bodies were pushed together. Silas' thigh had rested alongside hers for hours but at no time had he entertained an inappropriate thought. Not because his wife and son sat in the seat immediately in front of him but because his mind did not work like that. But Silas was worldly enough to know why the girl was taking her body to the port of Dar Es Salaam. He knew that for Africans there was a difference between political and economic freedom. He knew that people couldn't eat the vote and that political independence meant that another kind of repression took over. People had to sell what they had.

The descent to the coastal plain began. Zambia was far behind, three years had gone quickly. Silas and his family would be guests in Tanzania now, a country more attuned to his political thinking. Joshua did not share his father's optimism.

Joshua had grabbed the window seat. When the bus got up speed the draught from the window offered some relief from the heat. His mother was beside him, holding tightly to the handrail constantly afraid the next lurch of the bus would dislodge her from her precarious position. Joshua ignored his mother and father as much as he could. But he listened. He listened as his father spoke to the girl, he listened with growing resentment.

"You are very young to be travelling alone," said Silas. "Do you visit friends in Dar Es Salaam?"

"No. My family are in Kitwe, at the copper mine. I am going to work so I can send money back to them. It is hard now the mine is closed," she said.

"Aren't you afraid on your own?"

"No. I will soon make friends," she smiled.

"What will you do?" asked Silas already knowing the answer but not expecting the truth.

"I have heard there are jobs. I will work very hard. I am strong and I am lucky too." She continued to smile.

"It would be better if you stayed with your family," Silas advised.

29

"My father has done what he can." Her eyes became moist just at the thought of her father. "It is time for me to repay him."

Joshua's face prickled with rage. "Why is he concerned about her? She is nothing. If he had as much concern for me it would be better."

Joshua remembered how he'd heard his father refuse flights from Lusaka to Dar Es Salaam. His father told the men that they would travel on the bus like ordinary people. He said it was only fair. For days Joshua's mood had been incredulous.

A murmur went around the bus, people strained to look. Someone pointed. The sea came into view. The blue vista opened up in front of Joshua and he saw the sun's reflection on the water, like a million diamonds. His heart should have lifted but it did not. The bus continued its downward journey. Joshua hoped there'd be something for him in this place.

Kanu frowned. "Since the beginning you have caused much trouble Master Joshua. You have chosen a dangerous way. Nothing good can come of it."

"Just drive. No one will know," said Joshua, impatiently from the back seat of the of the Chinese made FAW saloon.

"We will be late. What will I tell your father?" asked Kanu.

"Tell him I came late from school," replied Joshua.

Kanu changed his argument. "It is too dangerous in this place, we come here too often," he muttered. He knew it was hopeless to argue. Resigned he drove towards the docks. Joshua sat back, closed his eyes and let his mind go back to six months earlier, to the day they'd arrived in Dar Es Salaam.

They'd been collected from the bus station and taken to a hotel. Joshua had never stayed in a hotel before. He liked giving instructions to the porters and was sorry in a way when in a few days they moved to their new home in Oyster Bay, an old colonial house that now belonged to the Government. It was different from the colonial houses in Rhodesia. Joshua heard somebody say it was in the German style. Joshua got his own room, an impressive big room that had doors that opened onto the veranda and garden. To Joshua the garden was a park. There were supposed to be servants. A cook and a housekeeper had come with the house. But his father had sent them away. He'd said that he would not have people serve on him. He would get his wife to do the cooking and washing.

In the first days a lot of people came to the house. They'd come in cars. Joshua soon learnt about different registration plates. Some cars had government plates. Others had CD plates. The CD cars brought Chinese people. They were the first Chinese people he'd seen and they all wore identical blue safari suits and had the same haircut. Joshua found them serious and not at all friendly although they smiled and nodded a lot at his father who spent many hours with them, locked away in his study. Joshua was not allowed into the study unless invited. It was a rule strictly enforced.

The Chinese had given his father the car. They said he needed it. Silas told them he couldn't drive so the Chinese sent a driver, Kanu. Kanu was Swahili and twenty-five years old. He moved into the empty servant's accommodation at the bottom of the garden.

Joshua was left alone most of the time. The house overwhelmed his mother and his father had endless meetings. He explored Oyster Bay, the suburb of Dar Es Salaam favoured by diplomats and Government officials. He found the beach and its golden sands, where, at the high water mark, stood giant palms, under which the spoilt adolescents of the privileged passed time. Bored with the world but engrossed with themselves they'd paid scant attention to Joshua once they'd established his lowly position. Joshua thought he'd be better accepted if he went to the English school in Oyster Bay but his father objected.

"It is decadent", he said dismissively.

Instead Joshua was driven by Kanu each day to the secular Asian school on India Street, a stone's throw from the city docks, a mystic area that irresistibly beckoned Joshua.

One day Kanu was late, only a few minutes, delayed by the traffic. It was enough. Joshua was drawn by curiosity. At first he was unimpressed as he walked towards the port. Decrepit lorries carrying precarious cargoes lurched their way along un-maintained streets. Ramshackle cars honked, circumnavigating water filled potholes of indeterminate depth. People on bikes or pushing overloaded handcarts tried to avoid motorised transport.

As he progressed towards the waterside the true character of the area revealed itself. Street vendors every few yards plied their wares. Fat women sat at street corners selling tiny piles of tomatoes or cobs of sweet corn. People were everywhere. Joshua's instinct told him this was a place where the sharp-witted thrived and the less gifted struggled.

He pushed on taking everything in, ignoring the smell of rotting vegetation and raw sewage that hung heavily in the humid air. He looked impassively at the dregs of humanity with their missing or deformed limbs as they begged from people who were a hair's breath from destitution themselves. He felt no pity for them.

A hand on his shoulder startled him.

"Master Joshua, I have been looking for you everywhere. You cannot come here alone! It is too dangerous."

"I'm not alone now. I'm with you. We can go on," said Joshua unconcerned.

Kanu's protests fell on deaf ears. Joshua walked on.

"Master, I will lose my job if anything happens to you." Kanu was anxious.

"Then stay close and look after me," replied Joshua.

They proceeded until the dockside and buildings almost touched each other and the hulls of the giant ships appeared to hang over the town itself. Joshua wove his way along the busy street, Kanu reluctantly following a step behind his charge. Giant steel hulls, streaked with rust, towered over the scene casting surreal shadows over warehouses with broken glass windows and peeling paint, their Teutonic design a product of the original colonial masters. Between the warehouses were dilapidated clusters of buildings whose architecture owed more to early Arabic traders.

Joshua was mesmerised by the incongruous union of steel and brick. He'd watched as ships discharged their cargoes onto the open quay only to see the packing crates whisked away by battered forklift trucks that disappeared into the milieu.

"Kanu!" came the shout from across the street. "Over here."

At the entrance to an alley stood three men, the tall gangly one who'd shouted stood out, his brightly patterned turquoise shirt and dark glasses in marked contrast to the drabness of the other two. Joshua stared at the man, instantly attracted by the pinched smile that had an almost threatening hint.

Kanu responded with a shrug and pointed towards Joshua.

"Hey Kanu, come on, we got some good stuff. Bring the kid," the tall one shouted.

"You know those men? What do they want?" asked Joshua.

Kanu leaned close to Joshua. "Don't cross the road," he warned. "They are not good men. It is better to keep away."

Joshua swerved and headed towards the men who responded with a whoop. "Hey Kanu the boy has more guts than you."

Kanu ran after his charge. "Master Joshua don't go there!"

It was too late. The man had his arm round Joshua's shoulder. He spoke directly to him. "Don't worry about Kanu. He's scared of everything. There's nothing to be worried about. We're all friends here. I'm McKay and this is my territory," he said. "Who are you?"

"Joshua, Joshua Sovimbo," he replied, "What do you mean this is your territory? And why do you have a name that is not African?"

The men laughed.

"You're a bold child. That's good", said McKay. "Come. I'll show you something." He led the boy down the alley.

Joshua coughed hard the first time. The smoke irritated his lungs. He'd struggled to get his breath and then he felt his head getting lighter. He looked around. Suddenly everything was clearer in his mind. People moved slower. He felt euphoric, like he'd never felt before. It was good. In the alley, away from prying eyes, McKay shared an improvised bench with Joshua.

"Don't worry about the coughing. Everybody does that at first," said McKay laughing and taking a draw on the joint himself.

"What is it?" asked Joshua.

"Dagga", said McKay. "It's Dagga. That's what we call it; others call it hemp or hashish. It has many names. But here we call it Dagga. But be careful. It is not allowed. The government says such pleasure is not for ordinary people. You must tell nobody of this place."

Kanu sat opposite, flanked by McKay's bodyguards. He'd tried to move but firm hands restrained him. The message was threateningly clear.

"Give me more", said Joshua with outstretched hand.

McKay held the joint in front of Joshua then quickly withdrew it.

"No", he said as if having second thoughts. "Enough for now. When you come next time you can have more."

McKay stood and moved off, his companions silently following. From that day Joshua became a frequent visitor.

The car stopped, Kanu turned off the engine. Joshua's mind came back to the present.

"We are here?"

Joshua looked and saw McKay at his usual place on the

corner. Joshua now craved the Dagga. McKay taught Joshua how to cup his hands and draw more smoke, how to hold the smoke in his lungs for longer to get more effect. Once he'd even shown him the hubbly-bubbly.

Joshua crossed the road with his usual expectant enthusiasm.

McKay looked over his head as if peering into the distance. His face was serious for a change. It was as if he were looking for something.

"McKay you alright?" Joshua was used to having his friend's full attention.

McKay continued to ignore Joshua.

"Something is wrong," said Joshua.

McKay shook his head.

Joshua took McKay's wrist. "Come, let's go down the alley."

McKay looked at Joshua. He shook his hand free. "No. I do not think we can have Dagga today."

Joshua stepped back. "Why, what is wrong?"

"No", said McKay. "It has become too much."

"What do you mean?" said Joshua smiling, "It is not too much for me."

"Maybe not", replied McKay, "But it is easy for you. You just come here and enjoy. I have to work all day just to give you pleasure."

"What do you mean?" said Joshua taken aback.

McKay lowered his head and spoke quietly to Joshua. "Do you think I get the Dagga for nothing? Do you think people give it to me? No," he said answering his own question, "I have to buy it. I am disappointed you have never once offered to contribute. I do not think we can smoke together anymore."

"I am your friend", protested Joshua. "For all this time you said nothing. Tell me what I can do. But please do not say I cannot have my Dagga."

"Do you have any money to pay?" asked McKay.

"Ah, you know I am at school. I have no money."

"Don't tell me that. You live in Oyster Bay. Everybody has money in Oyster Bay."

"You are right all people have money in Oyster Bay, except me. I do not come from a family with money."

"Then ask some of your friends in Oyster Bay for money," said McKay.

"Why would they give me money?" replied Joshua.

"Ah! I thought you were clever. Maybe I was wrong. Perhaps you are stupid."

"I am not stupid. Do not speak to me like that," said Joshua. "I want the Dagga. What must I do?"

McKay straightened up. He paused and took a deep breath. "I don't know." He shook his head. "Perhaps I am completely stupid myself." He withdrew a packet from his pocket, made from folded newspaper.

"There is Dagga in here. Do you want it?" he asked.

"Yes," replied Joshua, relief palpable in his voice.

"Take it then. But in seven days come back to me. Then you will pay."

Joshua took the packet. "But how will I pay?"

"Kanu will show you how to do it. He is a good teacher. He has done it before." McKay nodded in the direction of the car. Joshua saw Kanu flanked by McKay's guards, pain etched on his face.

Back in the car Joshua sat silently. Kanu drove slowly, he took short breaths. Every turn of the steering wheel was a pain to him.

"I think they have broken my ribs", he said. "It is truly a bad way you have gone."

Joshua was silent for a while. Then he spoke. "Turn back I will return the Dagga."

"It is too late for that. Now you're part of it."

Glasgow 1973

Duncan walked with his head down battling against the bitter Arctic wind that swept up the Clyde bringing lashings of horizontal hail. He was rushing to get home, such as it was. Even the paltry heat of the YMCA would be a respite from the tortures of this weather. January had lapsed into February but spring was still too distant to offer hope.

Winter had been hard in every way. There were no regular jobs for unqualified murderers. He existed on handouts from the dole and occasional casual work on the docks. Each morning he'd leave the YMCA and trudge to the dock gates. There he'd huddle with others waiting for the ganger to appear and select his men for the day. Duncan was a stranger without contacts and an accent that was not Glaswegian enough. He was picked only as a last resort. That's why he made a special effort on bad days when others preferred their bed. But today there were no ships and no work. He only had his daily trip to the police station to look forward to.

He turned the corner and was now shielded from the worst of the wind by the buildings. Only a hundred yards to go, Duncan raised his head to look. Outside the YMCA stood a green Austin Maxi. He instantly recognised it. An Army staff car. He stopped walking. His thoughts were of Military Police and back to Colchester. Instinctively he wanted to run.

"Murdoch!" boomed a voice.

Duncan hesitated. He could run but he knew that at best that would provide only a temporary reprieve.

"Murdoch?" shouted the voice again. "Is that you?" An overweight redcap appeared from a doorway where he was sheltering, a three stripe sergeant.

"Aye, it is. Who wants to know?" replied Duncan walking slowly forward.

"Major Cameron's inside looking for you," said the sergeant, "Look lively, he doesn't like to be kept waiting."

Duncan closed on the entrance of the YMCA and met Cameron as he exited. "Ah! Duncan just the man, just the man." His voice was welcoming. "Don't look so shocked. Did you think I'd forgotten you?"

Duncan looked at the Red Cap.

"Oh, don't worry about him. Al's just driving me around Glasgow, haven't got a clue myself. Now, where can we go for a bit of warmth?"

Duncan thought for a second. "There's a greasy spoon around the corner."

"That will do fine," replied Cameron.

The smell of warm, slightly rancid oil hung in the air. Duncan and Cameron sat opposite each other. An oversize ashtray spilt its contents onto the plastic tablecloth. They were the only customers in the café.

"Didn't expect to end up drinking stewed tea with you today," said Duncan.

"Bet you didn't," replied Cameron.

Cameron put his hands flat on the table.

"How are you finding it, fending for yourself? Not so easy I bet?"

"I'm managing," said Duncan with a less than convincing smile. "To be honest at times I thought it was a toss up which was better; this or prison. In the end I decided that this at least offers hope."

"You don't want to go back then?"

Duncan shook his head. "No."

"That's good," said Cameron, "But are you still pissed off with the Army?"

"I should be I suppose. I gave everything and they shat all over me. But what the fuck. What's gone is gone. No use looking back, it won't do any good. I am where I am."

"I'm not sure if I'd be as forgiving as you. But it is good. It means we can go forward. If you want to that is?"

Duncan nodded. "I do if it's an improvement on this."

"Alright, be outside the YMCA at eight tomorrow morning. Get yourself smartened up. Here's something to keep you going." Cameron passed Duncan a brown envelope. "It'll help get you sorted with some warm clothes."

Duncan left the YMCA at five to eight. Al was already outside waiting with the staff car.

"Get in," he said.

Duncan hesitated; he'd never been in a staff car before.

"What's wrong? Want me to cuff you or something. Get in," he smiled.

Al took Duncan unfamiliar ways, weaving through a labyrinth of terraced streets.

"Know your way around," said Duncan.

"Should do, been chasing AWOL's for twenty years around here. Always get them in the end. They go home. That's why they went AWOL in the first place. Homesick you see. Miss their mummies, that or lovesick. Not rocket science."

Al pulled the car left at a "T" junction. On the right Duncan saw the sign. 'Highland Light Infantry, Mary Hill Barracks.'

Al dropped Duncan at the gate and drove into the camp. Duncan waited in the guardhouse, sitting on a wooden chair watching the corporal filling in the logbook. Outside two soldiers in dress kilts and khaki battle blouses stood guard. Each nursed a Sten gun. Duncan smiled to himself. He'd done guard duty. He'd held a Sten gun. He knew that the soldiers had only empty magazines. It needed an officer before live ammunition could be issued. "Fat lot of good that is," he thought.

Major Cameron appeared at the door.

"Hello Duncan. Nice to see you're wrapped up. We'll walk, okay? I don't have an office here and what I have to say can be said on the move if that's alright with you?"

He never waited for a reply. Duncan followed.

"The visit to Colchester wasn't just sympathy for you," said Cameron, "I have a situation and I think that there is a possibility that we can help each other. Quid pro quo sort of thing."

"I've learnt never to expect anything for nothing," said Duncan. "But just what can I do for Army Intelligence?"

"We'll you're actually well suited in some respects, although you most probably don't recognise it. For instance did you know that in your Army entrance tests your IQ rating was above that of the average officer recruit?"

"With all due respect Sir, that's not so brilliant!" retorted Duncan.

Both men looked at each other and smiled. "Yes, I know what you mean," replied Cameron.

"Okay," said Duncan, "We're agreed I'm stupid enough."

"Then of course you have a working knowledge of the British Army and, more importantly, you're battle hardened, just." Cameron walked slowly. They crossed the parade ground and headed towards the sports field.

"You also have another important attribute. You can stand your own company. You have demonstrated your ability to manage alone in adverse conditions. I think that from childhood you learnt to be self-reliant."

As they walked Duncan let his mind drift for a moment, back to Stornoway and his secret craggy outcrop overlooking the sea.

"You're right I suppose," said Duncan, "I can be alone."

Cameron smiled. "I understand that you picked up other things as a child. You appear to have had a particular penchant for explosives I think?"

Duncan reflected again. He remembered his introduction to Chemistry at the hands of an over enthusiastic student teacher who'd produced a slightly louder than expected bang in the school laboratory. He'd quickly spotted the potential and applied himself to the subject. He knew the school curriculum was going to fall well short of his expectations so he'd set about persuading his mother to buy a chemistry set. Within days he'd exhausted the potential of the brightly coloured box. He sought to progress further. At the library he'd surprised the Librarian with his specific requests but she found a book that contained the information he required.

He soon had practical success utilising, to his own surprise and his mother's annoyance, precious sugar and pilfered fertiliser. Once started he was away. Whilst other boys in the locality hunted with dog or snare Duncan used his knowledge of chemistry. He was the scourge of the warren and became addicted to the excitement that preceded the bang and eruption of sod and soil as another burrow instantly became a crater. Unfortunately his efforts produced little for the table, the occasional shredded rabbit carcass being of little use for anything, not even the stew pot. He'd progressed to 'shifting' bushes, tree stumps and the occasional unwanted rock and had not exhausted his passion for ordnance by the time he enlisted. That's why he applied to be a combat engineer.

"It is amazing what results can be achieved with not very much," said Duncan almost to himself.

The men continued walking around the field.

Cameron broke the silence again. "I think you can see I've done my homework. You have qualities that are useful. Of course they have to be balanced against the negatives."

Duncan frowned at Cameron.

"At the end of the day you're a convicted murderer, continued Cameron. "That's a fact that cannot be undone. And a life sentence is a life sentence. Even with parole, which I hasten to add you're not supposed to have, your life is going to be pretty fucked unless something special comes up."

"What you doing. Building me up to knock me down again?" asked Duncan.

"No, just being frank. I told you I had a problem. I think you'll understand by the nature of my business I can't be too explicit. But now I'm confident my problem would be an opportunity for you."

"You want me to blow a few people up for you? Doesn't matter really because I'm already a convicted murderer?"

Cameron laughed. "No, nothing like that, in fact ironically your conviction might even be of assistance.

I want to place you overseas for a long time and I want you to send reports back to me as well as providing general assistance to colleagues from time to time."

"Overseas!"

"Yes. It's a nice place. You'll like it."

"Where?"

"You'll have to wait to find out. Not too long though. What do you say?"

"What are my options?" asked Duncan.

"Take the offer or hope I can swing it for you that your temporary parole be changed to permanent. Then you get to stay in the YMCA and make your own way."

"Great," said Duncan. "You give wonderful choices. "What's next?"

"It's a deal then," said Cameron with a smile. "I need to get you prepared. I'm sending you to the Shetlands for a while, to a small island. You'll be working for a private company. It'll prepare you for what I want. You keep your mouth shut whilst you're there and just do the job you're given. You'll get details before you go. By the way, you'll be signing the Official Secrets Act."

Oyster Bay, Tanzania 1974

Joshua sat at the table in the Kia, the servant's quarters, with Kanu. He'd sneaked from his room, using the veranda door, and crossed the garden.

Now he watched as the driver's experienced fingers worked deftly in the dull half-light. He used three papers from the packet, sticking two together side by side and the third across the top. He placed them flat on the tabletop.

"Quality is important," said Kanu. "We must only use proper cigarette papers and tobacco from Marlboro cigarettes. There is salt petre in good cigarettes; it helps keep the reefer burning."

He ran a razor blade the length of a Marlboro and let the tobacco spill onto the waiting papers. He broke the tobacco up with his fingers.

"You must only offer complete reefers. No loose Dagga. You make it easy for them and you can charge more."

"Do you think we will we earn enough to pay McKay?" asked Joshua.

"Maybe, if you listen to me," he replied. "When you go to the beach make sure there are only young people there. No more than four or five boys of your own age. Do not show them what you have. Stand a little apart. Do not try to sell anything. Keep in the shadows. Start to smoke yourself, but be careful. Do not take in too much of the smoke. You need to keep your wits about you. When they see you smoking they will come to you on their own. Offer the reefer to the one with the loudest mouth. He will take it in case the others laugh. He will say it is good. Then they will all want some. Still do not try to sell, wait for them to ask you, they will. When they do, tell them you will get some from 'your friend' tomorrow."

Kanu took a tiny amount of dry leaf from the parcel from McKay. He chopped it finely with the blade of the razor and sprinkled it evenly over the tobacco. In seamless moves he picked up the papers and rolled the reefer, sealing it by licking the gummed edge of the paper. He used a matchstick to compact the tobacco from each end. With cardboard he made a filter to keep one of the ends open and twisted the other end. He handed the finished item to Joshua with a smile. "Perfect".

"How much money do I ask for?" said Joshua.

"First lesson, you must take only US money. The people here all have Yankee dollars. Do not negotiate. Tell them they must only pay you what you have paid your friend. Tell them you paid $4 for each reefer."

"Why Yankee dollars?"

"McKay does business on the ships," said Kanu. "He likes dollars. Nobody on the ships will take Tanzanian Shillings. It will make him very pleased if you take him dollars. You should go now."

Joshua was back in less than two hours. Kanu was waiting.

"It was as you said. Tomorrow night I must take three reefers to them."

"Good. But we must be careful in case there is a trap," said Kanu. "You must not be caught carrying Dagga. In the evening I will come with you and hide nearby, in the shadows. You must tell them your friend does not want to be known. When they give you the money you will come and I will give you the reefer. It is better that the transactions are over before you yourself smoke."

Seven days later McKay was there, standing at the usual corner with his minders, sunglasses resting on his head revealing bloodshot eyes. He picked Joshua out of the afternoon crowd and smiled to himself.

"Little one you are on time. Seven days, as I said. That is good." McKay put an arm around Joshua's shoulder and guided him down the alley. "You have the money?" he asked.

"I have some," replied Joshua. He looked nervously around for Kanu. The two minders stood with him at the top of the alley.

McKay took Joshua to their bench, nestled between the alley walls, hidden from prying eyes. "Sit. Let me see what you have."

Joshua handed over the notes they had collected.

"Ah! Good, dollars. Let me count." He quickly fingered through the notes. "Thirty-six dollars," he said aloud. "Not as bad as it could have been." He folded the notes and put the wad into his shirt pocket. "Now we will have a smoke together."

"I should go," said Joshua.

McKay ignored the comment. He struck a match on a stone

and put it to the end of a reefer. Drawing deeply, the end glowed brightly. Slowly he exhaled letting smoke drift out through his nostrils.

"You," he passed it to Joshua. Joshua took the joint and inhaled himself. The effect was instant.

McKay spoke. "Do you know what a dock worker earns in a day?"

Joshua shook his head. "No".

"It is less than one dollar," said McKay.

"What about a domestic worker? How much do they earn?"

Joshua shook his head and took another drag.

"About eight dollars a month," said McKay. "They have to do a lot of work for that."

McKay took the joint back. "You go to school. You do not work. Does your father give you any money?"

"No. I asked for money but he refused," replied Joshua. "He said everything I needed was provided so I would only be feeding capitalists by purchasing unnecessary things."

"The kids at Oyster Bay, they have lots of good things?"

Joshua nodded.

McKay pulled out the wad of notes Joshua had just given him. He counted the money again and divided it. One pile went back into his pocket. He took five from the remaining $18 and handed the money to Joshua. "This is for Kanu. You must always pay the people who work for you well."

McKay slowly counted the remaining $13 dollars again. "Some say that thirteen is an unlucky number. But not for you." He smiled and handed the notes to Joshua. "This is your share. Be careful what you do with it. Do not attract the attention of your parents and do not tell Kanu what you have. That is important."

Joshua took the notes. It was the first money he had that was his own. It felt good. He fanned the wad, unable to conceal his smile.

McKay handed Joshua another tiny newspaper packet. "This is for next week."

Still smiling Joshua took the packet and slipped it into his trouser pocket.

"Listen to me carefully," said McKay. "You must always be careful. It is bad to be caught in this business. That is why the rewards are high. With all the time in school you will never make more than when you attend my 'college'. I will show you how to become rich. Go now. You are in business. Make friends with your customers. Find out what they like. Look for opportunities. Come back and tell me what they want. Do not smoke your profits. Remember you are Kanu's boss. If he gives trouble, tell me. I will see you next week."

Joshua felt the notes again. It was a good feeling. He started to walk up the alley towards the street. McKay called him one last time. "Joshua. An important lesson, if you cheat me I will kill you."

Glasgow April 1974

Duncan was taller and squarer. He'd never been broken, but he had been down and out. But now he wasn't down and he wasn't out. For Duncan confidence was the close companion of hope. His tanned face was evidence of exposure to the fresh Atlantic winds. Never had he looked or felt so good.

"If that's what ten months on a remote island does I'm off there myself," joked Cameron as he offered his hand. The smile was genuine and warm.

Cameron wore civilian clothes but his haircut and regimental tie were a give-away to the knowing. Nothing could change the indelible stamp of Sandhurst.

"Not very good for undercover," said Duncan.

"No?" Cameron laughed. "That obvious?"

The dark panelled lobby of the Buchanan Hotel, one of Glasgow's more established hostelries, was busy with the morning rush of guests checking out. A crowd clustered at the reception desk and the two men had to work their way around scattered piles of luggage. A lone elderly porter ambled around, seemingly oblivious to the chaos.

"This way," said Cameron leading Duncan to an alcove set back from the closed bar area. "It will be more private here."

"So tell me. What have you learnt? What was it like?" asked Cameron.

The broadness of the question caught Duncan off guard. He quickly recovered.

"It wasn't like the army for sure," he began. "Commercial blasting is just about shifting material and shifting it quickly. Personal comfort is definitely a secondary consideration. It's a crude business that requires little finesse. You lay huge charges to prise free giant slabs of sedimentary bedrock. That's what the island is made of. After the primary blast we'd rush in with secondary charges to break up the mass into manageable segments before the mechanical handlers got to work. It's amazing how quickly the landscape can be re-sculptured. In a few months we'd levelled the craggy outcrop and the site was ready for the erection of the tank farm and pumping station."

Cameron broke in. "Of course it's bonanza time in the North Sea. Money's no object."

"You earn your money though, there is nothing for nothing," replied Duncan. "And there's no town on the island, just the camp. Support vessels come and go and there's an occasional helicopter. That is the only contact with civilisation. We just worked all the daylight hours and when it was dark we set up arc lights. That's really weird. They cast eerie shadows over the rock formations."

"In the beginning I assisted a qualified blaster. I think it was just for them to get the measure of me. I did a bit if studying to familiarise myself with the tackle they were using. They took a copy of my army ordnance certificate and gave me a civvie ticket. Then I was blasting on my own."

A waiter brought tea in a pot, with china teacups. "Much more refreshing than coffee, don't you think?"

"A nicety that passed me by," replied Duncan more used to a tin mug.

There was a pause as Cameron drank.

"So are you going to tell me what it's all about? Duncan asked. "Or are you going to keep me in suspense?"

"First things first, let me tell you this is an informal brief. It is intended to give you the gist of the situation. Then you will have the choice to accept or reject. If you turn down the assignment I can't guarantee that you won't be returned to the Glasshouse."

"Hobson's choice then," said Duncan.

"It is really," replied Cameron. "Additionally I must remind you that you may never speak about this matter to anybody else without breaking your oath and contravening the Official Secrets Act. Clear?"

"I haven't anybody to tell."

"Okay then. I want you to go to Rhodesia and join the Army there," said Cameron. "You will fight in the war on the side of the Rhodesians. You will do your best to advance yourself. I want you to report back to me through a contact. I want not only specific information but also background stuff, civilian morale, effects of rationing and that sort of stuff. Simple enough?"

Duncan nodded silently.

"Additionally, there may be a time in the future when we would wish to carry out a military action, covert or overt. You would be expected to assist in any such operation if and when that situation arises."

Again Duncan nodded in silence.

Cameron looked at him, trying to gauge the reaction.

"Is that all?" asked Duncan.

"Just about."

"To be clear, you want me to be a spy? And just to set the record straight, don't they shoot spies in most countries?" asked Duncan.

"Only sometimes, and then only if they catch them," replied Cameron. "In practice we don't think they would shoot a British citizen because they rely a lot on the support of British public opinion. In your case we'd most probably do a deal to get you back."

"I know hardly anything about Rhodesia," said Duncan. "What do I base my decision on?"

"I can give you a quick potted history," offered Cameron, we've time.

"Go on," said Duncan.

"Right then. Rhodesia is landlocked. The Limpopo forms the southern border, shared with South Africa, and the Zambezi is the northern limit of the country. To the west are Botswana and the Kalahari Desert, to the east Mozambique. We'll get you a map so you can have a look.

Cecil Rhodes colonised the place, set the borders and gave the country its name, at the turn of the century. He used a combination of trickery and force to get the locals to sign a treaty handing over their lands. They've never forgiven him. Okay so far?"

Duncan nodded

"Two tribes occupy Rhodesia, the Matable to the west and the more numerous Shona to the east. They have never really got on. The Matable, descendants of the Zulu, used to raid the Shona for food, cattle and women on a fairly regular basis. That was their way. The raids stopped when the British came.

Rhodes wanted to encourage white settlement and so he offered free land to white settlers. One bunch settled at a place near Mount Hamden in 1890. They found fresh water and a nice climate. They raised the Union Jack and named the settlement Salisbury, after the British Prime Minister of the day. It became the capital of the new colony.

The Africans were left leaderless and, after being introduced to the Maxim machine gun and Lee Enfield rifle, put up little resistance. They did have one go at throwing out Rhodes and his crowd. The rising was led by a female witch doctor. They lost of course but the uprising is still referred to as the Chimurenga. Nehanda, that was the name of the witch doctor that led them, lives on for ordinary Africans in folklore. Every African will tell you she is coming back one day to bring them freedom.

Unfortunately or fortunately, depending on your viewpoint, Rhodes was strong of mind but frail of body. He came to an early end and was buried in the Matopas hills, the same place as Lobengula his arch African rival. Who said the old chaps weren't romantic?

Rhodesia became a model colony. In the First World War they raised a small army with an African contingent. They invaded German East Africa. Between the wars Rhodesia developed quickly. Roads, dams and all sorts of infrastructure were built. It became a nice place to live – if you were white."

Cameron sipped his tea.

"The whites took much of the good land. It became impossible for the Africans to live on what was left. Families were split as the able bodied men went to work on commercial farms and in factories. African women went into domestic service. One has to have sympathy."

"Why is that Mr Cameron?" asked Duncan with not a little sarcasm. "Your ancestors didn't have much sympathy when they did the same thing in the Highlands."

"Not quite the same thing really," retorted Cameron.

"What was the difference?" asked Duncan enjoying Cameron's unease.

Cameron ignored the bait. "White Rhodesians were confident. When Neville Chamberlain declared war on Germany the second telegram to land on Herr Hitler's desk, declaring hostilities, was from the Prime Minister of Rhodesia. Rhodesia became a training ground for the RAF. Hurricanes and Spitfires were a common site in the skies over Salisbury.

The country also provided a number of men. One Ian Smith became a fighter pilot who fought with enthusiasm. He was wounded and decorated. He is now Prime Minster of Rhodesia and leader of the rebellion against Britain. His staunch loyal background is the reason he has a lot of quiet support from the British military.

Colonialism has had its day though. British leaders realised this and had been getting rid of African possessions. But Rhodesia was a bit difficult, a pig in the poke so to speak. It was a self governing settler colony, just like Australia and New Zealand. So when it came time to discuss the subject of independence the white Rhodesian people expected to be treated like Australia and New Zealand. Unfortunately there was only a quarter of a million whites in Rhodesia but several million blacks. The whites were never going to agree to one man one vote. Not when they saw what was happening to other independent African countries. They didn't want to see their beautiful country go down the pan. Britain said it had to be one man one vote. And that is the crux of the problem.

Ian Smith, as Prime Minister of Rhodesia, unilaterally declared the country independent. He mutinied against the Crown. And there you have it, stalemate for the last twelve years."

"If there are so few whites why don't we just invade?" asked Duncan.

"Two reasons. The country is land locked. We'd have to cross somebody else's territory to get to them. Secondly there's a long association between the Rhodesian forces and our own, lots of old ties and that sort of thing. It wouldn't be the done thing."

"You're saying our lads wouldn't attack the Rhodesians?"

"I wouldn't put it that strongly, but you might say the motivation of some of our units might be questionable.

That's the history. Now the current situation, the blacks have become politically aware. The first black leader to emerge was Joshua Nkomo, a Matable. As could be expected the Shona set up a splinter group under a chap called Mugabe. To compound the situation the super powers have got involved. The Russians are supporting Nkomo and the Matable, whilst it looks like the Chinese are supporting Mugabe and the Shona. "

"So why are we bothered?" asked Duncan. "Can't we just bugger off?"

"Not quite that simple. It's more a question of what we don't want. What we don't want is two hundred and fifty thousand disgruntled, arrogant and penniless, white refugees landing on our shores. Remember the social upheaval in France when the white Algerians came home? That's not for us. That is what we have to stop happening.

So that's it in a nutshell. Of course if we go forward I'll get you a lot more detail."

"How do I fit in? asked Duncan.

Cameron smiled. "We're not expecting you to take on the Russians and Chinese or anything like that. In fact I'd be surprised if you ever see one. We just want eyes and ears for now. Go and live there and keep in touch.

That's it. What do think? It's your choice. But let me give you some advice. You're a man in your twenties, your whole life in front of you. You now have the choice of indefinite prison or adventure and hope. I know what I would choose."

"Okay," Duncan nodded. "When do I go?"

"Glad we got there," said Cameron smiling. "There will be a full briefing before embarkation. You'll travel as a commercial blaster. There's plenty of work in the mines. You won't need to hide your background. Renegades from the British Army are welcome in Rhodesia."

Duncan stood on the deck of the ship as it traversed the South Atlantic. "November 1974," he thought. Soon would come a new year and a new life.

There was unconcealed excitement on board. The Windsor Castle was less than twenty-four hours from its destination, Cape Town. It was as if the old girl knew she was nearly there. Her bows heaved and dug into the swell thrown up as the cold Atlantic waters butted against the warmer waters of the Indian Ocean.

The sea and wind were fresh on deck, gulls circled overhead. Duncan stood on the port side looking at the silhouette of the mountains. It was his first glimpse of Africa. For twelve days he'd listened to the steady throb of the engines that had pushed the vessel from Southampton and now his destination was in sight.

People on board said it was the end of an era. Soon the Windsor Castle would be retired, sold off to an uncertain future. The proud vessel was being made redundant by the Boeing 707. Since 1960 she had been the link between Europe and Southern Africa. Duncan would be amongst the last to experience her colonial opulence.

Dar Es Salaam February 1975

The pool area would have been in total darkness were it not
for the light that spilled through the patio doors. Evening brought no
respite from the humidity but it did bring to life a million insects and
a cacophony of sound. It was early. Joshua and Atu waited for the
others that would come later. Atu picked his way through shadows
on the patio, going toward the low brick structure that housed the
swimming pool pump and filter. He threw a switch. Underwater
lights illuminated the pool from below.

"Is that cool?"

"Yeah looks good," said Joshua, uncaringly between swigs of
beer from the bottle.

"You should have asked me to get you some imported larger.
This local stuff is shit."

"My dad got it, there's crates of it", said Atu apologetically.
"He likes it."

"Carlsberg is better. Your Dad should think of his reputation
when he buys beer. It can give the wrong impression." Joshua left the
empty bottle on top of the pump housing.

"Is she really going to come tonight?" a tremor of doubt
lingered in Atu's voice.

"Have you got the money?" countered Joshua.

"Yes, I got everybody else's too." Atu tapped the back pocket
of his trousers.

"Then she'll show", answered Joshua. "Guaranteed, a night
you won't forget."

"Oyster Bay hasn't been the same for the last two years, not
since you arrived. It's really crazy. But tonight is going to be the
tops."

"Your parents just better not show up that's all, or you're on
your own. One hundred percent on your own," warned Joshua.

"No problem. My Dad took my mother to Malawi for a
conference or something. They won't be back until Monday night."
Atu smiled. "I'll have time to clean up as well."

"What about the servants?"

"They got the weekend off. I gave them bus money to go
home. Nobody else around."

"It's going to be a long night." Joshua dropped onto a pool lounger. "Get me a cold beer," he demanded.

Joshua looked straight up. A million stars twinkled in the cloudless sky but the beauty of the night sky was lost on him. His thoughts never drifted that far. He'd made Oyster Bay his territory and that was the limit of his horizons.

Atu came back with the beer. "How long before the stuff arrives."

Joshua took the beer. "It will be here soon enough. The girl will come later, when the mood is right. Then we will see if your friends can live up to their big words."

Kanu bent over the table in the Kia. He worked quickly, trying to make up lost time. The traffic had been bad coming out of the city. The CD plates helped, but only when the road was clear. The trouble had been the clapped-out buses and improvised police checkpoints.

Each joint he produced was perfect. He wondered how many joints he'd rolled on the table over the last two years. A thousand? Perhaps two thousand? Behind him the door began to move slowly and silently. He didn't notice. Normally it would be locked but tonight he'd forgotten.

"So you are here?" said the female voice.

He was startled. His heart missed a beat. He looked around to see the girl staring at him.

He let his breath out slowly in partial relief.

"I told you to stay in the car," he said, the annoyance clear in his voice.

"I know what you're doing," she said laughing. "Don't get caught. It's big trouble."

"Don't tell me my business." He walked to the door and pulled her inside. "Why did you follow me? With somebody else you might have put yourself in danger."

"You left me there for so long. I didn't know if you were coming back," she answered.

"Don't be stupid. Of course I was coming back. You are needed tonight," said Kanu.

He pushed her towards the bed. "Sit there, don't speak. I will be finished soon. It will not be long before you start earning your money." He looked at his watch.

There was silence whilst he finished his work. Twenty

minutes later he scooped up the spillage with his hands. The package was complete. He looked over to the bed. She'd fallen asleep. For a moment he saw a child's face.

He tried to imagine her family. Before she started this life, she must have had a family. Would they take her back when her body was wrecked? He thought the future held little enough for her. Prostitution is only a transient existence. If she survived she might try to take her broken body back to her village but she would only face ridicule and rejection. He decided she deserved what peace came to her. He'd leave her sleep whilst he made the delivery of joints. Quietly he pulled the door closed as he left.

For a few moments she lay still, not daring to move, not till she was sure. Eventually she risked a peep to confirm he was gone. Then she worked quickly, listening, not knowing when he would return. Her search was practised. She looked in the usual places, careful not to disturb anything. There was precious little of value for her. Only money or jewels would do, things she could hide in the pocket sewn in the hem of her skimpy skirt.

The Kia was set back from the main house, hidden by banana trees and clumps of bamboo. In the darkness it was hard for her to make out the path. She worked her way towards the light. She walked quietly; keeping to the shadows but conscious that bamboo was a favourite place for green mambas to lurk.

If she could get close she might be able to pick up something through the open windows of the big house. The lawn of the courtyard was an open space before her. She waited and watched for signs of movement in the house. She was about to cross when the double louver doors opened spilling light onto the grass. She pulled back, retreating into the shadows. The silhouette of a man filled the opening. He looked into the garden. She stayed motionless; worried in case he should notice her. She need not have worried; his eyes had not adjusted to the dark before the phone rang. The man turned and went back into the room and picked up the receiver. She could hear his voice but not make out the words he spoke.

There would be no easy pickings here. She wanted to get back to the Kia before Kanu returned but something held her. There was a familiarity about the man. She'd seen him before. His hair had more grey and he looked older. His smile as he spoke was not new to her and she recognised his gentle voice. Then it came back to her. She'd sat next to this man on the bus journey from Zambia to Dar Es

Salaam, more than two years ago. She remembered he was a kind man. She wanted to go over to him but knew that was impossible.

She watched until he put down the phone. Only then did she retrace her steps to the Kia. Kanu arrived back when she was approaching the door. He surprised her.

"What are you doing here?" he demanded.

"I needed the toilet", she said.

He looked at her suspiciously. "It's around the side," he pointed. "Come straight back."

"It's a lot of money. What if I don't like it?"

Joshua pulled deeply on the joint. The tip glowed brightly. The Stones blared from the cassette player. Smoke gently drifted in the still room. He looked over to the youth who'd just spoken.

"If you don't like it? Well, if you don't like it perhaps you should consider a little boy next time. It might be more to your liking."

The others laughed. There were six now. Atu returned to the room with more bottles of beer.

"Fifty dollars each," said Joshua. "That's the deal. If it's too much you shouldn't be here."

They sat on the floor passing the joint around the room, drinking beer between draws. Atu gave him the wad of cash. Joshua counted the money then folded the notes before putting them in the breast pocket of his shirt, almost as if it were unimportant. He waited until the joint passed him once more then got up.

"I'll be back soon with the main event."

By the light of the rising moon he made his way down the long drive. He listened for a while before emitting a low pitched whistle. A moment later came the response. Kanu came out of the shadows, leading the girl by the hand.

"Where's the car?" asked Joshua.

"I left it at the Kia. We walked from there. I thought it better if the car was not seen here."

"You took her to the Kia?"

"What was I supposed to do?" replied Kanu.

"That was a stupid thing to do. Now she knows too much." He took her arm and led her forward towards the house.

"Keep to the arrangements. Be back here when I return."

At the top of the drive he stopped under the lone security light. He looked her up and down. She was pretty, there was something familiar about her, McKay had picked well.

"You don't look as bad as most of the whores. But I warn you, you had better be good or I will punish you."

They continued around the house. Without knocking he slid the patio door open and pushed her into the room. She resisted the shove, pushing backwards until she was again on the patio.

"What?" asked Joshua.

"I was told two people. There are six. I will not do it, not without more money."

"You have to. There is no choice," said Joshua.

"Six people for $20! I will not do it. I want $10 for each person or I go now."

. "Do not speak of money in front of these people." Joshua pulled her away from the patio doors. When they were alone he spoke. "The agreement was $20."

"Yes. But not for six people," she protested and started to walk away.

"Come back you bitch," he shouted. "We have a deal."

She turned to face him. "Sixty dollars in cash now," she said with outstretched hand.

"I will pay you," Joshua coincided, "but I will speak to McKay about this."

"Speak to who you want. I gave you the price, now give me the money or I will go."

"I don't have enough with me now," he lied. "You can have it when I get paid."

She hesitated and looked Joshua in the eye. Then she smiled.

"Wild thing, you make my heart sing….."

The words of the Troggs immortal song resounded loudly around the smoke filled room. Eyes, clouded by drugs and drink, watched as she walked amongst them. In the middle of the room she pouted her breasts and displayed her legs, tantalisingly apart. Somebody gave her a beer. She provocatively sealed her lips over the neck of the bottle and gyrated her hips to the rhythm of the music.

No one moved, they just looked as she performed for them, nobody wanting to disturb the moment. They may have been the same age but she was a woman and they were still children. She opened the patio door.

"There is a pool. I have never been to a house with a swimming pool before."

"You can swim if you want," said Atu. "Nobody will see you, except us."

She walked towards the pool. They crowded the doorway. She removed her clothes till she stood, with her back to them, naked. Not till she'd entered the pool did they go forward. At first they watched her nakedness as she swam. When she turned over onto her back they got first sight of her breasts and her lush triangle.

"Come in," she invited.

All but Joshua undressed and entered the water. He sat alone and watched as the youths circled her like nervous cubs, too scared to approach their prey. Slowly they gained courage from each other. Atu dared touch her first. The others quickly copied. Soon clumsy hands fondled, frantically exploring. She did not resist. In turn she worked magic with her hands. It became like a feeding frenzy. She broke away and climbed out of the pool, her body glistening as water ran down her naked black skin.

"Who will be first?" she coaxed.

"You must pick," said Atu.

"All right," she said, "that is good. If I can choose I will pick this one." Quickly she turned and pointed to Joshua.

Joshua stood up, "No, not me."

"Why? Are you scared? Is my body too much for you?" She rubbed her breasts with the palms of her hands to tantalise him.

"You must go with one of the others," he said.

"Go on," shouted Atu. "We don't mind. You can break her in for us."

The others cheered as she grabbed his hand and dragged him towards the house. Inside she found a bedroom.

"This will do."

"I don't want this," he said with anger in his voice.

She ignored his protest and closed on him. He tried to break free but she had him cornered. He felt her naked body press on his own. Her hands worked furiously. She pulled his shirt open; her hand went down his trousers. Frantically he fought to get free. Then he felt her hand on his shame.

"Ah!" she exclaimed with a smile. "Now I know why. Limp dick! That is your problem." She laughed into his face. "What a useless little sausage. Let me play with it. I will make it hard."

"Get away!" he shouted trying to conceal his embarrassment.

He always thought it was not normal, now he knew. He'd heard others speak, but there was nothing he could do. It had been his shameful secret. He felt rage building. She must not tell. His open hand came down hard on the side of her face. Her expression was of bewilderment. She went to the side, her legs buckled. She collapsed and her head hit the floor. Slowly she moved, turning to look up at him. She struggled to raise herself. On her knees, she tried to make the door. He grabbed her hair and pulled her backwards. She toppled again. He kicked her in the ribs.

"Bitch", he shouted.

She tried to curl up and groaned. He kicked again, her back.

"Bitch," he repeated. "Get up, GET UP."

Slowly she rolled over and struggled to her knees. He held her hair with one hand and once more he hit her face with the flat of his hand. Blood flowed from her nose and split lip.

"No, no more," she pleaded, managing to stay on her knees.

He felt it for the first time. Power, excitement. He felt the hardness, hardness like he'd never felt before. He hit her again and it felt better. He freed himself and forced it into her mouth. She gagged, but he held her head firm. The more she struggled the better it became. He withdrew and forced her onto the bed. He lost his virginity watching her bloody tortured face. For more than an hour he went on, inflicting pain, never wanting it to end. Then, in a seemingly unending eruption he came over her and then it was over.

It was minutes before he became aware of her whimpering body, which he still clasped tightly. Slowly he relaxed his grip and pushed her to the ground. He dressed and left the room.

The cassette had finished and the deck clicked off automatically. Nobody bothered to turn the tape over. Atu and the others were dressed. They sat at the patio table in silence. The spell was broken. Bottles of beer stood un-drunk on the table. Condensation formed on the cool outside surface and trickled down the glass. The screams of the girl had been heard by all. The piercing sound had broken the effect of alcohol and drugs. No one looked at Joshua as he threw their money back on the table.

"I made a mistake with this girl," said Joshua. "She is no good. I will get a better one next time. There is your money. You can have the Dagga for nothing. I will send somebody for her. Do not speak of this evening to anybody. Do you understand?"

The threat was clear, a response unnecessary. Joshua left the others sitting in silence.

At the gate he made the low pitched whistle again. Kanu appeared.

"It was quick. They could not hold their loads?" he laughed. The dull light hid Joshua's face.

"Where is the girl?" asked Kanu.

"She was no good," replied Joshua. "Get her from the house. Take her back to the docks. I do not wish to see her again."

"What about her money?" asked Kanu.

"She did nothing so she gets nothing. Just take her away." Joshua walked off into the night remembering his euphoria.

Mashava, Rhodesia March 1975

Diesel had made steam locomotives redundant in England. Not so in coal rich, oil starved South Africa. The two soot-blackened monsters belched steam and smoke as they dragged the long line of Pullman carriages out of Cape Town. The city that marked the convergence of the Indian and Atlantic Oceans was soon out of sight. The train traversed the narrow coastal plain and began its steep assent, along valley floor and through rocky gorge. Rails hugged the contours of the foothills; the locomotives struggled against the grade, until finally breaking out onto the Central Plateau where it began to gain speed. Only then was Duncan introduced to Africa's vastness. The Karoo, the barren undulating country that is the central plateau, became his scenic companion for a day and a half, the time it took to reach Johannesburg and its sister city, Pretoria, political capital of South Africa.

Duncan stood on the steps of the Rhodesian Embassy before 9am the day after the train arrived. The sign read 'Immigration Section'. He was not the first. Already a motley assortment of about a dozen men impatiently waited. A sense of anticipation pervaded. No doubt each man had their own special reason for wanting to gain entry to renegade Rhodesia. It was not a casual destination.

Precisely as the hour struck, heavy bolts could be heard sliding back and the great door slowly opened revealing an aged Consular Official, the stereo-typical product of an English public school.

"Good morning," he said, barring the way. "A good few of you today I see. All for immigration?" he asked.

Heads nodded and voices mumbled.

"Good. Then follow me." He led the procession through a hall and beckoned them into a side room that contained two rows of school desks.

"Please take a seat and do not speak to each other. There is a form and pen for each of you. Do not touch them until told to do so. Are there any people here who do not speak or understand English?" he asked.

Duncan smiled at the futility of the question which inevitably received no response.

A younger more astute man strode into the room. His presence demanded attention, he didn't introduce himself.

"I won't beat around the bush. My time is too precious; I do not propose to waste it."

"At the Embassy we know the position of Rhodesia better than anybody else. We are aware that the current situation of our country may make us an attractive proposition for certain undesirable individuals." He looked around the group.

"Here we vet and filter the people who want to come to our country. Some categories of people are welcome, others are not. If you are seeking adventure or want to start a new life you'll be welcomed. If you have some kind of military experience so much the better. We can even understand and make allowances for past mistakes, within limits.

However some applicants think that because Rhodesia has no diplomatic relations with the majority of the world it is a good place to escape justice for heinous crimes. Let me be clear. It is not.

We maintain unofficial contacts with international agencies. Individuals who have committed serious crimes against the person or sexual offences will find no safe haven in Rhodesia. Nor will malingerers be welcome."

He paused before continuing. "The process is as follows. Today you will fill in the form in front of you. You will leave the form and your passport on the desk. Tomorrow afternoon you will return to the embassy and either have your passport returned to you immediately or be invited to undergo an interview and medical examination. One week after that you can phone the embassy to see if your application has been successful. If it has you will attend the embassy to collect your entry and work permits. Additionally we will provide you, free of charge, a one way train ticket from Johannesburg Central rail station to Rhodesia. Any questions? Right, start filling in the forms."

Almost as an afterthought he spoke. "If you lie on the forms, and we find out, it will be considered a crime against the State. Be careful what you write."

Duncan lied on only one question: Do you have any ongoing affiliation, allegiance or obligation to any foreign military or intelligence gathering organisation?

Waiting slows down time. The two weeks passed slowly but

now at last he walked the platform at Jo'burg Central. The pristine royal blue Pullman carriages waited. They were embellished with a coat of arms and boasted 'Rhodesian Railways' in gold lettering along their length. The manufacturer's plate on the bulkhead, near the door said 'Made in Manchester England 1906'.

Duncan put down his suitcases and ran a hand over the polished panelling in the corridor. He could smell the bee's wax polish.

"Don't make them like this anymore do they?" The voice came from behind.

"When you're finished looking wouldn't mind getting a seat." The face was grinning. "How far you going?"

"Beite Bridge", answered Duncan.

"I'm for Salisbury myself, wouldn't mind a bit of company on the way."

Duncan picked up his bag and moved down the corridor.

"Grab the first empty compartment and spread out," said the stranger. "Bit of luck we'll get it to ourselves and then we can get some kip on the way."

Duncan picked the first empty compartment and placed his suitcase on the overhead rack. He held out his hand. "Murdoch, Duncan Murdoch."

"Pleased to meet you Duncan, I'm Rory," said his new travelling companion.

The stranger plonked himself on the sprung seat facing Duncan. "Just got your entry and work permits?" he asked.

"Yes," Duncan replied. "The embassy in Pretoria arranged for somebody to meet me at Beite Bridge. They said he'd get me fixed up with work and accommodation. Feels a bit hit and miss to me to be honest."

"What do you do Duncan?" asked the stranger.

"I've a civil explosives licence. I'm looking for mine work," he replied.

"Ah! No problem. That's the truth," said Rory. "But don't feel you have to take the first thing that's offered. There's a hell of a manpower shortage. You can take your pick. Your family going to follow?"

"No," replied Duncan. "I don't have much of a family."

Rory's face took on a serious expression. "Not one of these mercenary chaps are you? In the war for what you can get?"

"No," said Duncan. "I've been working in the Shetlands,

nothing but sheep for company and I need somewhere a bit warmer."

The stranger nodded. "Got some wild Scottish oats to sow then," he joked.

The guard's whistle pierced the air outside on the platform. There was a clatter as the slack in the linkages between the carriages was taken up and then the train began to move forward gently gathering speed.

Rory stretched his legs and eyed up his companion. "What do you think of the Kaffers then?"

"Kaffers?"

"Yeah, Kaffers, the black fellows."

"Oh," said Duncan shrugging his shoulders. "Don't know, never really got to know any except for a Nigerian who stayed in the same place as me for a while." Duncan recalled the honking black drunk in the next room to him in the YMCA with something less than fondness.

"The Kaffers you meet in England aren't the same as we got in Rhodesia. In Rhodesia they're hardly out of the bush. Take my advice; you don't want to be mixing with them. In any case the smell will be enough to put you off."

"Smell, what smell?" asked Duncan.

"You'll find out soon enough. They stink."

"You mean they're dirty?" he asked.

"Some of them wash but they still stink. It's their diet. Too much sadza. Their sweat is different to ours." Rory scrunched his face as if his nasal passages were being offended.

"I'm sure it's not that bad," Duncan laughed.

"You wait" said Rory before changing tack.

"Did anybody tell you about the Morality Acts?"

"What are they?" asked Duncan.

"It's the law. No marriage, no fornicating, no mixing between the races. Not that white people need telling. The law is to make it clear to the Kaffers, just in case any of them get ideas about our white women."

"Am I to take it you're not overly fond of the Africans then?" asked Duncan smiling.

"It's no joking matter," said Rory. "It's what the bloody war's about. We're not going to let a bunch of Commie Kaffers take over what we've built up over the last seventy years."

"I'm big enough to make up my own mind," said Duncan with irritation.

Rory stood. "You're not even in the country and you're telling us what to do."

"I didn't tell you to do anything," said Duncan.

"I think I'll go a bit further up the carriage," said Rory sliding open the compartment door and taking his suitcase from the rack.

"Great start," thought Duncan as he settled down for the journey alone.

Oyster Bay, May 1975

Joshua suspected it could only be very good or very bad. His father never wasted time on idle chit-chat. The sanctity of his father's study was rarely broken for social events, so the summons had made him nervous. He feared his father had found out his dark secrets. With concealed trepidation, after dinner, Joshua knocked on the door and waited.

"Come in." The call came quickly.

Joshua listened for a hint of intonation in his father's voice. He entered, still uncertain, and looked around the dull room, the place where his father spent most of his waking hours. Bookshelves lined the walls with volumes that could not have possibly been read. The lush Persian carpet was soft under foot. Silas Sovimbo sat behind the oversized antique desk in his favourite captain's swivel chair. A desk lamp cast a glow onto a letter that rested on the green leather desktop. Joshua strained to make out the impossibly small print. He could determine nothing beyond the coat of arms at the top of the page.

"Are you are trying to read the letter?" asked his father.

"No," denied Joshua. "It is just the strange picture on top of the paper that I am looking at. On one side of the shield is a lion. I recognise that. On the other is a strange animal. Like a horse with a horn coming out of its head. I have never seen such an animal before."

Silas smiled. "Nor will you see this animal except in pictures, for it does not exist. It is the figment of someone's imagination, a mythological creation. But it is special within the world of mythology.

Throughout history man has imagined many animals in his mind. Invariably these animals have some fearsome or threatening characteristic. But the unicorn is different. It is the product of a pure mind, because it has no bad features. It signifies only peace and harmony. It is therefore somewhat implausible that is appears on the coat of arms of Great Britain, the worst example of imperialism and colonial oppression that has ever existed." Silas laughed at the irony. "Sit down."

His father was in good mood. Joshua had little trouble

concealing his relief. Now it was fine, although in his heart Joshua knew that someday he would be found out.

"Mao said that the requirements of the collective good always override the needs of individuals and the family," Silas began. "This entails a sacrifice for all individuals and family members. I have guided our family according to Mao's words. This is why I have not been the father that you may have wanted. But you will always have the satisfaction of knowing the contribution you have made to the future of the people of a free Zimbabwe. I hope you will come to understand this."

Joshua nodded and wondered what gem his father had in store for him now.

Silas continued, "But this is not to say that you are ever far from my thoughts. Your teachers write to me and I get school reports. I am not ignorant of your progress. And now has come the time for me to say how proud I am of you."

Joshua's face lit up, but it was a mistake for Silas to interpret his son's smile as being an indication of pleasure or gratitude for the praise he was receiving. It never crossed his honest mind that his son drew amusement out of irony.

Joshua recalled his teacher, Mr Gupta's, practical lessons on methods and benefits of corruption in an education system. The lessons had started soon after Joshua had met McKay. One afternoon Joshua was struggling with the last hour of lessons. It was hot and boring as usual. Joshua divided his time between doodling and staring out of the window, contemplating his apparently insoluble problem: how could he get more free time to concentrate on his new business? He knew he was still dependent on his father who sent him to school. However he had little desire to waste time slumped over a desk scratching with nib and ink, listening to a 'wobble head' droning in monotone. Joshua knew there were better lessons to be learnt on the beach, more enduring and pleasurable lessons than anything he got from this classroom. He knew business generated money that money was power and power was freedom. Joshua wanted more free time.

Then Gupta, the teacher, had unwittingly provided the solution.

"Katz and Joshua, stay behind. The rest of the class is dismissed," Gupta had said.

When the others had left the classroom the teacher called the boys to stand in front of his desk.

"I believe you boys have been cheating. This is not good," he said, trying vainly to make his diminutive body appear authoritative.

"We have not been cheating," lied Joshua automatically, his mind going into overdrive. Joshua knew Katz was the least wealthy student in the class, he also knew that his financial situation was inversely proportionate to his academic ability. So as Joshua's cash flow became positive it was not difficult to get Katz to do some extra homework for a few Shillings.

Gupta produced two exercise books, one belonging to each of the boys. He opened them on marked pages and placed them flat on the desk.

"Identical writing you will agree. I think this is sufficient evidence of your guilt?"

Katz started to speak, burbling the beginnings of a confession. Joshua put a hand on his classmate's shoulder.

"May I look more closely?" he asked the teacher. "May I take the books to the window? The light is much better there. I want to make a proper inspection."

"You may look," said a suspicious Gupta. "But I am watching you."

Joshua took the books and crossed the room. He kept his back to Gupta and fumbled for effect as he removed two one-dollar bills from his shirt pocket and inserted them inside the offending pages, before returning the books to the curious teacher.

"It is my opinion that if you also look in better light you will see the hand writing is actually quite different. I think nobody has cheated."

Gupta shook his head but nevertheless took the books to the window. Joshua held Katz by the arm to stop him following the teacher. A few moments later Gupta returned to his chair.

"You are very clever Joshua. It is apparent in the 'clear light of day', so to speak, that you have not cheated at all."

He handed the books back to the boys. Joshua noted the dollar bills were gone.

"I think you can go," the teacher said to Katz. "Joshua you might like to stay a little longer. Gupta wore his most ingratiating smile.

They'd spoken as equals. The teacher said he wanted Joshua as a special friend and he was insistent that friendship was a matter of deeds, not just words. Gupta explained he had a family in India that would very much benefit from the receipt of a few US dollars now and again.

Exam times were a period when the depth of their friendship came to the fore. Joshua felt claustrophobic in crowded exam rooms, quite bilious in fact. He was pleased not to have to attend. On the other hand Gupta was bored with long hours of silent invigilation. He was more than pleased to sit an occasional paper himself, confident that the Oxford and Cambridge Examination Board would not be displeased to see an improving pass rate.

Over the following academic years the relationship blossomed. Joshua obtained five "O" levels. Unfortunately he only got a "C" in English Language, but overall the results were pleasing and he'd consequently progressed to "A" levels, confident of similar success.

And now Joshua sat in front of his father reaping the rewards of his malevolent industriousness.

"In a few months you will be finished at the Indian School," said Silas to his son. "I am hopeful you will do well in the examinations. The indications are that if you continue as you are things will be fine."

"The question is what will we do with you then? It is my belief that every Zimbabwean must contribute to the freedom struggle of our country according to their ability. You too must contribute.

What I have chosen for you is unusual. It will take you away from here, away from your home and family. I know you will suffer hardship and you will be forced to work hard but I believe it is the sacrifice you must make."

Silas picked up the letter from the desk.

"I have a letter here from the British High Commissioner in Dar Es Salaam. It is about you. I have considered the contents and decided the risks involved are worth it. The British want to curry favour with the leaders of the liberation movement. As part of this they are offering scholarships at British Universities for able students. Whilst we know that British society is in terminal decline they still maintain some of the best universities in the world. As part of the programme you are to be offered a place at a British University. Should I force you to go has been the question I have been pondering?

You will be exposed to a decadent self-indulgent society and it would be easy for you to be drawn into the bad habits of alcohol abuse and sexual promiscuity that pervade that society."

Joshua contained his feelings and struggled to keep his composure.

"I can see what is going through your mind," said Silas. "I have only one question for you. Do you feel strong enough to resist the temptations that will be put before you?"

Joshua wanted to shout "No fucking way." Instead he maintained his calm and said, "I think so."

Twenty-four hours, how twenty-four hours could change things. Joshua walked the Harbour Road, his anger barely subdued. "McKay will pay!" he thought, although he did not know how. Last night the world was in his grasp. His father had given him the key to all he wanted and was ready to open the door of opportunity. Now, McKay was trying to ruin everything.

He continued walking along the road. Shadows were long; the afternoon sun was dipping below the buildings, its day's work almost done. He pushed his way through the crowds, oblivious to the eyes that followed him. Adding to his misery, today there was no Kanu. Joshua's father needed the car. So he would have to go home alone, by bus.

Joshua had just had his first meeting with McKay since the night with the girl. They'd met alone in the alley. McKay faced Joshua, standing close, too close, using his height to intimidate.

"You will pay me," declared McKay, "I will have my share for the night and I will have compensation too. You must pay for damaging my property."

"But the girl was no good," protested Joshua. "I made no money myself."

"The girl was good when she arrived," said McKay, "She has been mine for two years. I trained her. I looked after her. She was my investment. Now her face is marked and her nose bent. She is useless. Even drunken sailors will not pay for someone in that condition. She cannot work the Europeans anymore. All she is good for is locals that have useless Shillings to spend. You will give me $500 dollars now if we are to continue as we were."

"That's impossible," protested Joshua. "I don't have that kind of money. I never earned that much since we became partners."

"Partners!" said McKay mockingly. "We were never partners. You delude yourself. Give me $500 now or you work it off with interest. These are your choices."

"But we are friends. You cannot make me do this. It is not fair." Joshua defended. His mind raced. "Resist," he thought.

"I will not do it. You are not the only one who can supply Dagga." Joshua's reaction was instinctive, without substance. "I can manage without you."

In an instant McKay pounced. Joshua was caught off guard and stumbled backward, struggling to maintain his balance. Then he was pressed tight against the wall. He felt the pressure of the unseen blade in his abdomen. McKay's breath was foul, his eyes dilated with rage.

He hissed. "Never threaten. Just do. Now you have lost the advantage. You are close to becoming food for the fish. Do you accept your debt? Yes or no? Be quick, or I will make up your mind for you?"

Joshua felt the tip of the knife pressing. He thought his skin would yield. He trembled and felt the muscles of his bladder relax. He fought to stop the flow of warm liquid down his leg.

"I didn't mean it. I was joking."

He feebly smiled in submission. "Please take the knife away, it is hurting me. I will do as you ask."

McKay gave the blade a last twist and watched Joshua wince before he relaxed his grip.

"Your jokes are not funny. Go now but come back in three days. I will tell you what you have to do then."

Joshua continued his walk, his mind was jumbled. The street was changing. The warehouses, the ships chandlers and shipping agent's offices were long passed. Now the street was lined with open fronted shops, the lairs of Arab traders. Joshua saw the Muslim proprietors in white robes and chuff head dress. They loitered almost nonchalantly, always ready to pounce on the unwary.

Something caught Joshua's eye. He crossed the road, weaving between the traffic and the crowds.

"What is it you see?" said the smiling Arab trader who'd spotted Joshua in much the same way as a spider sees its prey approaching.

"A prayer mat? You are a believer? No? No matter. What about this?" he said pointing to a carved hookah. "Too many hours of patient work have gone into these masterpieces. I can never get my money back. For you a very good price. No? What then?"

The shopkeeper was rubbing his hands and manoeuvring, positioning himself to block Joshua's escape from the store.

"I am looking for something special," said Joshua.

The Trader thought. "Ah, yes. What better display of manhood than a precious dagger? Ivory handle, curved steel blade as ordained by the Prophet. Perhaps a jewelled scabbard? Essential. It is good you don't forget the old ways. Let me show you. I have the best," he said pulling at Joshua's shirt.

"I know what I want," said Joshua resisting the trader's tug. He pointed to a display cabinet at the back of the shop.

The traders face fell.

"Not a weapon for a man," he thought as his customer led the way. He suppressed his feelings.

"Beautiful items," he said with well concealed scorn. "You have come to the right place; I am the only one in Dar Es Salaam that has this item."

Joshua smiled at the sales talk. He thought the next shop would also be the only one with this item! Preoccupied he missed the eyes that followed him and the neck that vainly craned to get a better view of Joshua's potential purchase.

The bargaining process began. The Arab feigned hurt as each offer was made and rejected. No Trader respected a customer that failed to follow the ritualistic bargaining process. The price was settled where Joshua knew it would end. He declined to have his purchase wrapped, just slipping it into his pocket. He stepped back onto the street and continued his journey to the bus station. Behind him feet walked quickly, making ground.

At the other end of Harbour Road the rusting bow of a giant cargo ship towered over the dock, its name 'SHEN FENG' written tall in white letters. Hidden under a coat of peeling black paint the silhouette of the original name of the vessel could be made out, "MV WICKLOW".

The sixteen thousand tonne freighter had been constructed on the Clyde in Scotland. For almost two decades it had run between

Europe and the Antipodes and it would have continued to do so had not an engineer from Lloyds of London, wielding his little hammer, noted too much flaking on the steel hull and decking. The insurance premiums increased and for the shipping company's accountants the sums no longer made sense. The vessel was sold to a Greek company as scrap only to re-emerge a year later as the "SHEN FENG", flying the flag of the Peoples Republic of China. Reincarnated the vessel plied the South China Sea and the Indian Ocean visiting ports that operated a more relaxed insurance regime.

They gathered in what had been the Smoke Room, the place where a generation of British Merchant Navy Officers had sipped pink gins at lunch time and played bridge and canasta during long evenings at sea. Now it was the ships 'Hall of Culture', a name more grandiose than the reality.

Tongogara the guest of honour and leader of ZAPU, the military wing of Robert Mugabe's liberation movement, stood in the middle of the room. Next to him was Silas Sovimbo. One a brilliant leader in guerrilla warfare the other a patient diplomat and ideologue. Both united in the common cause of liberation.

The Chinese Ambassador to Tanzania stood holding a ceramic cup ready for the toast. He wore the Chinese revolutionary uniform of denim and spoke in broken English.

"That we are here today is prophetic. The name of this ship is Shen Feng. Translated this means Victorious Wind. The cargo of military equipment being unloaded will ensure victory for the Zimbabwean people over their Imperial oppressors. It is the last piece of the jigsaw. For years our people have spoken and planned. Now it is time to act. With this last consignment of military equipment the framework for victory is complete. Training camps in Tanzania, staffed by Chinese Communist Party Members, are turning out Commissars who will disseminate the word and provide the ideological backbone to the struggle. As I speak military training bases are being established in the north of Mozambique. Volunteers from the Red Army will ensure that fighters progressing to the forward camps will be of the highest calibre.

I now propose a toast to our peoples. I have chosen the drink carefully. Maotai is an ancient drink. It is the product of blending two fermented grains together, wheat and sorghum. For me it symbolises the coming together of our peoples. The blend is distilled to produce a pure white spirit with a strong flavour. May Maotai symbolise our eternal relationship." He raised his cup high.

All drank.

Seven hundred miles away brakes shrieked metal on metal. The train ground to a halt with a shudder that only half roused Duncan from his sleep. He rubbed his stiff neck and looked out of the window onto the deserted station platform. The Guard unceremoniously yanked open the sliding door of the compartment.

"Messina, ten minutes if you want to stretch your legs. There's a bank to change money. I'm supposed to tell you that but the Rhodesians would rather you change on the other side." He slammed shut the door.

"The last town in South Africa," Duncan thought in his stupor. He'd hardly regained consciousness when the train started moving on the next leg of its journey.

For most of the year the upper reaches of the Limpopo ran dry leaving only a sandy riverbed to mark the border. But the situation would change quickly during the rainy season when tropical storm clouds unleashed their deluges that could instantly turn dry watercourses into raging torrents. Now was the rainy season and muddy waters swirled around the concrete pontoons of the combined road/rail bridge. The train made no attempt to build up a head of speed when leaving Messina. It clattered over the rail joints creating a slow steady metallic rhythm, the carriages coasting along almost effortlessly. The train broke from the cover of vegetation and crossed the steel and concrete structure at a leisurely pace and slid into Beite Bridge station on the far side of the river.

The sign read 'You are entering the Republic of Rhodesia'. Duncan stepped down from the carriage onto the platform and felt the warm dry breeze on his face. The sun cast long shadows and there was a profusion of tissue thin pink leaves on the ground, fallen from the Bougainvillea that lined the platform.

The porter from the train unloaded Duncan's cases. Before he could protest another black porter had picked them up. Duncan followed. At the door to the station building he was met by a European Immigration official wearing a white uniform more in keeping with the navy than any other service.

"I am obliged to give you this notice on arrival and ask that you read it and confirm you understand."

Duncan took the leaflet. Foolscap neatly cut in half. Top centre was the Rhodesian coat of arms.

"Welcome to Rhodesia. At the present time a state of emergency exists throughout the country. All persons within Rhodesia, whether Rhodesians or other Nationals are subject to the Emergency Regulations. All instructions issued by officers of the Police and Army are binding. Failure to comply with instructions will result in arrest and punishment in accordance with the specific ordnance of the Emergency Powers Act. Emergency Powers are intended to improve the security situation for all people within the borders. If you feel unable to comply with the regulations you should not enter Rhodesia. Please enjoy your stay."

"Clear enough," said Duncan.

"You coming in?" asked the Immigration Officer.

"Aye, I suppose I will, I've come this far."

Joshua hurried; he was close to the bus station now, just as darkness was falling. The stink of rank food from the street vendors pervaded the air and was only occasionally masked by the smell of burnt diesel as buses revved up and discharged clouds of black smoke that lingered in the still air.

Joshua dreaded using the bus when his father took Kanu and the car. He hated mixing with the dregs from the street. He worked his way across the square. Buses were parked side by side in bays. Joshua looked for his bus. It would be a good one, one with unbroken windows. The best buses were reserved for Oyster Bay. He walked around the back of the vehicles where there were fewer people. He suspected nothing till the hand came to rest on his shoulder. The lightness of the touch did not generate alarm. He turned.

"You! What do you want? How did you know I was here?"

"I followed you. You have been with McKay," she said. "He has thrown me out. He says I am no good anymore. Now I have no one to look after me and it is your fault."

"What do you expect from me? You have caused me many problems. Go away." Joshua pushed her away with one hand.

"You did this." She raised her head and pointed to the fresh scar that gave her a hair lip.

"They say I am scarred for life. I am no longer beautiful. How will I survive? You have a duty to help me."

Joshua laughed. "I must help you, a whore off the street. I would not piss on your burning body. Go away and die. It would be better for us all." He turned away not even harbouring a nagging doubt.

She shouted after him. "If you won't help me I know your father will. I will tell him about you. Does he know about the Dagga you sell?"

Joshua froze for a second and then went back to her. He grabbed her hair and pushed her down a narrow gap between two buses.

"Why do you speak of my father? How do you know him?" he shook her violently. "Tell me."

"I have seen your father, when I was in the Kia of your home. You will do well to treat me better."

"You are nothing to my father. He will not see you," said Joshua.

"I know your father is a kind man, he has not changed from the time I sat next to him on the bus from Zambia, coming to this place."

Joshua had thought there was something familiar about her, now like a mist clearing it came back to him. He could recall her face now. She'd changed, she'd aged and was no longer a green innocent, and her face was worldlier.

"On the bus from Zambia your father told me I could come to him for help. It may be time for me to do that."

Again he grabbed her hair. Now he banged her head on the side of the bus.

"You will not speak with my father. I forbid it." He felt a stirring in his belly and had to fight his arousal. He reached into his pocket, glad he'd told the Arab trader not to wrap the flick knife. He held it to her face. He pressed the button and the blade swung out and locked into position with a metallic click.

Still holding her hair with one hand he waved the switchblade beneath her nose and let the tip touch her cheek. He pushed until a droplet of blood appeared. She wriggled in an attempt to break free.

"Stay still or it will be worse," he warned. He wanted to go on, the feeling was good but he pulled himself back.

"Do not come near my father or me. Go back to where you came from." He pushed her to the ground.

"It will be bad for you if I see you again." He turned and went to look for his bus.

Duncan followed the directions he'd been given. They weren't complicated, there was only one road. It had taken him five minutes to walk. For Duncan motels were something from American movies. He'd never seen one before and he was disappointed. It was just a dusty courtyard with single story chalets on two sides and a low office block on the third. Each chalet had a small stoop and parking space in front. About half the parking slots were occupied.

"The Motel is to Rhodesia what the B&B is to England," said the Manager. "It's a cheap place to stay when travelling. Of course it does help if you have a car."

"I just arrived on the train. Somebody from Fort Victoria was supposed to meet me. But I got a message to come here."

The manager nodded. "You'll be going on the escorted convoy in the morning then."

"No chance of going tonight? he asked.

"No way," said the Manager. "It's only essential military night travel nowadays. All civilian travel is in convoy."

"Is it that bad?" asked Duncan.

"No, not really, most of the trouble is in the North and North East but we do have regular scares."

The Manager passed Duncan a key.

"Benjamin," he called. The black porter quickly appeared.

"Take the Boss's bags to number 22."

Duncan bent to pick up his case.

"Let the boy carry the case, don't do him out of a job, he'll get upset. Dinner is between six and seven."

It was more a rude thump than a knock on the door.

"You sleeping in there?" The voice was gruff and loud.

Duncan roused himself and opened the door. It was still daylight.

"If I was sleeping I'm not now," he said to the squat middle aged man in an ill fitting white suit and Panama hat.

"Sorry about that. I'm taking you to Fort Victoria in the morning, thought you might like to join me for a beer before dinner."

Joshua missed the first bus. Another quickly took its place. He sat at the back. Other seats were quickly taken, a scramble began. More people squeezed on. The aisle filled with standing passengers.

Joshua detested the forced intimacy of bus travel. He didn't like his space being invaded and the foul smell of humanity was abhorrent to him.

Buses left not by time-table but as soon as they were full – really full. Joshua could see nothing through the throng in front of him. He became impatient. At last the engine spluttered to life and he felt the clank as the driver selected first gear. He willed the bus forward. It was not possible for him to see the dishevelled girl who'd forced her way between two youths onto the running platform.

Natural light was now gone. Street lighting was a luxury preserved for few privileged areas. Most light along the bus route spilled from roadside shops and stalls and was meanly supplemented by the yellow glow of kerosene lamps that hung on the carts of street vendors. The bus progressed slowly, often not much faster than walking pace. People jumped off and on at will.

More people got off than got on and gradually the standing crowed thinned. Joshua's mind remained on McKay. Then it dawned on him he wouldn't have the money to pay Gupta to sit his exams for him now. The imponderable problem made him oblivious to the girl, who now had a seat, at the front of the bus. He never noticed as she occasionally glanced over her shoulder to look at him.

The bus passed the checkpoint that marked the beginning of Oyster Bay and the start of some feeble street lighting. The red and white pole of the barrier was raised and a uniformed soldier stood to something approaching attention outside the ramshackle guardhouse. The bus slowed but did not stop. Joshua stood and made his way forward. The bus stopped fifty yards short of Joshua's turning but he was glad to get off. He started walking as the bus pulled away. A few moments later the solitary brake light illuminated and the bus stopped again. He thought he recognised the girl that got off. He stopped walking and screwed his eyes in the half-light. Curiosity turned to panic. He began to run towards her. She continued onward. His heart was pounding. She was going to make good her threat to speak to his father. She would spoil everything. It would be the end. He ran harder.

Weeks ago the Government had sent a security guard to stand outside the house, twenty-four hours a day. Silas had been pleased at first. He said it was an indication that he was becoming effective in the liberation struggle. Then he'd seen that the guard noted all his visitors and he began to suspect that the Tanzanian authorities had another motive.

Joshua ran hard knowing he had to catch her before she got to the main gate and the guard.

"Wait!" he tried to gauge the level of his shout, loud enough for her to hear but quiet enough not to alarm others.

"Wait. Please wait."

In silent acknowledgement of the request she slowed and he gained on her. Eventually he was close enough to reach her arm. He pulled her to a stop.

"Are you going to hit me again?" she asked.

"Where are you going? Do you know what you are doing?" he said.

"You know the answer to both those questions," she replied. "Only your father will help me now."

Joshua's mind worked. "He will only give you the bus fare back to Zambia. What will you do then? You will be back where you started."

"What is my alternative?" she replied.

"I can do more for you. Come with me and we will talk," he said.

"I gave you that opportunity once. This is what I got for my trouble." She pointed to the mark on her cheek.

"I panicked. It was a mistake. I'm sorry. Come let's talk."

"Where?" she asked.

"The Kia. You have already been there. You can use the back gate. It is locked but I will come around and let you in. We can talk privately." He led her by the arm not waiting for a reply. She didn't resist.

"I won't wait for long," she said.

Fifteen minutes later Joshua fumbled in the dark with the key to the padlock. He could feel his heart beat and sweat ran down his brow. She appeared out of the darkness as he swung open the chain link gate.

Kanu was away, he'd checked. The key to his room was in its usual hiding place. He twisted the key in the mortise lock and the Kia door opened. He pushed her inside before turning on the light. They stood facing each other. For a moment there was silence.

"Well," she said. "What do you have to say now? What is your offer?"

Joshua had no offer. He had nothing to say. His hands were clammy.

She spoke again. "So your tongue is frozen. I will start. Do you have money to give me?"

"I will get money," he replied.

"I want money now, not a promise. I will not have a wasted journey." Her eyes were piercing and unyielding.

"Give me 500 Shillings now."

"I don't have 500 Shillings now but I will get it for you. I will bring it tomorrow."

She shook her head, contempt crept into her voice.

"You have nothing, you are nothing."

"Don't speak to me like that."

She pushed him further.

"The big man is not so big now," she laughed into his face.

"Don't laugh at me."

"It's different when you are the one being humiliated isn't it? You don't like your own medicine."

She walked towards the door.

He intercepted her. He put the key in the door and locked it.

"You want to make me a prisoner? You want to beat me again?" she goaded. "Touch me and I will scream. I am sure they will hear me in the house." She drew breath.

Before she uttered a sound he pounced. His hand was over her mouth. He tried to force her down. She resisted. They fell together. Then he was astride her. Again he felt power surging through his body and he was aroused. Instinct had taken over. He didn't need to argue with her. He would make her pay for the humiliation. With one hand he gripped her neck and pinned her to the ground. His free hand ripped at her clothes. She fought but by now he was invincible and she could not resist. Then he was in her. He built up to a crescendo and held himself at that high point. She no longer resisted. He raised himself on one arm; the knife was in his free hand.

The tip of the blade penetrated just below the sternum. He pushed it upward and gazed into her unbelieving eyes as steel ruptured her diaphragm and sliced into her left lung. The blade missed her heart but the aorta was punctured. Inside her chest cavity blood pumped furiously. She made a final feeble attempt to break free. It was useless. Blood erupted from her mouth and at the same instant Joshua ejaculated.

Beite Bridge, Rhodesian Border 1975

"What's C.A.P.C.O.?" asked Duncan pointing to the capital letters painted on the door of the BMW Cheetah parked outside Patrick Walkers Motel room. The two men walked across the car park towards the bar.

"Central African Power Corporation," replied Patrick Walker, his stubby legs taking two steps to one of Duncan's.

"It's who I ostensibly work for."

"Ostensibly?" asked Duncan.

"Well they pay me every month," he replied. "It's a unique job. I'll tell you about it sometime. You ready for that beer?"

Patrick Walker's height of five foot six inches was further diminished by a 46-inch waste. He puffed as they climbed the few steps to the bar and took a seat on the veranda.

The unflattering baggy cotton trousers clung to the last vestiges of a crease and his crumpled linen jacket was, improbably, too big. He fanned his red face with his Panama that had the primary function of protecting an almost bald scalp from the sun.

Despite, or perhaps because of his dishevelled appearance there was an aura about Patrick Walker. Duncan couldn't put his finger on it. Perhaps it was the round Churchillian face or maybe the highness of his forehead, or some intangible that betrayed the embedded arrogance of old England.

A waiter brought two bottles of Lion beer.

"Your first beer in Rhodesia?" he raised his glass, "Cheers. May there be many more of them."

They drank.

"Good?" asked Patrick.

"Very," replied Duncan. He put his glass down.

"I thought somebody from Consolidated Mines was picking me up?"

"That was the original plan but I happened to be on my way through and I know some of the chaps at Consolidated, so I volunteered."

"You're from Scotland then?" Patrick asked the obvious. "Do you speak any Gaelic?"

Duncan stiffened imperceptibly in his seat, "A little. Why do you ask?"

"I came across a word the other day. I wondered if you could help with it?"

"Try me," said Duncan.

"Ottrel? What does Ottrel mean?"

"Outsider. It means outsider. But that is not a Gaelic word," replied Duncan.

"No it's dialect from the Borders," Patrick replied.

Both men smiled.

"That's the formalities over. Now we can relax," said Patrick.

"Glad I remembered it all. These password sequence things are tiresome and frankly I find them a bit cloak and daggerish."

"I didn't expect to be contacted so soon?" said Duncan.

"It's what I do. At least now you know what I meant by ostensibly! We'll relax and get to know each other tonight. Tomorrow I'll brief you on a few things. One question though. How's Major Cameron keeping? Haven't seen him for a few years. Same school you know. I was a bit ahead. He was my fag at Repton. Useless little squirt. He's done well to pull things around for himself."

Next morning the sky was clear apart from a few puffs of cotton wool cloud. Duncan sat in the passenger seat of the BMW. He'd just watched Patrick annihilate a fried breakfast with child like glee. Now they waited. A uniformed police officer wearing a leather Sam Browne belt and holster for his service revolver walked the column stopping at each vehicle. A rifle hung loosely on his shoulder.

He came to Patrick's open window. "Done a convoy before?"

Patrick nodded, "Often."

"Guns? Ammunition?"

Patrick pointed to the back seat where an FN lay next to a couple of spare mags.

"Good. No firing unless ordered to do so or a terrorist is actually pointing a gun down your throat. Sound your horn if you're in trouble. Stay in your position, no overtaking, minimum ten yards between vehicles when we get up speed. Clear?"

"Perfectly," replied Patrick with the emphasis on the P.

The officer moved to the next vehicle.

"Nuisance these convoys," said Patrick. "Voluntary at the moment of course, it will be really inconvenient if they ever become compulsory. Make my work much more difficult."

Duncan pointed to the uniform, "Army?"

"BSAP," said Patrick. "British South African Police, the name is a hangover from the British South African Company that used to run the colony before the 1920's."

"Don't look much like police," said Duncan.

"They do a lot for police. In truth they put more men in the field than the Army and they have some formidable firepower to boot. There's rivalry between the Police and the Army."

Engines started. Patrick turned the ignition and the 1800 cc BMW motor came to life. The line moved slowly at first gaining speed gently as they climbed out of the Limpopo Valley. Soon the convoy settled at a comfortable forty miles per hour. Duncan kept his window open.

"Not good farmland between here and Fort Victoria," said Patrick. "It's too low and too hot. Lots of tics about, not good for livestock and cash crops don't do well either. It's mainly bush or Tribal Trust Land."

Duncan looked at Patrick.

"Tribal Trust Land is stuff reserved for the natives. No electricity, no irrigation and no proper roads. Primitive subsistence farming, difficult to make a decent living. Most of the men go to work for cash on the commercial farms or go to factories in the towns. The TTL is mainly kids, old folks, and the unable or unwilling and now the terrorists of course."

Patrick talked, Duncan listened.

"This area has been quiet up to now. The main activity has been in the north along the Zambian border and a bit in the north-east."

"Guerrillas. No not guerrillas," Patrick corrected himself, "Terrorists infiltrate from bases in Mozambique."

"What's the difference between a guerrilla and a terrorist?" asked Duncan. "Isn't it just the side you're on that determines the name?"

Patrick smiled. "As far as the Rhodesians are concerned anybody against them is just a terrorist. But I like to draw a distinction. For me a guerrilla is a fighter working behind enemy lines attacking and destroying military and economic targets. It's a type of legitimate warfare. A terrorist is different. A terrorist has no intention of military success. He'll actually avoid contact with military forces as much as possible. Terrorists only want to destroy the will of the enemy to resist. They attack soft targets, lonely farms, missions, any vulnerable group. Wives, children, priests, aid workers and even nuns. I don't know about you but for me that is morally unacceptable."

"I never thought of it like that," said Duncan.

"The Matable in the north are more guerrillas by nature. They like a good scrap and they're pretty good at it too. The Shona are a different kettle of fish. Not good. Like chalk and cheese."

"Suppose you'd like me to make my way to one of those areas?" asked Duncan.

"Not at all," replied Patrick. "I would like you here in the south, around Fort Victoria. In fact I think I have you fixed up with something that will suit you very well. I'll explain. If Salisbury and Bulawayo, the two main cities, are the organs of Rhodesia then the road and railways links to South Africa are the veins and arteries. Until recently Rhodesia had carried out most of its trade via the port of Bira in Mozambique. But soon Portugal, the colonial power, will pull out of Mozambique leaving the country to the Communists. It is inevitable the new Communist Government of Mozambique will close the border with Rhodesia. That means that the only real link that Rhodesia will have with the outside world will be via Beite Bridge, where we have just come from. This is going to be the real hot spot!

There's another factor. The area around Fort Victoria sits on the traditional tribal boundaries between the Matable and Shona. Both tribes will want control. It's an additional reason why I'd like you around this area. You need to wait, watch and listen.

But it won't be all bad. I can to tell you it's still a great place to live. The Rhodesians have really got the situation sorted out for themselves. Did you know, despite the problems, Rhodesia is still rated as the country with the highest standard of living in the world? No wonder they're hanging on so tightly. You got any questions?"

"What have you got arranged for me work wise?"

"Mashava, a few miles west of Fort Victoria. A great job, lovely area, good facilities. Get in there, settle down, sign up as a reservist - they'll snap your hand off with your military background and skills with explosives. You'll be a dream for them."

"Great," said Duncan. "What do they mine there?"

"Asbestos. It's one of the largest asbestos mines in the world. Not bad eh! Aren't you the lucky one?"

Oyster Bay 1975

"My instructions are to close the file. There will be no further action," Detective Inspector David Muzamindo spoke with a calm deliberance that contained a hint of both apology and finality. "I am authorised to say no more."

David Muzamindo, the most senior investigative detective in Dar Es Salaam's Criminal Investigation Bureau stood stiffly, refusing to sit. His credentials were as impeccable as his appearance. The son of an exiled Tanzanian academic he was brought up in the United States. Weaned on a diet of detective movies and criminal TV series, combined with inherited intelligence and a little support from the Rhodes foundation he was assured of his educational choice. Spurning prized academic placements he attended a criminal investigation course at no less a place than Langlay, home of the FBI. He not only drew attention to himself as a foreign black national but also by the fact that he, time and again, came top of his cohort, beating US students hands down. He was a prize target for US recruiters, but his gentle nature concealed willpower of steel. Nothing would deflect him from returning to his native Tanzania. Quickly he became the backbone of the otherwise disappointing Criminal Investigation Unit in Dar Es Salaam. Consistently he refused promotion over the years, declining both managerial and political positions, in preference to utilising his practical skills.

Silas Sovimbo sat before this man now. He was not satisfied. He rose from his chair to face the Detective eye to eye.

"A few weeks ago a girl was brutally murdered on my property. I am not convinced that it is a coincidence that the victim is known to me. I also do not believe it is coincidental that my driver disappeared that same night and with him went a substantial amount of cash and valuables from my residence. Further, your subordinates indicate to me there is to be an announcement of an important development. Then suddenly, today, I am told that the arrest warrant for my driver has been cancelled and the case is closed. You may think this is satisfactory, I do not. Further you must understand the whole incident has been traumatic for my family, not least for my son who found the body."

"Mr Sovimbo I am a servant of the State. I try to obey

instructions but I may have already exceeded my authority by coming to see you. If you are still dissatisfied I advise you to pursue the matter through other channels. The only thing I will add is some personal advice. On certain occasions, for one's own interest, it is prudent to walk away from an issue."

"I am a man of principle. I do not walk away." Silas concluded it was useless to pressurise the Detective further.

"Despite my disappointment I thank you for coming to see me. I hope you will understand that I do feel it necessary to pursue the matter through formal diplomatic channels."

Hiding outside, on the stoop, Joshua pressed up as close as he dare to the open doors and eavesdropped. "Why will he not leave the matter alone?" he thought. The question was rhetorical. Since the girl's death Joshua's time had been consumed trying to divert blame and salvage what he could from the situation but he knew he might fail because of his father's doggedness.

Two weeks later the letter came, delivered by courier. Silas retreated to his study and sat at his desk before breaking the embossed seal of the Department of Foreign Affairs. He withdrew the single sheet of parchment paper, the type favoured by foreign ministries for formal communications. In eloquent terms the letter invited Silas Sovimbo to attend the Department of Justice, where, in the presence of a representative of the Foreign Ministry, he would be permitted to ask questions of Detective David Muzamindo who in turn would be authorised to answer freely. Ominously the letter concluded by indicating that the results of the meeting might not be to Silas's liking.

The next day uniformed security guards accompanied Silas on his return from the Ministry of Justice. It happened quickly and Joshua did not see his father. If he had, the sight would have been of an ashen stooped figure, aged from the one that had left the house just two hours previously.

The guards came for Joshua. Without word they restrained him as his room was searched. When they were satisfied Joshua was pushed back into his room and the door locked. In the week that followed guards were never absent from his door. The window shutters were screwed closed from the outside and Joshua never crossed the threshold of the room. He was in solitary confinement. Food was delivered silently. Buckets were brought for his washing and ablutions. His cries and appeals went unanswered. Only once did others come into the room. On the second day the door opened. Two powerful guards pinioned Joshua onto the wooden floor. Their grip was harsh and unyielding. A doctor brandished a hypodermic syringe. Without care he dug under the skin of Joshua's arm searching for a vein and withdrew a sample of blood.

Silas too was in isolation. For the first time in memory his attention was diverted from the Struggle. For endless nights he sat in his study. More than once he saw the sun break the horizon without sleep having come. Only slowly did he regain his composure. Letters were written, phone calls made. He wanted to know all. But the full truth remained elusive. Only Joshua could tell that. He girded himself for the encounter.

Joshua lay on the bed, he lay on the bed a lot. Time passed slowly. Each day felt longer than the last. His possessions had ceased providing distraction from the monotony of confinement. He'd divided the day according to the routine that had developed around meals so the unexpected turning of the key in the lock triggered an internal alarm. The room suddenly filled with light. The guards entered without word and lifted Joshua to his feet. They flanked him as he was marched towards his father's study. Again he sat facing the great desk. The room was unchanged but the mood was incomparable.

The old man did not immediately look at his son but sat studying a piece of paper in his hand. The physical change in his father was apparent. The psychological one was not.

On the desk were piles of paper, typed letters and reports. A writing pad lay in front of his father and an expensive fountain pen lay on the pad, as if it had been discarded part way through a thought. Silas put down the piece of paper he was holding. He looked to a point on the ceiling, avoiding his son's eyes.

"You have been accused of many crimes. Some you are clearly guilty of, some are unproven. For days I have struggled trying to separate my emotions from the facts. At first it was hard for me to accept that your failures were not attributable to me. In the end I let logic prevail and came to the conclusion that the things you have done are abhorrent and against the principles I have lived by and tried to teach you. I believe that inside you there lurks an evil streak, placed by nature, for which I cannot take responsibility."

Joshua sat in insolent silence, realising the futility of

argument.

"I have looked at each charge against you. The work is complete to my satisfaction. You are guilty beyond any doubt."

Joshua spoke for the first time. "You have not asked me what happened. Do I not get a say? You told me the accused must have the opportunity to defend himself in a civilised society!"

"That is so," said his father. "You will have the opportunity to speak. However you are now a proven liar, so your word will carry little weight."

You are guilty of rape, murder, theft, living off immoral earnings and criminal deception. For rape and murder the penalty in Tanzania is death."

"I raped and murdered nobody!" Joshua protested for his life.

"I believed your story at first," said his father. "You said you heard a scream from the Kia and went to investigate. I believed it when you claimed you pulled the knife out of the girl only meaning to help. My heart was touched when you told me you tried to comfort her as she died in your arms."

"It is the truth father," said Joshua.

Silas shook his head. The police found that the knife used to kill the girl was very unusual. Only one trader in Dar Es Salaam sold that type of knife and he remembered selling one - to you."

Joshua cursed the Trader under his breath.

"You are right, I did lie to you, and I was scared and ashamed to tell the truth. I bought the knife but it was Kanu who forced me. He made me do it. He has bullied me from the beginning. I was scared of him."

"I don't believe this. You have never spoken about it before and it is too easy to blame a man that is not here. True Kanu disappeared the night of the killing and has not been seen since. He took nothing from the Kia yet the next morning I discover money and valuables missing from the house. You are the only witness to see him on the stoop that night. Then when your room is searched my missing watch is found. How do you explain this?"

Joshua listened, there was a long silence as his mind went back to the night.

He was sitting on the bed, the knife in his hand, looking at the girl, when Kanu had returned. Kanu gaped at the sight that met him.

"What have you done?" he shouted.

Blood had spread over the polished floor and it was slippery.

Reality kicked in for Joshua.

"Good, you're back," he'd said. "You must get rid of the body tonight. Nobody must know what has happened here."

"They will hang you for this." Kanu had said. "You have gone too far."

"Only if we are caught."

"I am not a part of this," Kanu stepped backwards, slipping in the blood.

"Not part of it? said Joshua. "Who brought the girl here in the first place? How did she die in your room? People have seen her with you before. Look there is blood on your feet. You cannot deny your part. Nobody will believe you. Not your word against mine."

"No. Not this time. This time you are alone. I will not be a part of it." Kanu was deliberate. He turned and walked out of the Kia.

Joshua spoke quietly under his breath, "Your part in it is assured."

Joshua's mind came back to the present.

"You asked for your chance to speak," said Silas, "What do you have to say?"

"Kanu hid the watch in my room to incriminate me. He is a devious person."

"You squirm more than a slippery eel," Silas looked at his son. "The doctors took semen from the dead girl. They were able to tell the blood group of her attacker. It is the same blood group as you!"

Joshua was quick. "What is the blood group of Kano? It could be the same as mine. Are they still looking for Kano?"

"No", conceded Silas.

"Then Father I tell you I did not kill the girl and you have proof of nothing more than my stupidity." Joshua's words were defiant.

Silas pulled a bundle of papers forward. He withdrew a school exercise book and an examination paper from the pile.

"I wrote to the examination board in England explaining my suspicions. They very quickly sent me a copy of one of your examination papers. I also have a school exercise book of yours."

Silas placed the two documents in front of Joshua. One displayed the student's untidy scrawl, the other the neat hand of Gupta the teacher.

"I believe you have been in a similar position on a previous occasion? Do you need to have an examination of the documents in the light? Mr Gupta explained all."

"Mr Gupta?"

"Are you going to tell me he forced you to do it?" asked Silas.

"No father. I am guilty of what you have now accused. But it is your fault. I did it for you. I know how you value success father and I know how much failure would disappoint you. You have expectations of me beyond my ability. I did it to make you happy. I am far more stupid than you give me credit for."

"I doubt that very much." Silas felt a hot flush in his face. "I am not taken in by this nonsense."

He pulled Joshua's "O" level certificate from the back of the pile and tore it in half.

"You have achieved nothing since you have arrived in this country. Now I will speak of your fate. If it were not for me you would now be languishing in prison facing the hangman's noose. However you have diplomatic status in this country because of my position. Under such circumstances it is not possible for the police to arrest or question you. For this reason and for the sake of the good name of the struggle, the Police have decided to suspend the case."

"However," Silas continued, "it is within my power to relinquish the diplomatic rights of my family. Should I do that the police will reopen the investigation."

"You wouldn't do that to me," said Joshua.

"It would be dangerous for you to think that." his father replied. Silas stood and walked around the desk. He paced the room, head bowed, hands clasped behind his back.

"In this place you have been hidden; protected from reality. To you the liberation struggle is merely a concept. You have been tainted with greed and decadence. I always envisioned a place for you in the liberation struggle, a place of influence where you could carry on my work. You have destroyed that dream. But at the same time I will not release you from your obligations so easily. I have decided you will be given the opportunity to prove yourself. You are going to volunteer to become a guerrilla. You will take up arms in the bush and you will share the hardships and deprivations of others. In this way I will ensure that the evilness that exists within you is visited on our enemies and not on your family."

"Volunteer?" said Joshua.

"Yes, you have a choice. You may decline to volunteer in

which case I will withdraw your diplomatic immunity. Then you will be treated just the same as any criminal in this country."

Chimurenga

Chifumbo Training Camp, Mozambique, 1975

Joshua Sovimbo observed. Fifty men, the whole group, dressed in battle fatigues, sat on wooden benches either side of trestle tables. They ate quietly, dipping lumps of sadza into pots of stew. For the first time talking was allowed at a meal, but the habit of silence was hard to break. As if fleeing the intense darkness of the surrounding jungle giant moths were drawn towards the pitch torches that burnt with yellow licking flames around the great hut. Occasionally one got too close and its wings would spontaneously ignite and the insect would disappear in a momentary flare and crackle. The torches were significant. Normally light came from dull bulbs that hung limply from the hut's cross beams. But tonight was a celebration, the group sat together for their last communal meal at Chifumbo Training Camp.

Joshua thought about the times he'd spent in the great hut that stood in the middle of the camp. He observed the building for what it was. Perilously thin Lupane poles supported an elephant grass thatch. A low wattle wall, not more than two feet high, ran around three sides. The space from the top of the wall to the eves was open; the floor was simply trampled mud.

It was not just the mess hall. Under the thatch he'd learnt the skills of war. He'd practised stripping and rebuilding an AK47. He watched as Chinese instructors, with the aid of nothing more than a blackboard and chalk, had explained the rudiments of trajectories for mortars and rocket-propelled grenades. He'd been shown how to set booby traps and told about the different types of land mines and their most effective use. Joshua knew they were the easy lessons, the ones he'd willingly taken on board.

But under that same thatch the Chinese instructors tried to force through a psychological metamorphous. This was where the minds of a group of individuals had been moulded into a single political will. The method had been proven to work in the war torn countries of North Korea and Vietnam. The group had been subjected to a monotonous and repetitive regime of Maoist theory. There was no escaping the rhetoric. They'd been made to listen to the same messages over and over again. From the moment they woke, before the break of day, till they lay their heads down, in the dark of night, they'd been subjected to the same relentless messages. Weakened by physical exertion and deprived of sleep their will to withstand had been quickly eroded. The Chinese instructors were confident in their methods. Only an extraordinarily strong mind could have resisted.

At this last meal, Joshua Sovimbo ate deliberately. It was part of the defence mechanism he'd developed. He toyed with a lump of doughy sadza. With his right hand he manipulated the material into a ball. When the sphere was near perfect he pushed his thumb into the centre so that a neat scoop like depression was formed. In a well-honed movement he dipped the scoop into the pot of soup and caught a fatty lump of meat and some juice. He raised the lot to his mouth. There was no spillage or mess and no need to use the sleeve of his tunic as a serviette, as most of his comrades did. Joshua discovered that if he concentrated on a detail, any detail of his own choosing and shut his mind to all else, he could ward off the continuous mind attacks. In this way he'd retained at least some of his own facilities.

Joshua looked over to the small table in the centre of the great hut. He watched the men who sat there, three Chinese instructors and an African, an unusual African, one with an aura of confidence. It was Tongogara, military commander of the Shona that listened intently to the Chinese instructors.

The man next to Joshua offered a plastic pail containing Chibuku, traditional maize beer. Joshua rubbed his hands on a palm leaf and took the container. He raised it to his mouth and gulped, but little of the opaque liquid passed his lips. He found it disgusting. For a moment the thought of Carlsberg and Johnny Walker crossed his mind. He passed the pail to the next man. More pails of Chibuku appeared. Joshua took his mind elsewhere.

The journey to Chifumbo had been unceremonious. He'd been a virtual prisoner on the supply truck that left Dar Es Salaam. For four days he'd sat on the back of the ancient three tonner. The trip was punctuated by involuntary repair stops. Joshua sat alone in the back, amongst the crates of supplies. The guard took the seat alongside the driver. The weathered canvas tilt offered Joshua little protection from the blistering sun and frequent tropical downpours. The torn material was supported by a series of metal hoops that lurched from side to side with each jolt. Comfort was an unachievable goal. He'd toyed with escaping but knew without money, or a place to go and the threat of hanging, it was not an option. He passed the time cursing his father and promising revenge.

The driver roused Joshua from a fretful slumber with the sole of his boot.

"Chifumbo!" he'd said unceremoniously.

Joshua stood in the open and looked. It was a clearing in the rain forest. He saw a disparate collection of huts, some European style, others of traditional thatch. A seven strand barbed wire fence ringed the camp, wooden towers stood at each corner. The Chinese guard had barely spoken. The welcoming procedure was stark and unfriendly. The shower was scalding, the DDT delousing humiliating. His personal possessions were taken.

"You will not see them again," said the guard. "They may prompt psychological regression. All that was before this moment no longer exists,"

The uniform was green cotton trousers and tunic. There was a Castro style cap and felt boots.

"The clothes are not yours. Every four days you will strip off and place your fatigues in the 'dirty pile' and take fresh fatigues from the 'clean pile'."

To Joshua it seemed the only thing that remained uniquely personal was his serial number. In Chifumbo even names were not necessary. The Chinese wanted a blank canvas to work with. The lessons were relentless. Mao provided the framework, Ho Chi Minn the details. They were taught the liberation struggle would be in three phases. Firstly came the politicisation of the people, when the masses would be made aware and forced to believe in the inevitable goodness of the cause.

In the second phase the enemy would be worn down by relentless surprise attacks on their way of life. The weapon was terror. There would be no attempt to confront the enemy in military terms. Instead the enemy would be forced to devote ever more of his resources to protecting what he held most valuable; civilians, women and children. It was a type of war that confounded Western conventions of fair play and morality, which made it all the more effective.

Only when the enemy was exhausted from protecting an infinite number of targets, demoralised by continuous atrocities and fearful for his loved ones, would the third and final phase commence. Conventional warfare would start. Tracts of land would be taken, military supremacy exerted. The enemy would be beaten on the battle field. This was the Maoist way to victory.

Joshua had liked some of the things he heard. "Here you are being taught to bring fear to the enemy. The qualities we seek are not bravery in the conventional sense. We need you to have the ability to generate fear and terror."

The Instructors continuously observed the group. Only Joshua had received a formal education. The others were fresh from the bush and had untainted minds. They were of peasant stock, people that had walked from Rhodesia, across the border. Not all were volunteers. Many had been coerced by commissars and political agitators that had infiltrated the Tribal Trust Lands and villages. This did not bother the Instructors, such unsophisticated minds would not be able to resist and the result would be reliable foot soldiers for the revolution.

In Joshua they saw somebody who had tasted the fruits of capitalism. This would normally have been enough to ensure his expulsion from the group. But the instructors saw something else in Joshua, something unique. They saw he had the natural ability to make others do his bidding. He was a natural leader. They also identified the callous nature of his personality, a quality that, if channelled correctly, would make him hated and feared amongst the enemy. But they knew his reliability needed to be tested. This was the topic of conversation at the small table.

Suddenly, without word the Chinese Instructors left the great hut. Tongogara stood, a tall confident figure, his presence felt by all. The murmur died away and the only remaining sound was that of the African night. All eyes rested expectantly on Tongogara. He spoke deliberately. His voice quiet, the audience straining to hear.

"Comrades you have reached the point where you have learnt all that our fraternal comrades have to offer. You are now ready for your real work to begin. Tomorrow you start life as true freedom fighters, members of your own fighting cadres.

You will make your way back to our homeland, not to some

foreign country. You are going to help expel the white interlopers who have stolen your land from you. When you arrive you will be hunted, because the white man will not easily give up what he has taken. Some of you will be captured and some of you will die. You must always remember that it is only something worth fighting for that is worth having. You can judge the value of the reward for victory by the level of resistance your enemy puts up to keep it.

Tonight I want to tell you of an omen that has come. An omen that you will understand guarantees victory. Nehanda, the mighty Spirit that led the first *Chimurenga*, is here."

A murmur rippled across the audience. The tale of Nehanda was embedded in the culture of all Shona.

Joshua recounted his own memories of Nehanda.

Long ago a Matable Chief stood above other chiefs. His name was Dingiswayo. It was he that had been tricked into giving away the Shona lands to the white man. The Shona, a peaceful people, did not understand that land could be owned by a single person. They would never agree to such a thought, but without military organisation they were unable to oppose the white man. But gradually resistance to the white man grew. The Shona eventually rose, with futile panga and spear; they attacked the white settlers, trying to drive them from the land. The settlers answered with rifle and machine gun. The rising was brutally surprised, only living on in the minds of the people. The *Chimurenga*, the great struggle, became part of Shona folklore. The leader was a woman, a spirit medium. She was called Nehanda. Nehanda had fallen during the rising, but it was said that when Nehanda returned the Shona would shake themselves free from the shackles of oppression.

Tongogara continued. "Nehanda is now with us again, you will be among the first to see her."

The silence was complete.

"The Spirit of Nehanda inhabited the body of a woman from the Mazoe valley. The woman, who has seen more than eighty years pass, walked alone from the ancestral lands. Nobody told her the way; she came close to this place by herself. She proclaimed herself to be Nehanda. She spoke, not as a frail aged woman, but in the powerful voice of Nehanda the leader. To all that would listen she revealed the secret of our destiny. She declared the coming of the second *Chimurenga*. All that listened believed her. I did.

94

When she had finished speaking she sat down, her back against a Baobab tree. Her last words were spoken quietly. She said she would wait there until the land was free. Then she should be carried back to her home, to a place where she could rest with the spirits of her ancestors. Then she closed her eyes.

That was six months ago. Today she still sits under the Baobab. She does not breathe but she remains patiently waiting. No beast or insect comes close and nature has not attacked her frail body, other than to harden the skin a little. She sits in her earthly form and waits for freedom. Now I tell you Comrades it is your duty to go from this place and win freedom for her. Then you shall help carry her back to our land. Tomorrow you shall see and touch her as you start on your journey to winning this mighty prize."

Tongogara paused for a moment, then continued.

"I have one other duty. There is also a sad truth. A shame hangs over us. Not all people who share the colour of our skin are strong enough to resist. They are the 'sell outs', the traitors, the ones in the pay of the white man. You must hate these people more than you hate the whites. The whites are our natural enemies and you must kill them but their black helpers are even lower. They are our brothers that have turned on us. There is nothing lower and there can be no mercy for them.

The traitors and 'sell outs' in our midst are dangerous and make it impossible for you to use your own name inside Zimbabawe. They will tell the white man who you are and where to find your family. So each of you will be given a new name, your *Chimurenga* name. It is the name you will be known as during the struggle."

Individuals were called to Tongogara. He embraced each and whispered their given *Chimurenga* name. Joshua never wondered if his new name had significance. It was not unusual for a *Chimurenga* name to be that of an animal. At another time, others would wonder, was it prophetic that he was called Makonzo, the Rat?

Bindura Farm, Rhodesia / Mozambique Border 1976

Shafts of the dawn's light penetrated the forest clearing. Smoke from the previous night's fires hung in the thatch of the great hut. The debris from the celebrations had been cleared but the trestle tables remained. An occasional bird shriek broke the morning's silence. It was the first day that Joshua Sovimbo no longer existed. It was the first day of Makonzo.

Tongogara appeared in front of the small group, fresh from sleep.

"I will give the briefing personally," he said. "My style in not that of the elders. I do not speak in circles and riddles. You will understand when I am finished."

It was the talk of a clear military mind without subtlety or care for feelings. Most Shona would have thought him bad mannered, elders would have found him insolent.

"Makonzo, you of the Cadre have been chosen to lead the first raid into our homeland. This is on the recommendation of the instructors. The instructors think you have qualities that are valuable but because of your background a question mark hangs over you. So this will be your test. It will be a raid where you cross the border, attack a target and then return. Four men will accompany you. Chimbodza, Sofala and Mbala were chosen because they are good fighters and have the quality of physical strength. This is important because everything needed for the mission will be carried on your backs. Tyoni, the fourth man, is chosen for his speed and agility. He will be your eyes and feet."

Makonzo smiled. The first three he did not know well, but Tyoni was different. Tyoni had attached himself to Makonzo at the beginning. He'd always fetched and carried and done Makonzo's bidding. Makonzo was happy to have his talisman along.

Margaret didn't know how to raise her voice, it was always gentle. She quietly called to her daughter.

"Come Susanna. It is nearly eight o' clock, time to leave your father alone."

Susanna kissed her father on the cheek and slipped off his knee.

Rudi's eyes followed his daughter, his love for her as great as it was for tiny Craig, his infant son, already in bed.

He got out of his chair and walked to the sideboard to turn on the valve radio. He waited for it to warm up. The tuner was always set to short wave. He fiddled with the dial, as much through habit as necessity. Back in his chair, he listened to the pips before the signature music began. The Oxford English accent never varied.

"This is the BBC World Service. It is twenty hours GMT. Here is the world news read for you today by ......"

Listening to the BBC news was a nightly ritual.

Rudi Barnadi was born in and had slept, almost every night of his 34 years, in the farm house. Ten years ago his father had died and Rudi became the third generation of Barnadi's to run the seven hundred acre farm in north-east Rhodesia. Victoria was Queen of England when Rudi's grandfather had walked to Rhodesia from the Orange Free State. He'd walked because he couldn't afford a horse. When he arrived in Salisbury he didn't rest till he'd registered a claim for what at the time was unwanted virgin bush land. Over forty years he'd worked relentlessly, pulling stumps, moving rocks, building and most of all growing God's bounty. He'd developed one of the best mixed farms in the north east. The farm was his legacy to his family, born of toil and the sweat of his brow. It was a legacy that would be cherished and protected by son and grandson.

Rudi had been taught well and learnt from his father and grandfather. The priorities were simple, family, farm and workforce, in that order. He saw native Africans as being at a different stage of development. He respected traditional ways, even if he did not agree with them. In return for labour he provided, to the satisfaction of his own conscience, a fair reward. He was benevolent and his workers content. But Rudi knew change was coming from outside and he did not sit back. He, like all whites, had a right to defend what was theirs. In the turbulent political times of the sixty's Rudi saw the best way forward being with the Rhodesian Front, the political party led by Ian Smith. His support for the Rhodesian Front was well known.

Makonzo led his men across the border on the first night of the full moon. For the next two nights they'd followed the dry riverbed till the moon had set. Then they slipped into the bush and lay up, hiding from prying eyes. On the third night they came to the row of giant electricity pylons that crossed the riverbed. They turned south, walking under the suspended electricity cables along the firebreak. They walked for not much more than two miles before coming to the point where the dense bush gave way to cultivated land. Even by moonlight the neat rows of lush green tobacco plants could be seen. They had arrived at the beginning of commercial farming. Makonzo led the group back two hundred yards along the firebreak and, disturbing as little of the undergrowth as possible, burrowed into the bush. They penetrated twenty-five yards before hacking a clearing for themselves, just big enough to bivouac for another day. For twenty-four hours they rested, but always one stood guard. Each knew they would need all their energy for the coming night's work.

They were all awake for the last hour of daylight. They ate their meal of bread and dried kapenta fish in silence. Only when they'd finished did Makonzo speak.

"You must check your weapons and make sure you have enough ammunition. Take only what you need for the attack.

Makonzo spoke to Tyoni privately.

"You have several tasks to perform this night. I rely on you especially. Are you prepared?"

"Comrade, I will not let you down," he replied.

"I hope that is the case. Now we wait for the moon to rise fully."

Rudi only spoke when the news was finished.

"Margaret, I have to go to Bindura tomorrow to pick up the new FM radio from the police station. Will you come with me?"

"Can't you send one of the boys?"

"No, the police have to show me how to work the thing. They'd train you at the same time if you came."

"I can't go with you. You can show me how it works later," replied Margaret. "I need to be here when the children get home from school." She put down her frame and needle on the side table.

"I'll think I'll go to bed now."

"I'll join you soon," he replied.

Rudi began his routine. He rarely spoke about security in front of the children. It unsettled them. But it was never far from his mind. He'd seen farms that had been attacked and knew others would be targets. He listened to government bulletins and took security advice. Improvements were ongoing. Recently the guerrillas had started to cut the telephone lines to remote farms before attacking. As a counter, FM radios were being issued. Rudi's set was ready for collection. He'd have it tomorrow.

He turned off the living room lights and pulled back the curtains, half expecting to see the dogs. But they were out of sight. A good sign he thought, if they were asleep there was no threat. He checked the doors again, back and front, leaving the windows open. They were protected by decorative wrought iron burglar bars. He returned to the living room and let the small lamp on the sideboard burn. Susanna slept lightly now but often she would tiptoe to her parent's room in the middle of the night.

Margaret had turned off the light on her side of the bed. Rudi pulled at the padlock of the gun locker that was bolted to the bedroom wall. It was secure.

The moon rose, revealing a cloudless sky. Tyoni was the first to leave the bivouac. He hurried, anxious to complete his first special task. The others waited half an hour before silently slipping into the darkness, keeping low, and skirting the perimeter of the tobacco field.

During the day a powerful diesel pump drew water from the farm's deep bore hole for irrigation. The old windmill tower, with its simple turbine, that dominated the farm was redundant. But Rudi couldn't bring himself to demolish the structure. As a child he'd helped construct it with his father and grandfather. For him it was a physical memorial to their relationship. But tonight it fulfilled a different role. It was the landmark that identified the rendezvous point for the attack. Just behind the tower was a natural mound, not more than ten feet high, a place of concealment and a place to meet.

The farmhouse was a single storey wood building with a red leaded corrugated iron roof. It stood in the middle of an enclosure bounded by a three-metre high chain link fence. The shortest distance from any point on the fence to any point of the house was the regulation twenty metres. The space around the building was kept clear to provide a field of fire. From the top of the mound Makonzo looked towards the gates. He could even make out the shape of the chain and padlock in the moonlight. His attention went back to the building. He looked at each window in turn. There was no movement. A single dull light shone in one window of the otherwise darkened house.

From the shadows came a low whistle. Tyoni emerged and scrambled towards them.

"I'm finished," he said. "The poison has done its job. It was quick."

A moment later came another low whistle. Chimbodza returned.

"The telephone lines are cut," he said.

"We are ready. Let us go," said Makonzo. They set off, crouching, moving from shadow to shadow working their way around the perimeter till they faced the kitchen, the only side of the house that did not front a bedroom.

Makonzo nodded. Tyoni withdrew the cutters. The first taut strand parted with a sharp crack that pierced the night air. Everybody remained still, looking for signs of movement in the house. They waited and watched like statues. No light or movement came.

Tyoni looked to Makonzo before cutting the second strand. Makonzo nodded. The crack from the next strand was not so loud but was still audible. Tyoni did not wait this time. He started to snip the individual links of the mesh until he had released a flap big enough for a man to pass. He slipped through. From inside his tunic he produced a yellow fertiliser bag and tied it to the fence. If they had to get out quickly there would be no time to look for the escape route in the dark. The yellow bag would guide them directly to the hole in the fence.

Tyoni turned to the house. He left his AK behind at the opening, only carrying a panga for defence. If he was discovered he would run for the hole, the others would cover him.

"Wake up Daddy," Susanna shook her father.

"What is it darling, have you had a bad dream?"

"No Daddy I heard a noise outside."

"It's just the dogs. You want to get in here with me and Mummy."

"No Daddy. It's not the dogs. I can see them they're asleep by the fence."

Rudi heard the second quieter twang.

"That's it again," said Susanna.

Rudi's heart began to pump but he concealed his alarm.

"Stay with Mummy darling, I'll be back soon."

Rudi slipped through the bedroom door. He went into Susanna's room and looked out of the window. He saw the shapes of Pixy and Dixie, the dogs, lying on the ground, close to the fence. He guessed they were dead, poisoned. He crossed the living room on his hands and knees. He didn't want the lamp to cast a moving shadow. Peering out of the kitchen window he saw nothing at first. Then it caught his eye, something light by the fence. "A marker bag," he thought. "They are already inside."

He quickly backtracked to the bedroom and shook Margaret with a gentle hand over her mouth.

"Get Craig. Stay here," the urgency in his voice was enough to stifle discussion.

"Lock the door till I tell you to open it. Call the neighbours if the phone is still working. Tell them we are being attacked, but be quiet, very quiet."

He felt along the top of the wardrobe for the key to the gun locker. The guns were loaded, ready to use. He withdrew his .303 hunting rifle and, as an afterthought, the Webley service revolver. Silently he made his way back to the open kitchen window. He slid the well greased bolt action off the rifle and a round slipped silently into the chamber. Shouldering the weapon he looked out the window, looking for movement, looking for a target.

Tyoni made a circuit of the house, ducking low as he passed windows. He'd heard or seen nothing by the time he'd arrived back by the kitchen door. Pulling a pen light from his breast pocket he pointed it at the hole in the fence and flashed the signal.

Makonzo saw the light. "Sofala, you go first."

Sofala rose and stepped forward. The hole was big enough

for him to get through. He was barely clear when the silence was shattered by the loud rapport of the .303. The round hit Sofala in the chest. Death was instant. From twenty metres it would have been hard to miss, even by moonlight. The force of the high velocity round knocked its victim backward, through the hole. Sofala landed on his back, staring skywards.

Rudi earned his marksman badge in the Rhodesian Regiment and maintained his shooting skills hunting wild boar and antelope. In a second he'd slid the bolt action back and forth. Another round was ready. His eyes strained. It was only a half movement, the flicker of a shadow, next to the motionless body. He took aim and let off a second shot. He wasn't sure, there was no reaction. He cocked the rifle and let go a third round. The result was instantaneous. From the shadows a man jumped up, breaking, running away. A second later two more shadows broke, chasing the first. Rudi sensed the panic of his attackers. They were going without returning a single shot. They ran like rabbits. He let go two more rounds and cocked the bolt action once more. This time only the spent case was ejected from the breach. The magazine was empty. There was no time to reload. He picked up the revolver, not that he expected to hit a moving target with the hand gun. He just wanted to maintain the attacker's panic.

Makonzo froze at the sound of the first shot. He watched Sofala fall back through the fence. Then the second round struck the ground in front of him, showering loose dirt into his eyes. The third shot passed straight through his tunic sleeve, miraculously missing flesh. Panic took over. Suddenly he was running, running as fast as he could. Mbala and Chimbodza followed their leader in the rout.

Tyoni remained alone and unseen, pressed tight against the side of the house. He was only a step from the kitchen window. He could see the barrel of the rifle sticking out of the window. He edged closer thinking that if he grabbed the barrel the others might have a better chance of escape. He was so close he could feel the heat from the muzzle flashes. Suddenly the gun barrel was withdrawn, to be replaced an instant later by an outstretched arm gripping a revolver. He was so close and so alert he could see the finger tighten on the trigger and the gun recoil upwards as a shot was fired. Before the second shot he reacted instinctively, swinging the panga in a wide arc with all his might. The blade sliced through flesh, bone and sinew effortlessly. The severed hand, still gripping the revolver, fell uselessly to the ground. Tyoni bent and retrieved the weapon.

Rudi was confused. He felt elation, thinking he'd driven off the attackers, but his eyes sent a different message. He felt the gun in his hand, and he was pulling the trigger, but there was no rapport and no recoil. There was no pain, but his eyes told him his hand was gone. Only blood spouted from where it should have been. He withdrew his arm and stared at the stump, trying to make sense of the scene. He looked up. In the window was a strange black face, pointing a revolver. His revolver. There was no time for a last thought of Margaret and the children. Just a blinding flash and then the end of Rudi Barnadi.

Tyoni ran as fast as he could, scrambling through the hole in the wire and over the prostrate body of Sofala. He ignored training and shouted for Makonzo. Makonzo did not reply. He found his leader and the others sitting on the ground behind the mound. Makonzo held his head in his hands.
"Is he wounded?" panted Tyoni.
"Only sand in his eyes. Nothing more."
"It is good," Tyoni laughed. "He's dead, I've killed the farmer. I have his gun. We have won."
Makonzo lifted his head and began to regain his composure. "What do you say?"
Tyoni recounted what had happened. "Come," he said. "It's safe. We can finish the task."
Cautiously they followed. Tyoni pointed out the severed hand. In the darkness it was impossible to see the body on the kitchen floor, but still their confidence grew. They broke the kitchen door and turned the light on. Rudi's body lay prostrate in a pool of blood. Makonzo went to the living room. Maliciously he swept the display of family photographs from the mantelpiece and threw Rudi's radio to the ground, kicking it across the room.
"This door is locked" shouted Tyoni.
"Break it open," replied Makonzo.
Mbala kicked the door. Its wooden upright gave way at the first attempt, the flimsy lock had shattered. Huddled, beside the bed, Margaret cradled her children. Makonzo looked down at the woman, there was no fear in her eyes, only defiance.
"You're so brave", she spoke mockingly. "Attacking women and children in the dark of night."

"Take the children" said Makonzo, "tearing Craig from his mother's protesting arms. "Take them to another room."

Without hope of success she clung desperately to Susanna. The child slipped through her fingers then she was alone in the room with Makonzo. She knew she'd never see her children again, not on this earth. She wished away her last mortal moments so that they could be reunited all the sooner, in a better place.

Makonzo dragged her to her feet and hit her across the face with the back of his hand. Once again he felt the stirring and once again he hit her. His hardness became unbearable. He ripped off her night-dress and looked at her nakedness before pushing her onto the bed. She lay impassively as he defiled her body. As an act of her contempt she refused to show emotion. She fought only to maintain her God given dignity for the final moments of her life.

When he finished he stood over her. She was haemorrhaging from between her legs. The white sheets were turning red. He took the knife from its scabbard on his belt. He looked her in the eyes as he ran the razor sharp blade deeply across her naked stomach. The skin parted to reveal her grey intestines, almost spilling from the exposed cavity. He grabbed her hair and lifted her head, forcing her to look. He laughed at the sight, leaving her to die alone.

The children huddled in a corner of the living room. The front door was open. Makonzo walked on to the stoop. Tyoni and the others were there.

Makonzo spoke. "We have to go, but first we must kill the children."

"Will I shoot them?" asked Tyoni.

"You have learnt little? We carry each bullet on our backs. They should not be wasted. You have proved yourself once tonight with the panga. Do so again."

Without word Tyoni returned to the living room, panga in hand.

The swish of the falling blade was clearly heard on the stoop. The children made no noise.

Mabala looked at Makonzo. He spoke with irreverence.

"Sofala our Comrade is dead because the Little One said it was safe when it was not. He must be punished for his error."

"I am the leader of this cadre and I will say who gets punished", Makonzo replied.

"You are not our leader," said Chimbodza, "You were the first to run. We no longer have respect for you."

Makonzo turned to walk away, ignoring the challenge.

Mbala pointed his gun at Makonzo. "Do not turn your back on us, Makonzo the rat."

"You are treacherous," said Makonzo reluctantly turning to face his tormentors. "You will pay for this if you do not put your gun down."

"Who will come to your rescue here?" said Mbala. "Who will know if we leave you behind, dead, company for Sofala?"

"I will," said Tyoni, standing behind Sofala and Chimbodza. "Put your gun down or I will shoot you".

Tyoni held the revolver.

"You are too small to scare us," said Chimbodza. "Go away whilst the men talk".

The words hardly left Chimbodza's mouth when Tyoni pulled the trigger. Chimbodza fell. The second shot hit Mbala in the neck. He dropped his gun, vainly trying to staunch the spurting blood with his hands. He fell to his knees and consciousness quickly ebbed away.

"When you were with the woman they wanted me to join them in killing you," said Tyoni to Makonzo.

Makonzo ignored the comment. "Have you completed your work inside?"

"I have."

"Then it is time for us to go. Get ready."

"I must do something first," said Tyoni, dashing to the hole in the fence, retrieving Sofala's backpack. He worked feverishly. In ten minutes he was finished. The two left, heading across the tobacco field towards the firebreak. In the two hours before the full moon had set they had already put several kilometres between themselves and the farm.

"He put up a hell of a fight. Took out three of them," the Police Corporal spoke to his Sergeant.

They were standing next to their Land Rover, parked outside the gates of the compound. Rudi Barnadi had failed to turn up for his radio and training the previous day. The telephone line was dead. Bindura requested local police to look in on the family. They'd known something was wrong as they approached. They saw the body at the fence and radioed for backup. Before it arrived they'd cut the gate open and the Corporal had made the preliminary check, looking for booby traps and seeing if anybody was still alive. Nobody was.

Within half an hour the place was crowded. Inspector Paddy McGuire took charge.

"One of the worst terrorist attacks so far," he'd said.

McGuire stopped a black corporal. "The dogs over there, they're starting to stink. Get them buried ASAP?"

The explosion wasn't loud. The African corporal was nevertheless dead, peppered with shrapnel from the mine. Tyoni had concealed it well behind a flowering shrub, the wire to the detonating cap unseen, beneath one of the dogs.

Kremlin Moscow 1976

Molenski laid the report on his desk, swung around in his swivel chair and stared out of the window. He looked at the River Moskva. It was where he always looked when he was contemplating. The river was flowing again, after the long winter freeze. The last of the ice clung to the grassy banks. It was quickly melting under the clear spring sky. Already green shoots were breaking through the sheltered ground. A father walked with his daughter along the embankment, the child skipping. Molenski should have been in a better mood.

Leonard Brezhnev had been good in the beginning, when he'd taken over from Khrushchev. But over time he'd changed. He lost interest in five-year plans, production quotas and grain harvests and turned his interest to super politics. Unfortunately he was not very good at it.

His attempt to bring the Chinese communists back under the tutelage of the USSR was a disaster. The split became total and irrevocable. War broke out on the border and the communist world was forever divided.

The Chinese, no longer able to rely on the USSR for raw materials, were forced to adopt a new foreign policy. They would have to scour the world for raw materials. They had to enter international politics. That was the beginning of the problem.

Molenski turned back towards his desk. Enough thinking, "Now I have the Chinese messing up all my plans." He spoke to himself as he pressed the button on the intercom.

Olga answered instantly, as she always did. "Yes Comrade Molenski?"

"Get me Sergi Andropov. I want him in my office within the hour." He let go of the intercom button before Olga had a chance to reply. He picked up the report again, he read it a second time.

Sergi Andropov came into the room and smiled. Comrade Molenski saw the physique of the perfect soldier in Sergi Andropov. Sergi kept to the rigorous KGB physical training regime. Most of his rank didn't bother; they slacked, letting their physical fitness decline as the perks of the job increased.

"I came as quickly as I could," he said.

Molenski pointed to the chair in front of his desk. "Sit. Have you seen the latest intelligence report and assessment for Southern Africa?"

"It is normal for you to get the reports first." Sergi explained the protocol that was well known to his boss. "However I guessed the reason for your summons and managed to get a copy, which I quickly read in the car coming here."

"Good. What do you think?"

Sergi took a deep breath. Open questions were dangerous. He needed an indication of what his boss might be thinking.

"It appears to be concise and well written," replied Sergi.

Molenski frowned. "You're not a bloody grammar school teacher! What do you think of the content? Can we regain the initiative?"

"Look," continued Molenski, not waiting for Sergi's reply, "it was enough when the Chinese got a foothold in Tanzania. Now they are spreading their wings. Last week one of our men watched as a Chinese freighter discharged a cargo of military equipment at Dar Es Salaam docks. There was not even an attempt to conceal the delivery. They are overtly supporting a rival faction in Rhodesia. A rival faction you assured me did not exist. They want to steal our victory. What are you going to do about it? How will you protect our interests?"

Molenski's voice raised an octave.

"What is more, our ally, yes our ally, Samora Machell, the President of Mozambique is going to give training bases to the Chinese and free passage for guerrillas to attack Rhodesia. This is bad. Once more, how will you regain the initiative? You didn't tell me yet." Molenski finished by thumping his desk.

Sergi knew it was best to let his boss get rid of his aggression. It was bad to interrupt when he was in full flow. He waited until there was a silence and then he spoke calmly.

"We are ready. An action is already planned. We are about to execute it. It will be a set piece. It has two objectives. Firstly it will tell the Rhodesians that they do not have control of their own country and secondly it will let the black population of Rhodesia know who is really winning their freedom for them, Nkomo and the Russians.

We will maintain the leadership of the liberation struggle and reap the rewards in the end."

"You need to be right on this," said Molenski. "I must not lose to the Chinese. It is politically unacceptable. Now tell me about your plan, in detail.

Three hours later Sergi Andropov was back in his Lubianka office, chairing his own departmental meeting.

"We will move quickly. Failure is not an option. Listen carefully because there is nothing on paper so far."

Sergi ran through the plan as he had explained to Comrade Molenski, in as much detail as he could recall. Overall he thought it was not a bad plan, considering he'd just made it up.

Tongogara had returned to Chifumbo Camp to be personally debriefed on the operation.

"Your report does not have the feel of truth. Yet I cannot disprove it." Tongogara looked Makonzo in the eye, trying to penetrate his mind.

"It is true you have done what was requested. You have struck fear into the hearts of our enemies, as no other has done before you. Look at this newspaper."

Tongogara pushed a copy of the Salisbury Herald towards Makonzo. "See what they write."

"ATROCITY: ENTIRE FAMILY BRUTALLY SLAIN"

"Police in Bindura have just released details of what they describe as the most brutal terrorist attack of the emergency so far. Farmer Rudi Barnadi (34), his wife Margaret (32) and their children Susanne (6) and Craig (4) were all killed in the attack that occurred four days ago.

Chief Investigating Officer Paddy McGuire said the scenes of depravation they had found were beyond the comprehension of ordinary minds. He went on to say that he believed that only a psychopath could be responsible for such an act of barbarism.

The Herald has learnt that Rudi Barnadi put up considerable resistance and managed to kill three of his attackers before being overcome. It is also reported that Margaret did not die immediately. She managed to write the name "MAKONZO" on the floor, in her own blood. It is believed that this is the name of her attacker.

A spokesman for the Government said that the security forces would leave no stone unturned in the search for the terrorists that infiltrated from Mozambique.

The attack has drawn condemnation from church leaders world-wide and even some Western Politicians.

Newspapers in the so called Front Line States however claim that the atrocity was carried out by undercover Rhodesian agents in a cynical attempt to discredit and undermine the liberation movement and the legitimate aspirations of the people of Zimbabwe."

"You have attained instant infamy," said Tongogara when Makonzo had finished reading.

"When I speak as a leader of our movement, I say that to terrorise our enemy is our intent. But I must qualify this by saying the value of such tactics can be lost if the atrocities committed are so vile that they turn world opinion against us. Your actions have brought us close to the edge in this respect."

Makonzo looked impassively at his superior.

Tongogara continued, "I will pass personal comment also. It is difficult for me to understand why you would condemn children to death by panga, to save only two bullets, or why you would leave a woman to die a slow agonising death from wounds you had inflicted on her.

It happens that your apparent bravery and leadership skills save you further criticism.

Now we must look forward. There is more work for you. But first let me remind you of our objectives. We are not just fighting to beat the colonialists or drive the white man out of our country. Our real objective is to take power for ourselves, so we can go forward with the revolution. We want to control Zimbabwe. It would be a hollow victory if a free Zimbabwe was born with our rivals taking the main prize. Do you understand this?"

"I do," replied Makonzo.

"Good. The time has now come to take the war to the south of the country. We have already won the hearts and minds of the people there. Now it is time to progress. It is unfortunate that in the south is land where the Shona and Matable mingle. We do not have the benefit of defined boundaries.

It is our belief that the Matable are beginning to fight in the same area and there is a worry they could become the dominant military force. This should not happen. So it has been said we need a man of notoriety to lead the struggle there, not only to fight the

Rhodesians, but also to inspire our own Shona people. The leadership have chosen you. I tell you this is the choice of the Council but it is against my advice. I believe you are not the one, but I am overruled."

Mashava, Southern Rhodesia

A pickaxe is the centrepiece of the Rhodesian coat of arms. Not a plough. This is because Rhodesia was colonised for its mineral wealth, not its land. Cecil Rhodes had hoped for a gold reef, like the one in the Transvaal, or another Kimberley diamond mine like the one snaffled up by DeBeers. But he never found his personal Eldorado. In that respect some said his adventure failed. It was not for the want of effort. Early prospectors walked out of the Limpopo valley behind ox drawn carts. They climbed till they reached the sub-tropical central plateau, four thousand feet up. Some made camp and pegged out their claims there and then. Others proceeded further into the interior.

Mashava was at the southern tip of the plateau. It straddled a complex geological cocktail. Nearby were scant gold deposits that, despite initial hopes, turned out to be barely mineable. Not far away nickel was discovered, further again chrome. But at Mashava was found the wonder material of the age. An easily mined and formed material, light to transport and possessing the amazing property of being almost totally heat resistant.

The Industrial Revolution was enveloping the world. It was fuelled by coal and powered by steam. The conversion of fuel to energy had to be efficient. Effective insulation of endless boilers, countless storage tanks and thousands of miles of pipe was essential. Without insulation, trains, power stations and ships could not have been built. The insatiable demands of industrialisation assured a growing market for asbestos.

It's something you don't forget. Duncan was grateful for that. Although he had not driven since the Army it took only minutes for him to regain his confidence. It was important because as Assistant Mining Engineer at Mashava he'd automatically received transport, a refurbished Toyota pickup. He'd be expected to drive himself around a large area.

The road from Fort Victoria to Bulawayo was eighteen feet wide and fully metalled. The bush had been cut back a further ten feet on either side. A single solid white line separated the carriageways and the sweeping bends were gentle. The Rhodesians had the best roads between the Limpopo and Cairo. Duncan drove slowly, not so much out of caution but just because he wanted to savour a feeling that he'd thought would elude him for ever when he sat alone in his prison cell: freedom.

The interview had been perfunctory. The job offer a foregone conclusion. Rhodesia, the second most developed economy in sub-Saharan Africa was in reality frighteningly fragile. More than one and half times the size of France the population was less than a quarter of a million white. Half of this number was women and children. From the balance, enough white men had to be found to occupy every position of responsibility in the civil service, agriculture, the mining sector and industry. Oh, and at the same time fight a war.

Rhodesian bosses had learnt to snaffle up what white labour came their way, see what ability and talents they possessed and then utilise them in the bast manner possible. In such an environment Duncan Murdoch was a rare and invaluable prize for his intelligence, training and abilities were real. Eight days ago he had crossed the border. Today he was moving into his house. On Monday he would start work.

Mashava Asbestos mine was split into three parts, The Workings, The White Camp and The Black Township. The White Camp was set back a mile or so from the main highway and accessed by a single track tarmac road. The turning was about thirty kilometres from Fort Victoria. Apart from the sign post all that was visible to passers-by were a few white bungalows scattered over a low hillside in the distance. The rest of Mashava was hidden from view.

The grating accent momentarily took Duncan back to another world. He had visions of the Black Country; Wolverhampton or West Bromwich. Leaden skies, lashing sleet, monstrous red brick mills, hunched, hurrying people. Sandstone spires, dyed black with the soot of industry, spewing from the stacks of 'dark satanic mills'. It was so far from here.

The Housekeeper's incongruous voice hung in the air. "Put the bags down." It was not a request. He put the bags down.

Duncan opened his eyes and viewed the apparition before

him. It didn't help that Vera Higginbottom was short. She stood square on, facing him, at the top of the drive, near the house, his house. Her hands were on her hips, or where her hips would have been if they'd existed. She had a fat arse – a seriously fat arse, although its true extent was not apparent at that moment. She'd also got a bulbous tummy and flabby bare arms. A blubbery neck supported her permanently puffed face on top of which sat a mop of curly chestnut hair, which looked very much like an ill fitting wig. But it wasn't a wig. This truly was not a vision of the master race.

If Vera were not in Mashava she would have been in her native Birmingham, travelling to work each day on a double-decker bus. She'd most probably have been a cook in some factory canteen or school, serving cholesterol reinforced mush to people who should be considered more victims than customers.

Instead chance, fortune and the desire to rule had conspired to bring her, and her husband, Douglas, a former works security guard, to Rhodesia, to a place where she was cute enough to realise she had one redeeming physical feature, the colour of her skin.

This qualification alone elevated her to a status of authority and responsibility that would have been unthinkable in her native land. She was the Official Camp Housekeeper. As such she had charge of the Guesthouse. She also managed and allocated accommodation to white staff and ran the all-important social club. Her position conferred considerable power and influence over the community.

Vera's husband had been appointed Head of Security for the Camp when in England. It had been his reward for unstinting service to the Grand Master of the Castle Bromwich Lodge of the Freemasons, whose brother-in-law, also a Freemason, had emigrated from the UK many years ago and now happened to be the Superintendent of Mashava Mine Estates.

She waddled towards Duncan who remained fixed to the spot.

"What are you doing?" she asked.

"I bought groceries. I was taking them into my house," he replied. "Is there something wrong with that?"

"We don't do it like that here. You do not carry your own shopping. That is what we have servants for."

Mrs Higginbottom turned to face the bungalow.

"ELIZABETH!"

The shout was disturbingly loud and the response amazingly

quick. Elizabeth appeared. The contrast with Mrs Higginbottom was immediately apparent and dramatic. Elizabeth was petite with soft Negroid features. She wore a simple servant's dress, buttoned at the front. The cool material hung loosely and shifted over her gentle curves as she hurried toward them. A headscarf of the same soft fawn material was tied at the back of the neck and complemented her blemish free coffee complexion.

Vera Higginbottom noticed Duncan's stare.

"Not a half cast," she said defensively, ignoring the presence of the servant. "Thoroughbred Matable, daughter of a chief. A handful to manage the Matable but good workers."

Duncan felt uncomfortable.

Vera turned her attention to the servant.

"Elizabeth, this is your new Boss. Mr Murdoch. You be good to him or you'll have to come and see me. Understand?"

"Madam," Elizabeth dropped a small courtesy to Vera and Duncan. Her dark eyes focused firmly on the ground.

Vera's voice rattled. "Elizabeth will come every day except Sunday. She will be at the house for 7am and will leave at 6.30 p.m. except Saturday when she can go at 2.30. Weekdays she has an hour and a half break midday. She's trained to do the housework, washing, ironing and basic cooking. She'll also sort out a vegetable plot for you in the garden. Saturdays, when you're not at work, she's to clean the pickup."

"What's left for me to do?" said Duncan with sarcastic astonishment.

The intonation was lost on Vera Higginbottom.

"You'll be busy enough with work and there are lots of other things to do. Golf, fishing, hunting, polo and we have great cricket and rugby teams. There is the Lions Club and some people are in the mine rescue team. They have a good social life. You'll find there isn't enough time in the day."

Duncan looked at Elizabeth but spoke to Vera Higginbottom. "It's a bit harsh isn't it?"

"Not at all. We treat our domestics very well. They're queuing up to get jobs. If we didn't provide employment they'd be in the bush starving. They are very thankful. Isn't that so?" Vera turned to Elizabeth.

"Yes Madam," replied Elizabeth.

"I don't know about this," said Duncan. "This is not what I imagined when I was told there would be help in the house. I think I might be more comfortable looking after myself. I've done alright in the past."

"Oh!" said Vera, "you want me to send Elizabeth back to the TTL? I don't think she'd like that. Would you like to go back to your village?" Vera Higginbottom's Brom voice was menacing.

"No Madam," Elizabeth's was quick to respond. For the first time she made eye contact with Duncan.

At that first glance, he knew he didn't want her to go.

"Now Elizabeth, take the bosses shopping. That's why I called you in the first place."

"Yes Madam",

Elizabeth bent to retrieve the bags from Duncan's feet.

"No! I'll take my own bags." Duncan intercepted the servant's hands.

"That's Elizabeth's job." There was annoyance in Vera Higginbottom's voice.

"I never had anybody to fetch and carry for me before. I don't need a slip of a girl to do my heavy humping." Duncan spoke.

"Mr Murdoch this is disgraceful. You have so embarrassed me in front of a servant." Vera seethed.

"I was hardly comfortable myself", replied Duncan.

"There is a system here Mr Murdoch. It works because we all keep to the rules. If you spoil your girl all the other servants will expect the same treatment. It will make life for everybody on the camp more difficult."

The Housekeeper smiled and softened her tone. "Perhaps we got off on the wrong foot. I understand you are new to the country. Don't worry you are among friends. There's not many of us and we stick together. We'll show you how to treat the African. They're very different from us. They're hardly out of the bush you know."

"Somehow I don't think I will be needing sociology lessons from you," said Duncan. "But Elizabeth can stay."

Vera's face flushed. "I'll get my husband to have a word. I just hope you don't turn out to be a kaffier lover. That's all we need." She turned and bumbled off down the road.

"How long you been at Msahava then?" asked Evans.

"About three months," replied Duncan.

"Liking it?"

"Yeah, it's good so far."
"Right shut up," said the sergeant. The trains coming.

It was the last easy place to intercept the train. From Bulawayo the eastbound railway line and road kept company till the Lundi River crossing, a few kilometres before Mashava. Then the railway veered to the south, hugging the contours of the escarpment, descending to the valley bottom and finally the border at Beite Bridge.

The six-man stick waited on the bridge over the Lundi River. The clatter of steel wheels could be heard long before the locomotive came into view. Sergeant Miles ordered the men to stand-by. They gathered their weapons and formed a dishevelled line. Trains travelled without lights at night, the first view would be of a hulking shadow, looming out of the darkness. The stick had to be ready. The train would only slow as it crossed the bridge. The Troopies had to board on the move, by torchlight. Three would travel up front in the locomotive, the other three with the guard in the caboose.

"Right, here we go." The locomotive crept over the bridge. Sergeant Miles tapped the first man on the shoulder as the loco was level. He scrambled along the ballast, catching the handrail and making the step. Two others followed in quick succession. The train was long. Before the caboose was in sight the driver had applied power and the train started to speed up.

"You first Evans," shouted the Sergeant, before jumping on himself. He turned to help the last man.

"Come on Murdoch. You don't want to be left behind."

They dropped their kit on to the floor of the caboose.

"Fancy a brew?" asked the guard.

There was only one proper seat in the caboose and that was for the guard. The soldiers sat on the floor drinking stewed tea from enamel mugs. The clatter of the wheels became more urgent. There was an intermittent squeal as the brakes were applied and the train began its descent of the escarpment.

Evans spoke. "Hey Murdoch, why did you sign up so soon?" Immigrants don't have to register for service for two years. You've only been at Mashava for three months."

"I don't do sports or any of that stuff; I'd only be sitting at home if I wasn't here."

"No family then?" asked Evans.

"No not here."

"There's the Club. You could go there in the evening. Or don't you drink?"

"Yea, I drink sometimes, but I like to choose my company."

"Heard you had a run in with The Foetus on your first day, that's why you don't go to the Club?"

"The Foetus?"

"Vera Higginbottom. That's what we call her. It's because of her good looks. She got up your nose didn't she?"

Duncan's annoyance was becoming obvious.

"Listen I signed up because I wanted to and it looked like I was wanted. That's it."

"Go on tell us, what The Foetus said to you?"

Sergeant Miles broke in. "Evans you're becoming a pest. Shut up and get your arse out the back and see if anything is trying to catch us up. Now!"

Evans shot Sergeant Miles a foul look. He got to his feet and moved towards the rear platform.

"Shut the door behind you when you go out. Don't want anybody seeing our lights."

"You're to be congratulated for signing up so quickly," said Sergeant Miles, "Anybody taking up a bit of the slack helps and don't mind Evans, he's just a nuisance. Doesn't mean harm, it's just we don't get many new people in the Camp and people are curious."

Duncan nodded.

"Thanks for that. As far as my personal life goes, I don't want to talk about it. I came here to get away from all that.

What's the score with this job?"

"Fair enough," said the sergeant. "I'll give you the background. It's all a bit new. The Portuguese just threw their hand in with Mozambique last year. Marxist revolution in their own country would you believe? Anyhow a commie, called Samora Machel, took over Mozambique, right rum bastard by all accounts. First thing he did was shut the border with us, which was a royal pain in the arse as most of our imports and exports used the port of Bira. He even shut the oil pipeline that used to bring all our fuel from the coast. Can you believe it?"

"Thankfully South Africa came to the rescue. They gave us a stack of old rolling stock and let us up the throughput over Beite Bridge. The railway to South Africa has become our umbilical cord to the outside world. We're surrounded by Commie countries, apart from South Africa that is. Because this route has become so important the *'Nobs up Top'* think it's only a matter of time before the terrorists have a go at the line. That's what we're here to stop. So once a week you get the privilege of escorting a train to the border and another one back, as far as the Lundi River. You only have to hope you're not on the one that gets attacked because fuck knows what we can do with six rifles against a decent assault!"

Mashava, Makonzo's Arrival

Wilfred Nogo stood on the brow of the hill slowly regaining his breath. No cloud or tree offered shade from the sun. In front lay the shallow valley he needed to cross to get to Beshawa village. Pushing the loaded bicycle up that last hill had been tough. There was not much time if he was to get there before dark. The bicycle belonged to the World Christian Union. Mounted on a rear carrier was a large wooden box. It was full, adding much to the weight.

Wilfred mounted the bike and let go the brakes. The bike gained momentum. Soon he was peddling with all his might. He hunkered down to reduce wind resistance and hoped that with enough speed he would get half way up the other side, without having to dismount and push. He felt the wind on his brow, it evaporated the sweat and felt cool. Soon his legs could not keep up, he freewheeled.

Out of the bush they stepped. They were at the very bottom of the depression, either side of the road, a Rhodesian army patrol. The corporal stood in the middle of the road, he raised a hand.

Wilfred cursed and applied the brakes. The forks juddered. His speed was too fast. He tightened his grip on the brakes. The back wheel locked. He prayed he didn't fall and spill the contents of the box. He skidded to a halt just short of the corporal.

"Good day sir," Wilfred greeted the corporal with a false broad smile.

"Passbook," demanded the corporal with an open hand.

Wilfred withdrew the dog-eared document from his breast pocket and handed it over. The corporal thumbed the pages. He studied the photograph and looked at Wilfred. One of the soldiers walked behind Wilfred.

"What's in the box?"

"Bibles," he replied.

"Show me."

Wilfred steadied the bike with one hand and used the other to flick open the catch and lift the lid of the box. His sweat was no longer due to exertion. The soldier peered inside before putting in his hand and withdrawing a copy of the New World Bible.

"You a priest?" he asked.

"No sir, only a messenger of God."

"You steal these?"

"It is not necessary to steal bibles sir. God will provide a copy to anybody who needs one. You may keep the copy that God put into your hand if you like."

Wilfred prayed that the soldier did not dig deeper.

The rest of the patrol laughed. Even the corporal smiled.

"You picked on the wrong one for that. He's beyond redemption."

The soldier threw the bible back into the box and turned away, his interest gone.

"You seen any terrorists on your travels?" asked the corporal.

Wilfred shook his head thinking of the naivety of the question. As if he was going to say yes there's half a dozen around the corner!" He bit his tongue, now was not the time to provoke.

"No sir, I don't think I've seen anybody that would interest you."

"Okay," said the corporal, handing the passbook back, "On your way."

"Good day, and God bless you sir," replied Wilfred.

He steeled himself for the long push. "Bastards," he thought as he felt fresh beads of sweat roll down his back. It would be hard to reach Beshawa on time.

Wilfred Nogo regularly collected pamphlets and bibles from the Baptist Mission and delivered them to the Tribal Trust Land villages. The American Pastor at the Mission, just about the only white to live in the black township of Mashava, praised the Lord for having given him Wilfred. He believed that without Wilfred the work of decades would have been lost. For nearly fifty years the World Christian Union had been sending young Americans to Africa. They came for a year at a time. Churches throughout the mid-west sponsored the volunteers. No self-respecting church failed to have a display board, proudly showing newsletters and photographs of the latest batch of 'missionaries'.

But in Rhodesia the growing intensity of the war had reduced the supply of volunteers to a trickle. Frequent attacks on outlying missions ensured the situation was not about to improve. The police not longer guaranteed the safety of volunteers. The programme was all but paralysed. The World Christian Union was trying hard to maintain its network until the emergency was over. Wilfred was key, he provided the only link the resident pastor in Mashava had with the outlying Christian communities. Tirelessly Wilfred cycled from village to village, keeping the faith alive with the literature of the Lord, or so the Pastor thought. He found in Wilfred a willing adjutant – by day. Darkness brought other duties.

Twenty-five thatched roundavals made up the village of Beshawa, the most remote settlement in the TTL. The biggest hut occupied the centre position and was reserved for the village headman, Upenyu. A Mopane pole fence encircled the entire village. People, goats and cattle were corralled inside the enclosure each night. Wild animals rarely attempted to penetrate the defences.

Each headman arrived individually and was greeted by Upenyu. Wilfred was the last to arrive. They all sat around a fire in the open, eight village heads. They'd come together at the behest of Wilfred. That night a stranger joined them, one that was known by reputation. Makonzo had arrived in Mashonaland a week before.

Upenyu spoke.

"When so many village head men gather together it should be for an Indaba – a council of elders. But nobody has called for an Indaba, so why do we come together?"

Upenyu looked at Wilfred, who had placed himself next to Makonzo. It was Makonzo who spoke first.

"It is I that asked Wilfred to call the meeting with you, and it is I who made Wilfred get the head man from each village to attend. Soon it will become clear to you why we have gathered. But first I believe there is some hospitality?"

"That is so," Upenyu clapped his hands together twice. Two women fetched a steaming three legged cauldron. They set it down near the men and served each according to tribal rank and precedence. Makonzo was the last to receive his calabash. He swore to himself that it would never happen in that order again.

They ate in silence. Only Makonzo leaned over to Wilfred and whispered. "Have you got it?"

"I have," he replied. "It is in the box on my bicycle."

Makonzo nodded.

There was no music, no dancing and no drinking. When the food was finished the men went quietly to the largest hut. It had been cleared. Even so there was barely room for all of them. On the dirt floor were grass mats, ready to sit on. Two paraffin lanterns gave yellow light. There was no fire in the centre but the thatch and timbers were blackened and smelt of old smoke. Makonzo made sure he was the last to enter. He pulled down the woven flap and sat, blocking the opening.

Without invitation Wilfred stood.

"The second Chimurenga is started, the struggle has begun in many parts of our land. Now it comes to you."

There was silence for a moment.

"You have forgotten your manners," said one of the head men. "Our host must speak first. We are in his house."

"No old man. It is a different time," said Wilfred. "We do not follow the old ways, not from now on."

"You may not speak to an elder in that manner," shouted another head man.

There was a growing commotion. The voice of Upenyu broke through.

"I agreed to the meeting so we could listen to your plans and, as elders, advise you. You will not receive assistance if you do not follow the correct ways."

Wilfred continued, he spoke quietly.

"We have followed your ways, the old ways, for a long time. It is because of your ways that we are in this position. You have had much time, many seasons have passed, and you have done nothing to improve the position of our people. Now your time is over, it is our turn."

Eyes shifted between Wilfred and Upenyu.

"Out!" cried the head man. "The meeting is over. You will not speak to me in such a way."

A shot brought instant silence. Ears rang. Makonzo sat with a revolver in his hand. Nobody had seen him remove it from his waste band. Now Makonzo spoke. His voice was strong and sure.

"We have come tonight to ask nothing of you. We have come to tell you. Tonight you will listen."

Upenyu protested.

"The young men of the village will come. They will chase you away. You will not keep us here against our will."

"Tyoni!" Makonzo shouted.

The flap over the door opened. The light was poor but the sight was clear. The grinning face of Tyoni filled the space. In his hands was the unmistakable profile of an AK47.

"Yes Comrade?"

"Stay outside. Stand guard. Kill any stranger that approaches the hut."

"Yes Comrade."

"Wilfred, go and fetch the package. Return quickly."

Makonzo got to his feet. He faced his captives.

"You will listen to me now. Before you leave this hut your position will be clear."

Wilfred returned with a hessian sack. Makonzo directed his speech to his host.

"Upenyu, I choose this village for the meeting for special reasons. Tonight a message will go from this place that cannot be ignored. For a long time we have been promising that freedom is coming, promising the end of colonialism. We promise you all the things the white man keeps for himself. These things will not come easily. But we do know that when black men stand united together against the white oppressor, we win. Do you all agree?"

There was a murmur of agreement around the hut.

"But agreeing is not a matter of words alone. We will not win when our own people help the white man. And we cannot win when you, the village head men allow your people to help the white man."

"Upenyu, stand up. Stand up now and face your accusers." Makonzo pointed his gun at the old man. Upenyu slowly rose to his feet.

"There is a man from this village. He is known by the name of David Mukadota. Is this correct?"

Upenyu replied. "There is such a man, but he is not here now. He is gone."

"Tell me more about this man," said Makonzo.

"He works far away. His family, his wife, his children, stay here. He sends money home for them. Sometimes he visits."

"What does David Mukadota do?"

Upenyu spoke quietly. "He is a policeman."

"A policeman? Do you wish to tell me more about him?"

"What more is there to say?" asked Upenyu.

"Maybe you could say that he is the son of your brother? Is that true?"

"It is true," replied Upenyu.

"David Mukadota is a *Sell Out* and you allow his family to exist in your village. This is wrong. I will show you the fate of *Sell Outs*."

Wilfred stepped to the centre of the hut and upended the sack. A bloodied head rolled in the sand, the head of David

Mukadota.

"Now get to your knees," Makonzo spoke to Upenyu.

The old man's eyes were fixed on the head of his nephew. He sank to his knees.

Makonzo put the revolver to the back of the old mans neck.

"This will be the fate not only of *Sell Outs* but also of those that tolerate *Sell Outs*."

He puled back the hammer of the revolver and gently applied pressure to the trigger. The head men watched in silence. Before the hammer fell Makonzo raised the barrel and the shot went harmlessly through the thatch.

Makonzo laughed. "Next time there will be no mercy."

Now Wilfred spoke.

"Makonzo has come to live among us. He will lead the fight. It is through him that we will restore what was taken.

We are fortunate that there are great nations across the seas that will help us with training and weapons, but it is we, ourselves, that must take the land back. And it is you that must provide men from your villages to join the fight. You send us your sons and we will return warriors. In the next two weeks you will provide twenty men from your villages. They will go to Mozambique for training. As soon as they go they will be replaced by trained fighters, who will live with the families of the recruits."

There was no resistance from the elders, the old men were told to stay in the hut. Like children they obeyed.

The next morning Wilfred pushed his bike towards Mashava. Makonzo and Tyoni walked alongside him. The guns had been returned to the secret cache. Success refreshed them.

"Do you have the photographs?" Wilfred asked.

"Yes," replied Makonzo. "Tomorrow you can put them in the pass books."

"The Pastor will be pleased I have found somebody to polish his pews."

Mashonaland, Sabi River

"Sorry you volunteered?"

"For this job or the Army in general?" replied Duncan.

The Sergeant didn't reply, just gave a wry smile that Duncan didn't see in the darkness.

"Right now I'd rather be in my bed," said Duncan after a pause, "Curiosity made me step forward for this one."

"You know what they say about curiosity?" asked Cunningham.

Rare southerly winds brought no good. In the dry season they came with the cold and frosts that threatened crops, in the wet season they brought the Drackensberg drizzle, conditions more usual in the Scottish highlands rather than southern Africa. Tonight it was drizzle.

Duncan wiggled his toes to keep the blood flowing and stop numbness setting in. He lay belly down in the foxhole, wrapped in an army groundsheet. Above, camouflage netting, supplemented by bits of vegetation, provided invisibility but no protection from the drops of rainwater that worked their way through. He pulled the groundsheet a little tighter and wished the Sappers had done a better job on the observation post.

Sergeant Rory Cunningham of the Field Intelligence Company lay alongside Duncan. His eyes were pressed tight to the eyepiece of the latest high-resolution field glasses that were fixed to a stub tripod. The tripod rested on a single line of sandbags laid out in front of them for protection. He began another slow sweep of the observation field. He stopped half way and concentrated on a single spot.

Duncan strained, looking into the dark. He moved a hand towards the handgrip of his FN that rested on the sandbags.

"Anything?" he whispered.

"Eyes, a pair of eyes. Too close together. An ant-eater out for dinner I think. You can relax. I get a bit edgy with the Matable. They're smarter than the other lot."

"Haven't had my first contact with Shona or Matable yet,"

replied Duncan. "Are they really that different?"

"Oh, you better believe it, chalk and cheese. The Matable call the Shona dogs because of the way they fight. They sneak up behind and bite you in the arse before running away. They're only brave against farmers and their families, or missionaries or cars travelling out of convoy. They see a uniform and they can break the sound barrier in bare feet.

When the Matable come out, which isn't very often, they're after confrontation. And they won't make you look good. Every Rhodesian schoolboy knows that. They're smart too. Did you know Zulu tactics are still taught at Sandhurst in the UK? And the Zulu's are cousins of the Matable?"

"How come you just set up an observation point here to watch them?" asked Duncan.

"You ask a lot of questions Murdoch," said Cunningham.

"Sorry, I'm only interested, trying to learn a bit."

Both men stared into the blackness for a while.

Cunningham broke the silence.

"Last week I was doing this same observation job facing the other way, east, trying to find the infiltration routes the Shona use from Mozambique. We've had a 'sanitation line' in place for six months. Caught bugger all. Then a few days ago we got a bit of mustard information from some friends overseas."

Duncan was getting the measure of Cunningham. He resisted the temptation to ask the obvious, "What friends?" He knew it would only be met by a rebuff. Duncan guessed that if he kept silent long enough Cunningham would volunteer the information.

It took less than five minutes.

"Did you know the Matable get their instructions pretty much directly from Moscow?" The question was rhetorical. "The Ruskies have quite tight control. They send all orders via the Russian Embassy in Lusaka – like a duck's arse that building, bristling with radio antennae though!"

Duncan knew that Cunningham was dying to tell him. He only had to keep quiet.

"It's our mates the Israelis. They got great radio interception capabilities, better than the Brits, and they can break the military codes – well partially in any case. They tipped us off! We're not really on our own!"

"Wow!" said Duncan. "That's amazing. I'm lying here in the bush because a few days ago some chap in the desert picked up a chance radio message form Russia."

"There was no chance about it," said Cunningham with self-assured confidence.

"So the Matable Army is coming this way and we're the early warning signal. When are we expecting them?"

"The information's not quite that precise. We know something's going to happen. Not too sure about the precise target or the exact time. That's the problem. Our friends will give us more information when they can. But you're right. We're part of the front line defence, how about that!"

"Why pick this place for the obbo?"

"During the rainy season the rivers fill, makes movement on foot difficult. The only safe way for an Impi to move about is to sneak across road or rail bridges at night. That or take massive detours through the bush. They'd be mad to do that."

"What's an Impi when it's at home?"

Cunningham laughed. "The Shona divide their men into Cadres. That's a political unit, an invention of the Chinese but for the Matable military tradition is important and the traditional Matable fighting unit is the Impi. In the old days an Impi could be as big as a battalion. Nowadays they would not be bigger than sixty or seventy men, smaller than a regular Army Company."

Cunningham turned onto his back and slid to the bottom of the foxhole. He opened a field green Thermos and poured himself and Duncan a coffee. Duncan sipped the hot drink.

"It'll be daylight in half an hour. We're not going to see anybody tonight."

Duncan continued to peer into the dark, his mind elsewhere. The only Matable he knew was Elizabeth, and yes there was something different about her.

An hour later the dawn chorus was over. In the bush the nocturnal animals had been replaced by their daytime counterparts. Duncan watched a troop of baboons march past the observation post, looking for breakfast.

"Time to pack up," said Cunningham. "Think you'll be volunteering for another stint?"

"So long as it doesn't clash with my regular stuff, I might," replied Duncan.

"You can come with me any time."

Matabeleland, Dingiskani's Kraal

The Kraal was filling. The summons had been passed by word of mouth to neighbouring villages. Those who could get to the Kraal at Shabani did. Men came form far afield. Elders and warriors in traditional dress milled around the Kraal. The cattle and goat pens had been emptied to make room for the visitors. Shepherds protected the animals in a makeshift stockade outside of the compound. Youths drew water from the deep well for the women and children. Men drank maize beer and kashasha.

The Kraal had only a single entrance guarded by Warriors with spears and shields who ensured only guests and villagers gained entrance. A more substantial guard composed of guerrilla fighters armed with AK47's remained concealed in the bush, some distance away. Sentries posted on the distant kopjes kept lookout against intruding police and soldiers.

Unseen drums began to beat as the last rays of red light faded on the horizon. At first the beat marked time. Slowly, almost imperceptibly, the rhythm and sound grew and with it the sense of anticipation.

The ground at the Kraal's centre was raised. On the mound stood the largest hut, the hut of Dingiskani. Outside the hut cow skins and soft hide pillows, stuffed with bird feathers, had been laid ready for the Chief. From here Chief Dingiskani, the direct descendent of Shaka and Lobengula, would direct the ceremony.

To one side a whole bull was being slowly turned on a giant spit. Men operated the crude iron crank. Children danced around the pit of glowing embers. Only one ceremony demanded the sacrifice of a precious bull. It had been seventy years since the Spirits had been invoked in a war ceremony.

Dingiskani sat inside his hut with his two sons. The mood was serious.

He spoke.

"I am troubled. Not since the days of Lobengula have we fought as a nation. Although seventy years have since past the harsh lessons of that time remain sharp in our memory. Your grandfather witnessed the scene. All the days he was Chief he counselled caution and bade my father and me do the same. I have followed his word, until now, when with white hair and long tooth, I go against his counsel and wisdom."

Tembo grinned.

"It will not happen the same way again Father. The last fight was uneven. Then the white man had rifles and machine guns. We had only spears and shields. Those times are gone. Now we are at least equal in weapons. Maybe our equipment is even better. You know we have been away and learnt the way of the white man. For two years we suffered in a land of snow, under a red flag. There we learnt the craft of war from the best army in the world."

Morgan, his twin brother, nodded in agreement.

"They are still guiding us, our friends in Moscow. They have given us a great plan to follow. We have received detailed instructions. What we are about to do will open hostilities and set down a marker for the whites."

"Still petulant monkeys," said Dingiskani. "You always know everything."

The old man smiled.

"Are you laughing at us father?" asked Morgan.

"No, I don't laugh. I just recall your youth. Since you were babies you were indistinguishable in looks and inseparable in behaviour. Will you never disagree with each other?"

"Never." said Morgan. Tembo nodded.

Dingiskani's smile faded, "But you were so hard with your sister.

"Only when we were young father, when we did not know better. Now we cherish her. She is second only to you in our thoughts. Our debt to her can never be repaid but it will never be forgotten." Tembo spoke, Morgan nodded.

"When your mother died Elizabeth was only nine years old. She was so strong. She buried her own grief with her mother. I was weak, she became my strength. You were needy, she was your support. Always she was there, wise beyond her years."

"It is sad that she is not here to see this," said Morgan.

"A messenger was sent to tell her. She knows and her spirit will be with you."

"That is good, for it is the sprit of Elizabeth that is the embodiment of the Matable and that which makes us embark upon our adventure. The white man took our traditional lands. We moved to harder areas and scraped the sandy soils. We watched sturdy

Matable soldiers, weakened by hunger, become scrawny tillers of dirt. We looked on as our women walked barefoot to fetch water and kindling so that we might eat and drink. The white man killed our cattle, taking not only our food but also our pride. If that was not enough it became necessary for our best men and women to leave the villages, to find money work, so that others would not starve. Slowly they eroded our way of life and traditions. Tomorrow we start to take them back. No longer will our sister, a Matable Princess have to be the servant of a white man. When Elizabeth returns to the village triumphant, we will have won."

Dingiskani spoke, his words slow and deliberate.

"You are only partially right. I let you go tomorrow, not in the hope that you will restore the past. What is gone is gone. Lobengula is dead and will not return. The days of the white man are also nearly gone. This is clear to all except the white man. What you start tomorrow will help chase him off our land, but even without you, he will go. Your real task is more important. You must win for us the right to sit at the great table. We must have a voice in the councils that will decide the future of this land. The greatest danger to us is that one oppressor is replaced by another that is even more evil. Beware the Shona. They have eyes for what is yours. These are the real enemy. Listen to me carefully. If they become our masters we will soon pray for the return of the white man. Mark my words well".

Dingiskani lent forward and picked a tiny assegai and shield, perfectly formed miniatures. Reverently he offered Tembo the symbolic weapons. Head bowed in submission Tembo accepted the gifts with both hands. He did the same for Morgan.

"Now we go outside. The ceremony must begin. The spirits will be evoked to fight alongside the Impi. You and your men will eat the flesh of the bull and take his strength."

Two days later Tembo and Morgan walked together, the last warriors to leave the Kraal and head towards the sacred site.

The Matopas, a place of giant rounded bare rocks, stood over the surrounding bush. Millions of years of exfoliation have produced dramatic and improbable formations. From a single gigantic slab of metamorphic rock, erosion produced a maze of deep canyon like paths and gullies. A myriad of secret hollows and sub-terrain caves had been created, but most astounding, the balancing rocks stood high and proud. Often three, four or five giant boulders sat, one on top of the other, precariously balanced, apparently ready to topple and come crashing down.

Generations of witch doctors, unaware of the processes of erosion and unable to explain the massive geological feature, attributed spiritual qualities to the place. The Matopas became a mystic place for the Matable, the gateway to the next world and a sacred burial ground. It was also a good place to hide.

Forty chosen men gathered in the hidden cavern. Each had secretly made their own way to the place. They worked in two groups, two fighting Impies of twenty men each.

Kerosene lights, hung from steel spikes set in the rock, cast dancing shadows as men hurried, preparing the tools of war. Grease was cleaned from guns, actions were checked, explosives primed. No orders were given; each duty was known and practised.

All around were wooden packing cases, some opened, their protective tarpaper lining folded back, contents exposed. Assault rifles, RPG's, machine guns and grenades and the paraphernalia of war lay everywhere. To the rear of the cavern were more piles of unopened cases, the origin clearly stencilled on the wood: *"Product of the Deutsche Democratic Republic"* and *"Made in the Peoples Republic of Chezslovakia"*.

In the cavern it was cool and dank, outside the sun still shone. They had to wait till it had sunk before they could start their long journey.

When it was nearly time Morgan and Tembo came together by a pile of packing cases. Men gathered around, organising their packs, ready to move out. They carried the minimum for the journey they would be unburdened with explosives, heavy weapons, large quantities of ammunition and rations. If they were discovered on the march they would not stand and fight. They would disperse and scatter in the bush, each man making their own way home. Only when close to the target would they become a cohesive fighting force. It was their chosen strategy.

Morgan spoke to the men for the last time.

"This cavern has been a good hiding place for our cache of weapons. Now it becomes more, it is our operational headquarters, our base in Zimbabwe and the place from where we start our first major mission in the east. From this chamber we emerge and when our business is complete, it is to this place to which we will return.

Over there is a bank of radios. An operator sits at the desk.

He will be our contact with the outside world. When we have been successful it will be from those radios that the official communiqué will be sent.

We are ready to begin now. We have the weapons and the training. We are few men but enough. Our first mission will be dramatic. The Rhodesians and the rest of the world will see. It will be a statement to our enemies, and a test of our determination and endurance.

We have not chosen an easy route to our target. There will be many days of hard marching. We will suffer, but it will give us the element of surprise. They will not expect this."

Morgan took over.

"It is possible that some of us will not return from the adventure. But those who do not return will live on in our folklore. Future generations will remember us. Pamberi! Forward!"

Forty men raised their weapons above their heads and in unison answered, "Pamberi!" They filed into the dark of the night.

Mashava, Patrick Walker

It was the only remaining vestige of a doomed union. The fact that it survived in such a hostile environment can only be put down to the fact that money talks. In the 1950's, misguided and naïve politicians, had attempted to form a federation between Rhodesia, Zambia and Malawi. The concept quickly collapsed in the face of African nationalism, but not before the Kariba Dam project was born. The Central African Power Corporation, or CAPCO, was established as the company to finance and run the gargantuan project.

The completed dam straddled the Rhodesian / Zambian border. About half the power station was in each country. When the border was closed, as virtual hostilities broke out between Rhodesia and Zambia, neither side was willing to pull the plug, so to speak, on the power station.

As a result CAPCO remained the only company to work either side of the hostile border. The main shareholders and financiers of CAPCO were based in London, so it was a simple job for the British Government to get Patrick Walker appointed as CAPCO's Southern Africa field representative. He alone enjoyed freedom of travel in both countries.

"We'll keep contact to a minimum," Patrick Walker had said. "But keep me informed about everything."

Duncan shook his head at the ambiguity of the statement as he sat in his office looking over the asbestos works. In the yard a white fitter supervised black labourers as they prepared a Mitsubishi front-end loader for the mine. Cynics said the Japanese overtly supported international sanctions against Rhodesia because it gave them a clear run at the black market. Duncan thought that was a good assessment.

He unfolded a scrap of paper and picked up the receiver. He dialled nine for an outside line and waited for the purr. He dialled the rest of the number.

It rang twice. A young female voice answered.

"Good morning, CAPCO. How may I help you?"

"I'd like to speak to Patrick Walker please."

"I'm afraid Mr Walker's out of the office this week. Can I take a message?"

"Tell him Duncan Murdoch called will you?"

"Of course Sir. Duncan Murdoch", she repeated. "I'll make sure he gets the message." The line went dead.

Duncan concentrated on the giant A2 piece of paper on the drawing board. He began filling in the squares, taking information from his note book. With luck he'd finish next weeks blasting plan before lunch.

A few minutes later the black Bakelite phone on his desk rang.

"Hello, Duncan Murdoch."

"Duncan? Patrick here, Patrick Walker."

"I was just told you were away for the week."

"I am. Coincidence I called the office just after you. Handy really, I was meaning to make contact myself. I'm in your neck of the woods tomorrow. Thought I'd drop in to your place. Catch up on things, see how you're settling. Say about 5.30?"

He didn't wait for a reply. The line went dead. Duncan replaced the receiver.

He left work early. He wanted to catch Elizabeth. He always felt awkward in the kitchen, when she was there. It was as if it were her domain. He almost wondered if he should knock.

"Elizabeth. I'm having a visitor tomorrow. Can you cook for two?"

Elizabeth was at the kitchen sink. She half turned to face him. The sun was low in the sky and shone through the window. He could make out the silhouette of her body through the thin material of her dress. He stared and felt his face flush.

"Yes, there will be enough," she said.

He was sure she'd noticed.

She turned back towards the sink. Duncan wanted to believe he'd seen the merest curl of a smile on her lips. He lingered for a moment, his eyes unable to avoid her hips. He felt a rare warm glow.

Until recently it had never crossed his mind. He'd always been alone and never contemplated otherwise. That was the way it was. Somehow, Elizabeth, without intent, had stirred something inside. He liked it and wanted to explore more, but he knew it could never be more than a thought, especially in Rhodesia.

"I never gave you my address, said Duncan opening the door to Patrick Walker.

"It's my job to know things like that," he replied. "Bit early, sure you wouldn't mind?"

Duncan thought Patrick Walker had put on more weight.

"No, come in. The foods not ready yet. We can have a beer on the stoop if you want."

"Better inside actually. Prying eyes and all that stuff," replied Patrick.

Elizabeth brought a tray with two bottles of Castle and glasses. Duncan watched Walker's eyes follow Elizabeth. As she leaned forward to put the drinks on the coffee table he strained, for a glimpse of cleavage.

"Looks like you're pretty well set up here," said Walker, his eyes following Elizabeth as she left the room.

Duncan ignored the comment.

"I'm changing my status with the army. I've been doing voluntary duties so far. Now they're going to assign me as a full reservist, Rhodesian Light Infantry, Combat Engineering Company. They say I'll most probably get a stint of training in Salisbury."

"The RLI," said Walker. "Almost as bad as the French Foreign Legion these days; that many foreigners."

"I'm also going to keep the extra duties locally, if I can," added Duncan

"They'll like you, that's for sure."

Vera Higginbottom had her uses. Elizabeth trained in the Guest House under her condescending eye.

"You may eat with your fingers Elizabeth but civilised people use a knife and fork. It is very important how they are placed on the table!

Sadza may be all right for you, but educated people normally eat meat and potatoes. That's a big difference between us."

Duncan didn't know about the humiliation, he did however appreciate that Elizabeth produce a good cottage pie on a tidy table.

Elizabeth appeared. "The food is ready."

"Shepherd's pie, my favourite," said Walker.

"Cottage pie," corrected Elizabeth.

Patrick stared at Elizabeth, she'd broken the rule. Servants don't speak unless spoken to.

"Same thing," he retorted.

"Minced lamb for shepherd's pie, minced beef for cottage pie. This is cottage pie." Elizabeth looked Walker disrespectfully in the eye.

"I'm sure it's very good, whatever it is," Duncan broke in.

"Thank you," said Elizabeth as she turned for the kitchen.

"Bit feisty," said Patrick.

"With character," defended Duncan.

Patrick changed the subject.

"So, go on, speak. What news have you got for me?"

Duncan talked, Walker ate.

Walker finished mopping his plate before he contributed to the conversation.

"It's always been suspected that MOSAD was collaborating with Rhodesian Intelligence. What you say adds to the belief that the Israelis have close ties with Rhodesia. That's really good information. Your chap needs his arse kicking for letting that one out of the bag."

Elizabeth hardly dared breathe. She stood, pressed tight against the wall, listening. She committed what she heard to memory.

Walker spoke.

"The Africans are trying to put up a united front. We think it's a load of old tosh. African tribal loyalties will surface in the end. For sure Nkomo doesn't like this new chap, Mugabe. Fellow is stealing his thunder and possibly more. Anything else for me?"

"One thing. Might not be important," said Duncan. "Had a briefing at Battalion a couple of days ago. The brass is getting worried about the Beite Bridge railway. Security is going to be beefed up. The trains already get an escort, but from next week there is going to be a Company of Troopies either end of the line, permanent stand-by. That's quite heavy duty stuff.

I'll still be on regular escort duties of course. I'm roistered for every Wednesday.".

"Inevitable really," said Walker. "Vulnerable route. I'll let the powers that be know. By the way, Major Cameron sends his regards. I'm sure London will be pleased with your work so far."

She'd had enough and edged herself away, heart pounding. She slipped out of the house, unheard, disappearing into the night. "I must contact them," she thought to herself. The Twins should be warned.

Fort Victoria, Mashonaland

The driver saw the barrier ahead. He doubled the clutch and dropped from fifth to fourth. He didn't need to double the clutch, it was a fully synchronised gearbox, but he thought it was better for the gearbox. The engine raced as he eased the clutch out, the vehicle slowed. He dropped to third, the truck slowed some more. He applied the brakes and brought the vehicle to a standstill in front of the red and white pole that blocked the road. A sign proclaimed *'Welcome to Fort Victoria'*.

The driver jumped from the cab. He wore the green coverall uniform of the Parks and Wildlife Department, his breast pocket had yellow embroidery proclaiming *'Assistant Warden'*. Lovemore Hove had passed through the checkpoint before, but this time he was nervous.

Two African policemen stood next to an M60 machine gun in the sandbagged emplacement, on the side of the road. A rusty corrugated roof gave protection from both the rain and sun. Lovemore recognised the machine gun, he knew it was useless in action. A sustained burst would result in a jam. If the operator was rough in clearing the jam, which he would be if somebody was shooting at him, the firing pin would, in all probability, snap. Then he'd really be in the shit. The M60's predecessor, the Browning Automatic Rifle, was actually a superior weapon. The Russians had taught him this.

The white police officer, in charge of the checkpoint, leaned against the outside of the sandbag wall, drawing on a cigarette.

A third black policeman approached the truck.

Lovemore had spent nearly half his thirty-one years working for Parks and Wildlife. He began as a messenger and worked his way up. His record was unblemished, he'd only had a single period of prolonged absence. That was recently, when he'd claimed his mother was dying from cancer. The absence lasted the better part of six months.

"Passbook and papers," demanded the policeman.

Lovemore had them prepared.

"What are you carrying in the crates?"

"Crocs. For the crocodile sanctuary at Lake Kyle." he replied.

The policeman looked at the papers and walked to the back of the truck. Lovemore followed a pace behind. Four long wooden crates were stacked on the flat bed. Two on top of two. A few one inch breathing holes had been drilled in the crates. The policeman went on tiptoes, trying to peek through one of the ventilation holes. It was too high and too dark for him to see anything.

"Open it," he said.

"You open it," replied Lovemore.

"I want to see inside," said the policeman.

"Fine. I'll get you a crow bar."

"Wait here."

The policeman returned with the white Officer.

"You are refusing to open the crates?" he asked.

"I am," replied Lovemore.

"I can arrest you if you continue to refuse."

Lovemore thought for a while.

"Arrested is better than eaten."

The Officer shook his head and turned his attention to the crates. He mimicked his colleague, trying to look through the breathing hole. He banged the side of the crate with the brass end of his swagger stick. Nothing. Finally he pushed the tapered end of the stick into one of the holes. The reaction was instantaneous. The crates jerked violently, threatening to break the restraining ropes. A side panel on one developed a crack. The Officer stepped back sharply, his swagger stick abandoned in the hole.

The reptile eventually became still. Lovemore stepped forward and removed the remnants of the swagger stick, now six inches shorter. He returned it to the Officer without comment.

A cream Morris Oxford halted on the other side of the road. The Officer recognised the female driver, the wife of a friend.

"Let the truck through," he said, turning his attention to the car.

Lovemore's racing heart beat slowed a little as he pulled away, swinging the truck onto the highway south. Fort Victoria soon disappeared from his mirror. There was little other traffic, just endless bush on either side, green from the recent rains.

A few miles on a troop of baboons sat in the middle of the road, they stood their ground. Lovemore drove at them, smiling. At the last second they jumped clear. Lovemore heard their shrieks of protest.

As the sign for Lake Kyle came, he slowed. There was nothing ahead and the rear view mirror was clear. He drew close to the junction. Then he pushed his foot hard down on the accelerator, the big diesel engine responded and the truck lurched forward, gaining speed. The junction passed. Lovemore checked the mile pegs, he saw the 118 mile marker. At the 121 mile peg he slowed, almost to a crawl, carefully scanning the right verge. He saw what he was looking for, two barely visible strips of concrete disappearing into the bush. He stopped, checked for traffic again, engaged low-ratio and swung the truck ninety degrees, till the wheels were on to the narrow concrete strips. The cab pushed up against undergrowth, he revved the engine. The bush gave, branches bent and rubbed along the side of the truck which miraculously disappeared into the vegetation. Only a sharp eye would tell where the truck had left the road.

The first roads connecting towns in Rhodesia were simple affairs. Two parallel strips of concrete, wide enough to take the wheels of horse drawn and early motor traffic, single carriageways with infrequent passing places. There were low level bridges or fords crossing rivers, impassable in the rainy season. There were few cuts and embankments, roads followed the contours of the land, twisting and turning to avoid even minor natural obstructions. Not until the twenties did the Rhodesians begin to lay proper highways, but when they did, they were good. Sections of strip road were by-passed and abandoned during the construction of the highways. It was on to just such a section that Lovemore had driven his truck.

Not much distance was covered in half an hour in low gear. The truck lurched from side to side when wheels hit collapsed bits of strip. Lovemore knew he was getting close when he felt the truck begin to descend. He was entering the depression that skirted the Longo River. The thick vegetation gave way to the expanse of the hidden Mopane forest.

Mopane trees normally fail to grow above four meters high because elephants eat the leaves and rub away the bark, resulting in stunted trees. Only in the absence of elephants and where climate conditions are perfect, would Mopane trees achieve their full glory, growing to eighteen metres or more and producing a fantastic top canopy. It was not without reason that the rare natural occurrence was referred to as *Cathedral Mopane*. Under the dim canopy Lovemore manoeuvred the truck between the trees, searching for a level place to make his camp.

Two full days of toil passed before he'd finished. Only then did he stand back and admire his work. Firstly he'd used the HIAB crane, on the back of the truck, to unload the crates. He'd released the hungry crocodiles. Instinct made them head for water. They soon disappeared, heading for the river. Then he'd draped the truck in camouflage netting. From fifty paces nothing could be seen. The field aerial for the radio was extended. Then came the slog, building the enclosure that had to perform two functions, to hide and to protect.

He foraged for bracken and dry bush. He dragged branches and saplings to the camp. He drove uprights into the soft ground, wove a barrier and draped it with foliage. It was six feet high and, laced with strands of black thorn and embedded with split green bamboo saplings. The camp was big enough for forty men.

Finally, at the right time, he switched on the short wave radio and tapped out the message in Morse code. It was short, only four letters from the phonetic alphabet. Golf. Oscar. Oscar. Zulu. In the hidden cavern, under the Matopas hills, the operator was waiting for the signal. He responded with "Tango Bravo". All clear and understood.

Mashava

Elizabeth left Duncan and Patrick talking at the dining table as she slipped into the night. She hurried toward the hostel that was her home, running the last hundred yards. She was panting by the time she'd got to her room and closed the door. She wanted to write but the only proper table was in the communal dining room. That was no good, so she sat on her bed, using an old magazine for support, as she printed the draft message onto a sheet of writing paper. She thought for a while before adding a second sentence.

The rules of the code were committed to memory. She worked methodically. Accuracy was important or the code would make no sense. It was an hour before she was satisfied and began to print the final version on a sheet of good writing paper. Satisfied she put the message in an envelope, addressed to Mr Tuti c/o Shabani Bottle Store, Gwanda. Mr Tuti didn't exist, the bottle store did. It was the bus stop nearest to Shabani, her village. Messages could be left at the bottle store for collection. She burnt the rough workings on an enamel plate. She knew nobody must see what she had written, the hostel might be full of Matable but there was still the chance of a sell out or a Shona spy. It was dangerous for her to send a message but she needed to warn the twins about the soldiers – and maybe protect Duncan as well.

Sleep was short and fitful. Even before light she was up from her shallow slumber, roused by her own excitement. She drank water, having neither time nor appetite for food. In the half-light of dawn, as the cockerels crowed, she hurried down the broken road.

Life at the bus terminus had started before she arrived. Already people were coming, the first bus had already left and others were revving smoky diesel engines. She wandered around the packed ranks of buses, looking for her vehicle.

The bus terminus, in the centre of Mashava had once been in good condition. It had been surfaced and the lanes marked, but the low quality asphalt had crumbled under constant use. There was no money for repair. Now it was just an area of hard standing, a dust bowl in the dry season and a quagmire in the rains. The oldest part of the township, colonial buildings, with dilapidated Dutch gables, surrounded three sides of the terminus, housing open fronted shops, exclusively occupied by Indian traders.

For forty-five minutes she searched without success. The place became more crowded. Buses came and went. People with improbable large loads vied for position in queues. Cases, crates, trunks and animal cages were tied onto roofs. Arms hung out of windows and faces were pressed up to glass. On the fringes street vendors, in shanty kiosks, made from corrugated iron, or pushing barrows, made from old bike wheels and scraps of wood, worked the crowds. Glasses of milky instant coffee were available next to carts of buns thickly coated in shocking pink icing sugar, while alongside stinking bags of dried kapenta fish were on offer.

Hustlers were trying to scrape a living on the edge.

"Where to?" asked a Tout suddenly blocking Elizabeth's way. His breath stank of sour milk. She winced.

Touts eased journeys, at a price. With brawn and bribe they guaranteed the client a good seat and ensured luggage was properly loaded, even on the most overcrowded bus. Touts were hated yet could make a journey palatable for a few extra dollars.

"Nowhere," said Elizabeth. "But I want to find the Sunshine Company bus for Bulawayo. Have you seen it?"

Every morning a bus left for Bulawayo before eight. It was nearly that time now. The bus took a circuitous route around many townships, arriving at Shabani late in the day.

"Maybe," he replied with a black toothed smile. "I could help you for 50 cents."

She didn't hesitate; already she'd looked for too long. Fifty cents was okay.

"Alright."

"Over there," the Tout pointed with one hand, holding out the other for his money.

Elizabeth was not gullible.

"Show me," she clasped the 50 cent coin.

"Come quickly," the Tout huffed, pushing a way through the throng.

The bus looked good, the yellow paint was fresh and bright. Unfortunately mechanical condition and appearance are not interrelated. The bus had, at some time toppled over, done a summersault. Undoubtedly the accident was due to a combination of overloading the roof and sharp cornering. The bus had been miraculously resuscitated, brought back to life, unlike many of its passengers that day. No amount of pulling and hammering could remove the kinks from the chassis. The result was a vehicle that crabbed down the road at an amusing and improbable angle. Oblivious or uncaring, passengers packed the notorious vehicle for its daily run.

The driver was climbing down from the roof, he'd been checking his cargo. Forgetting this task was not a mistake he'd make a second time.

"Driver wait! I have a job for you." She stepped in front of him. "I need your help. Do you remember me?"

"Yes, I remember you."

"I need you to take something for me to the Bottle Store at Shabani."

"I have no room for extra parcels today," he replied. "I am full and will leave immediately."

"It is only one small letter. When you give it to them at the store they will give you $5. It is a lot of money for one small letter."

"True," said the driver. "It must be an important letter. I will take it at that price."

"Be careful with it." She said handing him the envelope.

Elizabeth stood and watched as the driver started the engine and edged forward. Begrudgingly the crowd parted and let him through. Her attention turned to the one with bad breath, who was standing with outstretched palm.

"My money."

She handed him the fifty cents and turned to go. Bad Breath pocketed his coin and waited till she disappeared into the crowd.

"Why would a Matable be so anxious to pay so much to send a letter," he thought aloud. Quickly he cut a diagonal path across the parking area. He caught up with the bus before it reached the open road and jumped onto the open platform, to speak to the driver.

The Mopane Canopy

The boy wore only shorts as he ran along the riverbank. Warm mud oozed through his toes as he went. When he was clear of the village and was sure nobody would see him he slowed down to a trot. It was a long way and he needed to pace himself. A few minutes earlier he'd stripped off his school uniform. Now it was neatly folded and hidden together with his shoes, in the hollow of the dead tree he always used, not far from his school. He would not go to school today, he had other things to do, but he would return to the hollow tree in time to put on his school clothes and get home without his mother knowing.

Katz knew his mother would beat him if she found out he had missed school again. She told him all the time he had to learn so he could go to the city and get a good job when he was older. Then he would be able to send money home to help look after the family. It was his duty. But Katz didn't want to go to the city, he liked the village and the bush. So he reckoned if he missed school he would not have to go away. He wasn't thinking about that now though.

A cloth bag hung from a piece of string that he used as a belt. It banged on his side in rhythm with his steps. Inside the bag was an old hacksaw blade that had been especially shaped on a grinding wheel. It would be inserted into holes in the trunks of Mopane trees and used to wheedle out sweet Mopane worms. Big sweet ones that would hiss and sizzle in the hot fat and get a good price at the market. Everybody loved deep fried Mopane worms and the boy knew that fifty fat worms were worth more than a hundred thin ones. Katz always had the fat sweet ones. On the way back the cloth bag would be full and he would earn more than two dollars. The two dollars would be added to his secret stash, the money he was saving to buy a hunter's knife. Not an African Panga that anybody could get, not one of those. He was going to have a real American hunting knife like the one Jim Bowie used and he'd seen in an old magazine. The thought spurred him on.

Katz had learnt that worms got bigger and sweeter the longer they were left in the tree. The trouble was that everybody took them early from the trees that were close to the village. He travelled far in his search for Mopane trees that nobody else knew. One day he travelled a long way down the river, out of the TTL and into the park and game land. There he discovered the strange Mopane forest with its "roof" and dark interior. It became his secret place. It was off the TTL and a place where it was forbidden to go.

After an hour of running the riverbanks changed. The soft mud was replaced by yellow sand. It was firmer under foot but it was sharp and would have cut feet that were not as hardened as his.

There was only a few hundred yards to go when he saw the first one. He stopped and held his palm over the print in the sand. His whole hand did not cover even half the impression. "This is big," he thought, "I have never seen one so big." He walked on keeping away from the water's edge as a precaution. Here the river ran slowly and deeply, it was just before the rapids and a good place for crocodiles.

Twenty yards on he saw the next trail, even bigger than the first. The footprint was cracked and dried. It had been made more than a day ago. He found four more sets of prints. "Four big crocodiles," he said aloud knowing something had happened. It was impossible that he'd missed them before. He knew this river too well. He would follow the tracks backwards and see where they had come from.

Crocodiles were not agile on land, their spoor was unmistakable, clawed pads and swishing tail. Katz followed the tracks into the Mopane Forest.

The crocodiles had travelled in a straight line, following their noses, searching for water. Soon he began to hear it. The familiar sound of a panga hacking on wood. This only meant one thing, there were people around. He crept forward, more cautiously. The trail went in the same direction as the hacking. Katz had learnt how to stalk prey. He knew what to do now he was stalking human quarry. He had to be quiet and unseen because humans had good hearing and sight. But there was no need to keep upwind because humans did not have a good sense of smell.

He went lightly from tree to tree, making no sudden movement, until he saw the man between the tree trunks. Katz watched in silence for a while, staying hidden. He recognised the plain green uniform of the National Parks and Wildlife. They had come to his village once to catch a wild leopard that made its home where the villagers dumped their rubbish. They captured the animal alive and took it away. The National Parks and Wildlife did not bother the people, not like the Army and Police.

Katz knew that men do not often work alone so he watched and listened for others. Only slowly did he begin to believe that this one was without company. He worked like a demon, even in the dull light under the canopy Katz could see the sweat glisten on the man's brow as he chopped at undergrowth, freeing branches.

He followed as the man dragged the liberated branches deeper into the forest. He was close before he realised that the man was walking towards something he was building. It was good. It looked just like a natural thicket. Katz watched as the man carefully wove in the branches he'd just dragged over. When he had finished he picked up his panga and went to get more.

Katz closed on the barrier. It was safe. He could hear the man had returned to his hacking in the distance. Katz saw the black thorn and green bamboo. Bad muti he thought. He walked around and found the entrance. "Ah! A kraal, a hidden kraal". It became clear. He went in slowly watching and listening. Nobody was there. It was a big compound. To the left he saw the lorry. It was partially covered with netting like the soldiers used. There was a awning on the side, attached to the lorry. Wooden cases were stacked nearby. One crate lay on its side, shattered. It smelt of fish. He knew it had been used to transport the crocodiles. He could even make out the crocodile tracks. Two poles held up the awning. He saw the holster hanging by its belt from one of the poles. Without thought he went over and lifted the flap. He withdrew the pistol. It was the first time he'd handled a weapon, it felt heavy and cold to the touch. It would be much better than the knife he dreamed of.

The hacking stopped. Knowing the man would be returning soon he slipped out of the compound and moved away as silently as he could. Before the man had arrived back at the kraal Katz was running hard, making his way towards the riverbank clasping his trophy. He didn't stop until he was back at his village and the secret hollow tree.

His heart was pounding as he pulled on his school clothes. He bent to fasten the shoes that had cost his mother so much and that he hated to wear. He would leave the gun in the hollow tree, hidden for another time. He thought of firing the weapon, of hunting for game. He was lost in his own excitement as strong black hand's grabbed him from behind. He froze with fear and was unable to struggle or shout. The hands turned him around and he looked his captor in the face.

"Father!"

The American Pastor lowered his newspaper. "They call it 'Necklaceing'. Can you believe that? Can you believe how inhuman man can be towards his fellow man? If people could apply fifty percent of their ingenuity to curing the world's problems as they do to devising ways to inflict pain the world would be a much better place. What do you think Wilfred?"

Wilfred was not expecting the question. He did not reply, he just continued picking bundles of leaflets from the store cupboard in the Pastor's office.

"Oh," said the Pastor. "I never thought. You probably don't even know what I am talking about. You don't get the newspapers. Apparently some new terrorists have turned up around here. A bad bunch. They specialise in killing their own race by covering an old car tyre in petrol before putting it around the victim's neck and setting fire to it. Can you just imagine that? Horrible, just horrible."

"It is unusually cruel," replied Wilfred who had no need to imagine it. "The people in the villages must be very scared."

"You know I worry for you Wilfred, said the Pastor. "If it's not safe for a policeman to travel in the countryside how safe is it for you? They have killed five black policemen in two weeks."

"It's six actually," Wilfred corrected. He knew because he had been present on each occasion.

"Perhaps I should confine you to the Township for your own safety," said the Pastor.

"I really don't think that is necessary. They won't hurt a man doing God's work," replied Wilfred.

"They have killed missionaries in the past you know," said the Pastor.

"I will let you know if I am in danger. I really think others have more to be worried about than I do," said Wilfred truthfully.

He left the Pastor to finish his newspaper

Makonzo worked in the panelled corridor of the mission hall. He pushed a long handled brush back and forth. A soft cloth wrapped around the head polished the parquet floor. The room smelt of lavender polish. Wilfred walked past carrying his leaflets. He motioned Makonzo to follow him.

In the garden Tyoni swung a slasher back and forth, cropping the grass. Wilfred walked past, Makonzo followed.

"Watch out for us," he said.

Tyoni nodded.

"What is it that cannot wait," asked Makonzo as they stood concealed by the lemon trees.

"One of the Comrade's came this morning. He gave me this." Wilfred pulled his jacket back to reveal a pistol sticking out of his belt. "The Comrade told me his son had taken it from men in a camp on a distant part of the Sabi River. Outside the TTL."

"Could they be our men?" asked Makonzo.

"No. We have nobody in this place and besides the pistol is Russian."

Makonzo thought before he spoke. "I want to know what is happening. You must find out the truth."

Wilfred nodded, "I already have a plan. We will know soon." Is there anything else?"

"Yes," said Wilfred. "A man, not a Comrade, comes, he seeks a reward. He watched a woman pay a bus driver $5 to deliver a letter. For his own greedy purposes he wanted to know what was so important it was worth $5. He thought there was profit in it for him and so forced the driver to give him the letter but he did not understand the content. So then he brought it to me." Wilfred produced the letter from his pocket. "It was to be delivered to a bottle store near Gwanda, in Matable Land".

Makonzo took it. He withdrew the single sheet of paper. The words made no sense:

letrderisoarreodes.ootakensaihris.
AlBieBigtannwcryamdslir.DntatcWdedyngttan.

"Code! Things become interesting. The person who sent this is careless or the message is important. Why else would she entrust this to a stranger?" said Makonzo. "Make an exact copy of the letter. Give the original to the bus driver to deliver. Tell him he dies if he speaks of us. We don't want anybody to know we have seen the content. Then send the copy with the next messenger to Mozambique. They will break the code."

"Is it not better to radio the message?" asked Wilfred.

"No. It is too long. We must not compromise our radio." Makonzo thought for a while. "Tell your informer to find out who sent the message. Tell him to be careful, she must not know we are watching."

Matabeleland

Morgan stood still, hiding under an Acacia tree, on the second day of the march. The tree would never grow to its full potential, the ground was too arid, but there was enough green foliage for concealment. He was thankful he'd agreed with his twin that they would only fight in the rainy season. True, the swollen rivers would be difficult but at least there would be vegetation to hide them.

The single engine Cessna droned overhead as it made wide sweeping circles. After a few minutes the plane turned away and the noise of the engine faded. Still nobody broke cover, they knew better. Morgan slipped out of the shoulder straps and dropped his pack onto the sandy floor, using it as a seat, leaning back on the trunk of the tree. He cradled his rifle and patiently waited. The others in his group were in line of sight. Three sat under separate acacias, the last, Edison, had been caught in the open. He'd no choice other than to fall onto his stomach when the plane came. He'd slithered to the nearest cover, a giant cactus and lay face down in the sand, hoping his camouflage did its work. The material of his tunic rubbed against the base of the cactus. It was so gentle Edison didn't feel it, but the rubbing was enough to activate the defensive mechanisms of the cactus.

Experienced observers in spotter planes looked for clues, they could read the land. Spooked antelope, restless flocks of birds, even the comic stride of a gangly giraffe were telltales. Minutes passed, the sky was silent but everybody remained alert. Morgan shut his eyes and concentrated.

The two Impies had split up, taking slightly different routes. Morgan had gone to the north, Tembo to the south. Parallel lines, ten miles apart. They would stay separate till they arrived at the rendezvous, near the target.

Somewhere a bird shrieked and a previously unseen flock rose into the air, almost as one. Morgan opened his eyes. A lone kudu, not more than twenty feet away, broke cover from his hiding place. It bolted east. Morgan knew that meant the plane was coming from the west, out of the sun. He could tell the pilot was good.

The speeding shadow raced across the ground. The gruff roar of the Cessna's flat four engine at full throttle was deafening. The plane was low, very low. Morgan could clearly see the Rhodesian Airforce markings on the underside of the wings.

It was an old trick, a medium height sweep. Disappear over the horizon, then a long slow turn, losing height, finally coming out of the sun at zero height, max speed. If the observer saw anything the plane would climb back to five thousand feet, get a fix and call it in. But the Cessna didn't climb. It just continued on and disappeared over the horizon.

On day three Tembo's Impi was already ahead, they'd not been interrupted. Tembo was pleased, another two nights and they'd be on the plateau. Tembo marched the men in extended line, one man on the point, two hundred yards ahead. At times they trotted, but mostly they walked. Every hour they rested for five minutes.

Tembo sat alone, under a black thorn, near the ridge of the escarpment. He looked back, the way they'd come, over the falling land and across the vastness of the plain they'd traversed. The people were told the war was for land yet Tembo knew they'd marched for seventy-two hours and not seen a human being. He wondered if the people would ever really understand it was not for land they fought. Truthfully there was enough for everybody.

It was the afternoon of the next day when the trees began to give way to shrub and bush. The cover was becoming thicker. Late in the afternoon a whistle came from the front. Everybody stopped and crouched. Tembo moved forward and met the point man coming back.

"What is it?" he asked.

"Track ahead,"

Tembo checked his map, a perfect copy of a captured Rhodesian Ordinance Survey Chart.

Tembo followed the contour lines with his finger, and then checked his compass.

"Cattle track. We are near, very near."

A light gust of wind passed over them. There was warmth in the air. It was a sign, a bad sign.

"We have been fortunate so far but now I feel it coming. The rain will be here soon."

He looked at his watch and spoke to the point man.

"We move forward, to the dip, over there." He pointed to a hollow two hundred yards on the left.

"Then we wait for radio time. With luck we will beat the rain and be in camp tonight."

Lovemore was in the camp; he sat by the truck, at the radio. The batteries were at fifty percent. That was enough, no need for a charge. He wanted to avoid running the generator.

Eighteen hundred hours, his earphones came to life. Quickly he jotted down the signal and sent the reply. It was over quickly. One column was close. Lovemore waited to see if the second column was also close. After five minutes still no message, he shut the transmitter down.

Light was failing. It would be dark in twenty minutes. He worked quickly. The infra red beacon took a few seconds to warm up; he unpacked the night scope as he waited. They'd explained about infra red to him, all about visible and invisible bands of light, but he'd never understood. He knew the beacon lamp got hot though. With one hand he carefully picked it up by the handle and carried it towards the river, placing it in a clear area. Only somebody with an infrared scope would be able to see it. He hid in a clump of sprouting saplings and hoped he would not have long to wait.

Morgan looked down on Edison, his best soldier, one with specialist skills.

"You should have told me straight away."

"I did not want to cause a delay. I thought it would go."

"Ah! You know better. Cactus barbs do not go away by themselves. They are more persistent and annoying than an old wife."

Edison lay face down, his bare back exposed. A man was working by torchlight, his face only an inch away from Edison's skin. He scrutinised every pore.

"That's more than two hundred," he said as the tweezers withdrew another barb from the inflamed area around Edison's right shoulder blade.

"I have never seen so many in one small area. The rough shirt rubbed them till they bled. He has a temperature already."

"Infection. This is not good," said Morgan. "I don't want to leave him here alone and I do not have spare men to take him back.

Make sure you have removed all the barbs and apply the antibiotic powder. We will stay here till the morning and see what the situation is then."

Edison looked up.

"Go without me. I will make my way back, alone."

"It is not over for you yet, you have important work to do and I will not abandon members of my Impi so easily," said Morgan

He cursed the spotter plane of the previous day. It put them far behind Tembo, by now he would be very close!

By morning the inflammation had subsided, a crust was forming on the yellow puss. Edison's temperature was falling. The antibiotic was doing its work.

Tembo picked the strongest man. "This is the last obstacle, you will go first, take off your pack. Leave everything except your weapon. It is the only place to cross, the river is wide and the water fast but it is not deep. A strong man can make it."

The man tied the rope around his waist and waded into the water, rifle above his head. The current was strong, he lent forward to keep balance. The water did not come to his chest, the bed was solid under foot. On the far bank he pulled the rope taut and secured it to a tree. The rope sagged in the middle, below the surface of the water, but it would do its job.

Two men followed across. Once on the far side they moved quickly in the direction of the Mopane forest. The first carried a canvas pouch around his neck. It was becoming dark. They stumbled onwards. The front man removed the infra red scope from the pouch. He fumbled for the switch before raising the scope to his eyes. Immediately, straight ahead he saw the beacon flashing. He moved forward.

"Lovemore! Lovemore!" he called.

From the left came a voice. "Password? What is the password?"

"Ah! Don't be an arse Lovemore. It is I, your Comrade."

"Password. Or I shoot you, Comrade or not."

"Our leader would be proud of you, nobody else would be though. Strike, strike is the password."

"And Fear is the response," said Lovemore.

The darkness was broken by a flashlight. The men came together, they laughed. Lovemore spoke.

"Quickly fetch the others, come and see what I have prepared for you."

As he spoke, the first distant roll of thunder could be heard.

Morgan looked at the radio operator's rough note.

"Tembo is there before us," he said.

"Shall I respond?" asked the operator.

"No. It is unnecessary. We do not need to give anything to the enemy. It is enough that we know Tembo has arrived. At least they will sleep comfortably tonight. We shall have another night in the bush."

The radio operator packed his equipment. Morgan concealed his disappointment. Edison had tried; he'd walked unaided and carried his own weapon. The others shared his load. He'd refused extra rest and sweat ran down his brow all day. But his effort was not enough. They had not made up the lost time. Morgan gathered the men.

"We will not make the camp tonight. We will rest here. When the moon rises we will walk again. Then we will sleep for two hours before the sun comes up. It will be hard."

No one complained. They drank water and ate what they had before finding a place to lie, on the sandy ground.

Morgan did not sleep though. He saw the distant sky light up, a sure indicator of the approaching storm. Later he could make out individual bolts of lightning, and then came the thunder. A distant rumble in the beginning, it grew louder. He roused the men.

"We must move to higher ground and look for shelter."

By torch-light they marched for almost an hour. They came to a low kopje. On its steep slope they found shelter under overhanging rocks. Twenty men huddled into the space as the first drops fell. Within a minute it was a torrential downpour. They sky was lit by sheet lightning; the crack of thunder came closer until light and sound were simultaneous. The raindrops hit the rock with force so hard they rebounded into the air. For two hours the heavens opened.

Then it stopped suddenly. For a while there was only the sound of running water.

The rain didn't bother Morgan so much, it was the runoff that would cause the problem.

Tembo was comfortable under the truck's awning. A tall earthling pole had been stuck into the ground to save the vehicle from lightning. The canopy of the Mopane forest gave cover, directing water into channels. One channel fell onto the awning. Somebody used a branch to lift the sagging canvas. A rush of water fell to the ground. Tarpaulins were strung between trees. Each man found a dry place to bivouac. Kerosene lanterns hung from poles. Lovemore stirred a three legged pot hanging over an open fire. Despite the deluge they would all eat hot food and sleep safe. No prying eyes would come that night.

Tembo rested uneasily knowing his brother was on the wrong side of the river. He knew it would soon flood and be impossible to cross. He would have to start the work without his brother and that would mean added risks.

Daylight arrived. The air was fresh, the humidity gone and the clouds dispersed. Early heat evaporated the moisture from the rocks. Wisps of gentle mist lingered. Morgan stepped into the open. As if in gratitude for the rain, plants emitted a sweet fragrance that permeated the air. He inhaled, it was good, he liked the morning.

But his mind quickly came back to the day.

"Edison. How is Edison this morning?"

"I am ready," Edison's voice was clear.

"We will move closer to the river but I cannot be sure what we will find there."

They marched for four hours, finally reaching the cattle path that Tembo had crossed. They went to the same depression he had used to rest.

"The grass is still flat. This is where they stayed before us. You will wait here. I will go ahead on my own to see the state of the waters."

He followed the trail left by his brother. He heard the waters before he saw them. They were muddy and angry. Even before he'd cleared the bush and had a clear view his feet sloshed in shallow water. He went forward holding on to trees as his feet sank in the shifting sands.

At last he came to the edge of the bush. Before him the river was in flood, a swirling mass of breaking water dirty with sediment. The river banks had been broken, only water existed from the bush line on one side of the river to the bush line on the other side. Morgan knew that his brother would have left a rope. It was somewhere under the water.

The Mopane Canopy

Two heavy machine guns stood on tripods, mechanisms tested and ready for action. They'd been removed from the hidden compartment, under the flatbed of the truck. Boxes of ammunition and bags of grenades were neatly piled on the ground, recovered from the tool locker behind the cab. The explosives were more problematic. Sniffer dogs could easily have detected their presence. The idea of hiding then in false bottoms in the stinking crocodile crates was good. The plan had worked well, all the ordnance was delivered, intact, just four miles from the target.

Tembo finished his inspection and spoke.

"You did well, your preparation was thorough and you chose a good site.

"It is the best I could do," replied Lovemore.

"Unfortunately we will be short of men until Morgan and his men arrive," Tembo continued. "You will have to guard the kraal whilst my men get on with the preparations. Can you do it alone?"

Lovemore smiled and picked up his weapon, he needed no further instruction.

The child's directions were good, it was impossible to miss the place, even if the crocodile trails had been washed away in the previous night's rain. Wilfred was dressed as a priest; he wore a cassock he'd borrowed from the Pastor's locker. He openly carried a bible. It was an unusual sight that entered the Mopane forest. He made no attempt at concealment as he wandered around, trying to be seen. He soon got his wish.

"Stop! Put your hands in the air." The command was strong. "Do not turn around. I am pointing a gun at you."

Wilfred the 'priest' slowly lifted his arms, raising the bible high into the air.

"I am unarmed. I am a friend."

A few rays of midmorning sun penetrated the canopy.

"Who are you?" asked Lovemore.

The priest didn't answer. He sensed the voice was coming

closer.

"What are you doing here? What business brings a priest to this place?"

"I was told you were here, I came to find you."

"How did you know I was here?" asked Lovemore, concealing the alarm he felt at having been discovered so soon.

"A boy from the village saw you. Don't worry, he has been sworn to secrecy. He will not speak. But I would like to speak, speak to your leader."

"What makes you think there is a leader?" asked Lovemore. "Why do you think I am not alone?"

"I have something of yours. May I return it?"

"What?" asked Lovemore.

The Priest undid the middle buttons of his cassock and reached inside, slowly. With his free hand he withdrew the handgun and held it above his head.

"The boy took this. He will not steal again, you can be sure of that."

Lovemore took the gun out of the Priest's hand.

"Ah. I thought I had lost it in the scrub."

"The writing on the gun. It is Russian. By this I know you are a Freedom Fighter. You are one of us. There are people close by who will help you."

Lovemore realised the boy had been in the Kraal. The mission had been compromised.

"Get on you knees. Put your hands behind your back."

The Priest obeyed, unsure.

"Do not shoot a man of God, one that means you no harm."

"I will not shoot you," Lovemore produced a length of twine and a green field bandage from his kit bag.

"You will be blindfolded and tied before we go further."

Lovemore directed the Priest from behind. They stumbled through the forest for fifteen minutes. Lovemore had not stopped the Priest till he was dangerously close to the Kraal. But he did not want him to know that. So he chose to walk in circles until his prisoner was disorientated.

Tembo considered the man sitting in front of him. The blindfold had not been removed. He knew it was better to keep the stranger in darkness, but he would not trust a man till he'd seen his eyes.

"Remove the blindfold,"

The priest squinted as his eyes got used to the light. He looked around and thought the boy's description had been accurate. It was a big compound; there was a lorry and an awning. He sat under the awning now. His captor sat opposite, on an upended ammunition box. Tembo spoke.

"Who knows we are here besides you and the boy?"

"The boy was alone when he found your camp. He told his father and his father told me."

"And who have you told?"

"I have told the head of our Cadre," replied the Priest. "He is a good man and fights for the freedom of the people. He sent me to meet with you."

"So what is your message?"

"The leader thinks you are an independent Cadre or maybe a wandering Matable group. In any event, if you fight for freedom a hand of friendship is offered. My leader would like to speak with you, to see what help he can give."

"Why does he not come himself?" asked Tembo.

"He thought it would not look good if armed people approached you. He thought a man of the cloth, as a messenger, would be better. Times are treacherous."

"And where do you propose we meet?"

"It is easiest if I take you to him."

"You think times are less treacherous for us? Tembo laughed.

The Priest had not expected that to work. He waited for a while, as if pondering. Then he spoke again.

"At the edge of the forest, the way I came, there is a clearing. In the middle there is a great bamboo. It is easy to find. I will bring my Leader to this place. He will come alone, except for me. You should come with one man only. We may talk there."

"How far away is your Chief?" asked Tembo.

"Not far. If you take me back to where you found me and let me go, I can return to the bamboo in three hours."

Tembo thought. What was more dangerous, to meet him or ignore him?

"I will be there." Tembo turned to Lovemore. "Put back the blindfold and take him back to where you found him."

Tyoni returned first, he spoke to Makonzo.

"They are suspicious and careful. More than once I was nearly caught."

"I don't believe that. You are too clever for that to happen," said Makonzo.

"It is true," replied Tyoni. "It is only the fact that they were distracted by the priest that made it safe for me. Thank the Lord."

They both smiled.

"So what have you to report?"

"The place where they stay is well hidden. It is not a simple place to rest. It is clearly a forward base. I would guess there are not less than fifteen men. I am sure they plan to carry out an operation from this place."

"Can they be 'sell outs', maybe Sealous Scouts?"

"I do not think so"

"What weapons do they have?" asked Makonzo.

"I could not see all. The men carried AK47's, modern, wooden stock."

Makonzo nodded, "Uniform?"

"Not Rhodesian, but not ours. It has a pattern I have not seen."

"I believe that Wilfred the priest will say they are Matable," said Makonzo. "If he says that, I believe we are strong enough, so we will attack and take them! Prepare your men. Be ready to move."

Less than an hour later Wilfred, still in his cassock, sat before Makonzo.

"They believed me, that's all that matters," said Wilfred.

"I have already spoken with Tyoni. Now tell me what you think."

Wilfred began.

"They spoke in a dialect of the Matable. I have no doubt of that. They foolishly removed my blindfold in the compound. I saw everything. The compound is strong, made with much black thorn and bamboo. As well as the truck there is much equipment, not only weapons but ammunition and explosives. More than I have seen in one place for a long time."

Makonzo smiled. "Tell me, how many men do you think?"

"I saw no more than ten. Maybe there are one or two more," replied Wilfred.

"That is all? We are thirty, we will surprise them."

"Make your preparations."

The Mopane Canopy

Lovemore returned. He spoke with Tembo. "Your mind is fixed? You will meet them?"

"Ah! It is not good but I have no choice if the mission is not to be abandoned. If I cannot make an arrangement all our planning and efforts will have been wasted. When I meet the Shona I will tell them I am waiting here before an attack on Fort Victoria. I will say we have much preparation to do. Then if necessary I will strike the real target tomorrow, even without Morgan's men. The last words my father spoke to me were not to trust the Shona. His words have always been good so I will not trust them and I will not share the glory of our work with them, but for now I must talk."

"I will come with you to the meeting?" asked Lovemore.

"No. I will take another. I have more important things for you to do. You will be the insurance."

Tembo turned to the radio operator. "I go now. When I return there are important messages to send, messages on which our mission depends. Be sure that the equipment is ready."

Tembo spoke secret last words to Lovemore. Then he picked a man to accompany him. "You will watch out for me. Make sure your weapon is ready."

Tembo checked his own pistol and fastened it in its holster. Outside of the kraal they moved quickly following Lovemore's directions.

The Mopane trees ended abruptly and gave way to a clearing covered in grass green from the recent rain. In the middle of the clearing a clump of bamboo erupted as The Priest had described. Tembo stood in the shade of the last Mopane trees. He waited and watched.

Few birds visited the Mopane forest. There was little accessible food in the sodden acidic soil on which the Mopane thrived, but on the edge of the forest, where light penetrated, birds sang.

Tembo looked towards the centre of the clearing. The bamboo's sprouted skyward, some as much as thirty feet tall and as thick as a man's thigh. They wafted in the breeze, the breeze that eluded the forest. Hanging precariously from the sagging tips were a profusion of the cocoon like nests of Weaverbirds. Some of the inhabitants darted backward and forward holding unwieldy twigs in their beaks for building and repair work to their homes. Others carried food for their young families. Tembo watched, not admiring the industriousness of the birds but looking for signs.

From the far side of the clearing came a squawk of alarm. Birds rose as one, seeking safer perches. Movement came from the bush. A figure emerged from behind a cluster of thorn. He stepped into the open; there was no weapon to be seen. Tembo recognised the Priest.

"You know what to do. Stay here, out of sight. Watch my back. It is up to you to protect me." Tembo unbuttoned the flap on his holster and folded it back. He lifted the pistol slightly and let it drop back to make sure it was free. He flicked the safety to off. There was a round in the chamber, Tembo only needed to pull the trigger.

The Priest shouted. "Are you alone?"

"One man as agreed," replied Tembo.

A moment passed. Another man stepped forward. He stood behind the Priest. He held an AK across his chest.

"We will meet in the middle", shouted Tembo. "Just you and I." His words were for the stranger.

The two walked towards each other. Tembo looked to the eyes of the Shona but the Shona avoided his stare. Tembo lowered his gaze to the man's AK. He recognised the model. Chinese pressed steel, wire stock, different to the quality Russian weapons of the Impi. As they closed Tembo could see the slide mechanism caked with black grease. Days had passed since the weapon had seen cloth or oil. The tip of the barrel was encrusted with mud.

They were less than ten feet apart. The first movement was almost imperceptible. Maybe the tightening of the man's grip on the stock, maybe some other movement. Tembo could not say what it was, only that the hair on the back of his neck stood up. Then the Priest stepped back into the bush.

The barrel of the AK began to raise. Instinctively Tembo reached for his pistol. His hand was still in motion when the barrel of the AK47 came level with his stomach. There was no time to think. Only the words that his father spoke came. "Don't trust the Shona."

The muscles of his belly tightened. He anticipated the bullets tearing into his flesh.

The thump never arrived. There was only the metallic click of the action sliding forward. The two had eye contact. Each wondered what happened. Tembo was first to realise his adversary a second later. His opponent tried to clear the blockage but Tembo had the edge. he raised his pistol and pulled the trigger. A single shot to the chest. It was enough. The bullet penetrated clothing. It broke skin and met no resistance till the sternum, which gave way easily. The heart of his opponent was torn; irretrievably damaged. Unconsciousness was an eternal few seconds in coming. He wavered on his feet before legs gave way. A corpse landed on the ground.

Adrenaline accelerated Tembo's thoughts. The danger had not passed. He was exposed, he needed cover. He crouched. A single shot. The bullet passed close by, over his head. Tembo turned. His man broke cover looking for a target. A new gun rattled, from a different direction. His man fell to the ground. Tembo was alone.

"Stop or I will kill you." The voice was sure. "I can kill you now. It is better you surrender."

Tembo knew he had no chance. He stood upright. Two men emerged from different parts, the priest and another. Both pointed AK's at him. The situation was hopeless. Tembo dropped his gun. The men came forward.

The priest spoke. "Let me introduce my leader. Makonzo."

Tembo looked at the one he had shot.

"Another hero of the struggle. A new name for hero's acre, "said Makonzo. "Did you think I would by so stupid as to endanger my own life?" He laughed. "I will not kill you yet, there are things you must tell me before I give you that release."

"Tie his hands Wilfred."

.

The needle flickered just above the red mark. The charge was not enough. The batteries were almost flat. There was no option if he were to transmit. He would have to start the generator.

The radio operator swung the crank handle of the two pot Lister diesel generator as fast as he could before flipping a compression lever. The engine spluttered. He threw the second compression lever and the engine popped into life, accelerating to speed and then settling into a steady rhythmic thump.

Nobody in the Kraal heard the distant shots from the bamboo clearing.

The Cadre were prepared. They'd worked their way around. They'd come from the east and entered the forest at its highest point. Tyoni liked the advantage of height. Now they waited, ready to ambush.

The scout had been quick. They had seen them leave the Kraal and followed. They had gone in the direction of the strip road, the same strip road along which Lovemore had driven the truck. The undergrowth was still broken. It was an easy trail for an experienced tracker.

The scout knew they must return the same way. He guessed what they were doing. He'd hurried back to tell Tyoni.

Tyoni had picked the place. The trees were tall and thick, the trunks wide enough to conceal a man. From ahead came voices, careless voices. Each man of the Cadre stood silent, hidden as the voices came closer.

Tyoni crouched, peering through the growth. Three men, strange fatigues. Two carried a wooden munitions crate between them, each holding a rope handle. Tyoni could see that the crate was not heavy. The two men were arguing, their guns slung uselessly on their backs.

They were not looking. Tyoni waited till the last moment. They came closer, unaware. He stepped in front of them, his gun pointing. In unison his men followed. The chattering stopped the men stood still, surrounded. Tyoni smiled and motioned the men to put down the crate and guns.

The lid of the crate was loose. Tyoni looked inside. Trenching tools. He looked at his prisoners fingers, caked with mud. They had been working with their hands in the soil. As he thought, the men had been laying mines and traps.

Tyoni calculated, he had three men prisoner, two had gone to meet Makonzo. There should be no more than four of five men in the Kraal. Then he heard the diesel engine spluttering into life. It was enough for him, he would seize the opportunity. They moved quickly.

Tyoni spoke to three of his men, "Quickly, take the clothes of the prisoners. Put them on and tie the prisoners up."

He left a guard with the prisoners. "If they give trouble use the bayonet. Do not shoot. There must be no noise."

The imposters led the way. They walked towards the sound of the engine. The Cadre followed, keeping to the cover of trees. They found the entrance to the Kraal. Lovemore had overlapped the walls when he made the entrance. Nobody could look in from outside, just as nobody could look out from the inside. They walked into the compound, their arrival unacknowledged.

The stolen fatigues had earned a few seconds, long enough for them to cross the compound.

Then. "Who are you?" The voice was already too late.

The alarm was barely heard above the diesel engine. The radio operator looked up. He knocked the compression levers to vent. The engine revs fell away. Attention was on the three men. Nobody moved for a moment. Then pandemonium. Tyoni ran forward, his men flooded through the entrance. It was over in a moment not one shot had been fired.

Lovemore had gone quickly at first, running. As he approached the clearing he'd slowed and stepped carefully. He could see light through the trees. He was close. He went to the right, working his way to the North. He came out of the Mopane forest, not into the clearing but into an area of bush. He was careful.

He'd learnt how to track animals. They were more difficult to follow than humans. In the Department of Parks and Wildlife he'd stalked elephant and rhino. Sometimes he'd chased the big cats. His animal senses were developed and finely honed. Some creatures could feel the vibrations of footsteps through the ground.

He'd had too little time. When Tembo arrived he'd scouted less than half the area. He'd heard Wilfred and Tembo shout at each other across the clearing. He tried to work his way around to the Shona, towards Wilfred's voice. The giant bamboo obscured his view. He heard the shots but could not see. Frantically he backtracked trying to bring Tembo back into his line of sight. It took minutes. Tembo was tied and being led off into the forest before he was ready.

When Lovemore thought it was safe he broke cover and ran across the clearing. His Comrade lay bleeding. Flies were already congregating and settling on the open wound. He was still not quite dead, eyes rolled high in their sockets exposing bloodshot whites. Lovemore knelt beside his Comrade. He held the hand of the wounded man and felt the last pulse of life ebb away. The man was already beyond worldly comfort.

The man's gun was gone. Lovemore checked the corpse's pockets. There must be nothing that could be traced. He stood and looked for a last time. The animals would eat him before the Whites came.

Lovemore followed the group into the forest. He'd hoped to overtake them. He would warn the compound. But they were too fast. He only caught a glimpse through the trees. He pushed on, darting from side to side, always under cover. He closed up. They were not careful. No rear guard. Tembo was in front. They prodded him with a rifle and moved in the direction of the Kraal. Lovemore did not understand. It dawned slowly on him. The camp had already been taken.

Fort Victoria, Rhodesian Army HQ

"It's been missing for three days."

"So why did they only report it today?" Lieutenant Walters was agitated.

The police inspector explained for a second time. "They only reported it missing this morning but it's been gone for three days. This is actually the fourth day. It left Bulawayo empty. The driver was on his was to the National Game Park at Wankie. He was supposed to set up camp for an elephant cull. He never arrived at the site. They have been searching the Game Park themselves."

"The driver's most probably drunk in a beer hall or running his mates around. Might even have been eaten by a lion. Never know your luck," said the Lieutenant. "You know what Kaffers are like."

Twenty-two years old, pimply faced, ginger hair, Walters held an unsupportable belief in his own abilities. A full time regular, he commanded a part time Company of the RLI. He was based at Fort Victoria. He didn't like sharing barracks with a battalion of the African Rifles, a black regiment. He didn't bother hiding his contempt. "Blacks are blacks, they might be on our side but they'll always be unreliable and untrustworthy, most probably worse." He didn't like the Police either, which was a shame because his main function was liaison and support of the BSAP.

The police inspector hadn't wasted time on a radio message or phone call. Walter's reputation for inaction was well known. He went in person to the barracks. The Police Inspector wondered if they were on the same side at times. There was no respect – either way.

"There are a couple of points." The police inspector explained. "The driver's been with Parks and Wildlife for fifteen years. Reliable as clockwork - until recently. Last year went off to look after his dying mother. Gone for six months. Came back right as rain. But the word amongst the boys is that there was nothing wrong with his mother. Intelligence has nothing but it is possible he could have been training with the nasties. Also, the truck was logged going through one of our roadblocks a couple of days ago, here in Fort Victoria. The driver answered the description of the regular driver. Had a load of crocodiles. Said he was going to Lake Kyle. All his paperwork was in order. Just that Parks and Wildlife don't have any projects at Lake Kyle."

"You sent patrols around Lake Kyle yourselves?" asked Walters.

"Not ground patrols. Swept with a spotter plane. Nothing. Sending a couple of Land Rovers out now. Resources, that's the problem. Looks like they're not going to find anything. Our best chance is local farmers. They'd report anything automatically but we'll get nothing form the local Africans. They will be too scared to say anything."

The Inspector continued. "I think there's something about this missing truck. More than a gut feel. It's too suspicious. That's why I'm asking for the army's help."

Walters shrugged. "What are one black and a truck going to do?"

"I think it needs to be taken more seriously. It's no ordinary truck that's gone missing. This thing is a self-contained field unit. Messing facilities, radios, first aid, communications, tools, the lot. It's better than anything you or I have at our disposal."

Walters scribbled on a piece of paper. He wore an almost pained expression. "Okay. I'll organise something. A patrol, if not today tomorrow. But if the truck's that good and it is found I might just keep it for ourselves."

The Police Inspector turned and left unconvinced of Walters's sincerity.

Walter's would bring it up during the evening briefing. Ask for volunteers. See who was available, who fancied a ride out.

Mopane Canopy

No grass grows under the Mopane canopy. Newly fallen leaves cover the ground and quickly start to decompose, releasing nutrients back into the soil. The only green plants that survive are the ones that require little light for photosynthesis; some thorns, vines and parasitic plants.

Lovemore wriggled through the layer of dead leaves until he was nestled up to the compound wall he'd constructed. He got too close, a blackthorn barb penetrated his sleeve. It drew blood and made him silently curse. He couldn't see inside the Kraal. It was too dangerous. He listened, straining to make out words. For twenty minutes he lay still. At first there were just ants, tiny Pharoes ants, harmless as they crawled over his skin. Then came the centipedes, less numerous but troublesome. They bit and spat acid into the wound they left. He could not stay, slowly he crawled backwards, ruffling the leaves with his hands to conceal his trail. When he was twenty-five yards away, hidden by trees, he dared to stand. There was nothing he could do alone. He went to the riverbank.

The level had fallen, but not enough. He cursed that the waters were so quick to rise and so slow to fall. He checked the rope. The two ends were out of the water, the rest was still submerged.

"Morgan must be close, with his men, maybe waiting on the other side," he thought. But he knew he would be well back from the river bank and wouldn't know anything was wrong until the evening radio check. By then it would be too late.

Lovemore ran along the river bank. He tore six leaves from a banana tree and uprooted leafy saplings. With his bare hands he dug a hollow in the gravel. He wrapped his AK in the banana leaves and placed it in the depression. He emptied his pockets into another leaf and covered the depression with the saplings.

His feet sank into the soft sand, he looped his arm over the rope and began to work his way across. The water was too powerful, his legs were swept from beneath him. He hung by his arms, the rough rope burnt but he dare not let go, the current would take him away forever. It was useless, the river was too strong, he worked his way back.

Soaking, he went to his stash and dug up his rifle. He unwrapped the banana leaves and removed the canvas shoulder strap from the weapon, before returning it to its hiding place. He looped the shoulder strap around the rope and then through his belt. He tied it off, pulling hard on the knot. Again he edged off the river bank, into the water. His feet lifted, he relaxed his arms and let the strap take the weight. It was better. He worked his way across, fighting to keep his mouth clear of the foaming water.

Half way it became harder. He was pulling into the water, waves washed over his head, he fought for breath. The hemp rope cut his hands till they bled. Finally he felt the bottom again. Not enough to grip at first. He pulled some more. At last he gained his footing. Clear of the torrent he untied himself and collapsed on the bank, gasping for air.

Edison's fever had subsided, the skin on his back was no longer inflamed. All the cactus barbs had been removed. He was happy Morgan had not sent him back, but he knew Morgan had good reason to keep him.

He worked his way down to the river every two hours, always to the same spot. He'd marked a tree that stuck out of the water so he could monitor the level. Down another four inches. For a while he sat concealed in the undergrowth, watching.

He saw the marks coming out of the water, a few feet away from his hiding place and then the canvas strap, still hanging from the rope. In a moment he'd found the prostrate body. He thought it was a corpse at first, then he saw the chest rise. He went closer.

Lovemore tried to lift himself and turned his head. Edison recognised the face of his Comrade.

"We must not stay here. The Shona have the other bank. They tricked us and have taken our camp," gasped Lovemore.

Tembo, with his men, was forced into the squat position, in the middle of the Kraal. His hands were tied behind his back. Nylon twine cut into his wrists, the more he tried to loosen the knot, the deeper the twine cut. He closed his eyes, concentrating, trying to put his mind above the pain. Speaking was not allowed. The back of his legs hurt, the circulation was cut. He lost track of time but could see that darkness was coming. The guards walked around watching and waiting.

He cursed his stupidity. How easily the Shona had taken them. He knew the mission and their lives were forfeit as he watched the Shona ransack the camp in an undisciplined frenzy. They riffled everything, the truck, the stores, the packs. Only the ones called Wilfred and Tyoni, tried to maintain order.

Tembo thought that the indiscipline gave hope. He watched as the leader, the one they called Makonzo, came close. He spoke to a guard. Tembo could not hear the words. The two men looked at the prisoners. Tembo's saw into the eyes of Makonzo. Dilated and glazed, they were not the eyes of the rational.

Makonzo moved back to the truck. He sat on an empty packing case, under the truck's awning. He spoke to Tyoni and Wilfred.

"It is too late for us to leave. Darkness is coming. We will stay here tonight and enjoy what hospitality the Matable have to offer. What do you say? They can provide entertainment. We will make them talk and watch them die. After tonight the message will be clear. No Matable will come to our part of the world again. We must only choose one to live and spread the message."

"If we kill the prisoners we lose what we have gained," said Tyoni.

"How so?" asked Makonzo.

"There is so much equipment here. Not only what the men carried, but everything from the truck also. More than we alone can take away. All from the Russians or their friends. It is the best equipment we have seen. Much better than what we receive from our Chinese Comrades."

"We have no choice but to leave what we cannot carry," said Makonzo.

"That would be a sadness because the whites will find it and use it against us."

"We already have our own cache of arms and more comes all the time."

"Yes. Every bullet carried on the back of a Comrade, across the Mozambique border. Too many trips would have to be made to bring such equipment to us. It is our duty to save it."

"What do you have in mind?" Makonzo asked.

"We make a new cache, a place, no more that one day's

march. That is far enough. We hide everything we have won. We move it all quickly, before the white man comes."

"This is a lot of work."

"Yes. But not for us," Tyoni laughed, "We have Matable donkeys to do the work." He looked to the squatting prisoners.

"They will do it."

"You will deny me my entertainment?" asked Makonzo.

"You will still have your entertainment. But not tonight." said Tyoni.

"Maybe it is not such a bad thing," he said. "But if I agree to your request others might say you have no stomach for the kill."

"You know that is not true. I have proven myself and I will prove myself again. I will draw the first blood from the prisoners, but only when we have our new cache safely hidden."

"You will do it and I shall be the witness!" Makonzo smiled.

Tembo looked at each of his men in turn. Some weakened, the ones that remained strong nodded. Only one could not signal at all. Fatigue had overtaken him. He swayed on his haunches, his balance obscured by pain. Behind the wavering man stood a Shona guard, rifle held high with both hands, ready to bring down the butt onto the wavering man. Such a blow, to the nape of a man's neck, would kill. Tembo tried to will his man back to consciousness. The man's eyes were open but he saw nothing. He wavered, leaning too far forward, beyond the point of no return. For a moment he tottered, partially aroused by the threat of the fall. He fought to regain balance. It was useless. He fell.

Even before he toppled the guard raised the butt of his gun higher. He readied to bring the weapon down using the force of both arms. The guard focused on the proud third vertebrae. The rifle butt started its downward arc. Tembo gathered his strength and pushed on stiff legs. He sprang upwards and sideways, his shoulder aimed at the distracted guard. The butt had not made contact when the full weight of Tembo's body struck the guard. Both men fell, Tembo on top, arms still tied. The guard and Tembo lay face to face. Tembo could only head butt his opponent. The guard's nose split, like a ripe fruit. Blood flowed. The guard was blinded. But with bound hands the situation was hopeless. Tembo pulled himself to his knees. He fought to gain his feet. The guard tried to retrieve his dropped gun. Tembo kicked the weapon away.

Other guards moved in. They came at Tembo from behind. Tembo felt their presence and turned. He lurched towards the nearest. The guard side-stepped the attack. Tembo tripped. Nothing broke his fall. He landed face down. Only the softness of the earth saved him from injury. He tried to rise again, then came the first kick. The boot buried itself into his ribs. The crack was audible. He cried in pain. Air was forced from his lungs. For a second he was paralysed, unable to inhale. Slowly his diaphragm relaxed and he took an inward gulp of air. The recovery was short lived. A boot came down on his neck, pressing hard. His cheek was pushed into the soil. He felt the cold metal on his temple. It needed no explanation. He tried to look from the corner of his eye. He wanted to see the face of his killer.

Makonzo came forward. He watched the fracas. His pistol was drawn but he offered no help. The guard had Tembo pinned down and had his finger on the trigger. He looked to Makonzo. Makonzo hesitated. The guard pulled his gun away.

"He will die soon enough. Leave him for now. You will have extra fun with him later. It would be too easy to let him go now."

A final boot connected with the soft tissue that covered his unprotected left kidney. There was a blinding flash and then black spots danced before his eyes. The pain burst over him. He could not suppress a cry.

Makonzo looked to the guard. "They must work tomorrow. Let them sit."

Fort Victoria Barracks

Lieutenant Walters was sitting at his desk. He didn't raise his head he just continued writing as if nobody was there. Duncan and Private Rory Quinn had been standing at attention for too long, past the point of common decency. Duncan didn't normally have problems with officers, even young ones. Walter's was the exception. Not that Duncan would say anything. He knew better than that.

Duncan looked at the map that covered the wall behind the Officer. It was marked "SOUTHERN COMMAND", "Masvingo and South Matabeleland Operational Area". Coloured pins marked the latest operational situation for all the lands south of a line stretching from Bulawayo to Fort Victoria.

The Lieutenant concentrated on his paper work. Duncan cast a glance at Rory. Neither spoke. Duncan was impatient; he had work to do at the mine. He didn't need to watch an acne-faced kid scribbling. Finally Walters signed the bottom of the paper with an exaggerated flourish. Duncan then watched part two of the ritual. The Lieutenant painstakingly separated the copies. The carbon paper was removed, smoothed and placed at the back of the pad. The Lieutenant carefully folded the top white copy and four flimsies. He put them in his out tray and let go a sigh of relief as if he had accomplished a major task.

"Five copies are stupid. Doesn't matter how hard you press, the bottom two copies are illegible," said Walters.

Duncan wasn't sure who the Officer was talking to. It could have been the ionosphere. In fact it was most probably the ionosphere. Finally the Lieutenant raised his head and looked at them.

"At ease men," his first overdue words to them.

"Not stand easy," thought Duncan. "Only at ease. Bastard."

"It's not your normal briefing. Something's come up. I was going to mention it tonight but thought I'd collar you two instead."

"Sir", said Rory.

"I have another duty for you. Pain in the arse job, should suit you two." Walters laughed.

"Had a visit from the local police this afternoon, appears

176

Parks and Wildlife have lost a truck. Police want us to find it, not that we don't have enough to do, fighting a war and all that."

Walters went through the story without enthusiasm. "We need to make a bit of a show. Brass doesn't like it unless we make a bit of a fuss of our police colleagues. Army co-operating with the police and all that shit," said Walters. "So I want you two to take a run along the Beite Bridge highway, down as far as the Lake Kyle road. Go to the lake. Potter around. Be seen.

It's almost certainly a wild goose chase, nothing to suggest any activity in this area. At worst the driver got pissed and ran off the road. He's most probably dead in the bush somewhere, would be nice to get our hands on the truck though. Want you to start in the morning, check both sides of the road for anything suspicious."

Duncan interjected. "I'm a part timer. I'm supposed to be working at the mine tomorrow."

"I know. And I know you're over your allotted hours. But that's war. I've spoken to the mine superintendent. You're released from work. No problem. Any other objections?"

"Don't we get a say in this?" asked Duncan.

"As much say as I did," replied Walters.

Rory spoke. "We're roistered on train guard duty tomorrow night. We'll be knackered."

"You can sleep on the train." said the Lieutenant, "Nothing happens on that duty."

Mopane Canopy

"By morning it will be safe to cross the river," said Morgan. "But we cannot wait till then. Every hour is precious. We will cross in the dark and attack before daylight."

Morgan led his men forward under stars and a clear sky.

"There will be no rain tonight," whispered Edison as he helped Lovemore attach himself to the rope once more.

Lovemore pushed off into the water. The others watched and waited their turn. It was not so hard. The water had dropped further. His feet touched the bottom nearly all the way across. More land on the far bank was exposed. It was easier for Lovemore to scramble free and make the tree line.

The other men followed. One at a time they fastened themselves to the rope and quietly slipped into the water. They edged forward, rifles wrapped in plastic groundsheets slung across their chests attached to the webbing. The AK47 is not an accurate weapon at any distance but it is robust and will function in any condition. Morgan had said tonight its reputation was to be tested. He's also said that there was to be no retreat. They would carry their packs with them. Standard plastic liners would keep them afloat and would help the men when their clothes became waterlogged. Morgan was second last across. He slid into the water only when he was sure the others were safely landed.

On the far bank each man unwrapped his rifle, groundsheets were folded and stowed, backpacks were left close to the river. They would be retrieved later. They carried weapons and enough ammunition. Bayonet scabbards were loosened and blades ritually tested. When everybody was ready Morgan led the line forward into the Mopane forest. They went only two hundred yards, stopping in the lee of a natural fold in the ground and still out of sight of the Kraal.

Morgan lifted the leather cover of his wristwatch and whispered to Lovemore. "Four am. Two hours to daylight. Whichever way it goes it will be over by the time the sun rises. Take Edison and go forward. Observe and return. Be bold and take opportunities. We will wait here for one hour, then we come with or without your signal. Go now and the Spirits of our forefathers go with you."

Tembo lay on his side, alert. His whispered orders had been passed from man to man. They must only feign sleep. He believed rescue would come. Morgan would not let them down, they must be ready. Tembo was sure the Shona did not suspect the existence of the second Impi. As time passed hope did not fade, it grew. Tembo would willingly die for his brother and he knew Morgan would do the same for him.

The fire had burnt brightly in the first hours of darkness but now there were only glowing embers. Two dull bulbs, powered by the truck's battery, hung from the frame of the awning casting only a dim glow. The camp had drifted into silence broken only by the snores and grunts of sleeping men.

Two guards had been set. One watched the prisoners the other was outside the Kraal.

The prisoners guard had walked around at first but when he'd tired of stumbling in the gloom he sat down with his back against a tree, nursing his gun. The punishment for falling asleep on guard duty was death but the sanction had never been enforced. Nobody stayed awake to check the guard. As the minutes became hours the guard's head became heavier and began to sag. His mind slipped into that disturbed space that is mid point between sleep and awake.

Outside the Kraal the guard found a place to hide himself, in sight of the entrance. It was too dark to walk. He would rely on his hearing for protection, picking out the warning signals from the sounds of the night.

Lovemore led Edison away from the river and into the forest. Soon they could no longer hear the water the only sounds were those of insects and frogs and the hoots of distant owls.

Lovemore went to his knees. Edison followed. He was close enough to touch Lovemore but could see nothing more than a shadow. Every few yards Edison scraped his foot deep into the mat of dead leaves marking a clear trail. Lovemore slowed, Edison could feel the tension. Then he picked up the faint smell of burnt wood. They were close now.

Edison thought they had come to a bush but slowly he realised they were at the edge of the Kraal. Lovemore felt for his hand. With a finger he passed the message. He traced a large circle, the compound, then an arrow to the left. Edison closed his hand twice, the signal for understanding.

They went left along the wall, crawling on their bellies. They heard snoring. Lovemore stopped and pulled Edison forward. In the distance was a dull red glow. He thought it was the eye of an animal. Then the light moved and became brighter. A careless guard pulled on his cigarette. They backtracked to the rear of the compound. Lovemore wriggled forward, pushing into the thicket wall. He felt for the soft spot.

The thicket fence was to protect. There should be only one defendable entrance. This was an anathema to Lovemore. He had worked with animals too long. He knew the danger of being trapped. There should always be an escape.

Lovemore gently pulled back the leaves and exposed the shallow gully that went under the fence. It was safe. No blackthorn, no bamboo. It was not big, just enough for one man to squeeze through. He pushed. Inside to the right he could see the faint glow of the bulbs. Men lay around, resting on their packs. The meagre light was just enough for his sharp eyes to make out the one leaning against the tree with his gun, the prisoner's guard. He withdrew. Again he held Edison's hand and fingered his message. Edison clenched his hand and began the journey back to Morgan following the marks he had scraped in the leaves.

Lovemore silently removed the bayonet stored in the stock of his AK and tucked it into his belt. He pushed the gun ahead of him into the gully and followed through the thicket. Snake like he slithered forward.

Twenty minutes and he had reached the first man. Lovemore touched his leg. He felt the muscles tighten and relax. Lovemore looked to the guard still sitting nodding, unaware. The twine yielded to the sharp blade. It took longer for the circulation to restore feeling to numb fingers. Lovemore rolled to face the other direction. He reached a second man.

He worked as the stars faded but before the first pre-dawn hue began to garnish the sky. He passed the bayonet. The prisoners lay motionless but free. Lovemore stayed with them. Still. They waited for the signal that they knew would come.

Edison returned to the fold in the ground and spoke to Morgan, the tone urgent. Morgan looked to his watch. He whispered orders that were passed down the line. They moved off, each man following the next, crouching, behind Edison's lead. Even eyes accustomed to the dark could hardly see. They went slowly.

At the thicket wall three men went to the right, feeling their way. They found the hollow. Others worked their way to the front and waited in the darkness.

Kato was content with the perch he'd found for himself between the twin trunks of a stunted tree. He'd wedged himself into the "v" and smoked. It was more comfortable than it looked and would have provided a good view if there had been light.

It is said that the last hour before dawn is the worst. That period just before the promise of a new day is fulfilled. For Kato it was the time to think of home and his family. They were foremost in his mind.

Kato was another unwilling volunteer that did not want to fight. The Shona army had no conscripts, or so it was said. He'd come from Morandera, a village in the east, in the heart of Shona land. His father worked in the giant Hunyani paper mill at Norton. He was always away so that the family could live well. Kato stayed on the TTL with his mother and grandmother. The women grew maize and tended goats on a hectare of land that had been purchased with wage money sent by his father. It would have been fertile if there was irrigation. Instead, in the dry season, water came from a deep well and much time was spent carrying plastic buckets to the fields to maintain the scant crops.

Sometimes his father visited; Christmas and one other holiday in the year. Kato could not remember exactly when but knew it was in the rainy season. The family would go down to meet the bus. His father would bring presents and money. It would be a time of happiness and they would all eat meat. Kato wondered if it would be such a time of happiness when he returned home to his mother.

He liked the magazines his father brought, the coloured ones with shiny paper. It made him want to work in the city. He wanted a job like his father. Then he would wear Western clothes. His father said he would put him forward for a job in the mill when he was past

15 years old. That time would come soon enough.

It was nearly two years ago that a stranger had come to the village, a Commissar in the Liberation Struggle. He said he was going to bring freedom for everybody but all had to work together. The land would be a wonderful place when the struggle was won and everybody would be rich like the white people.

He came again. This second time he brought other people, Comrades who carried guns and pangas. The Comrades were angry with the Head Man and elders. They picked out one of the village men and made him stand before the village people. The Comrades said his son was a "Sell Out" who worked for the Police. Because of this all his family had become the enemy. The Comrades said the punishment for the man and his wife was death because they had brought such a bad person into the world. People were angry and scared. The Commissar had said the Party was kind and forgiving. So in this instance the mother and father would only be beaten and driven out of the village. But that was on condition that the Elders joined in the struggle. The Elders agreed but only to save the life of the man and his wife.

The Commissar came to live in the village. He took the house of the Head Man. Everybody was given duties. Everybody had to attend meetings. The village only had to provide food at first, for the Comrades. Later the Comrades said that young men must be given over for training, to become great soldiers of the Chimurenga – the struggle.

Kato didn't want to fight. He didn't understand the Commissar. The Elders had spoken though and he had to obey. At the training camp in Mozambique he only dreamed of going back to work in the city. He survived on a promise. The promise he could go to the city as a hero when the Struggle was over. He wished it was over. He wished he was a hero. One of his wishes were about to come true.

Edison came from behind. He selected the serrated edge of the blade.

The human neck is complex. A crowded part of the body. Two carotid arteries take oxygenated blood from the heart to the facial muscles and brain. The de-oxygenated blood is returned by the jugular veins. The trachea connects the mouth and nasal passages with the lungs. It is made of tough cartilage so that it does not collapse. The trachea also supplies air to the wind box. It is important to completely sever the trachea to stop the victim screaming. Then there is the oesophagus, the muscular tube that passes food from mouth to stomach, lastly the spinal column, a hollow stack of bone and cartilage that houses the lower brain stem and nerves.

In his trance Kato heard nothing. In a single movement, Edison pressed his left hand over the youth's mouth. Edison jerked his victim's head back and simultaneously ripped the serrated edge across the exposed throat. He felt the serration rip through cartilage. Blood erupted. Kato tried to yell but there was only a hiss as air from his lungs escaped through the severed trachea. The brain sensed a lack of blood and shut down of its own accord. Unconsciousness was immediate, death of life and dreams followed quickly.

Edison lowered the limp body to the floor. High in the canopy a bird chirped, the first note of the dawn chorus.

They moved forward, poised either side of the entrance. Morgan waited a few moments. He wanted some pre dawn light.

The three at the rear began to crawl through the hollow. The first sidled through effortlessly. The second followed. He made no noise but his presence was enough to make the dozing guard lift his head. Through bleary eyes he saw a man crawling. Another was coming through a hole. He stood. Before he shouted a burst of automatic fire felled him and woke the camp.

Everywhere men moved. The prisoners were up and running. They fought with bare hands. The Shona were too slow. Morgan led the charge through the entrance. They fanned out, rushing the defenders. Morgan went to the left. Lovemore had described the truck and the awning. Makonzo was up. He scrambled for his pistol but was too late.

"Put it down," said Morgan.

Makonzo dropped the weapon. Morgan kicked it away. It skidded under the truck. Tyoni watched but could not get to his master. He was locked in his own struggle.

Morgan's strong arms pulled Makonzo. "Up!" he demanded.

"I have no weapon. Don't shoot me," pleaded Makonzo.

"Tell your men to stop", ordered Morgan. He prodded a rifle into Makonzo's chest. "If one of my men dies you will follow him."

Morgan pushed the gun forward to reinforce his statement.

No further encouragement was necessary. "STOP! STOP!

yelled Makonzo. His voice was heard above the fracas. "Do not resist, it is useless."

Men still fought. They became fewer in number. The struggle had ended. The tables had turned.

"Tonight?" said Tembo.
"Tonight," said Morgan.
"Send the signal," Tembo spoke to the radio operator.
"We have work to do," they both agreed.
Trussed like chickens the Shona were now the prisoners, they lay on the dirt floor. Only an hour since dawn.
"What shall we do with them? Do you have any idea?" asked Tembo
"Yes. I have an idea," replied Morgan. "But that is for later."

Orders were issued. Men moved.
"You have the timers?" asked Morgan. "Show me".
Four men stood in front of him. As well as weapons they carried satchel packs.
"We have them," said one. He undid the buckle and lifted the flap of his satchel. Morgan looked and saw the cardboard box marked "CASIO". "Digital watches make perfect timers," he said.
"How many pylons are prepared?" asked Morgan.
"Four pylons will fall. Two legs from each pylon will collapse." the man replied. "The charges are set for nineteen hundred hours."

Rhodesian industry was booming despite or maybe because of sanctions. The hydro-electricity from Kariba was not enough. Electricity was imported from South Africa on a 32kV high tension line. The pylons traversed the bush from the South African border to the electrical switching station outside of Que Que. Disrupting this line would plunge large parts of the country into darkness for many days. This itself would be a dramatic demonstration but it was not the main target, only a distraction.

"Do not make a mistake with the timers. Go now. We will meet you at the rendezvous before six o'clock."
Four more men left before noon. They headed for the railway

carrying the explosives needed to prepare the line.

Fort Victoria Barracks

"All I got that's not allocated," said the mechanic pointing to the Land Rover.

"We might have to go off road, what about that Eland," said Rory pointing to an armoured truck parked in the corner of the garage.

The motor pool mechanic shook his head. "It's a three man crew and I can only see two of you. Besides you're not trained. You'd have it on its side in ten minutes. Thing's top heavy."

"It's the Land Rover then. Don't suppose it's mine proofed?"

The mechanic smiled. "Yeah, and its got reclining seats and a cigar lighter too. What do you expect for a "63 model? Racing trim?"

The Land Rover was old. The new stuff was kept in reserve or given to the regulars. The only new thing on the LWB ragtop was the green and fawn paint work. The doors creaked when they were opened.

"You can drive if you want," said Duncan. "I'll observe."

"Thanks bud. That's very kind of you."

The Land Rover had been designed for use by farmers. It used a lot of aluminium because of its availability after the war in Britain. Steel was in short supply due to reconstruction. The Army were quick to spot its usefulness and adopted the vehicle. The biggest design fault, as far as the army was concerned, was that the driver sat on top of the fuel tank. Not a great situation if you run over a mine.

The Rover had been fitted with a field radio ten years ago. It hadn't worked for the last eight. They'd been given a back-pack VHF set instead.

The Armoury sergeant was more forthcoming.

"Take a couple of these. They're great." He pushed two Rhuzi's across the counter with half a dozen magazines. "Handy in an emergency. Scares the shit out of anybody on the wrong end."

"Not very good when you're on the right end either," said Duncan remembering his training session with the Rhodesian version of the Israeli Uzi sub machine gun. Pull the trigger and the whole magazine empties. There's no stopping it.

"Take a grenade launcher as well."

Rory drove over to the Ops Room for an intelligence report, nothing special. Just the general alert that had been in force for weeks and was taken for granted now.

They started the patrol from the Fort Victoria checkpoint, the last place the Parks and Wildlife truck had been seen. Outside town there was nothing to see and hardly any traffic, just endless bush either side. Rory drove slowly. The vegetation appeared greener and thicker since the previous night's rain. The bush responded quickly to water.

Twenty klicks out they encountered a Highways gang cutting back the growth either side of the road. There was a tractor and trailer for the boys. Rory pulled over and spoke to the Boss Man. He'd seen nothing.

A few more klicks and a troop of baboons occupied the crown of the road. They were unwilling to yield to the Land Rover. Rory didn't want to spook them. He slowed and drove through the troop at a crawl. The baboons parted begrudgingly.

They came to the Lake Kyle turnoff; Rory took the left turn and joined the narrower road. The vegetation had not been cleared back, branches brushed against the side of the Land Rover. They crossed a brow. The land fell away. The distant waters of Lake Kyle glistened in the sun. The lake was only fifty percent full. Much more rain was needed to fill it.

They drove down to the water's edge, to a small cluster of European houses, each surrounded by a high chain link fence. They stopped at a large bungalow. The security gates were open. A Rhodesian Ridgeback bounded towards their vehicle. It barked but kept its distance. A young woman in flowery dress came to the fly screen front door. She smiled.

"Its okay", she said, "It's only trained to attack kaffars."

It was an incongruous comment. Duncan thought there was something sad about the words tripping so easily off such sweet lips. They stayed for tea. She'd seen nothing.

Duncan took the wheel. Despite its age the old Land Rover pulled up the incline without effort. A big truck going off the road here would have left a lot of evidence thought Duncan.

"I don't think it came down this track," he said.

They headed back to the junction with the Highway. Duncan stopped for a while before turning left.

"Where you going?" asked Rory. "It's right to Fort Vic."

"Perhaps the driver missed the turning and came a cropper

later on. We can take a look. There's plenty of time."

"We're off plan now," said Rory.

"Don't worry about it."

"Suit yourself", answered Rory. "We've nothing better to do." He slid back in the seat and pulled his bush hat over his eyes. "Siesta time! Call me if you want me."

Duncan smiled and shook his head. He'd go for half an hour and then throw a "U" turn if he'd seen nothing by then. He settled back concentrating on the road.

It wasn't long. The marks were clear and fresh. The rain had not hidden them. On the left verge an arc made by tyre tracks that had veered off the road for a while. Maybe a sleepy driver he thought. Duncan stopped to check it out. He picked up his rifle and left his partner snoring. It was probably nothing.

They were more like tractor tyre marks. A few days old. The crushed grass was beginning to stand again. Duncan looked on the other side of the road. More tracks. The truck had not accidentally veered off the road. It had made a sweeping right turn. Duncan walked over. He could see the strips of lichen covered concrete. He checked the vegetation. The marks where branches had been broken were clearly visible. He walked forward, pushing his way through the undergrowth. It was easy. In a few steps he had entered another world. Clear tyre tracks stood out, not accidental skid marks. The truck had come this way deliberately.

He walked further. The hair on the back of his neck stood up. He was alert. The strip road was easy to follow here. It went to the right. Something at the bend made Duncan stop. He looked. It glistened almost like a single gossamer thread of a spider's web. Only spiders did not spin single lines across roads. It was a fine nylon trip wire. He followed it with his eyes.

The line ran to the trunk of a young tree, not much more than a sapling. He stepped into the bush and came around the back of the tree. Most of the vegetation was lush green only a few leaves close to the tree were browning at the edges. He bent forward and lifted one. It was loose. Underneath was a square green box. Exactly eight and a half inches long, six inches high and five and a quarter inches deep. He knew the dimensions by heart. He could not read the Cyrillic writing stencilled onto the box in black paint but he knew what he was looking at. A standard issue Russian anti-personnel mine. Freshly laid.

He backtracked, checking for other trip wires. He came back

to the road. Rory was leaning on the side of the vehicle smoking. "Been for a shit?" he asked.

Mopane Canopy

"I must do it myself," said Lovemore picking up two bricks of plastic explosives. "I have lived with her for so long it is only right she dies by my hand."

It was difficult for him. The truck had been his life for fifteen years. To him it was no inanimate object but a machine with life that had been his faithful servant. Tonight it would cease to exist, blown into thousands of small pieces by his own hand.

Morgan spoke. "I know it is bad for you to lose your truck, but it is worse if the enemy uses it against the Comrades!"

Little was left to do. The camp was no longer needed. Soon they would leave. The last hot meal was prepared in the field kitchen, onwards there would only be food from ration packs.

Edison joined them. "You asked for this" he said, handing Morgan an iron bar. Morgan took the tool and placed one end into the glowing embers of the fire, soaking in heat.

Morgan and Tembo stood before their Shona prisoners. The prisoners had seen the explosives placed around the Kraal. They had seen the timers set and they saw the Matable prepare to leave. They knew that yesterday they had planned to kill the men that now held them captive.

"We would be justified in killing you," Tembo spoke aloud for all to hear. "You would not have shown us any mercy of that I am sure."

"But that is your way," said Morgan, "We think differently. If we kill you, the White men will find your bodies. They would find out what happened and they would make sure that the world knows how primitive black men fight among each other. They will justly say black men are not civilised enough to govern themselves. They would ensure that the news overshadowed the actions we are going to take this day."

Tembo took over. "So we have decided not to kill you. But that does not mean we forgive the treachery of our meeting. For no good reason, one of our men and one of yours lie dead. This is the fault of your leader."

"Bring him to me", said Morgan.

Makonzo sat amongst his people. He did not raise his head. Two guards lifted him by his arms and dragged him to the front. He refused to stand, staying on his knees.

"Take off his tunic," said Tembo.

The guards tore the tunic away. Makonzo hunched forward.

"You have problems standing?" asked Tembo. "Then do you have anything to say?"

Makonzo remained cowed.

Morgan spoke to the prisoners. "I will show you how brave your leader is."

He turned to Edison. "Bring me the iron."

Edison wrapped a rag around the cool end of the iron bar. He withdrew it from the embers. The hot end glowed cherry red, small sparks jumped.

"We will teach you a lesson."

"Hold his head up", Morgan said. A guard pulled at Makonzo's hair.

"Tell me your name." Morgan waved the bar in front of Makonzo's face.

"Makonzo, my name is Makonzo", he mumbled.

"Makonzo the rat. That is apt. Makonzo I think your name is well chosen. But don't you think you are more like a dog? A Shona dog."

"Are you a Shona dog?"

Through history the Matable had dominated their Shona neighbours and had always considered them as inferiors, no better that the packs of wild dogs that roamed freely in the bush. For a Shona to be called a dog was to be reminded of past humiliations.

Makonzo did not answer.

Morgan held the glowing iron close to Makonzo's face. Gently he let the tip touch his forehead. The man screamed. A pink dot appeared where the melamine in his skin had been destroyed. It would be forever visible on his forehead.

"What are you?" asked Tembo.

"I am a dog. I am a dog. Do not burn me again."

He handed the iron back to Edison. "Put it back in the fire. It must be hotter."

"We are glad you agree you are a dog."

"You," Morgan pointed to one of the prisoners. "What does a dog do?"

"Dogs bark," he replied.

"What else does a dog do?"

Tembo turned his attention back to Makonzo. "Let me see what you think a dog does."

Makonzo was assisted with a motivational kick. On all fours he crawled.

"That is good, but faster", said Morgan, "I can't hear you."

Makonzo barked.

"Keep moving, keep barking."

Makonzo moved. He barked. The Matable laughed and clapped.

"Faster! Louder!" shouted Morgan.

Smiles came to the faces of Shona prisoners.

"Enough", said Tembo after a few minutes. "Bring him to me. Hold him still."

Strong arms gripped Makonzo.

"All that are here know you are a dog but it is important you yourself do not forget the lesson of this day. You must carry a mark until your death as a reminder. Give me the iron."

Makonzo struggled uselessly. The guard's grasp was too strong.

He lowered the tip. His hand was steady. There was a hiss as hot metal came into contact with skin. The smell of burning flesh was accompanied by screams. He dragged the iron across the skin of his chest, tracing the simple child like profile of a dog's head.

Makonzo's screams were piercing. He struggled against restraining hands. Tembo finished his work. "It is done. This is more mercy than you have shown your victims. Let it be your lesson. Tie him up."

Morgan spoke to Lovemore. "We go now. You will stay to guard the prisoners. Two others will stay with you. At 1600 hours leave for the rendezvous. Make sure the prisoners are secure and check the charges. They must be set for 1900 hours. The booby traps must all be primed. Be sure all the unwanted Shona weapons are inside the vehicle and cannot be retrieved without triggering the booby traps. The Shona must know about the traps."

"Take one prisoner with you. Travel quickly. One hour from the camp let the prisoner free. He must have just enough time to come back and release his comrades. Advise them to run away quickly. Soon after many Rhodesian soldiers will come."

Fox Railway Siding

"Now we wait here for one hour. It is important to stick to the timetable," said Morgan. "It's a mile away we are safe from prying eyes. This place is not patrolled. But you will still not smoke.

The men obeyed and unslung their packs. Morgan sat on an exposed rock, the others sat on the ground, resting. They had marched four miles with heavy loads. One passed a water bottle to Morgan. He drank. The water was from the flooded rived and tasted of grit, but it was cool.

"If this target is so important why have we not attacked before?" asked one of the men.

"Because things change," replied Morgan.

"How so? The line has always been here."

Morgan considered for a while before he spoke. He took more water. "When Ian Smith led the Rhodesians to declare independence he felt very strong. Although Rhodesia was land locked South Africa and Mozambique were friendly, Botswana was only an unimportant desert. Of all the neighbours only Zambia was hostile, but Smith was not worried because the Zambians needed to export their copper ore and the only way was through Rhodesia.

"Then one time Kaunda, the Zambian President, said bad things about Rhodesia. As a punishment Smith closed the border with Zambia, stopping all imports and exports. But by doing this Smith did great harm to his own railway system. Firstly half the goods transported on Rhodesian Railways were to and from Zambia. With the border closed the railway was making big losses. On top of that Smith did not realise that when the border was closed half of the Rhodesian Railway's rolling stock and locomotives were actually in Zambia. Rhodesian Railways needed them back. Under pressure Smith reopened his side of the border."

"So what happened then?" said the man.

"Kaunda was not so easy. When the Rhodesians opened their border gates the Zambians shut theirs. The tables had been turned on the Rhodesians.

"But what about the copper exports?"

"The Chinese intervened! They built a new railway line from the copper belt in Zambia to Dar Es Salaam. A complete new route in less than a year. Zambia was no longer dependent on Rhodesia."

Morgan continued. "It got worse for Smith. The fascist Portuguese Government in Lisbon fell to the Socialists. The first thing the Socialists did was to give all the Portuguese colonies independence. And the first thing the new Government in Mozambique did was close the border with Rhodesia. The situation was completely changed. Now this place became important, it is the only remaining railway line out of Rhodesia.

The railway from Beite Bridge to the Midlands is single-track with passing places. The passing places are sidings where a train can be held whilst trains going in the opposite direction pass. Each siding has a signal box and most are in remote places. They are perfect places for us to attack. You my friends are going to close the railway line! Now let us prepare to go."

Each evening a fuel train entered Rhodesia from South Africa. It carried petrol, diesel and kerosene to fuel the war. It was the only way for fuel to enter the country. Thirty miles before the Sabi River crossing the train slowed and was diverted into the Fox Siding. It waited till the Johannesburg bound express sleeper passed.

"Alfred! Alfred!" It was an urgent whisper.
Alfred looked into the darkness."
"Alfred, do not be alarmed, remain quiet."
The old railway worker peered into the dark, holding an empty kettle in his hand. He'd come down the wooden stairs from the raised signal box to fetch water from the standpipe. It was teatime.

Alfred was old. For nearly forty years he'd worked for Rhodesian Railways. An Assistant Signalman, as high as an African could go. He worked the Number 9 box. Always the night shift, the helper of oversized Arthur Sullivan, the white Signalman who sat upstairs in a well-worn swivel chair, his bulky frame squeezed tight between the wooden arms. On a table beside him was his nightly supply of food. Few trains travelled at night. Arthur found eating helped pass the time.

Only the two worked the night shift. Arthur rarely spoke to Alfred, except to give orders. Not that Alfred needed orders. After forty years he knew everything, more than Arthur. Now it was Alfred's time to make the tea. It was always the same. Arthur had never made a cup of tea in the twenty-five years he'd been with the

Company.

"Who calls my name in the dark?" Alfred kept his voice low.

"Do not be alarmed Alfred. I mean no harm." Morgan stepped from the shadows. His gun in view.

Alfred stepped back.

"We have business here tonight Alfred. You will help. It will be easy for you so do not resist."

Alfred's thought of his beloved railway. Morgan was ahead of him.

You must only think of your wife Edna. Tonight she sits in your house in Melsetter. She has your two grandchildren, a Comrade is with them."

"You know much about me." Alfred was frightened. "How did you find this out?"

"That is of no matter. We have our ways. First, you wait here while we take the signal box. Then you will receive your instructions."

Morgan signalled. From the shadows two more men emerged. Silently they crept up the outside steps.

Arthur didn't attempt to get up when they entered the signal box. He stared, holding his sandwich. His mind had been far away. There was no resistance. He was tied and bundled into the storeroom. He missed his tea.

Four men returned. Their breathing was heavy. They had been running along the track. Morgan spoke. "Tell me," he said.

The tallest spoke. "One thousand metres. At the beginning of the embankment. The pressure pad is set. At 19.00 the timer will activate the circuit. The first train that passes over the pressure pad after that time will set off the charges. There are four charges. All on the same rail. Fifty metres between each. They will cause the train to fall to the left, down the embankment."

Morgan was perplexed. The unexpected radio message had exposed the mission so it must have been important but he couldn't understand why and was about to ignore it. The message was to attack only on a Wednesday, but he could not afford to wait another day. Never the less he would be prepared to fight and kill the soldiers on the train.

"Alfred," said Morgan facing the signalman. "You must give

me information."

Alfred stood at the back of the signal box, guarded and still not trusted.

"Is the Johannesburg train on time?"

"Ah! The Green Mamba? Yes, as far as I know. It should pass here a little after 9.30." replied Alfred. "It gets priority."

"The Green Mamba?" said Morgan.

"Yes, Now we use a South African Loco, Class 4E. It's painted green and very long. We call it the Green Mamba because it's like a snake", said Alfred, "very quick."

"You know a lot about trains," said Morgan. It was a statement.

"It is my job," replied Alfred, puffing his chest out.

"Good. Tell me about the petrol train."

"Every night it comes, only the length changes, it is always the same locomotive and rolling stock."

"And?"

Alfred smiled, happy to share his knowledge. "The locomotive is RR class DE2 built by the English Electric Company of Preston England. Its number is 1218. It is written on the plate. I see it every night! The wagons are very old. From 1928. Ones the South Africans no longer want. Type XP2. Each holds 30 tons of fuel. There is a speed restriction because of their age."

"Is that all?" said Morgan.

"There is a guard's van. Type V14. Big. The guard likes it. But now he has to share it with the soldiers. It's not so comfortable."

"How many soldiers?" asked Morgan.

"I have seen six on the train. Not more. Three in the locomotive and three in the guard's van. We pull the train into the siding. It waits for the Green Mamba to pass. It is here for at least half an hour. The soldiers from the locomotive join the ones from the guard wagon. They smoke and drink tea at the side of the track. I tell them it is not safe to smoke so close to the fuel but they ignore me. They always stand around the guard's van."

"It is enough," said Morgan. "Now you will run this signal box till we go. Do you understand?"

"I do, "said Alfred. Despite years of service Alfred had never pulled the levers that operated the points and signals. He had never been allowed to spin the handle of the telegraph and press the signal bell. That was work for white men. Tonight he would get his turn and in a way he was happy.

Morgan marshalled the men along the track. Sentries had been set. He knew where the Rhodesian soldiers would gather. He marked where the guard's wagon would stop. He picked the place for his men carefully. He needed a field of fire, cross fire, but the petrol tankers must not be hit. The plan was not to destroy the train, not here in any case.

The guard's van would stop next to the water tower. The water tank was on legs. The top of the tank looked down on the siding. Steam trains needed lots of water. Giant Garrett locomotives were thirsty beasts. They would top up with water from the tower. Morgan placed two men on top of the tank. They would be shooting downwards.

Another two men would come from the far side of the track. They would hide in the bush. Nobody would look under the wagons. As they saw the soldiers walk from the locomotive they would go under the train and come out the other side. They would shoot parallel to the train.

Opposite the guard van, square on, hidden behind a pile of loose coal, would be the machinegun. The fire would riddle the guard's van and anybody inside. It would be enough. Impossible to escape.

Sabi River Bridge

"He's just being stupid," said Rory.

"Admittedly he doesn't appear to be the sharpest knife in the drawer on this one," replied Duncan.

"It's the closest anybody's come to a contact in this sector and he just says leave it with me. He's off his bloody trolley."

Duncan and Rory stood apart from the rest of the Stick that waited to join the routine Tuesday journey of the Green Mamba on its journey to the South African border. They'd only just made the Sabi Bridge. Lieutenant Walters had kept them hanging about. When they'd left him he was painfully typing a report with two fingers on his ancient Olivetti typewriter. The sun was going down.

Duncan reflected. The past hours had been a comedy show.

Rory hadn't believed Duncan at first. "What do you mean you found a terrorist booby trap?"

"I have, in the bush over there." Duncan pointed to where the truck had left the road. "Come on, I'll show you."

Rory had stubbed out his cigarette and reluctantly followed Duncan. There was no mistaking the booby trap. "Holy Joe, we got a contact. Better call it in quickly."

They tried. They drove the Land Rover to a higher spot to help reception. "HOTEL QUEBEC ONE, COME IN HOTEL QUEBEC ONE." No response. They repeated the call, still no response.

"Try a different channel."

Still nothing.

"Try an open channel," said Duncan.

"I'll do channel 16, that's for emergencies."

In less than ten minutes and the batteries were flat.

"Fat lot of good this set is". Rory threw the hand piece to the floor in frustration.

"What about the Land Rover's set?" Shall we give it a try?"

"I've been trying to juice it up while you've been calling," said Duncan. "It's totally useless."

"Phone or back to HQ?"

They drove back to Fort Victoria. Knackered Land Rovers have little in common with performance cars. The ride would have been amusingly perilous in different circumstances. They drove like the possessed.

"We need to see Lieutenant Walters immediately," they'd told the black orderly who scurried off sensing the urgency

He came back and told them Lieutenant Walters said they should have used the radio if it was that urgent. It was fifteen minutes before they got into his office. Walters was sticking pins in his map. Duncan made the verbal report.

Walters nodded. "Did you follow the track into the bush?"

"There were only the two of us Sir. The place was clearly booby-trapped. The priority was to make others aware," replied Duncan.

"You didn't bring a lot of information for me to go on," said the Lieutenant now collating his report forms and flimsies before inserting them into his typewriter.

"Righty-ho then. Leave it with me. I'll get a report off a.s.a.p."

"Don't you think Sector Command should be alerted?" said Duncan.

Lieutenant Walters looked up from his typewriter. "Do you know what these are?" he asked pointing to his shoulder straps.

"Pips Sir," replied Duncan.

"Correct, and that means I get to say what happens. Don't you men have a train to catch or something?"

"Sir."

"And keep your mouths shut. Don't want rumours spreading and causing panic. Clear?"

"Sir."

"Off you go then."

Incredible.

The stick began to close up on the bridge. They could hear the train approaching. Duncan and Rory picked up their packs. The Sergeant grabbed a man by his webbing and pushed him gently in the direction of Duncan and Rory. "You three in the last carriage. Don't be making yourselves too comfortable. I'll be up front with the other two."

They prepared to board. A puny car horn sounded off, down the road. In the distance headlights came into sight. They bobbed around frantically. Somebody was driving like a lunatic towards the bridge.

Fox Railway Siding

The bell rang once. Alfred looked towards Tembo seeking approval.

"Do what you must but be careful. You have a family to think about,"

"The first bell is just to draw attention," said Alfred. He walked over to the wall mounted telegraph and tapped the brass key once. "That tells them I am alert."

Tembo watched. "Tell me what is going on."

"Rhodesian Railways use the English system," replied Alfred almost proud that anybody would take an interest in his knowledge. "The track is divided into blocks. Only one train is allowed into a block at a time. A signalman controls each block. He communicates with signalmen up line and down line by electric bell signals. In a passing block, like this one, the signalman has to make sure the up train is out of the block, safe in the siding. Only then does he let the down train into his block."

He was interrupted. The up line bell rang again. 1 – 2 – 1. "Train approaching," said Alfred. He sent the same signal back as confirmation.

"I must set the signals and points now." Alfred moved over to the bank of levers that overlooked the front of the box.

Grabbing one of the levers, he leaned back using his body weight to pull it forward. "I am opening the 'up line' signal. This will allow the train into my block." He selected another lever. "I am opening the points to the siding. This will take the train off the main line. Only when I can see the train in the siding can I let the down train into my block."

It was the first time Alfred had pulled the levers. It was a good feeling, an ambition fulfilled.

The diesel-electric locomotive was unusual. Diesel locomotives were only used on cross-border trains. Rhodesian Railways stuck with steam locomotives when possible. Coal was plentiful, diesel scarce.

The driver sat high in his cab, the twin 500 horse power Ruston diesels throbbed behind him. He strained his eyes, the new night restriction was difficult, he didn't like it. No lights on the main line. He had to concentrate.

He passed the first signal. Green. Open. He eased back the throttle. Only 20 mph on this block. The train slowed. He saw the second signal. A double. The left one open. Going into the siding, just like every night. He could hit the light switch now. The track lit up in front. His eyes took time to adjust. He checked the speed. Still too fast, only ten MPH for the points. He applied the breaks. The screeching was like a banshee in the darkness. The front bogies entered the points, the train shifted to the left. Steel rims clattered as they crossed the joints. The signal at the end of the siding was closed, red. The driver brought the train to a halt twenty-five yards short of the signal box. Same spot every time. He doused the main light and took his foot off the dead man's peddle. There was a sudden loud hiss as air pressure was released from the braking system. The Rustons barely ticked over now, missing the occasional beat. Half an hour stop normally. He'd let the engines idle to keep pressure up in the pneumatic system.

"Going for your smoke?" said the driver.

"You bet," said the sergeant sitting beside him. "I hate these fuel trains. No smoking in the cab and all that shit."

"Make sure you're past the guard's van before you light up. I'm going to see Arthur in the box."

The driver and sergeant exited the train backwards, careful to get their footing on the ladder rungs. There was no platform, just stone ballast running alongside the track. Walking was difficult. Two young Troopies jumped from the rear door of the loco and joined the sergeant. They stretched. Moments before they'd been asleep. The three men shouldered their weapons and walked toward the back of the train. A row of incandescent lights gave just enough light for walking.

The smell of fuel oil was strong. Some of the tanks were so old they leaked drops of their precious cargo.

The sergeant saw the men from the guard's van. They were already on the track smoking. He pulled a thirty pack of Kingston's from his tunic pocket. Rhodesian grown Virginia tobacco, best in the world. Watching eyes went unnoticed.

Morgan stood in statuesque silence. He was behind one of the water tower stanchions ready to give the signal.

Tembo pressed his back against the rear wall of the signal box. The lights inside were dimmed but he still kept to the shadows.

Tembo watched the soldiers as they walked to the rear. He saw the driver amble forwards towards the signal box. Alfred also watched. He looked to Tembo. Tembo put a finger to his mouth. "Quiet, just carry on." he whispered.

They heard a thud as the driver's boot landed on the bottom step.

"Hey Arthur. You still eating you fat bugger?" They heard him climbing the steps.

A bell rang. Single stroke. Alfred stepped towards the telegraph. He hit the brass response key.

The train driver came into the signal box. The up-line bell rang again. Four strokes. Express passenger train approaching. Alfred went to the levers. He checked the points. They were set for straight through. He pulled the lever that opened the southbound signal. The line was clear for the express.

"Hey! What are you doing? Where's Arthur?" said the driver. His voice was gruff. Company Regulations were strict, union rules inviolate.

"Where's Arthur?" he demanded again.

Tembo stepped forward out of the shadows, his gun pointed at the driver. The driver stopped for a second, taking in the sight. Without further hesitation he spun and disappeared out of the door with the deftness of one many years younger. Tembo resisted the urge to fire. He quickly followed.

The soldiers walked the last few steps more quickly.

From the far side two unseen shadows came from the bush and crossed the line. They kept low and slipped under a wagon. The noise of their boots as they scuffed the stones went unheard.

Morgan waited. Just a few more steps and the six troopes would be together, bunched.

They heard the driver's shout but he was too far away for them to make out what he was saying. He passed under a bulb. They could see he was running towards them waving and shouting.

Then they made out the dark figure that followed. Did he carry a gun?

Together they dropped their unlit fags. There was only a moment of confusion as they un-shouldered their weapons.

It was enough. Morgan signalled. The Russian PK machine gun stuttered, spitting lead at a rate of 30 rounds per second, drowning out the noise of the diesel engine.

The three second burst discharged 90 bullets, 60 of them hit the three targets standing next to the guard's van. They cut a more or less horizontal line at chest height. The bodies offered little resistance and the bullets continued through the flesh until they became embedded in the wooden side of the van in a shower of splinters. The first three soldiers slumped. The last three fared little better. They managed to get their guns off safety. One managed to get a round into the chamber but he never got to pull the trigger.

One of the Matable came from under the wagon. He fired till his magazine was empty. The two guerrilla fighters on top of the water tower fired downwards. The crossfire was merciless. The soldiers lay in a crumpled bloody mass.

The driver stopped running and raised his hands into the air. Tembo was behind.

Alfred did not look. He'd never seen anybody killed before. He stayed in the box only just remembering the last bit of the sequence. He tapped the telegraph four times, signalling the line clear signal for the express. Unknowingly he's just condemned to death many more people than had just been shot outside.

They wasted no time. Morgan supervised the placing of the charges on each of the petrol tankers.

Mopane Canopy

Trussed like a chicken, he lay on the ground, arms behind his back tied with a slip knot to legs folded back. The more he struggled the tighter the slipknot became. Escape was impossible. His chest burnt and he could feel dead skin tightening around the marks. He wanted to scratch, he wanted to pour cold water on the wound. Blisters were forming, opaque balloons stood proud on his black skin. Transparent liquid oozed from the wounds. Minutes lasted for hours in his mind.

He twisted and looked around. He could see the truck. "When would it explode? When would his man return?" Others lay trussed and scattered around the compound. There was no talk. Makonzo looked for Tyoni. He could not see him.

Lovemore led the group. Only three of the four carried weapons. The fourth's hands were bound. The pace had been fast. Without warning Lovemore called the group to a halt.

"We have walked for one hour now. It is time to let you go." Lovemore spoke to the Shona prisoner.

"Did you pay attention? Can you find your way back?"

The prisoner nodded. "I can," he said.

"Our war is not with you. We want only to chase the white man out of our country. Go back to the compound and release your people. Do not go near the truck or the explosives. They will detonate if you disturb them. Remember if you betray us once more you cannot expect to be treated so easily. Next time we will not let you go."

Lovemore cut the rope from the prisoner's hands with a bayonet. He gave the weapon to the prisoner.

"Free the men with this. Leave the Mopane forest quickly. Soon white soldiers will be there," said Lovemore.

Without a word the man turned and began to run, retracing the path they had come along. He was quick.

Before entering the compound he circled once to make sure it was clear. Only then did he enter. Everything was as it had been when he had left. He cut the first man free. The sharp blade sliced the cord easily.

The man rolled onto his back and shook himself clear. He pulled his rescuer forward and whispered. "Do not free Makonzo. He can no longer be our leader."

The man stared. "It is a dangerous thing that you ask. It is not for me to decide who is our leader."

"Then give the blade to me, I will decide who is released."

The blade was passed to Zenger. He worked quickly. He went from man to man, whispering to each.

Makonzo wriggled to face the man. "Release me," he demanded.

Zenger ignored the plea. He continued releasing others. Makonzo shouted. "Untie me now. I am you leader." His cry was left unanswered.

The last man was freed. Makonzo still lay on the floor. The freed men watched. Nobody spoke for the leader. Only one man moved, deliberately and unnoticed by others as authority ebbed away from Makonzo.

Zenger looked at the freed men. They listened. "There is little time for discussion. Soon this place will explode. I say our leader has disgraced us. Makonzo barked like the dog he is. The Matable are right. We can no longer follow him. We have seen his character."

He turned to Makonzo. "You now carry the sign of the dog. I will not stand with you because of that. You should have died rather than let the Matable humiliate you like this.

When you gave orders we obeyed. We willingly risked death. When you told us to execute our own people in the name of the struggle we did this for you. We have passed all tests put before us. But you? You have failed. You are the coward."

Now you will have the same right you give to prisoners in your kangaroo courts. The verdict is clear before the start. You are guilty and will die. We will leave you here and you will disappear with the explosions. So what do you have to say?"

The two men stared at each other. For a moment Zenger saw dull fear in Makonzo's eyes. But suddenly Makonzo's eyes brightened, fear evaporated, strained lips relaxed, the wisp of a smile appeared. Zenger believed Makonzo was finding courage.

But he was wrong.

Zenger never felt anything. He never heard the bang or felt the powder burn on the nape of his neck. The bullet went into his brain stem. He just dropped to the ground, motionless. Blood splattered over Makonzo where he lay. He'd seen Tyoni come from behind.

In the stillness a wisp of smoke lingered around the end of the barrel. Tyoni looked at the men.

"Who gave Zenger the knife?" he demanded.

Nobody spoke but all eyes went to one man. Tyoni walked towards the man.

"Get onto your knees".

The man obeyed, the one who could have saved himself but instead had run back to save his Comrades.

Tyoni put the gun to the man's head. He did not hesitate. The shot echoed through the Mopane trees. The victim fell forward.

"Who else joins rebellion? Who else does not want to follow Makonzo?" he demanded waving the pistol above his head.

Nobody moved.

"Release Makonzo," Tyoni spoke with authority, "Move quickly. Anybody who speaks of what happened here today will suffer the same fate as these two," Tyoni pointed to the bodies on the ground. "And the same fate will also befall your families. Do not test me on this. Now quickly, go. Split up and make your way back to your villages. You will soon be called again. I will take Makonzo."

The men left. Tyoni pulled his leader to his feet and helped him move forward, out of the compound.

"Come, I will carry you. It is fortunate I saw where the revolver fell during the fight."

It was less than one hour later they heard the explosions. The compound was no more. It was already dark but they knew they had to keep moving. If the white soldiers came they would be tortured for information and then buried alive. It was their way.

"Run that by me again," said the Major unable to hide his incredulity. "Speak clearly."

It was an uncomfortable phone call for Lieutenant Walters, he squirmed in his seat. The twenty four hour clock on the wall read 18.22.

"About 14.30 hours today two of my chaps found heavy tyre tracks going into remote bush a few clicks beyond Fort Victoria. They believed the tracks belonged to a missing Parks and Wildlife truck.

When they followed the tracks into the bush they came across recently set anti personnel mines. They reported the mines to be of Russian manufacture. I reported the find to Battalion."

"When did you send the report to Battalion?" asked the Major.

"It was logged at 18.10 hrs?" replied Walters.

"Would you consider discovering active terrorists in your area significant?" asked the major.

"Yes Sir," said Walters.

"Why did it take you so long to make the bloody report?"

"Communications difficulties," Sir.

"Do the communications difficulties extend to the civil authorities?" asked the Major.

"No Sir".

"So you have told the police and they have alerted the local population."

"No".

"No, the police haven't alerted the local population or no you have not notified the police?"

"No I have not notified the police."

"Why not?"

"I didn't want to spread alarm among the civilian population."

"When I first spoke to you I thought you might be a half-wit. But I was wrong. You're totally witless. In fact you're actually a complete fucking moron," said the Major.

"When the discovery was made we had four hours of daylight left. Now it's dark. I'm speaking to the Sector CO now. I'm recommending a Company strength response. They'll come from Brady Barracks. I expect your replacement to be with them. Is that clear enough for you."

"Sir."

"Make sure the Troopies who found the mines are available."

Walters hesitated. "Can't Sir. I sent them on train escort duties. Won't be back........"

"Just get them. NOW! I hope to Christ for your sake nothing goes down tonight."

The line went dead.

The maximum evening demand of the Rhodesian Electricity grid peaked just before 1900 hrs at 1100 Megawatts. Five hundred megawatts came from Kariba. A further 240 megawatts came from Bulawayo and Salisbury coal fired stations. A couple of tiny local stations generated a trivial amount. The deficit of 350 megawatts came up the South African line.

The 330KV border transmission lines were buzzing. Bits of condensation that formed on the porcelain insulators crackled in the dark giving off blue sparks.

At the foot of four pylons, LCD timers counted downwards. They reached zero simultaneously. A minute electoral impulse was generated. This was amplified on a solid state printed circuit board. The output was sent to an independent relay. The relay activated and released the energy stored in a high voltage capacitor. The 5000 volt shock ignited detonators embedded in blocks of TNT. The TNT exploded and tore away the legs of the pylons to which they were attached. Unbalanced, the pylons toppled into the bush. The cables that the pylons supported were made of a central steel core wrapped with high conductivity aluminium strands. They were not strong enough to withstand the tension put on them and snapped. The dead end of the cables fell limply into the bush. The live ends thrashed about wildly showering sparks in all directions.

No power grid is robust enough to lose twenty-five percent of its supply in an instant. The protection system built into the grid tried to make up the sudden shortfall by drawing more power from other sources. But they were already running at full capacity. The power stations were fitted with giant circuit breakers designed to protect the generating equipment. One at a time the breakers started to trip. It was a systems engineer's nightmare, a cascade failure.

In the National Control centre outside Que Que the Shift Charge Engineer looked in disbelief at the mimic board that hung from the wall. Indicator lights changed from green to red. The system was shutting itself down. Then the lights in the National Control Centre itself went out. A few seconds later the emergency lights came on courtesy of the backup generator. For the first time since electricity arrived, more than sixty years ago, most of Rhodesia was plunged into darkness. The Shift Charge Engineer scurried round looking for the Emergency Procedures Book.

Many tributaries feed the Sabi river. Most of the year they run dry but during the rains they quickly fill and overflow. Over thousands of years vast flood plains were created. Nineteenth century railway engineers avoided the obvious temptation of running their lines across these huge flat areas. They skirted around them, keeping to higher dry land.

The main line to Beite Bridge carefully followed height contours. In places it ran on embankments and ledges carved out of hillsides. One kilometre south of Fox siding was just such a place. To the right of the line the land rose towards the watershed. To the left it fell away sharply towards the flood plain.

The green locomotive belonged to South African Railways. It pulled five sleeper cars, a first class day carriage and a restaurant car on its whites only, journey through the African night.

The term 'express' was used loosely. The journey took twenty-three hours and 15 minutes. The train pulled out of Salisbury station at exactly 15.05. It was scheduled to arrive in Jo'burg at 14.20 the next day. Track restrictions meant that much of the journey was undertaken at less than forty miles per hour.

Rhodesians Railways were pedantic. They advertised the service as non-stop, and this was one of the reasons why the train only slowed to a walking pace at the Sabi River crossing where it picked up the soldiers.

When he got the all clear from the guard that all the soldiers were aboard, the driver opened the throttle. Not much. No point going too fast. They'd soon be going down gradient.

The soldiers walked the length of the train. Part of the job was to be seen and give reassurance. There were ninety-three passengers on board.

Barnadi, the train driver, was an Afrikaner from South Africa. He didn't care much for his Rhodesian assistant, Stokes. Barnadi like most Afrikaners had not forgiven his Anglo neighbours for the Boer War. The two didn't chat. Barnadi begrudged speaking English. At Beite Bridge the Rhodesian co-driver would be replaced by a South African. Barnadi's tongue normally loosened from that point onwards. He looked at his watch. Just after 7pm. The train approached the passing block.

For security reasons Rhodesian Railways had their own back up power supply. Neither Barnadi nor Stokes noticed the flickering signal light as the emergency power supply kicked in.

The signal was green. Barnadi reduced speed from forty five miles per hour to thirty five, the maximum allowed in the sector for an express. They passed the stationary fuel train. The signal box was in darkness, the siding lights out. Nobody was in the loco cab. There was nothing to indicate the carnage that had just occurred on the other side of the fuel train.

They cleared the sector. Barnadi opened the throttle a little more. The tone of the engine deepened as it took the extra load. The speedometer crept to the maximum permissible speed of forty miles per hour.

At the same time as the pylons fell, another digital timer at the side of the railway track activated an electric circuit. A small cavity had been scooped from under one of the sleepers. Inside the cavity a tiny micro switch, connected to a load cell had been inserted.

The next train that crossed the sleeper would exert enough pressure to activate the load cell. This in turn would set off charges further down the line.

The wheels of the train ran over the sleeper. Instead of darkness ahead there was a blinding flash. They felt and heard the shudder simultaneously. The train left the tracks. It tilted to the left. At forty miles an hour the one hundred and twenty tonne locomotive had vast inertia. Over and over it went, trying to break free of the carriages. Ahead lay a giant boulder, twice the mass of the locomotive. The cab slammed into the ancient basalt rock. Driver and co-driver were instantly pulped. Rescuers would be unable to distinguish the fleshy mass. To the rear the carriages agonisingly reared and twisted. Lights went out, bodies were flung like dolls in the dark. Nobody was unharmed, only the seriousness of injury varied. As the noise of the collision died away the debris found unstable equilibrium. From the wreckage voices broke the unexpected silence, voices crying for help.

It would be many hours before help arrived. Many would never see it come.

At Fox siding the dead Rhodesian soldiers had been stripped of their weapons. All arms were welcome, even ones from the enemy. Morgan chivvied his men along. He scrambled onto the locomotive and went to the cab where Edison sat proudly in the driver's seat. He smiled at Morgan. "Just like the one I drove in Zambia. No problem," he said.

"So it was worth saving you after all," said Morgan returning the grin.

"We are ready to go now", said Tembo. "You must set the signal and points correctly."

"It is done," answered Alfred. "I must only send the telegraph signal."

"The train driver is with the fat one in the storeroom. They will not escape. Now we must think of you," said Tembo. "If we take you with us or just leave you here it would not be good. The whites will want proof you resisted. Forgive us for what we are to do. It is for your own good. When the war is won you will be remembered. You too will be a hero."

Tembo nodded to two of his men. They came forward. "Alfred, which arm do you use?" said Tembo.

"Right", answered Alfred.

Tembo looked to the two men. "Break the left arm and tie him up."

"Let me send the signal first," said Alfred. "Then you will be safe on your journey."

The fuel train left the siding and rejoined the main line less than five minutes behind schedule.

The Mopane Canopy

In the barracks at Fort Victoria a group of Rhodesian soldiers studied maps.

I'd say they camped somewhere around here Sir," said Duncan resting a finger on the map, not far from the forest. "I'd also say they have an alternative escape strategy."

"Why do you say that Pvt. Murdoch?" asked Major Copeland.

"One set of tracks. In only. Mined the route behind themselves. Obviously no intention of coming back that way. According to the map there is no suitable alternative route for a vehicle. They most probably dumped the truck and are making their escape on foot."

Lieutenant Walters butted in. "Nearest border is this one." He pointed. "Suppose they are making for that. I could organise a block."

The Major lifted his head.

Duncan spoke. "That's the South African border Sir. I believe the South Africans are on our side. That would make it an improbable destination. Mozambique or Botswana would be the destinations if they were leaving the country, that's a long hike either way. They most probably have a base inside Rhodesia."

"Good. You're a thinker Murdoch," said the Major. He turned to Lieutenant Walters. "Murdoch must be tired. Organise some tea for them for him. That would be useful."

"Power cut sir!" said Walters. "No electricity or hot water."

"I know there's a power cut Walters. It's dark in here. That's why we're in the briefing room using tilly lamps. I also know the reason we have a power cut is because of you. You sent men on a remote patrol with no backup and no working radio. You then failed to report a serious situation. Finally, you tried to send Murdoch and Quinn, the only people who knew what was happening, on a train journey. I should be sending you for Court Marshall not to make tea. I might just do that in any case. In the mean time just fuck off and organise the tea will you."

"Sir", Walters snapped to attention. "How many sir?"

"Many what?" said the Major.

"Sugars in your tea Sir."

"Just go."

"I wasn't supposed to do that in front of you," said Major Copeland as he turned back to face Duncan and Rory. "You two have been on the go for a long time but I need you in the morning. Get some rest after your tea."

The African orderly produced a couple of field cots. Duncan lay down and closed his eyes. Only a couple of hours to go before daylight returned.

He recalled the events of the evening. The train had been in sight. Duncan and Rory were ready to board. Then they'd seen the staff car careering towards them on the Sabi Bridge. The breathless sergeant panted the message as if he'd run all the way. Only four soldiers got on the Green Mamba. Duncan and Rory were on their way back to barracks.

They were travelling up Main Street when the lights went out. Streetlights, shops, houses the lot. Duncan looked at the dashboard clock. Exactly 7pm. Sabotage. Saboteurs set their timers to go off on the hour by force of habit. It was a dead giveaway. The chances of an accident happening on the hour were 59 to 1.

Major Copeland was waiting in the briefing room at the barracks when they arrived. Lieutenant Walters was with him, face flushed.

"Right", said Major Copeland to Duncan and Quinn. "I want a full debrief. "D" Company of the RLI is on route. I think we have a serious contact here."

The major's questions were sharp. "How'd you spot it? How'd you know it was Russian?" He shot the questions. Duncan's answers were just as sharp.

The convoy set off from the barracks before sunrise. They passed Lake Kyle as the morning sky turned red. Duncan and Rory travelled in the back of Major Copeland's Land Rover.

Duncan watched for the entry point in the bush.

"Ahead, on the left", he said.

The convoy came to a halt. Copeland jumped out.

"You sure this is the place?"

"Yes Sir."

"Right," Major Copeland said to the driver. "Set up a CP here. You show me what you found Murdoch."

Duncan led. He pushed through the bush showing Cropland the broken branches and tyre marks as they passed. He went forward, Copeland stayed close. Duncan stopped. He pointed out the almost invisible trip wire. Copeland struggled to see it even after Duncan pointed it out.

"Of course it's not too bad with a bit of dew glistening on the wire", said Murdoch.

"Good eyesight?" said Copeland.

"Not bad Sir."

Duncan walked parallel to the trip wire. He lifted the ferns to reveal the box. "Nasty thing. Take the legs from everybody within a 25 metre arc."

"Okay, I've seen enough. I'll call in the engineers to disarm it."

"Oh you don't have to bother with that Sir," said Duncan producing a nail from his pocket. "Knew we were coming back so picked up a few things at the barracks." He knelt down next to the mine. He grabbed the trip wire confidently and tightly with his left hand.

"Mustn't let go now," he said. "That would be bad." Slowly he put tension on the wire. More wire unreeled out of a hole in the side. Then it snagged. Duncan gave it a sharp pull.

Major Copeland pulled back. "Hope you know what you're doing Murdoch." he said.

"Yes it's fine. Look."

Copeland looked over Duncan's shoulder.

"See that? It's the end of the firing pin. Spring loaded. Let go now and the lot goes up. But watch." Duncan pulled again and the pin came out further to reveal a small hole drilled through the bar. "The hole is used as a safety feature during the priming stage. You're not supposed to be able to pull the pin this far after it's primed but if you give it a bit of a yank it normally comes. Duncan took the nail and slipped it into the hole. Gently he relaxed his pull on the wire and the pin went forward until the nail fouled on the hole. "Right," said Duncan. "Safe as houses."

Copeland was sweating. "I'd rather you didn't do that again when I'm around. Where did you learn that trick?"

"Aldershot Sir. Bomb disposal course."
"Sir?" The voice came from behind, Major Copeland's driver.
"What is it?"
"You're needed on the radio urgently Sir."

Duncan was surprised at the speed that things had been set up. The Company radio was mounted on a twin wheeled trailer, a self-contained unit with generator and extendable antennae. The operator sat on a fold up chair in the open fronted canvas tent. "Battalion Sir".
Copeland put on the headphones and listened. The shock was clear. He gave the headphones and handset back to the operator.

"He spread the sector map on the bonnet of the Land Rover. "Hold the edge Murdoch. Driver get the Section Leaders here now." He studied the map, his finger tracing the line of the railway.
"Here, this is where they did it," he said to nobody in particular.
"Did what Sir?" asked Duncan.
"Took the Green Mamba express out last night. Lots of casualties. Rescuers just getting there."
"Wow, I should have been on that one Sir", said Duncan.
"Copeland looked at Duncan with raised eyebrows. "Lucky escape."
The Section Leaders arrived.
Duncan looked at the map. His eyes traced the railway line. It dawned on him. "Fuck," he said out loud.
"What is it?" asked Copeland.
"It's not over Sir. They haven't finished".
"What do you mean?"
"Sir. I think there's a good sized bunch of them. It's too much for one or two people. We already know they never intended to escape using the truck, hence the mines over there. They've taken out electricity pylons around here," said Duncan pointing to a spot on the map. "Then they marched along here to the railway line and did their business with the Green Mamba."
"We know this," said the Major. "What's your point?"
"Look. Just up from the crash site there's a siding, where they park goods trains to let passenger services through. I think there is a good chanch they're going to hijack whatever's in the siding and make their escape that way."

"It fits. You might just be right." Copeland hurried away to the radio tent.

"Get me battalion quick!"

"They're already on for you Sir."

He listened.

"Yes. I know about the signal box. We worked that out for ourselves. But there might be another danger." Copeland reiterated Duncan's thoughts.

Bulawayo Railway Line

It was mid morning. Edison was alone on the train. It was the way he wanted it. Everybody else had gone. He too hoped to make his escape soon.

The fuel train had left Fox siding on schedule, continuing its normal journey. Now it was entering the last block before the Bulawayo marshalling yards. "Nearly there," he thought. Once in the siding he would set the timer at five minutes and leave. That was the plan. They would not have time to do anything to stop the explosion in such a short time, a whole fuel train exploding in the largest marshalling yard in the country. That would be good. The loco approached the Environs Signal Box.

"Not too fast," Edison spoke to himself as he sank in the seat. He prayed to keep up the deception a little longer. The engine clattered across the complex series of points. It had to run past the signal box to get onto the branch line.

Even as he looked up Edison knew it was over. He recognised the BSAP uniform of the man that stood at the top of the steps looking down into the cab. A policeman in a signal box? No, it was not misfortune. They were looking out for him. They had been warned.

The detonator cable ran the length of the train. It was connected in series to the detonators in each charge. The end was tailed off at the timer in the cab, next to Edison. It was pre-set to five minutes; he only had to flip the toggle switch. But that preset wouldn't be any good now.

He lifted the safety cover on the timer and moved the dial anti-clockwise to zero. Now when he threw the toggle switch the explosion would be instantaneous. He'd decided not to live.

Every signal was on red. He ignored them and opened the throttle. The train gained speed. The risk of derailment was unimportant, nothing mattered now. He would get as close to the marshalling yard as possible.

He didn't see the khaki clad figures. He didn't know the

policeman at the signal box was just confirming what they already suspected. He kept low in his seat as if hiding would help.

Maybe he thought he would be safer hidden by the cab door. Unfortunately the sheet metal was not strong, indeed less resistant than the glass of the window. The bullets passed through the 16 gauge metal easily. Edison took body shots. His right side didn't hurt. It became numb but he couldn't stop the muscle spasms as his nervous system was thrown into convulsions. He could see the crimson foaming puddle spreading on the cab floor. He tried to keep his foot pressed on the peddle. It was hard. He reached for the toggle switch with hands that would not obey instructions. Unconsciousness came quickly, descending over him like a blanket. He slumped forward; his foot slid off the dead man's brake, his last thought of the switch.

As soon as the pedal raised, fuel was cut off from the engine and the safety switch tripped, cutting off power to the traction motors. Air was let out of the pneumatic system with a massive hiss. Brake pads came into contact with the metal wheels. The train shuddered to a halt in less than half its own length.

It had not reached the marshalling yard. It was still in the high-density suburbs. Houses and shanties crowded up to the track's edge.

It was a selfless action by the soldiers of the African Rifles. They could not have known the explosives would not go off. They just saw charges attached to fuel tanks. They ran from one to the next pulling detonators and cable free of the explosives. They threw the tiny aluminium detonators as far as they could.

The final part of the mission was denied.

"I told you didn't I? I told you ages ago. Them Matable are a shit load of trouble," said Rory Quinn with childish glee. For once in his life a prediction of his had come true.

"Yes, you told me. Now shut up and keep your eyes open. There may be another booby-trap. That would wipe the smile off your face," said Duncan.

He'd found four more already. One anti personnel, a claymore, and two buried HE land mines. Big enough to destroy an armoured vehicle.

Rory was quiet for a while. After half an hour they had

reached the Mopane canopy. Here tracks criss-crossed everywhere. Duncan picked his head up for the first time. "Okay, clear." He called forward the lieutenant who was thirty yards behind with his section.

"It's safe for you to go on now sir," said Duncan. "But I can smell burning or something from that direction. You might like to check it out. For sure there have been a lot of people around here recently. Our orders are to report back to Major Copeland once we cleared the area. We'll go now, if that's all right with you sir."

"That fine. Thanks," the Officer turned to his men. He shouted. "On me. Extended line. Let's sweep the area."

Major Copeland was still at his command post. It had grown and now straddled the width of the road. There was no traffic. The highway was closed to all but military and police traffic. An Alloeutte helicopter rested on the tarmac. Its blades hung limply, geltly flopping in the light breeze. Copeland spoke to another officer. Pip and a crown, a Lieutenant Colonel. No flashes on the epaulettes. Not a staffer, a line officer.

Major Copeland saw Duncan. He broke his conversation and called him over.

"Tired Murdoch?"

"Yes Sir."

"Think you could muster enough strength to salute the Battalion Commander?"

"Sorry sir." He snapped to attention and made the best attempt he could at a salute."

"The chap I told you about," said Copeland to the Lieutenant Colonel "The situation is bad but it would have been a lot worse if it wasn't for this man."

"Well done", said the Lieutenant Colonel. "Private Murdoch? We appear to have missed you at induction. I think you can expect to hear from your CO. Sooner rather than later. Good work." He turned away.

"Get yourself a lift back to Fort Victoria. You're relieved as of now," said Copeland.

The fuel train had travelled slowly so an not to arouse attention although everybody in the Impi's was anxious to get back. Two of the three objectives had been destroyed. They would not hear about the third till they were back at their Matopas base. Now they just needed to report their success to Lusaka.

At its closest point the railway line came to within twenty miles of the Matopas. Edison had slowed the train to a crawl and the men jumped clear in the darkness. The march had been difficult with tired legs. It was mitigated in that they carried little on their backs now. The ordinance and rations were gone, used. Only personal weapons remained. The mission had been costly in equipment.

They stuck to close formation till light came then they dispersed into two's. Each couple made their own way and was responsible for masking the spoor they left behind. The first men arrived after eleven, the last at 1400 hrs. Men only wanted to eat and sleep, but Tembo and Morgan did their duty first. They sat at the radio and ensured the report was sent.

For want of something better all sides listened to BBC World Service. Unbiased it was not but it did embody a type of self deprecating naivety that made it somehow acceptable.

The operator flicked a switch to change from headphones to loud speaker. He fine tuned the dial to improve reception. The voice was always the same, synthetic Oxford exuding a 'better than thou' tone. It was as much to say that if the BBC broadcast it, it must be true.

"This is the BBC World Service. The time is 2000 hrs GMT. Here is the World news."

"Large parts of Rhodesia were plunged into darkness last night when fighters loyal to Joshua Nkomo's ZIPRA Party attacked the main electricity distribution system. Disruption is widespread. Many factories remain closed and important irrigation systems have been turned off. It is expected to take more than seventy two hours before full electrical supply is restored."

"In a related attack the main railway line connecting South Africa to Rhodesia was sabotaged. An express passenger train was derailed. There are unconfirmed reports of casualties."

"Rhodesian authorities in Salisbury said that in a contact between their ground forces and terrorists a number of their soldiers were injured. A mop-up operation is in progress. The spokesman was unable to be precise about terrorist numbers but claims casualties were high amongst them."

"In a separate incident reports are coming in of an attempted attack on the railway marshalling yards at Bulawayo. A Rhodesian Police spokesman said the attack was easily thwarted. There were no casualties amongst the security forces but all the terrorists had been killed. He emphasised that at no time was there any danger to the general public or infrastructure of Rhodesia."

"In London a Foreign Office Spokesmen said that the events in Rhodesia signify a major escalation of the conflict. He added that intelligence reports from the area had predicted the likelihood of such incidents. He also said he expected the situation to get worse and called on all parties to return to the negotiating table."

Mashava Township

Mashava Township was still. It was the dead of night but Wilfred barely slept. He could only wait in his rooms for news.

The tap was tentative. Wilfred knew it would be safe, despite the hour. The police knocked with their feet. He opened the door just enough to see who was there.

"Tyoni! It is you. Quickly come in, do not let people see light spilling into the darkness. Tell me what happened. I was beginning to fear I would not see you again."

"Ah, it is good to see a friendly face. Give me some water, I have a great thirst."

Tyoni's hair was matted. There was dry mud on his clothing, his complexion had a grey pallor, his cheeks were sunken. He slumped into the only armchair in the room. Wilfred fetched the water and passed it to him in a chipped, handle less mug that he'd recovered from the Pastor's waste bin.

"It is dangerous to travel when you are in such a condition. It is clear to everybody you have been up to no good. Do you carry your pass book?"

Tyoni shook his head between gulps of water. "No."

"The white soldiers will take you if they find you. What you do is too dangerous. It is also foolish. There are many patrols around Mashava in the last days. The soldiers are very angry over what has happened. It is said six of their own were killed. Many people have been taken from the villages in revenge. It has been too dangerous for even me to go and find out what happened."

Tyoni ignored Wilfred. "It has taken me three days to get here without being seen. I am tired but there's no time for rest. You must come with me to fetch Makonzo. He is injured and needs help. I had to leave him some distance away."

"Is he wounded? Was he shot? What has happened? I have no information from the time I left him at the bamboo clearing."

"He is not shot but he is very sick. Maybe he will not live. I will tell you later what has happened but first we must go and fetch him. He cannot stay where he is. When the sun rises he will be found."

Wilfred spoke. "We will bring him here, to the servants quarters. The Pastor will not know."

The hand cart was well known to people of the Township. In the past it had been the grim visitor to many houses. It was the vehicle for the last mortal journey. Shona tradition demanded that the dead should be laid to rest amongst the remains of their ancestors. It was the only way to free the Spirit. But White administrators of the new township ridiculed traditional beliefs. They forced families to surrender their dead for burial in the European manner. They said it was for the health of the living but all Africans knew such matters had not been a concern before the White man came. Why should it be a concern now? Could it be the whites were scared to let the Spirits run free?

In the still of night the cart, little more than a gurney, would be pushed to the homes of the dead. The bereaved insisted the bodies be taken and buried before the sun rose, lest the Spirits see what had happened. That was acceptable to the rules of the Whites. They called it an Ordnance.

The cart had two large pneumatic tyres and leaf springs. There were wooden handles back and front. It rolled easily over rough ground even with a heavy load.

Prying eyes might see but they would not speak.

With only a torch it was difficult for Tyoni to find the spot where he'd joined the main road. He looked for the broken shoots he'd left as a sign.

Eventually he stopped. "Follow me," he said, "I am sure this is the place."

A few yards through thin vegetation Makonzo lay where Tyoni had left him. He didn't respond to Tyoni's touch.

"He is worse."

Wilfred knelt and shone the torch into the face of his leader. Beads of sweat rested on his brow. His cheeks were hot to the touch.

"He has the fever. We must get help for him quickly."

The two men picked up the dead weight and carried him to the cart. They stumbled through the long grass. They pushed the cart and listless body. The only sign of life was an occasional low moan. Within the hour they'd arrived at the front of the church. Wilfred went ahead and checked. He returned. "No lights in the Pastor's house. We can go."

They lay Makonzo on a straw mattress in the corner of the room.

"We must get his clothes off and bathe him," said Wilfred. "It is important to cool the fever."

He unbuttoned Makonzo's tunic. The material stuck to his chest. Slowly he peeled it back. "My God! What is this abomination?"

He shrunk back. "I have never seen a sight like this."

"The Matable branded him with a hot iron", said Tyoni, "They wrote on his chest. They said it was so he would not forget his own treachery."

"He may not have to remember it for very long," said Wilfred. "His whole chest is infected."

The blisters on his chest had broken but the open wounds had not scabbed over. They had festered in the humid bush. Yellow puss oozed from the infection and mingled with trickles of blood. Wilfred leaned forward and smelt the wound.

"That is a good sign. There is hope. It is not rotting yet. I smell no gangrene. But we must get a doctor or your efforts of the last days will have been in vain."

The doctor was young. He worked in the African clinic treating African diseases. He'd been trained in South Africa but only to treat black patients. White students studied all races but black students were forbidden from seeing a naked white women, even in death. The absurdity made young educated minds fertile ground for rebellion. He wanted Makonzo to survive.

"He will be ill for several days", said the doctor. "Only if his fever breaks and his temperature falls can you be sure of his recovery. You must keep him lying on his back. Sprinkle the powder from the sachets on the wound every four hours. Wipe around the wound regularly. Use only boiled water that has a capful of this mixed in it."

The doctor handed over a bottle of Dettol. "It is all we have in the African clinic. I have given him an anti-biotic injection. It is working now. I will come back tonight and give him another injection. For now do not worry about food but you must force him to drink. This will be the secret of his survival. If he drinks he will have the best chance. There is no more we can do."

For three days the men tended their Comrade and leader.

One was always at his side. Tyoni and Wilfred had much time to talk. Tyoni told the story of the Mopane Forest. He told of how Makonzo had been humiliated and about the mutiny. He told of the men he had shot and the threats he had made.

"Truly it was not a good time for us," said Wilfred. "But I think the White man is confused. I have heard he is worried that we are working together. It is good they don't know of our troubles. They would use it against us."

Tyoni shook his head. "If Makonzo recovers it will not be long before the White Man becomes aware of the problems between Matable and Shona. I fear Makonzo will seek retribution on the Matable above all else."

The inflammation around the wound began to retreat, his temperature began to fall. It was days before he ate but he never refused drink. On the fifth day Makonzo sat up, his eyes once again clear.

"The Pastor knows you are here", said Wilfred. "He wanted to visit. I told him you have river fever and that it is contagious. It will keep him away for a while. I need to check your wound. It is time for it to be cleaned."

Makonzo placed a hand on his own chest.

"I have seen it many times," said Wilfred. "You will carry the scar for the rest of your life. There is nothing that can be done about that."

"Give me a mirror. Let me see what they have done," said Makonzo.

He peered into the shaving mirror. A scab had formed and the bright red inflammation was turning pink around the edges. The wound was no longer wet but the writing was clear. Makonzo stared at the mirror image for a long time before speaking.

"This mark will be the nemesis of the Matable. As long as there is breath in my body I will extract a heavy price for this humiliation."

He slumped back. "Do what you have to do," he said to Wilfred. "I need to be strong."

Fort Victoria, Chevron Hotel

No mosquitoes but lots of gnats. The shortage of DDT gave rise to improvisation. The female mosquito lay's her eggs in standing water, suspended by a slender thread just below the surface. Rhodesians discovered that if a bit of petrol is poured onto the water, the surface tension is broken and the eggs fall to the bottom. No mosquitoes, no malaria! The petrol evaporates in the sun and everything is hunky-dory. But it didn't work for gnats unfortunately. They just multiply out of all proportion. So Duncan waited inside, in the lounge bar of the Chevron Hotel, Fort Victoria the usual place for his meeting with Patrick.

He pulled the letter from the breast pocket of his shirt. He read it again as he waited for his beer to arrive.

Mixed feelings. He was perversely proud and somehow disbelieving. When it had arrived he telephoned to check if it was true.

The envelope was franked Salisbury. The return addresses KG5 Barracks, the Army Education Corps. The letter confirmed his place on a six week Officer Conversion course.

Nobody had spoken to him at Fort Victoria. His CO was gone. The new one had not arrived. It was considered inappropriate for an NCO to tell a private he was becoming an officer. So it was down to a civilian administrator to explain over the phone.

Duncan's promotion to Lieutenant could not be confirmed until he'd completed the course. The administrator explained his inclusion was unusual. Candidates for the course were normally senior NCO's. She couldn't recall a private being nominated previously. She congratulated him.

He didn't speak to anybody about it. He had to sort out the dilemma in his own mind first.

Patrick Walker's phone call was a surprise. It was not time for his normal visit. It tempered Duncan's euphoria. The conversation had been characteristically abrupt.

"Duncan. How are you? Passing through tomorrow. Thought I'd see you. About 7. Normal place. I'll see you then?"

A waiter came with his beer. Duncan folded the letter and put it back in his pocket.

"Excuse me Sir, are you Mr Murdoch?" The African had a strange English accent.

"I am", replied Duncan.

"A gentleman is waiting for you in the restaurant. He asks will you join him?"

The waiter led the way.

The corner table was more suited to a courting couple. Patrick Walker rose as Duncan approached. He offered a puffy hand.

"Good to see you again". The voice was typically exuberant.

"Please. Sit, sit. Wine. Nice red. VAT 10, local. I normally drink South African, Stellenbosch if I can, but this Rhodesian one is quite good. Have a glass?"

"I'll stick with the beer," replied Duncan taking his seat.

The waiter laid a serviette on Duncan's lap and offered a menu.

"I wasn't expecting to eat," said Duncan.

"Celebration time. Congratulations in order don't you think?" said Walker.

"For what?" asked Duncan.

"Don't be coy now. Not often a trooper gets a commission. In fact never heard of it before. Well done. Knew you were of the right calibre. Apparent all the time."

It hadn't crossed Duncan's mind to tell Patrick Walker the news, not yet. He might have got around to it in a few days or at their next regular meeting, when it was confirmed.

"How did you know?" asked Duncan.

"It's my job to know. It's what I'm paid for. I am rather good at it don't you think?"

"But I detract. What you did was a jolly good piece of work. No wonder they want to promote you." Patrick lifted his glass.

"Toast! Here's to Lieutenant Duncan Murdoch, Rhodesian Light Infantry, saviour of Bulawayo."

"It hasn't happened yet. The promotion."

"It will." Patrick gulped his wine. "The papers are signed."

Walker quaffed at his glass. "I've always been attracted to red wine. It was greed that started me, not taste. My love started when I realised you got a bigger glass when you choose red."

Duncan thought there was more than an element of truth in that thought. He drank his beer.

Patrick signalled the waiter. "I've been waiting for you before ordering. I'm starving. Going for the Piri Piri chicken for starters and then the "T" bone. What about you?"

Duncan cruised the menu. "Kapenta and a fillet steak."

Patrick spoke between mouthfuls. "Promotion can be flattering in almost any circumstance," he said. "Let me give you an example. Did you know that three days before the end of the war, with the Russians knocking on the door of Berlin and Hitler dead, the remnants of the Nazi leadership were still queuing for the top job. Amazing, absolutely amazing don't you think? You'd have thought they'd all have been running a mile, wouldn't you?"

Duncan shrugged. "Has this got something to do with me?"

"It doesn't hurt to stand back a little and see which side of the bread is buttered. It's perfectly clear that the end is gong to come to this regime, most probably sooner rather than later. Bearing this in mind it might be a mistake to get too drawn in. A bit like signing up on the Titanic if you know what I mean."

"Are you suggesting I should refuse the Commission?"

"No. Not at all. Quite the opposite. You will be privy to much more information from now on. But it would be prudent if you maintained access to your lifeboat so to speak. I think you'd agree?"

"You're talking in riddles. I'm not sure what you mean." said Duncan.

"Simply old chap, I don't want flattery to go to your head."

Duncan felt a flush of anger at Walker's presumption. "Is this meeting to remind me of my past? To let me know I'm a "lifer" on parole? To keep me in line?"

Walker was uncomfortable. Duncan's reaction was too direct. His forehead glistened with sweat. He sensed the conversation might get out of control. He dabbed his brow with a serviette.

"I would not put it so crudely. I'm sure there's nothing to be concerned about. I personally have complete faith in your loyalty. It's just that my superiors in London, people who don't really know the situation, might like some reassurance of your reliability. Worried about you going native sort of thing."

Duncan sat back in his chair. He spoke quietly and deliberately.

"Why should I feel loyalty or gratitude to an Establishment for freeing me when it was that very same Establishment that unjustly imprisoned me in the first place?"

Duncan was angry now. "My loyalty is not and will never be, to a system that prejudiced me from the beginning. I will not be influenced by any threat from that Establishment. My appreciation is limited to the individuals that championed my cause and I will not let them down"

Duncan continued, he was in full flow. "Let me tell you some other things. I have seen the communist way. I fought against it in Aden. I have seen communists force their beliefs all over the world but nowhere have I seen the system bring any benefit to the people. For me, as long as the Rhodesians are fighting communism, my position as a soldier in the Rhodesian Army is justified."

"But do not think because I am anti-communist that I approve of the Rhodesian system either. Rhodesia is only a romantic renegade state, a figment of the white man's imagination. For the blacks Rhodesia is a place of squalid oppression and fear. I cannot approve of that. Be assured I find racism as reprehensible as communism, but till something better comes along tell your people in London they are assured of my co-operation. Your threats are quite unnecessary."

Mashava Mine, The Pit Head

Duncan was the first Mine Deputy to arrive. The rescue team had already descended the shaft. He paced the pit head. It was strangely quiet, too quiet, for a major accident. The great spoked wheel of the winding gear was stationary. The cage was at the bottom of the shaft. There would be no news until it returned to the surface. He could only wait.

Six weeks had passed since his last meeting with Patrick Walker. Longer than normal. He'd been absent from the mine, on the Officer Induction Course in Salisbury. He'd learnt to eat properly with a knife and fork and pick the right wine glass at the dinner table. Most importantly he had been taught not to splash Willard's Tomato Ketchup over his chips. He'd learnt to pour the sauce on the side of the plate and dip his chips into it individually. Thus prepared for bush war he returned to Mashava.

He'd sensed a difference on his return. He thought it was him that had changed but quickly realised it was something else. The atmosphere around the mine had changed, tension had been building. Everybody knew something was going to happen. Now, on a Saturday morning it had. Tired of pacing, he sat on a wooden bench. He thought about his first trip down the shaft, into the bowels of the mine. He recalled almost verbatim, the blurb he'd been given.

"The mine at Mashava is the largest Chrysolite Asbestos working in Africa. What's hauled out of the ground at Mashava should not be confused with the Amphiboles or blue asbestos mined elsewhere. There was not a single case of asbestosis in the mine's medical records despite many of the staff having worked at Mashava for more than thirty years."

"Asbestos is an under-utilised material. It is easily manipulated and formed. When pressed into sheets with gypsum it is impervious to water. It is a good insulator of both heat and electricity and is resistant to wear. It does not corrode and above all it is cheap and plentiful."

Duncan had learnt quickly. The basics were easy. In Mashava asbestos was found in huge underground pockets, trapped like bubbles, within the iron ore bedrock, just like a honeycomb. The trick of extraction was to blast through the bedrock into the pockets without pulverising the trapped fibre. It was a delicate job made worse because asbestos was dry mined. The dust problem was incredible.

Duncan had quickly picked up the routine. The duty Mine Deputy, the Operations Manager and the Geologist would meet on Monday morning. The production schedule would be agreed and the blasting plan set. For the rest of the week core holes for the explosive would be drilled in the bedrock and the blasting cables run. Only on Saturday morning would the charges and detonators be placed in position. Then, after lunch, when the mine was clear, detonation would take place. The mine would then be left until Monday to allow the dust to settle.

Saturday was the big day. Before noon all residents of the White Camp and Black Township would take in their washing. Windows would be shut, children brought indoors.

Sometimes, not often, the calculations would be wrong or the geology would be not quite as predicted. Then there was a problem. The pressure in the underground workings would increase, suddenly and dramatically, forcing air and plumes of asbestos dust upwards till they erupted through the main shaft and air vents. It was a spectacle dreaded by adults but eagerly awaited by children. The dust could erupt upward for hundreds of feet. The wind would catch the dust and carry it along. Slowly the particles would settle, like a white blanket, over the countryside. It would take weeks to disperse naturally. That should be the worst that could happen - in theory. But today something worse had happened!

Duncan had been in bed. It was 8am. He was not roistered but was the senior man at the workings. A deep rumble disturbed his slumber but not enough to wake him.

The first thing he was aware of was Elizabeth. She was standing in his bedroom, by the door, looking at him. In the twilight zone, between sleep and wakefulness, it seemed so natural, almost like she belonged there and he wanted her there. But it was not natural. She had never come into his bedroom before, not when he was in bed.

"Boss you have to wake up," she spoke softly.

He sat upright.

Duncan slept naked. Now he was covered only by a cotton sheet. For a moment, chest exposed, he felt erotically vulnerable. The serious look on her face made him quickly dispel any such thought.

"There has been an accident at the mine," she said. "They want you to go quickly."

Instantly he was alert. Elizabeth gave no indication of leaving. He wanted to get out of bed. Their eyes met. She was mesmerised, her gaze fixed on his naked torso.

"Elizabeth. I need to get up."

She turned and left the room without a word.

Suddenly he was back at the mine head. The whine of the giant electric motor starting brought Duncan back to reality. He was on his feet. High above, the big wheel began to turn, slowly at first. He looked towards the shaft. The cables were vibrating as they did under load. The cage was coming up.

Some of the experienced cage operators could judge the size of the load by the degree of vibration in the cables. Duncan did not possess such skill but he didn't have long to wait for the cage to arrive.

The giant shackle that connected the cable to the cage passed, slowly. Two bells rang and the cage stopped in a jerky motion. The operator unhitched the Bolton Gate, slid it open and lifted the drop bars on the cage itself. Half a dozen ghost like figures toppled out. The whole rescue team had come up. They were covered in asbestos dust. The tallest man walked over to Duncan and peeled back his face mask. "It's impossible down there. Can't see a bloody thing. Our air filters kept blocking up. Not much we can do until the mine is vented and the dust settles."

"You didn't find anything?" asked Duncan.

"Oh no. We found plenty and it's not good. There's a stack of bodies at the bottom of the shaft. I'd say most of the missing people are there. We fetched a couple up in the cage," he pointed backwards with his thumb. "Poor bastards suffocated by the look of it. But their eardrums ruptured first. It was the pressure from the explosion. Blood running down their faces before they died. They must have been in agony as they choked."

"Any idea of the cause?" asked Duncan.

"Certainly not an accident," was the reply.

Mashava Township

Mashava's Township Beer Hall stank of sour maize beer. It was dim and muggy inside. Old smoke hung in the air from the night before; giant louvered vents built into the eaves didn't work. The rows of wooden tables and benches had been cleaned and the tile floor was wet from its recent sluicing. A whiff of carbolic came from behind the high counter that supported the banks of chromed beer taps. There were no windows in the hall, what light there was came through a few semi-translucent sheets set into the corrugated asbestos roof. A filthy door that had at one time been white, led off to a small back room where the atmosphere was even more claustrophobic.

Makonzo and Tyoni sat silently waiting for news. A fat woman brought sweet Nescafe in glass tumblers. She placed them on the wooden table without word. The explosion had happened. They'd heard the emergency siren wailing for an hour. Now it had stopped.

Makonzo sat in the only wooden chair with arms, Tyoni, to his right, on a bench.

"The work of clearing Mashava of Matable has begun," said Makonzo confirming the obvious to his companion.

The metal doors of the main hall clattered as someone came in. Determined and hurried footsteps echoed on the tile floor. They got louder.

Wilfred appeared at the open door. He was short of breath. He sat on the bench opposite Tyoni, the expression on his face serious.

"You have something to tell us?" asked Makonzo, not waiting for Wilfred to get his breath back.

"Yes. But not what you expected," he replied.

"What then?" asked Makonzo with a frown of suspicion.

"Do you remember, before the train, we intercepted a message? A message that was in code. A message from a woman on the Gwanda bus."

"Yes, I remember. But what does that matter now? Many

things have happened since then, and many things are happening as we speak. I don't want to be distracted by side issues."

"But this is interesting, very interesting," said Wilfred persistently, "not a side issue at all."

"What then?" said Makonzo. "Speak. But be quick."

Wilfred unfolded a piece of paper. "I have the translation of the code," he said. "The message says, *"Normally six soldiers on train. Three back three front. Better not to attack on Wednesday's"*." He put the paper flat on the table. "The code breakers said the code is a simple Russian system, a system most probably taught to the Matable."

"So, what does this mean?" asked Makonzo with a shrug.

"It means we have a Matable spy in Mashava and that spy has been working with the group in the Mopane forest, the ones that harmed you! If the woman who sent the message is still here there is an opportunity find the culprits in person and exact revenge!"

Makonzo ran fingers over his shirt, feeling the outline of the scar on his chest.

"You think the woman is nearby?" he did not wait for an answer. "Find her, bring her to me."

The heat of the day had passed when the meeting convened in the crowded Mine Deputy's office. Duncan stood at the back of the room.

Rossi, the slightly built police inspector was of obvious Italian extraction. He spoke.

"This is a police matter and I will chair the meeting. Mr Finnegan, you've been down the mine today, give me your report and appraisal of the situation."

"I'm speaking as the Rescue Team Leader. I'm not an investigator although I've worked on the mine for several years. "I'd just like to say…….."

"It's Tom isn't it?" broke in the Inspector, "Not a court of law. Just tell us what you saw for now."

"Okay, sorry. There was not one blast but several and they all occurred at the same time."

"Three new caverns were supposed to be opened this morning. As far as I can see the caverns were opened up according to the blasting plan. If they were the only explosions the miners would probably have survived and the incident would have been considered an accident. But there was actually another bigger unscheduled explosion. That explosion occurred in the main access tunnel, not far from the cage. Under no circumstances should there be explosives in that location."

"Could the blasting crew have simply been moving explosives around or forgotten about them?"

"No. The blasting crew are smarter than that. They wouldn't leave their exit compromised.

In any case the official charges were laid yesterday. The blasting crew was not due down the mine till 9.30 to fit the detonators. The explosion was recorded a little after 7.30 am."

"So you are saying the explosion had nothing to do with the blasting crew?"

"That is exactly what I am saying", said Tom. "And there's more."

"Go on."

"As of now we've recovered thirty bodies and no survivors. All the dead come from two of the working Gangs. This is really strange."

"Why?"

Tom had his audience. "It's how we organise the labour. Each cavern is allocated to a gang, a gang of about fifteen men that work under an elected Gang Master. The Gang Master gets a lump sum for clearing the cavern and distributes the money to his men more or less as he sees fit."

"Right, so there were two gangs working this morning", said Rossi.

"There should have been four!" answered Tom.

"Two gangs didn't turn up?"

"No. That's not correct." Duncan interjected. All eyes turned to him.

"I was at the pithead immediately after the explosion and the first thing I did was check the numbers down the mine."

"Go on," said Rossi.

"We keep two records of workers. Firstly they sign on at the gate as they arrive at the mine, that's just time keeping. Then we run a tally board at the pit head for people actually down the pit."

"This morning four gangs clocked on at the security gate on time and as scheduled. But I found the tally boards at the pit head had been messed up. The tallies were thrown about all over the place. So I went back to the Gate House to see what I could find. It was clear that thirty of the men had signed off at the gate earlier than they should have, much earlier than their shift normally ends! And they didn't ask or even let anybody in authority know."

"What's the explanation for that?" asked Rossi.

Tom spoke. "As I said the gangs are run by Gang Masters. The Gang Master picks his own men. They are split on tribal lines, about fifty/fifty between Matable and Shona gangs."

"So?"

"There should have been four gangs working this morning. Two Shona, two Matable. Only the Matable were underground at the time of the explosion. It was the Shona that had signed off at the Gate."

"A deliberate attack against the Matable then?" said Rossi.

"I think so", said Tom "although I don't suppose the Shona would have minded too much about the damage to the mine, so long as we don't stop their wages that is."

The phone rang loudly. The Deputy answered.

"It's for you", he said giving the handset to the Inspector. The Inspector listened for a while then returned the handset to the cradle.

"Perhaps the mine was not the primary target," said Inspector Rossie. "You may will be right" he continued looking toward Duncan. "People are being put out of their homes in the Township and houses are being torched. I'd wager they are Matable homes that are being destroyed."

"That's a bit rough," said Duncan.

"Can be unusually cruel to each other, the Africans, been fighting since before we got here and will still be fighting when we have gone!"

"That's ongoing. You'll be busy sorting that out then?" asked Duncan.

"Not likely," replied Rossi. "That's the Department of African Affairs problem."

"What will they do?"

"Nothing, not till Monday I don't suppose. That's when the offices open. Their policy is not to interfere in these things. Let nature take its course sort of thing. But I tell you I wouldn't like to be a Matable this weekend!"

"Okay then", continued Rossi. "To sum up; thirty dead, no survivors, nobody trapped. Almost certainly sabotage probably directed against the Matable. Agreed?"

No dissension.

"I'm declaring the mine a crime scene and putting a guard on the pit head.

We'll review it on Monday when chaps from the Mines Safety Board have had a bit of time to do their thing."

Duncan drove the pickup quickly. He had a hollow feeling in his stomach. Though not disposed to such sentiments he had what most would describe as a bad premonition. He hoped she was still there. His mind was running ahead of things, he hoped. She could not go back to the Township for now she would have to stay at his house until things had calmed down. It was too dangerous to let her return to the Township.

He pulled the truck into the drive a little too quickly and it began to slue sideways on the gravel. He became aware of his own anxiousness but didn't slow down. In a few steps he was on the stoop, at the front door. It was locked. He didn't fumble for keys but almost ran around to the back door hoping to find Elizabeth in the kitchen. He turned the knob. The kitchen door was unyielding, also locked. He fumbled for his keys, even feeling a tremor of panic as he opened the door. He liked her when he first saw her but his shyness, her aloofness and the law stopped a relationship developing. But now, when she was in danger, his suppressed feelings began to bubble over.

"Elizabeth!" he shouted.

There was no response. She should have been there. It was not time for her to go. The kitchen was tidy on the table was a note. He recognised the neat missionary taught hand of Elizabeth.

He read.

"Shit!"

Mashava Camp, Duncan's House

The whistle was shrill. She stopped taking the washing from the line and went to the side of the house. At the bottom of the drive next to the gate stood the old man, the one who had whistled. He would not come through the gate uninvited. A lowly African found in a white man's garden without good reason ran a risk. Better to whistle or shout for attention.

She thought it was a hawker, before she recognised the old sun dried face. He often came to the hostel, asking for work or just begging. Elizabeth walked towards him.

"What do you want old man? The Master is away and there is nothing he would want from you." Her words were kindly.

"I do not want the Master. It is you I am looking for. I have news of a message for you. I came especially," he replied.

She looked at him, suspiciously. "What message do you have for me? Be quick, I am working."

"It is a message that came to the hostel. A bus driver from Gwanda brought it," said the old man, exposing decayed teeth through a lopsided smile. She wondered how he managed to whistle so clearly. "Give it to me, tell me the message."

"No, I can't do that. You have to fetch it yourself. The driver would not tell me. He said it is too important. He is waiting at the hostel for you. He says he will only speak to you."

"He only wants to extract a reward before he will tell me what he has already been paid for," she said. "Tell him I finish at six today. Tell him I will see him then."

"He won't wait. He said you have to come now or he will go away with the message."

"Can't you see old man? I am working. The Master will be home soon. I will be in trouble if I leave before he returns."

"That is up to you", said the old man, "I have done my job, but I think you make a mistake." He turned to leave.

Elizabeth hesitated. A message from Gwanda, she could not take the risk. It could only be something from her father. She had no choice.

"Wait, I will leave a note and come with you. You can take me to the driver. I will only be a few moments."

The old man smiled.

Despite her hurry she penned the note patiently and left it on the kitchen table.

The old man set off at a pace surprising for his years. Elizabeth lengthened her stride to keep up. He kept a half pace ahead of her. They walked, without speaking, along the dusty road towards the Township.

She saw the smoke drifting over the settlement even before the first shanty buildings came into view. As they got closer she smelt the burning.

"What is happening? Tell me old man. Why are there fires and why are there no people on the street? It is Saturday, there are always people on the street on Saturday."

The old man looked back and shrugged. "It is not far now. The bus driver waits for you."

They approached the crossroads, the centre of the Township. Here a few people stood in a group, quietly whispering as if afraid they would be overheard. A shopkeeper was closing the shutters on his windows.

"Why does he close so early?"

"It is nothing for you or me to be concerned with," replied the old man.

He walked straight on, across the road. There was no traffic. Elizabeth stopped. "That is not the way. The hostel is up here, to the left. Where are you taking me?"

"I am taking you to the bus driver", said the old man.

"You told me he was at the Hostel," she replied.

"He was, when I met him. But he went to wait at the Beer Hall. That is where he is now."

"You never said that before." Elizabeth slowed.

The Old Man came back to her. "Come. We are nearly there now." He took her by the arm and led her forward.

She'd never been to the Beer Hall. It was not a place for a Matable woman, or any woman of repute. She looked across the road.

The single storied building with its grey corrugated roof was set back from the road. A low wall signified the beginning of the garden, a large plot dotted with fixed concrete benches and tables.

Some tables had giant red and white umbrellas for shade, the only dash of colour in the garden. The ground was compressed dusty soil that should have been grass but instead was something that turned to mud during the rains. Any grass that had grown was long since worn away by the steps of drinkers who cared little for what was underfoot. No table in the sunlight was occupied. She saw only a lone man sitting at a bench. He was out of place, more watching than drinking.

Tyoni sipped the opaque beer from its plastic pale as he peered over the rim. He'd been waiting a long time on the concrete bench and was becoming restless when they came into view. He saw the old man holding the woman by the arm, leading her. She came forward reluctantly.

"Pretty," thought Tyoni, "Makonzo will have fun with her." Maybe before the inevitable necklace of fire he would also get a turn. He waved a hand at the two men waiting, leaning against the wall on the opposite side of the road. They moved toward the Old Man and Elizabeth.

Tyoni waited and pictured the final scenes, a sight he had often witnessed.

The "flaming necklace" had become a feared trademark but Makonzo would extract what he wanted first. Stripped naked she would be held. He would torture and defile her till she confessed or he became exhausted. If she had not broken he would allow others to follow him. In the end all confessed, guilty or not. Only then would Makonzo give the signal, but she had to be conscious. It was no fun if the victim was unaware of their fate. If she was unconscious water would be thrown on her and they would wait. Then she'd be bound to a post and a tyre doused in diesel would be hung around her neck. Petrol burnt too quickly. Diesel took time to get it burning but slowly the flames would creep around until the circle was complete. The hair was always the first to go. The smell of singeing hair combined with that of burning rubber would fill the air for a short while, a unique combination. The victim always closed their eyes and held their breath, instinctively trying to survive, to extend life by a few seconds more. But the end was inevitable.

The pain of burning would become so intense, the victim would eventually scream for one last time. The great exhalation would be followed by an intake, not of air but of fire. The flames, drawn down the bronchial would instantly blister the moist membrane of the lungs and render the organ useless. The victim could no longer breathe and it was suffocation that caused death, but not before the flames had inflicted even more pain. Tyoni was amazed at how long a person continued to writhe. He'd timed it once, more than four minutes. To the victim it most probably seemed a lot longer.

Instinct made the hairs on the back of Elizabeth's neck stand up but still she walked on, led by the old man. It was wrong. She felt it. She saw the two men walking towards them, their step quick and too intent. One face was familiar to her. Suddenly it came. She remembered. The bus station, it was him, the one with bad breath. Caution turned to alarm. She twisted herself free from the old man's grip. He tried to hold on, his faltering grip hurt. He was not trying to lead her anymore, just restrain her till the men arrived. The men began to run the last few yards. Elizabeth broke free, turned and ran, back towards the crossroads.

Tyoni was on his feet, shouting as he ran, "Catch her! Do not let her escape."

At the crossroads she glanced backwards. They were close.

Makonzo had left the Beer Hall. He had work to do. Today he'd finish what he'd started weeks ago. The roots of tribal hatred had not been destroyed by the war of liberation, they merely lay dormant, just below the surface. Like a weed they just needed to be watered for the shoots to break surface and flourish once more.

For weeks past Makonzo had ensured that old tales had been resurrected and passed from one mouth to the next, rekindling old fears. People were reminded of past Matable raids, of the pillage of Shona grain and cattle, the murder of those who dared defend themselves and the taking of Shona women to become the slaves and concubines of the Matable Impies.

Makonzo now asked any group of Shona that would listen, "Do you want the White Masters to be replaced by Matable Masters? Do you want to go back to the old days?" He looked at the crowd and saw men from the mines, youths and women from the Township.

The antagonism he had fostered over the past weeks had erupted, triggered by the explosion at the mine. The crowd knew what to do, to make the most of the opportunity, to rid the township of the Matable plague forever.

Outnumbered and disorganised Matable women had no time to worry or search for their husbands who'd gone to work in the mine that morning. The wise ones fled before the baying crowd, leaving behind all they owned for the looters or fire. The few that decided to stay perished in the flames of their own homes. Once started the frenzy was unstoppable by reason.

When Makonzo joined the mob they listened, they acknowledged him as their leader. "You have done well. The job is nearly complete. The Matable pestilence has almost been eradicated. Many have run into the bush, we will chase them back to Matable land. They go with nothing but their lives and even those they will lose if they are not quick."

He continued. "In the township there is only one group remaining. A number have taken refuge in the hostel. They have barricaded themselves in. It is our final task to kill off the last infestation. Go to the hostel now. Soon men of the Cadre will come, men to finish the job."

Elizabeth turned right at the crossroads. She wished she'd stayed in Duncan's house and not been fooled. Elizabeth knew that the hostel offered her only chance now. The rough road rose steeply. It was harder to run, the men were gaining. She gave an extra push. Ahead she saw the crowd but she dare not stop. There was little choice but to push through; that or be captured. Now at least she knew where all the Township people were.

From behind came a shout. "Stop the Matable whore. Don't let her get to the hostel". Tyoni was no longer running, he was screaming at the top of his voice. People heard and turned, but Elizabeth was running fast, too fast for most. She side stepped feeble attempts to grab her. She wove between people unaware or too slow. Finally ahead, between her and the hostel, stood one more obstacle, a gangly man of awkward movement. Alert he'd seen how she slipped by others. He'd not be fooled so easily. As she came close he dodged, first to the left, then to the right. Elizabeth looked him in the eyes, seeking a sign. There was none. She was upon him. Her first twist was to the left, he made to follow. At the last moment she veered to the right, ducking low. She sensed freedom and pushed one more time. But he was ready.

It was as if she had hit a wall. Her head stopped dead. An arm across her mouth, hooked from behind. Momentum carried her body forward. She fell backwards and into the grip of her captor. The crowd were watching, a few came forward to help. Elizabeth sank her teeth into the hard black skin that held her head so tightly. A gush of warm blood filled her mouth. Her captor shouted with pain and released his grip. She dropped to the ground, fighting to regain her feet. There was not enough time. The crowd was coming. It was hopeless, all appeared lost.

Then the surging crowd stopped as the barrage of stones and rocks hit the ones in the front. From the hostel, defenders, had run forward. Strong arms lifted her. Elizabeth knew they were not hostile, she did not resist. She was dragged the last few yards until she was inside the hostel. She lay on the floor, exhausted. Someone held a cup of water to her mouth. She drank, her dry mouth welcoming the relief. .

"Thank you", she said.

The man who had pulled her into the hostel looked down on her.

"You saved my life," she continued.

"No I have not done that," replied the man, "I have only prolonged it for an hour or two. Not more."

"Why? What is happening?"

"We are all that is left of the Township Matable. All the rest are gone – gone or dead. The crowd outside only offers the same for us. We will resist as long as we can but no help will come and we only have sticks and stones, even as we speak the crowd gets bigger and angrier."

"The police will come", said Elizabeth.

"Ah! The white police will not risk themselves for us and the black police are too scared to come."

"We must do something", said Elizabeth.

Makonzo outwardly remained calm but struggled to contain his rage. Tyoni knew this was when he was most unpredictable and dangerous. "She was too quick," he said.

"This is a black mark against you," said Makonzo. "You are sure she is in the hostel?"

"I saw her pulled in with my own eyes. She is there."

Makonzo rubbed the blade of his panga on the side of his leg. "I will have that woman alive. We must go carefully I do not want her to die without knowing the reason."

"Night will come in a few hours. When the light fails we will attack. You must listen carefully." Makonzo drew in the sand with the tip of the blade. "Behind the hostel is an open plot, more than one acre. It is surrounded on two sides by bush and one by buildings. This will be the killing ground. Tyoni, you will take the whole Cadre, all the trained people to the open land. You will hide in the bush and buildings around the plot. You will wait."

"Your men must have pangas. There should be no shooting. The white men will know that there are Comrades here if they hear the guns, so kill without guns."

Makonzo pointed the blade at Tyoni and spoke. "You have the chance to redeem yourself. You will lead the group and you will find the woman. You will bring her to me unharmed."

"How will you get them to come to us across the open ground?"

"I will be in front of the hostel. The crowd will surge forward. Hidden in their numbers will be boys with petrol bombs. We will set fire to the front of the hostel. When the building is on fire they will try to escape across the open ground."

"Go now and gather your men."

Mashava Camp, Duncan's House

Duncan looked at the note again. It said she'd be back by two, now it was gone four. "Why did she go to the Township when it was so dangerous?" he thought. "Maybe she had not heard or perhaps she wanted to fetch her things?"

He was surprised by his own anguish. He was restless and couldn't sit in the house. He went into the garden. The Township was three miles away. He listened but could hear nothing although he fancied he could catch the faint whiff of burning on the still air and he was sure he saw wispy clouds of smoke rising above the Township in the distance. It was only now, with the thought of losing her that he realised how attached he had become. No word of affection had been spoken between them but now he realised there was no other he was closer to in this place. In his short life there had been only three women he became comfortable with, his mother and Mary Scobie were two. Elizabeth had unwittingly become the third. He cursed that his awkwardness had not let him display his feelings more. He yearned for female company.

"Why hadn't Battalion mobilised? Surely the Army reserve would be called to pacify any problems even if the police didn't want to interfere." He decided to phone.

"What do you mean no orders? There's a riot going on, right now, a couple of miles from here." Duncan struggled to contain himself.

His rage grew. "I don't care if the police haven't asked for assistance. People may be dying and we're not even being stood-to? It's ridiculous."

"Call Brigade and let me know what they say" He put down the phone without waiting for a reply. The sky was darkening. He was sure that if he did nothing he'd never see her again. He tossed the idea back and forward in his mind before deciding.

The locker had been fabricated in the mine workshops from quarter inch sheet steel. It had been an exercise for the apprentices. What it lacked in aesthetics it made up in strength. Duncan removed both padlocks and pulled back the hasps. The door creaked as he pulled it open.

From the top shelf he picked up his service revolver, still in its leather holster, he grabbed the FN rifle but had second thoughts. He put it back and took the pump action 12 bore. "Better in crowds," he thought.

He checked the magazines of each weapon. Six rounds in the revolver, six cartridges in the shotgun. He pulled the belt from the webbing that hung in the locker and put it around his waist. He filled two of the pouches with .38 shells for the revolver and put spare shotgun cartridges into his pockets. He'd try the hostel and hope she was there, he didn't know where else to look.

He reversed the Land Cruiser out of the drive and headed for the Township. His heart was thumping. He had gone a good way, and was only half a klick to the township when he saw the roadblock. Duncan slowed. He wound the window down. A white officer stepped in front with raised hand.

"You can't go through. There's trouble in the Township. Natives are a bit restless. Kaffers knocking seven shades of shit out of one another actually," he said with a grin. "You'll have to use the main road to get around the Township. Bit inconvenient I know. But there you go."

"I don't want to get through the Township I want to get into the Township. My "domestic" is stuck in there," said Duncan.

The Officer was bemused. "It's pretty hot in there at the moment. You can get another domestic you know if worst comes to worst. Besides not sure if I can let you through. Never occurred to me that anybody would be foolish enough to want to go in there. Why don't you go home and see what's left in the morning?"

"Fuck off. Just because you're a fat lot of good doesn't mean I'm going to sit on my arse."

"Wooooo there! No need to take that attitude. I'm trying to help you. If you're that bothered and intent on suicide I'll radio HQ and see if I can let you pass. Wait here." The officer walked towards his Land Rover.

Duncan didn't wait. He was holding the Land Cruiser in gear. As soon as the Officer was clear he gunned the engine and let out the clutch. The Land cruiser leapt forward, rear wheels spinning. A constable raised his rifle.

"Don't shoot", shouted the Officer. "He's got enough problems coming as it is. I hope she's a good shag at least." He watched as the vehicle disappeared into the Township.

His was the only vehicle that wove down the deserted

potholed road. He used dimmed sidelights for guidance. There was no electricity in the town. Duncan thought it had been turned off. A few shanties and slums yielded shafts of yellow kerosene fuelled light into the descending darkness. He needed no directions. He'd spent days pouring over survey maps of the area for it was deep beneath the ground that the vast empty worked-out asbestos caverns lay. And he'd been here before. Once he'd been making a field tour and he came through the Township. He had been driven by some subconscious force and curiosity to see where she lived. He knew the building. He slowed to a crawl as he got to the crossroads. "Left for the hostel, up the hill," he thought as he selected first gear to pull around the corner. A bonfire burnt high on the hill, close to the hostel. He stopped and heard the chanting through the open driver's window. Quickly he reversed out of the crowd's sight.

Getting out of the Land Cruiser he walked to the corner, shotgun in hand. He could see the extent of the crowd and crossed the road to try and get a view of the hostel, to see if it too was burning but his view was obscured. "God, I'm too late," he thought.

From the shadow he saw the flicker of movement. Wedged in a tiny gap between two buildings he saw the shape. Duncan pointed the shotgun. "Come out, come out now," he said.

A scrawny figure emerged. He wore coveralls from the mines. His hands were raised comically to their full extent. "Don't shoot me Boss," he pleaded.

Duncan stepped forward and grabbed the man by the arm and dragged him to the Land Cruiser.

"I won't shoot you if you tell me what is going on," said Duncan.

The man spoke without hesitation and with unexpected eloquence. "The last of my people are trapped in the hostel. I have been listening. Word has come that the hostel is to be burnt, then they will all be killed. I have a plan, I am trying to save them."

"Who is in the hostel, who is to be burnt?" asked Duncan.

"The last of the Matable," replied the man, "The hostel is full, all the rest are gone or dead. Have you come to help as well?"

Duncan did not answer the question. He was thinking, trying to find a way. "How many people are inside?" he asked.

"I'm not totally sure, sixty or seventy. No more."

"And what is your plan?" asked Duncan.

Elizabeth stood in the hostel courtyard. She spoke to Oliver, her rescuer. "How many people," she asked.

"I have counted he replied. We have eight men, twenty-six children and thirty-two women, 33 with you. Sixty-eight people in total. That is all that is left."

In a corner sat a few women with suckling babies, the youngest children, oblivious to the danger, seeking succour from their mother's teat.

"We must make a plan. What are our options? There must be some."

"The men are at the front with some of the older children. They gather stones and throw them back at the crowd to keep the mob at bay. But I do not know how long they can hold out if the Shona make a serious charge. At best they only give us some time."

Elizabeth nodded. "What about escape?"

"This is our only hope. There is open land at the back of the building. If we can get across safely and make the bush, we then have a chance of getting away, some of us at least. The biggest danger will be crossing the open ground. We need the cover of darkness for this."

Elizabeth shook her head. "The Shona are not stupid. They will have thought of this. If we leave the shelter of the building they will attack us. It will be the end. Nobody will make it to the bush."

"Then what?" asked Oliver. "Do we stay here and perish, for no one will come to rescue us, that is sure."

"We must hold on as long as we can. In such a situation things change very quickly. My father taught me this. Success comes to those who stay calm and are ready for the opportunity that dawns."

"I do not believe an opportunity will come but I will stay as long as I can. Then I will run. I will carry one child under each arm. That is all I can do. If all the men do that we will save some of the children."

"Who will choose the ones to stay?" asked Elizabeth.

Oliver shrugged.

"I will stay with the children. I will not leave them. But you must help me prepare to resist as long as possible."

"Tyoni must be ready now. His men will be in position," said

Wilfred to Makonzo.

The two men stood on the flat roof of the building opposite the hostel, looking down on the crowd and the blazing bonfire.

"We will wait a few minutes more. The men inside are still throwing stones back at us. Every one that comes at us makes the person throwing more tired. None of them will have the strength to run soon." He laughed.

Wilfred nodded. "I will go down and get the boys ready with the petrol bombs. I will stand by the gates, by the post on the left." He pointed. "When I see you wave I will send the boys forward. Then the end will begin." Wilfred went down into the crowd to make preparations.

The main square was quiet. Shopkeepers had put up their shutters to protect their businesses. Stray dogs, sensing an opportunity to scavenge freely wandered. Duncan drove slowly with dipped lights. His companion pointed. He'd seen what he was looking for. Three buses were parked, in darkness, side by side, waiting for the dawn and another day's work.

Duncan picked the nearest, a bright yellow Leyland. *"Sunshine Bus Company"* was written down the side in foot high letters. He pulled up alongside. Within seconds he was trying the door. It was wedged shut. From within a bleary eyed driver, was roused. The sight of Duncan waving his revolver was sufficient to attract his attention. Reluctantly he opened the door.

"Keys!" Duncan demanded.

The driver pulled a key out of his pocket. It was attached to an old wooden cotton reel with a piece of blue twine.

"How much fuel in the tank?"

"More than half. Enough to get to Salisbury in the morning." stuttered the driver.

"You're not going to Salisbury," said Duncan snatching the key from the driver's hand.

"I hope you can drive," said Duncan to his new friend. "Otherwise the plan is useless?"

"No problem Boss," he said taking the key.

"Lock yourself in and follow me. You know what to do."

Duncan turned back to the bewildered driver. "Out."

"My things?"

"Thirty seconds. Move."

The driver needed no further prodding. In under half a

minute he stood with coat, bedding and bag, watching his bus trundle out of the terminus.

Makonzo was ready to give the signal. Wilfred was in position at the wide gateway. Red milk crates were by his feet and he was surrounded by adolescent children champing for the instruction. Makonzo raised his arm and let it fall. Wilfred started handing out the Molotov Cocktails.

"They are coming!" Oliver came quickly from the front of the building. "They are throwing petrol bombs. Get the children ready we will leave now and take our chances."

"No, wait," said Elizabeth raising her voice.

She knew it would be difficult to get men to listen to a woman. That was African culture, but she had to try once more.

"I am the daughter of Dingisgani. I speak with knowledge. You must listen to me."

"You may be the daughter of a great chief but what do you know of fighting? You are a woman."

"True," she said, "I have not trained as a soldier and I have never served in an Impi, but I have spent many nights, too many to remember, listening to my father and the elders discussing strategy and tactics. You should at least listen to me."

For a moment the men were quiet in respect of the Princess.

She continued. "I know that if I was in the position of our attackers nothing would give me more pleasure than to lure the occupants of this house into an open space. The ground at the back of this building is such an open space. It is nothing more than a killing field. Would we not want to do the same thing ourselves if their positions were reversed? I wager that even as we speak our attackers have their best people lying in wait. We must not leave that way."

"So what do you propose then? What is your plan?"

"We have no option but to stay and fight. Better to die fighting than be hacked down from behind, running like the Shona dogs."

Oliver did not answer her, instead he spoke to all in the room.

"Get the women and children ready. We will leave soon, out of the back. If by running like dogs we can save some of the children we should run."

The crowds emotions had been building for this final

moment, the elimination of the Matable in Mashava. A youth ran forward from the crowd holding a bottle with a blazing rag stuffed into its neck. He stopped and brought his arm forward in a sweeping arc, releasing the missile at the top of its swing. The flaming vessel continued and dropped just short of the building, breaking on the floor and splashing a ball of flame against the wall of the building. The crowd cheered as the youth returned triumphant to the crowd. Another youth ran forward with another missile. From the shadows of the building a lone Matable defender stepped out and hurled a stone at the attacker. It flew wide of its mark, falling uselessly on the ground. The crowd laughed at the feeble defence. Another fire bomb flew. It was only time now, a short period of time.

Nobody in the crowd heard the engines coming from behind so intent were they on the task in hand. The Land Cruiser led, the bus followed. The drivers had taken a run at the hill, they drove at the crowd. They knew to slow down was to lose momentum and the element of surprise. They would not swerve. It was for the people to move and the people would have little warning. Until the last second, both vehicles travelled in darkness. A few yards from the hostel Duncan turned on his lights and pressed a hand on the horn. It was almost too late for the crowd. To all it was clear the vehicles were not going to stop. Panic broke out, people pushed and jostled to get clear. Some were luckier than others.

It was over in seconds. People were hit, some knocked to the ground. Miraculously nobody went under the wheels. The path cleared quickly before them and suddenly they were through the swathe of people, crossing that narrow piece of unoccupied land before the gates.

Duncan drove through the wide open gap and veered to the left. The bus followed, along the side of the building and into the courtyard that was protected on three sides by buildings. Already flames jumped from the front of the building, a section of the roof was alight, shedding welcome light in the courtyard. Inside smoke was filling the corridors. The fire was taking its grip. Wooden beams crackled as they burnt. The intensity of the flames increased and mysterious metallic echoes came from above as the corrugated iron roof began to buckle under the intense heat. Mothers fought to control panic, children had fear in their eyes. Men shepherded women and children to the back of the building. Soon there would be nowhere to go.

But Elizabeth had not given up hope. Alone she dodged the spreading fire and kept watch on the front. From the crowd outside the youths continued dashind forward to throw their missiles. She knew it was their intention to watch the Matable burn to death if they did not run out the back. Suddenly she noticed a change in tone from the crowd. It was as if their jeers had changed to howls of panic. The crowd parted and she saw the vehicles. It was too dark to see the driver but she thought she recognised the Land Cruiser. Her heart filled with hope as she made her way to the back of the building. It did not need to be explained to her. She ushered what people she could find before her. The opportunity was clear. She knew they would have to be quick before the Shona crowd recovered.

She got to the courtyard. The bus had stopped and was already turning. The Land Cruiser was out of sight. Matable men saw the bus and hardly dared to believe their eyes. No orders were given. Men surrounded women and children, providing a shield.

Mashava Township, The Hostel

From his place on the roof of the building opposite Makonzo had seen the vehicles coming. He'd shouted to the crowd but his voice had been lost. It was only when the vehicles were inside that Wilfred, still at the gate, turned to look at his leader. But he did not need instructions; Wilfred knew he must stop the vehicles leaving.

Makonzo came down from the roof. He called the youth that had thrown the first petrol bomb. "You have more important work to do. At the back of the hostel, around the waste ground, before the bush, our Cadre wait. You must go and find Tyoni, the leader, and tell him what has happened, tell him about the bus. Tell him he must attack the back of the building immediately. Go as quickly as you can. They must not be allowed to escape."

Duncan did not wait with the bus. He drove the Land Cruiser towards the front of the building, stopping between the crowd and the blazing building. In a second he was out, of the back of the vehicle, brandishing his 12 bore for the crowd to see. He hand dropped to his side to feel the comforting reassurance of the service revolver, still in its holster.

Momentarily the crowd was subdued at the turn of events. But then a child ran forward and hurled a stone at the vehicle. It struck the windscreen and the glass cracked. The lowly child's act of defiance encouraged the mob. Another ran forward and hurled a missile. The crowd regained confidence as each second passed. Duncan looked over his shoulder, it was too soon for the bus, he knew. He focused forward again. Another fearless child darted forward from the crowd and hurled half a brick at the Land Cruiser. Had he more strength it might have posed a problem but the missile fell short. The next one bounced on the bonnet with a metallic thud. He didn't see where it came from. The crowds howls grew in intensity, their courage fed by their own noise. Others ran forward. Somebody climbed a gatepost and goaded the crowd further forward. People behind began to push. Duncan knew that at any second the line could break. There would be a rush and then there would be no stopping the flood of rioters. He needed more time.

He pumped the slide action under the barrel of the shotgun and let go two rounds in quick succession, over the mob's head. Momentarily they were taken aback and retreated a few steps. But it was only seconds before the stones started again. He traversed the barrel of the shotgun, stopping and pointing at the more threatening characters. But the shotgun was no discouragement for the reckless bravery of youth. Children ran forward, shaming their elders into following. The man on the gatepost leapt from his perch. Now he stood in front of the crowd gesticulating, urging the people forward. Duncan aimed. He'd made up his mind. A sacrifice had to be made. He prepared to pull the trigger. He was ready to shoot.

At last, from behind, Duncan heard the revving engine and horn of the bus. He turned to look. It was coming. The driver was low in his seat, head and eyes barely visible. Duncan signalled the bus through. It was a mistake to take his eye off the crowd. His eyes saw a flash of red as the stone hit him square on the temple. He felt warm blood trickle down his face. Black spots danced in front of his eyes and there was an overwhelming desire to vomit. He struggled for balance, wavering on the back of the truck. The bus came on. He knew it must not stop. The crowed sensing Duncan's vulnerability began to surge. The bus drove into the crowd; they were not willing to yield. Stones broke windows and sticks beat against the side panels. Duncan, by strength of will forced himself back into consciousness. He aimed the shotgun above the heads of the crowd and pumped the mechanism.

The shots barely silenced the crowd this time but the bus didn't falter, going forward it even managing to accelerate. The sound of stones bouncing off the bus increased, like a storm of giant hailstones. On the floor and between the seats women and children cowered for protection. Men with sticks were ready to beat any that tried to enter the vehicle. When he could not see Oliver drove by instinct. Everybody's life depended on his luck and judgement. Those at the rear of the crowd were becoming angry and frustrated. They pushed forward. A woman at the front slipped, her scream was piercing as the front wheel of the bus crushed her legs. A man was knocked flat and disappeared under the chassis. The bus went on. In what seemed like an instant there were less people and more hope. Gravity assisted as the bus ran downhill faster. For a while the mob ran alongside beating the vehicle and shouting. Gradually the numbers fell off and it became clear it was too late to stop the escape.

Duncan's mind was clearing. He recognised the danger of his own isolation. He knew he must follow the bus quickly, before the crowd turned all their attention on him. He jumped to the ground but before he could get into the cab the provocateur, the one that had stood on the gate was in front of him, waving the eighteen inch blade of his panga.

He charged forward. It was suicide. Duncan pulled the revolver from its holster. One shot. It hit the man in the chest. The attacker dropped the panga and fell to the ground. Nobody came forward to take up the charge. Blood spurted from the attackers wound, the liquid looked black in the flickering light of the burning building. Wilfred died doing his master's bidding.

Duncan did not wait. He took advantage of the crowd's respite and drove the Land Cruiser at the crowd. He hit people, many, he did not know how many. He didn't see the boy come from the side. He didn't see him lunge with the fence post. Later on he couldn't recall the side window breaking but he did remember the explosion on the side of his head, the feeling as darkness descended and consciousness slipped away.

He awoke in bed. His head throbbed. It was like a hangover. It took time to recollect events in his mind. He touched his temple. It was sore. There was a lump. He heard the clock tick at the side of his bed. He turned his head to see the time. The room was too dull. The curtains were drawn. He lifted himself and strained. Eleven thirty. Daylight breached gaps in the curtains, darts of light penetrating the room. It was morning. The fog lifted from his mind, parts of what happened came back to him, but not all. The Township, the crowd, the bus, it wasn't a dream, it was real enough. Elizabeth! His heart missed a beat. He pushed himself up in the bed once more. Where was Elizabeth? He swung his feet around and sat on the edge of the bed, for the first time aware of his nakedness.

The bedroom door was ajar. He heard a noise in the kitchen. Instinctively he knew it was her and he was relieved. He wanted to stand but his head swirled. He slumped back. Nausea swept over him again. He closed his eyes, time passed. He didn't see her come into the room. Her voice had softness, a softness he hadn't heard before. She spoke with a gentle familiarity and he felt good.

"It's good you have woken at last. Now I know you are

getting better. But do not be ambitious, you must rest more, lie down, I will bring you something for the headache."

"How do you know about the headache?" His voice was hoarse.

She smiled. "You deserve to have a headache after last night."

"I do have a headache."

Elizabeth leaned over him and pulled the sheet higher. He caught the waft of sensual musk and despite his condition he felt stirrings. He tried to dispel the thoughts but his eyes followed her involuntarily as she left the room. He knew it was not just her voice that was different, her whole demeanour had changed. He felt good as he drifted off once more.

The clock said four when he next woke. The headache had lifted, the lump remained. He stretched his body, arching his back, and took a deep breath, life coming back into aching muscles. He watched the ceiling fan slowly spinning. It was like a dream.

Elizabeth came into the room carrying a tray. She placed it on the chest of drawers. "I will help you," she said.

Duncan didn't need help but he let her come to in any case. He wanted to feel her closeness and smell her again. Her arms were strong, her hands soft. She pulled him forward and arranged the pillows.

"I need a shower," he said.

"Eat first. It will give you strength. Then I will help you shower."

He was not shocked at the suggestion, only compliant to her will. She fed him soup, a soup he had not tasted before.

"What is this?" he asked.

"It is traditional. It is the meal we give to returning warriors. It is to give you back your strength."

"It's good," he said between mouthfuls.

He was in the shower. She directed the stream of warm water over him. He stood motionless and she washed him with gentle hands. It was natural and beautiful. She dried him with a towel as tenderly as a mother treats a child. For his part he stood like an obedient child and let her work unhindered. She made him sit, wrapped in a towel, while she changed the bed sheets.

"You suffered last night. For a time I was worried and thought I would have to call the white man's doctor."

"But you didn't?"

"No I wanted to make you better myself. What you did for me was good, it became my duty to care for you."

She helped him back into the bed. He lay between the fresh white sheets still naked.

"You are doing this because it is your duty?" he asked, disappointment tingeing his words.

She looked into his eyes. "Just because something is a duty, it does not mean it is not also a pleasure," she smiled. "When a mother takes care of her family it is a duty but nobody other than a mother experience's the pleasure she gets when she sees her child happy and contented. Sometimes it is not only an honour but also a pleasure to fulfil a duty."

Her words brought back memories of his mother's lonely and forlorn existence on the bleak and desolate Scottish hillside. Carefully she had nurtured him with little hope of physical reward, now he knew he was the only pleasure for her.

She looked deep into his eyes and saw the depths of his sadness and knew she had inadvertently touched a suppressed emotion and exposed a childlike vulnerability in the man. It made her want to be closer to him. Without further words she stood before him and undressed. He looked at her, he wanted to hold and touch her, but not because of lust. Naked she pulled back the sheet and slipped in beside him. For the first time their naked bodies touched and it was if it were natural, there was an emotional symmetry in their union.

In her mind she said that she was with him because he needed her. She was justly giving him what he deserved for the risks and actions he had taken on her behalf. But inside she knew that what she did was not an act of charity or thankfulness, it was more to do with her own deep desires. He pulled her close in an embrace, his lips gently brushed hers and felt their soft warmth. His hands travelled and marvelled at her silky skin. She was perfect in all ways. For her too it was the first experience of carnal love and although her thoughts were pure, she could not and did not want to resist the desires of the flesh.

She ran her fingers over the toned muscles of his chest. She kissed his neck and her hands explored. For an eternity they gently caressed each other. Eventually they were ready. He gently pushed and she lay on her back, she did not resist. He entered her and she pulled him closer. He moved and felt her willing response; there movements were in unison, a perfect harmony. Slowly their rhythm increased, building to in fervour. They embraced to make themselves as one until their feelings broke in an eruption, a magic crescendo of emotion and love. Afterwards they lay silently entwined in each other's arms each inwardly celebrating the perfect union of uninhibited happiness.

There existed a paradox in their unity. He was the Master and she the servant, yet it was he that came from common stock whilst royal blood ran through her veins. In the paradox they found unity as they were temporally freed from the fetters imposed by a prejudiced topsy-turvy society. For hours as they lay in each others arms and, somehow liberated, each whispered to the other their inner feelings in a way they had been unable to with any other person before.

Elizabeth, since the death of her mother had had to repress her feelings. She fell into the role of a "rock" that gave emotional strength to her father when it was her that was most in need of such support. But she had existed in Matable culture, a culture unsympathetic to women. Women were supposed to carry their burdens in solitary silence.

Duncan, by skin colour and accident of birth was not part of this repressive regime. Elizabeth was free to communicate with the culturally blank canvas of his mind. She opened her heart and mind to him and he was a receptive vessel. She explained about the great loss that the death of her mother had been, the greatness and vulnerability of her father and her devotion to her twin brothers. She spoke not only of good times but also of hardship. Her words contained a deep truth only achievable through modest serenity.

Duncan listened to her gratitude for the work he gave her and how the money she earned meant so much to so many. He felt guilt at his selfishness for the way he jealously guarded his wealth compared to the selfless generosity she displayed, although she had so little. He'd always felt uncomfortable at the privilege afforded him by being white, but now he felt the shame of his meanness, made worse because Elizabeth never complained. That was another of her qualities. He was taken by the proud sincerity of her words and most of all her intelligence. Now he knew she was more than an intellectual match for him, and almost all the white people on the settlement too. He remembered how she had stoically tasted and swallowed the bitter pills given so regularly by the truly inferior and bigoted regime of the Camp Housekeeper.

When she'd finished talking there were tears in his eyes

because he knew what she had spoken was from her innermost heart and in this confession it was implicit that he would have to do the same.

He began his story on the barren windswept hillsides of Stornoway, a climate difficult to comprehend to people who only knew sunshine and warmth and where footwear was an option. He described a cold stone crofter's cottage that made her thankful for her African rondarval. He told of depravations and hardships that black Africans thought white people never had to endure. He explained how as a child he would sit, alone, looking out to sea and dream of adventure. All she had known was the community and bond conferred by tribal life and the feeling of belonging. She felt gratitude for her good fortune, for her escape from the torture of isolation and loneliness. It was clear to them both how inverted their lives were, yet in the diversity they had found a bond that was unifying. They were in truth master and servant yet it was Elizabeth who was the princess and Duncan the pauper in so many ways.

When Duncan finished his story the irrevocable bond had been completed and they consummated their relationship once more with passion.

The sun had gone. They lay together, naked flesh touching naked flesh. Slowly he drifted away. For the first time in his memory his mind was in communion with another soul and the feeling was good. When he awoke in the morning she was gone.

Lusaka Airport, Zambia 1976

Perspiration ran down Silas Sovimbo's brow and his shirt stuck to his back. He was the sole occupant of the decrepit VIP Lounge at Lusaka International. Nobody came to Lusaka airport unless they had to; Zambia was bankrupt, strangled by the Rhodesian war. He looked at the silent air-conditioning units and the motionless ceiling fans and shook his head. The only relief from the stifling humidity was the draught from the broken windows.

He was becoming impatient with the heat and waiting. He picked up an ancient Lusaka Times from the complementary stand. The head line said it all. "Blacks Fight Blacks Whilst Whites Look On" The editorial ridiculed the guerrilla movements for the inter-tribal rivalry and fighting. "News?" he thought. "What news, this is our entire history." He discarded the paper.

The silence was broken as three men entered the room, two uniformed Immigration Officers and a third in a freshly pressed safari suit. The one in the safari suit wore black framed sunglasses and walked with a swagger that it would have been comic if the man were not to serious about himself. Their footsteps echoed on the tiles as they walked towards Silas.

One of the immigration men held out his hand. Silas handed over his red diplomatic UN passport. The official made a show of looking at the photograph and checking it against Silas's features.

"You're not Chinese?" said the man with sunglasses.

Silas looked sarcastically at the back of his black hands. "No. You're right. I'm African."

"But you are the official Chinese representative?"

"Yes. The Chinese don't think that black men need yellow men to represent them. They think we can speak for ourselves so they sent me," replied Silas.

"The Russians are sending a proper representative!" said the taller Immigration man.

"That's the Russians. But don't you think a black man can be a 'proper' representative?" Silas held out his hand for his passport. "No stamp," he said, "Nobody should know I have been here."

The Immigration Official handed back the document and left.

The tall man in the safari suit spoke. "My name is Longa. I am with International Affairs. I will look after you during your visit. Now we go to the Guesthouse. It is nearby."

"You were late," said Silas, surprised by the absence of an apology.

"No petrol for the car," replied Longa. "Even Government cars have to buy on the black market now. It takes time. It's the way here. Besides it's no matter, the other visitor has not arrived yet." Even as he spoke the sound of jet engines winding down on the apron could be heard.

The Tupolev 104 was the first Russian passenger jet. It bore a remarkable resemblance to the De Havilland Comet. In fact Mr Tupolev had an uncanny knack of coincidentally coming up with designs similar to many other Western planes. Unfortunately the similarities, in the case of the TU104, were very much restricted to the visual. When the plane first came into service Western observers thought the reason it stopped at every major airport on its route was because the Russians wanted to show it off. However it soon became apparent that the frequent stops were required because of its very limited range. The fuel tanks were too small and the engines too greedy. It got the nickname 'roller coaster', continuously up and down.

Sergi Andropov was on his first visit to Africa, first trip outside of the USSR in fact. He thought the TU104 was very good and the 23 hour journey from Moscow to Lusaka with fourteen stops quite normal. Then again he had nothing with which to compare it. He'd sat alone and hadn't spoken to anybody for the entire journey. Russians rarely spoke to strangers, it was too dangerous. Uncle Joe might be dead but the Gulags were still open. The plane had more than fifty passengers when it left Moscow, only half a dozen remained when it arrived at Lusaka. As the plane taxied to a halt a stewardess came to Sergi. "Wait here. Let the others get off first."

Sergi watched his fellow travellers disembark and be ushered onto a waiting bus.

"They are ready for you Comrade," said the stewardess at last. A Zil pulled up at the bottom of the steps. The product of the Moscow Motor Works the Zil was the Soviet Union's response to the American Cadillac. The uniformed driver held open a door for Sergi. The two indifferent Immigration Officials who had just seen Silas now stood by the Zil at full attention. They nodded Sergi through. This was the extent of formalities for an important Russian visitor.

The Zil was designed to give a luxurious ride around the well paved roads of the world's capital cities. The ability to negotiate crumbling tarmac and Zambian potholes was not in the design specification. The wild rocking motion and the thuds as the suspension grounded on its rubber stops made for an uncomfortable ride. Sergi felt there was more turbulence on the ground than in the air. Work was impossible, concentration difficult. It was all he could do to hold on and look through the darkened windows at the impoverished decaying world outside. On first impressions it did feel as though he had just left the world's first Socialist Worker's Paradise.

The building was still called Federation House even though the Federation was a distant memory. It was designed to reflect the real-politic of the period when it was built. Three self contained wings with sleeping and dining facilities, joined at the hub, like the spokes of a wheel, each wing named after a country of the Federation; Rhodesia, Zambia and Malawi. The central hub contained conference rooms and communal areas. Its location close to the airport was ideal from the planned clandestine meeting, away from the prying eyes of Lusaka and the media.

Silas rose to his feet as Longa ushered Sergi into the conference room next morning. It was a mannerly but not warm meeting. The men faced each other over the conference table that was only a few feet wide, but the real distance between them was an infinite ideological chasm.

"First the formalities. I need your Official Credentials gentlemen," said Longa.

Each man handed their host a sealed envelope.

"Please sit and wait. We will begin soon." Longa left the room. Silent minutes passed slowly. Suddenly the double doors were flung open. "Gentlemen! Gentlemen! Gentlemen! How good of you to come. Please don't get up."

Kenneth Kaunda, President of Zambia, stood in the doorway, arms raised in a dramatic gesture more suited to a cabaret act.

"I will sit here," said Kaunda, picking the chair at the head of the table. The two men suppressed their surprise in diplomatic fashion.

"I will start gentlemen as it was I that orchestrated the meeting."

Many were disarmed by Kaunda's extrovert personality but beneath the extrovert façade lurked a shrewd political negotiator. "I know you did not expect to see me. Please accept my apologises for the surprise, but I need you to know the importance that my government and I attach to this matter."

Kenneth Kaunda was born in 1924 the son of a Presbyterian Preacher and was brought up in various missions. He became a teacher and taught in missionary schools for many years. Throughout his life he never shook off the habit of talking to people as if they were school children, even if they did happen to be national leaders of countries often more influential than his own. During his period on the copper belt he became politicised and was imprisoned for his troubles on many occasions. Eventually he led his country to independence, becoming its first black Prime Minister. He supported the independence struggles of his neighbours, often to the detriment of the Zambian people. He allowed both the Matable and Shona to have offices and military bases in Zambia.

Kaunda spoke as an admonishing teacher. "My people are making great sacrifices for their brothers in Zimbabwe. The sacrifices are made so that ordinary black people may become free, not so the political leaders can fight for power amongst themselves. I have a single demand. The tribal fighting stops now. This is my non-negotiable position. Anything else we can talk about."

"Now," he continued, "you two are sent as representatives of the paymasters of the war. Russia and China declare they are helping the liberation struggle for ideological reasons. I am inclined to believe this although there are others who are more cynical."

"Sergi Andropov, you represent the USSR and support the Matable. Silas Sovimbo you are here on behalf of the Chinese who support the Shona. Together China and the Soviet Union finance the totality of the liberation struggle but the help is strictly divided on tribal lines. To a simple man like me it seems that such a situation creates the environment for a competitive not co-operative dynamic."

"I want you to tell me your positions, for undoubtedly you have a brief. But first, Silas, you are a Shona. I invited China to send a representative. Explain to me why do they send you?"

Silas squared his back and looked directly at Sergi. With the conviction of twenty years adherence to Maoist principles he spoke.

"The Peoples Republic of China strongly believes that self-determination is the right of all nations. They have gratefully accepted your invitation but want you to accept me as their official envoy because they believe only a Zimbabwean can speak for Zimbabwe. They believe it is insulting and condescending for the subject people to be ignored in important discussions."

Sergi reacted to the provocation. "Nonsense! This is political rhetoric!" He banged the table with the flat of his hand. "The so-called Peoples Republic of China refuses to sit together in any forum with the USSR because they cannot accept the USSR as the leader of the International Socialist Revolution. The lie that was just spoken is easily exposed. If they were so concerned about self-determination their soldiers would not now be marching into Tibet, crushing by force a two-thousand year old civilisation. China is colonialist when it suits."

Silas was on his feet. "How can your pampered leaders present themselves as Socialists? Exclusive shops stuffed with Western luxuries for Party members whilst the People go hungry, Dachas in the countryside when ordinary people live ten to a stinking room. The Russian Leadership feed at the same trough as the Imperialists!"

Sergi now stood. "You are no more than the lackey of your Chinese masters; a messenger boy."

The two men faced each other and became aware of the gentle tapping of Kaunda's fingernail on the polished wooden table.

"You took the bait too easily. Please sit down." He spoke in a gentle voice.

Both men sank back into their chairs.

"Good." Kaunda smiled exposing his brilliant teeth. "There is nothing like a frank exchange of views to clear the air. Now everybody knows where the other stands. This will make discussions much easier. Let us have some nice Kenyan coffee and I will tell you about my family before you get to work with my officials".

Nine hours later Kaunda returned. He read the document. "This is good gentlemen. Yes very good. I am sure it will be acceptable to all parties."

The document was the result of the day's talks between Sergi and Silas. Kaunda went over the main points.

"One. For the duration of the liberation struggle the military wings of all political movements will be united under an umbrella organisation called the Patriotic Front."

"Two. The Patriotic Front will assume a joint military command for the conduct of the war and ensure that conflict between the rival guerrilla groups is avoided."

"Three. The political organisations will continue to work independently but will put the suffix PF to their names. So the Shona Zanu Party will be known as Zanu PF and the Matable Zapu Party will be known as Zapu PF."

"Now gentleman we should see if we can finish on a good note. Each of you should request a token gesture from the other, something small but significant. This is so both of you can go home and claim that you have not returned empty handed. Silas what would make you happy?"

Silas thought for a moment. "In Tanzania we have bases for both Chinese and Russians, yet in Zambia you only have Russian bases. If you would allow a small Chinese base in your country this would be very pleasing and seen as a positive move by my sponsors."

Kaunda looked to Sergi. "What do you say to that?"

"My superiors would be unhappy with that. It would be difficult for me to make such a concession."

Kaunda smiled. "Then you are fortunate. It is not a concession for you to give. It is a concession for me to give. So you are asked to give nothing. I, as President of Zambia, will grant this request."

"Sergi?"

"My request is practical. You have a fighter on your side. A person of, shall we say a particular enthusiasm. One who at times has difficulty identifying the enemy. I request he be withdrawn from the field. He is known by the name of Makonzo. You may be aware of him?"

Silas maintained his composure, concealing the bitter disappointment and shame of fathering the most loathed liberation fighter.

Selebwi Pickwi Refugee Camp, Botswana

"It's all over, rest now." The soft Irish accent of the Nurse was reassuring.

Elizabeth lay back. The pain had subsided, waves of tiredness swept across her mind but sleep remained elusive. The old iron framed hospital bed was a luxury. She closed her eyes to satisfy the nun but her mind continued to race.

She knew it was impossible but it was not a mistake. Common-sense said she should not have given herself to Duncan, but for once common-sense had not prevailed. She knew there were laws, white man's laws, laws that forbade Duncan to her. And there were tribal rules, traditional laws, which forbade her to Duncan. She knew that as she slipped from his arms while he slept, they had no future. She took $20 in notes and change from his wallet and trouser pocket. She left a note saying she would pay it back even though the wages Duncan owed her more than $20. She took bread and cheese for her journey. Without daring a final look she left the house and walked as the sun rose.

There was no going back to the township. Mashava meant certain death, that life was over. She would return to her tribal village, to the home of her father. Her journey would be long and dangerous. She walked in the "wrong" direction to avoid the remnants of the rioters. She avoided the main paths and relied on her instinctive knowledge of the bush for direction. It was a long walk. She dared not stop for rest. The sun was at its peak before she chanced breaking cover and joining the main road. The traffic was almost non existent. It was more than an hour before she saw what she wanted. The ramshackle Bedford mini bus slowly trundled towards her. The front near side suspension had collapsed and that corner of the bodywork was perilously close to the ground. At the wave of her hand the vehicle shuddered to a halt. The rusty side door slid open. Elizabeth pushed her way into the rear, joining the other passengers. The driver took the 25 cent fare before forcing the column change lever into first. The tired under-powered engine spluttered as the unofficial bus pulled away. There was a menacing clang as the driver yanked the gear lever into second. Despite the nature of the transport Elizabeth was grateful to be moving away from Mashava.

The news of the Shona attack on the Matable spread quickly. Dingisgani's heart hurt with fear for his precious daughter. The Twins wanted to take the Impi and rush to Mashava Township to search for their sister. Their father counselled against the idea.
"The fighting is stopped those that are dead are dead. There are no prisoners, nobody to rescue. Maybe some escaped. They will be making their way back," he spoke more in hope than in conviction.
"An attack on the Shona now will only attract the wrath of the Rhodesian Soldiers. You will end up fighting the wrong people and lose."
"But we must have our vengeance," argued the Twins. "They must pay for what they have done."
"You are right, they must and they will pay. But we will not present them with the bill until we know the full cost. No, we will bide our time and actions. Retribution will be planned and deliberate."
Despite wise words Dingisgani fought to control his emotion. As the days passed the hope of seeing his daughter again faded but just as all had seemed lost she finally returned.
Dingisgani was lifted by Elizabeth's return. For days he would not let her leave his side. The twins stayed in the village too. They had orders not to attack. Momentous changes were taking place far away. In the village they did not know it yet but the war had been lost by the White Man. White Rhodesians no longer looked for victory, only for what they could retrieve from the ashes. They were being defeated not on the field of battle but by the treachery of their main ally, South Africa. The apartheid regime, south of the Limpopo, anxious to maintain control, was bowing to pressure to withdraw support from the Rhodesian rebels. The time was fast approaching for the Rhodesians to seek a settlement and salvage what they could. But Rhodesians were obstinate and slow learners.
Whilst the political leaders sought a way Dingisgani rested with all his children. For a time there was a joy in the Kraal that had been absent for many harvests. Dingisgani pretended that bygone days had returned but he knew it was only a reminder of what had once been. It was no real surprise when the "big talks" failed and the Twins were recalled to the Matopas. The fighting would continue for

now. But Dingisgani did not suspect Elizabeth would once again leave him.

As a woman does, Elizabeth knew when the blood did not come the first time. But she waited for another moon cycle to pass. Still the blood did not appear. In the village the Nanga, the spirit medium, was the keeper of secrets. She alone could withhold truth from the King. She spoke wise words and was custodian of the oracles that guided the tribe. Only here could Elizabeth confide.

The two women were alone, they sat cross legged, facing each other over the fire. As the flames of the Spirits gently danced, Elizabeth confessed her story, prayed for forgiveness and sought advice of the Wise Ones. When she had finished talking the Nanga looked up, for the first time moving her gaze away from the flames.

Her words were not of admonishment, they were kindly and gentle, "Since the time you drew you first breath I have known you. Then I had not this shrivelled face but never did I possess the beauty of your dear mother, whom I knew well and of whom you are the mirror."

The Nanga looked again into the flames.

"I can see your life, I can see you. I know the story you told and the feelings are the truth. You are honest and whole of heart. This is good and will help you in the future. Your strong heart is the foundation of your life, you must be true to it."

"The days ahead will be difficult. Of this there is no doubt. There are decisions for you to make. Tell me what is in your heart now."

Elizabeth moved uneasily but looked directly at the woman opposite. "I feel a glow inside. It is a good feeling. When I lie down at night I feel not despair but happiness for what is growing. But then I shake myself from this romantic dream. I am wrong to feel this way. I know I bring great shame on my father and the people of our tribe."

Elizabeth continued. "I have heard you have the power to take this glow away. Although it hurts my heart I believe that this is the best."

"Oh child, you do not listen." The Nanga spoke. "I told you to be true to your heart and now you speak with your mind. Inside you is not a glow, it is a child. It is your child and what you feel is the beauty of motherhood. It is a good thing. Yes I have the skill to kill this baby in the womb. It is not magic and it carries danger for you. I have done it in the past and seen the results. Believe me as a woman, not as a Nanga, this is a bad path."

"But what of the shame I bring?"

"This is truly a problem as well. It is not only the shame. When the people realise the father is a white man they may kill the baby. Because of this I believe you must go from here and have your baby. I have heard of a place. To the west lies the country of Botswana. It is not like this country. The people do not fight, they do not have an army. But there are camps that accept people from our troubled lands. They are strict about who they accept. No soldiers or liberation fighters may enter. Only people in need are welcome. You are in need and must go there."

"But what about my father and my people?" said Elizabeth, "Will I ever see them again?"

"When the time is right you will. I alone will know where you are and when it is good I will send for you. You must trust me. I will clear the path for your return."

Elizabeth looked into the flames. She sorely wanted to stay, to be close to her father and people but knew the words of the Nanga were good.

"I will do it," Elizabeth said her eyes tearful for her father.

Suddenly the dying fire crackled and a shower of sparks erupted. Elizabeth leaned back in alarm.

The Nanga looked into the fire, a new yellow flame danced. She sat mesmerised. Her gaze was fixed and her eyes became cloudy. Slowly came the curl of a smile. She raised her head. "It is a hard road you will follow, I will be with you along the way but not at the end. There will be bad things on the road but in the end it will be good."

The Nanga stood. "Go now, I am finished."

The Nurse returned and handed Elizabeth the baby wrapped in a white sheet. Elizabeth cradled her child for the first time.

"He's healthy enough," said the Nun, "and strong but he's very pale. Maybe he'll darken later. Have you thought of a name yet?"

"Yes, I have", said Elizabeth. I want to call him James."

"James? Where did you get that from?"

"You don't like it?" asked Elizabeth.

"It's a Scottish name. We're Irish here. What about Patrick or Sean. They're good names."

Elizabeth shook her head. "No I will call him James."

The nun shook her head. "All right, James it is. Now let's not see you malingering in bed. I want you back in the college in a couple of days. Not everybody gets the chance to advance their education like you."

Purgo

Chimoio Gorge, Mozambique. 3rd September 1979

It felt like Elizabeth lived in his mind, always ready to step forward whenever his concentration lapsed.

Duncan was taking his turn as lookout, watching the gorge that was the choke point in the valley that led from the coastal plain to the interior of Mozambique. They were five miles east of the guerrilla camp, they waited in the place where the strategic road and railway routes criss-crossed. It was hard to stay focused on the deserted iron bridge. Something evoked the memory of her smell, the scent that had lingered in his imagination since that night. He remembered reaching out for her and the feeling of emptiness when he realised she was gone. The reality of the note that at the same time, said nothing and everything. Deep in his heart he believed their stolen time together had been as special to her as it had been to him and that one day they would be together again. He knew she was only being realistic when she went. When the fighting was over he would look for her and she for him, but for now he lay in wait, ready for what everybody knew would be the last major incursion of the war.

Duncan recalled the briefing. A date for the new talks had been set. Soon all the leaders, black and white, would meet at Lancaster House in London. It was clear the meeting was only to discuss the terms of surrender. But they were being asked to make one more effort, to give Ian Smith a position of strength in the negotiations, to show the world that the white regime still had the military will and ability to continue – even if it was not true.

"Lieutenant, I need to go down to the river and fill the water bottles. Is that okay?" A camouflage uniform crawled up beside Duncan.

"No. You have to wait till dusk. If you've no water have some of mine." Duncan pushed his water bottle towards the corporal.

Being an officer sat comfortably with Duncan although the
training had been minimal. A few weeks at Salisbury then a posting
to the Combat Engineering Company. He'd settled into his war
routine quickly, six weeks work, six weeks active service. Always the
same. For nine months he'd followed the routine without a break.

There'd been incursions before but this last one was going to
be the biggest, everybody knew that.

"Can't I go to the river before the mosquitoes come out? The
bastards bite me to death."

"No. It's too dangerous. Blow our cover and the whole
operation is compromised."

The corporal changed the subject. "This hanging about is
killing me, how much longer?"

"When we get the signal we go. Not before. Think about the
Sealous Scouts, they've been here five days longer than us," replied
Duncan.

"I didn't volunteer for the Scouts and I don't get their pay
either."

"That's enough whinging. Shut up now, I don't like old
women in my unit. This is a silent oppo."

"I need some warm food. Cold rations for all this time isn't
good."

"Corporal, just shut the fuck up. That's an order. Go and see
how the other two are doing and check out your kit whilst you're at
it. That C5 better go bang when we want it too."

The corporal sidled away. Duncan raised his field glasses and
looked down the hill. He lay on the lip of a small fold in the slope.
Top cover came from thinly spaced trees and the grass was high. The
dip was a perfect hiding place. The trees were not so thick as to stop
him seeing the river which wound its way along the valley bottom
about a hundred yards ahead. He could just make out the railway
track as it followed the course of the river. He focused his attention
on the metal structure, the combined road rail bridge that spanned
the narrow gorge at the neck of the valley. Duncan had reconnoitred
the bridge twice already. He was sure of his target.

Each year the tail of the monsoon drifted over the Indian
Ocean and dropped its watery residue on southern Africa. This was
the rainy season and when it happened everything came to a halt.
Rivers overflowed, roads and railways flooded, aircraft were
grounded and movement on foot became a mud laden nightmare.

That is why they waited at their jump off points. They needed a forecast of three clear days from the Army Meteorological Office. Everything else was set.

Rhodesian Air Force planes, bombers, fighters and transports, were armed and ready. Two companies of the RLI had arrived at their forward base inside Mozambique. Everybody would go on the signal *'Aztec'*. Once broadcast there was no turning back, the automatic sequence would have started and the main Shona base at Chimoio, central Mozambique, would be destroyed.

Duncan was about to lower his field glasses and allow his thoughts to return to Elizabeth when he saw the elephant grass to his right quiver in the still air. There were wart hogs around but they were noisy. Duncan let out a low pitched whistle to warn the others. Slowly and silently he cocked his FN and watched for more movement. Suddenly he felt steel pressing on the back of his neck. The sensation was unmistakable. It sent a shiver down his spine.

"Gotcha" said the South African with a chuckle. Duncan remained still. Then his assailant grunted. For a second there was no sound or movement. Then the corporal spoke.

"No. I got you."

Duncan rolled over to face the barrel of the Scout's gun. Behind the Scout was Duncan's corporal with his unsheathed bayonet pressing into the South African's back.

Duncan smiled. "Well done Corporal. You've redeemed your self."

"It was your whistle that warned us sir."

"Fuck off," said the South African, "We weren't trying in any case."

He let out a croak remarkably similar to that of a bull frog. A grinning black face popped out of the grass, just where Duncan had been looking. He joined them making sure he kept below the ridge line.

"You lot getting bored? Testing our guard now?" Duncan asked the Scout.

"Nope. But got some news. Change of plan. Didn't want to put it on the radio net."

Sealous Scouts were almost renegades. They acted alone in the enemy's rear. Army rules didn't apply. They were mixed race, even had black officers. Their unofficial motto was: *"Don't give a shit"*.

Sticking to the plan was not a priority. They were opportunists.

"What is it?" said Duncan.

"We identified a juicy target. When *Aztec's* signalled we're going to take it out," said the Scout. "Going to try and pick us up some Chinese prisoners."

"What you got?" asked Duncan.

"Communications centre, top of hill 104, guarded by Gooks, operated by Chinks. Quite a coup to have some Chinkie prisoners back in Salisbury don't you think?"

"What about us?" asked Duncan. "We're supposed to blow the bridge to cut off the route for reinforcements and rendezvous with you to get out of here. That's the plan."

"Yea it's really the same. You go to the rendezvous but now you get to hold the position and wait for us."

"Bollocks," said Duncan. "You're there for a reason. You're a stick of twelve men and supposed to be cutting off retreating terrorists. You're trained for that. We're combat engineers not soldiers. There's a fucking big difference."

"Listen bud, we checked out the trail almost all the way to Chimoio. The last rains have made it almost impassable to vehicles. If anybody does come your way it's going to be a couple of stragglers on foot. You lot can handle that and it's only going to be for a few hours. In any case it's not a request, I've just come to tell you. You'll be all right."

"You're a bunch of bastards," said Duncan.

"Yeah, we know."

Chimoio Base, Evening 3rd September 1979.

The scent of victory pervaded the ZANU forward camp at Chimoio. Everybody spoke in almost mystical terms of the Lancaster House Conference, the time and place where the Rhodesians would at last surrender. As light faded the MAN diesel generator was started and the camp lit up. Guards sauntered to their posts. Nobody expected an attack, nobody was watching as the Rhodesian reconnaissance party did its work. The gently rustle of leaves, the bending of boughs was missed as the vanguard of two Companies of Rhodesian Light Infantry marked their start positions.

Silas Sovimbo had travelled by train to the derelict and half deserted town that gave the Camp its name. The main street of Chimoio was empty. Grass grew in the once busy main street. Paving slabs had been lifted by strong roots and the gables of the ornate Portuguese colonial buildings were streaked black and moss laden. As light faded Silas completed his journey to the guerrilla camp in a Lada jeep. Entering the camp he was taken directly to the command bunker where Tongogara waited. The briefing was slow. Tongogara was uninterested in political intrigue and chicanery, preferring action. The Shona Chief of Staff was unique. He was a fighter and the only black military leader truly feared by the Rhodesians.

As they spoke through the small hours Silas heard the constant chatter from nearby radio sets. Adjutants came and went with scraps of paper. At last one message caught Tongogara's attention. He contemplated the note for a while and spoke.

"No rain for three days. That is the forecast. I will leave now." He stood, effectively cutting off Silas in mid sentence.

"Three days without rain is enough time to visit the camps in Tete, to the north. I have been waiting for this opportunity."

Silas also stood. "What about Makonzo? We have not discussed that situation yet," he said.

Tongogara looked Silas in the eyes. "Your son? He survives at Chimoio only because of the respect I have for you, his father."

Silas could not respond to the bluntness of Tongogara's

words.

Tongogara continued. "Your son is still proud of his actions, of the slaughter of innocents and wanton brutality that cannot be excused by the contingencies of war. He is unable to accept his excesses. Without acknowledgement of his error there is no place for him under my command."

"Then what should become of him?" asked Silas.

"I understand he desires to go back to Zimbabwe. This to me would be a grave mistake. After the war must come peace and reconciliation, concepts beyond his understanding. To me he is a danger. Normally I would dispose of him as a common murderer. If he stays here, under my control, that will be his fate. But out of respect I will let you decide his fate so long as he is taken away from this place and not allowed into Zimbabwe. That is my decision. Now I must go. You may use my quarters whilst I am away. You will have privacy."

The two men shook hands as comrades but not friends.

Tongogara's Spartan quarters, a bunker dug into the heavy clay soil, provided a claustrophobic atmosphere for the meeting of father and son. For an age the two sat opposite each other in silence.

The only exit from the bunker was a short passage leading to the Operations Room. The corrugated iron roof was propped up by thick wooden posts that concealed and supported eighteen inches of compacted soil that was designed to absorb a direct hit from a mortar round. There was no natural light. Air came through a six inch galvanised pipe that broke surface several yards away. At this place, next to the vent, Tyoni lurked, concealed by the shadows, secretly listening to the conversation of father and son.

Makonzo gripped the edge of Tongogara's map table. His were the first words. The quiver in his voice betrayed his anger. The accusation was direct.

"It was you. You were the one. You are the reason I was recalled."

"No. You are the author of your own destiny," replied his father. "You were given freedom and responsibility. You abused the situation so that even our allies could not work with you."

Makonzo did not hear his father's words. He spoke only what was in his own mind.

"I did not want to go to the war. You forced me. Then when I succeeded and left you in the background you used your influence to bring me back down."

Silas looked at his son and shook his head. "All my life I have worked with a single aim and I believe that I am respected for my efforts. You on the other hand have only earned the crude respect that is generated by fear, the kind of respect that a man has for a venomous snake."

"I will not wait here any longer. Tomorrow I will go back to Zimbabwe with or without your permission. I will not miss the victory."

"You will not go back," said Silas.

His son stiffened. "Old man, you are jealous. You have failed. It is the gun and my way that has won this war. I have surpassed you and you do not like it." Makonzo stood. The veins in his temple were raised. He shouted "You will not rob me of my victory!"

As his son raged, calm descended on Silas and he made up his mind. When Makonzo had finished ranting Silas spoke with a resolute calmness.

"You have no choice. You will be taken from here to Dar es Salaam. I will have you arrested and you will be locked up. On my word you will be tried for murder. Your life lies in my hands alone. You will atone or die."

"This is because I killed a few Matable pigs?" he ranted, "It is what they deserve."

"Do you think I do not know your motivation? I have heard of the mark of shame on your chest that you justly earned. You seek revenge on innocent people for your own dishonour."

The white's of Makonzo's eyes bulged. The confrontation with truth was too much. Silas saw the release of uncontrolled rage from his son for the first and last time. There was no physical contest, the result was assured. Two hands clasped Silas's throat in a clamp like grip. Thumbs pressed into the soft pockets below the ear lobes. The Old Man struggled but could not escape the manic hold. The carotid artery was crushed, the brain starved of blood. There was little pain. Resistance soon stopped. Darkness fell like a veil as Silas closed his eyes for the last time.

Minutes passed before Makonzo relaxed his hold. His father's limp body slumped to the floor. He felt nothing for the prostrate being. His senses returned with the metallic click of the pistol being cocked behind him. Makonzo turned to face the entrance. Two adjutants pointed weapons at him. A third officer stood behind. He was the one who spoke.

"Tie Makonzo up. I will try to speak to Tongogara on the radio. Keep him here for now."

Tyoni listened at the ventilation pipe. He knew he had to do something quickly. He slipped into the darkness.

It was still dark. Only a feint reddish hue on the horizon gave indication of the impending dawn. They walked slowly in line, abreast, almost feeling their way. Duncan and his men moved towards the barely visible bridge.

"Down! Wait!" Duncan ordered in a whisper.

The men sank in unison.

African dawns come quickly. Ten minutes separates darkness from light. Before their eyes the shape of the steel structure began to solidify.

It loomed larger as they drew closer.

Birds began to sing, a few at first, then many, heralding the new day. In the distance a troop of Blue Monkeys screeched as they began their search for breakfast. Duncan heard what he had been waiting for. The distant hum was distinctive. The drone of twin Pratt and Whitney radial engines was clear. The Dakota containing Red Leader had arrived over the target and would circle high above, as if taunting those below. Operational command would remain 17 000 feet above the battle.

"Show's on," thought Duncan. He knew what was coming next. The distant drone was suddenly overwhelmed by the roar of un-suppressed jet engines as the four B2 Canberra Bombers of the Rhodesian Airforce made their bomb run towards the Chimoio Camp. The planes' route was a low sweeping ark as the planes approached the camp from the 'wrong' direction. Reveille for the camp would be several five hundred pound general purpose bombs with their deadly fragmentation qualities.

Duncan stood and moved forward. Orders were not necessary. Two men on the flanks went either side of the bridge to provide a watch and covering fire. Duncan and the corporal went straight for the structure, each taking the foundation of a supporting buttress. According to the plan they had less than thirty minutes to complete their work.

Tyoni had waited till dawn was nearly breaking before making his move. Now he worked his way towards the command bunker, possessing an objective but no clear plan. Then he heard the drone of the Pratt and Whitney engines. He immediately knew what it meant and thanked the God he did not believe in for the distraction. He quickened his pace. His AK47 no longer hung casually across his shoulder, he loosened his side holster.

The command bunker was at the centre of a series of communication trenches radiating outwards, ready for use in the event of an attack. Normally the trenches were avoided, particularly in the rainy season when the bottoms became waterlogged. Instead wooden foot bridges and duck boards were thrown over the gaps to enable swift surface travel. It was easy for Tyoni to drop into the safety of the trenches and travel unnoticed.

As the roar of the jet engines became deafening, the ground shook. Bombs dropped from the Canberra's wings. Explosions racked the camp, the air was thick with shrapnel. Tyoni cowered safely at the bottom of a trench. As the sound of the last explosion died away he knew he'd have to move quickly.

The guard at the entrance to the bunker pressed his hands hard against his ears. The pain was obviously intense, his eardrums were perforated. He'd failed to open his mouth during the explosions to equalise the pressure. Disorientated and deaf he didn't recognise the Type 64 silenced pistol pointing at him. It was an unusual weapon to find in a guerrilla camp. Normally it was used by Chinese special agents for close quarter work. It discharged especially heavy ammunition to cause maximum damage and make death more certain from a single shot. It could be used in semi-automatic or automatic mode. This morning it was set at semi-automatic. This detail was lost on the guard. Neither he, nor the people inside the bunker, heard the shots. There was no flash to see either, the suppresser had done its work. Tyoni holstered his pistol as the guard was dropping.

Tyoni knew the layout of the bunker. He'd been there often. He removed the pin from a fragmentation grenade and pulled the bunker door open a few inches. He pitched the grenade through the gap. It went unnoticed as it rolled along the duck boards. The fuse was set for the minimum three seconds. He stood behind the door jam.

Fragmentation grenades almost always inflict fatal injuries

within a radius of five to ten yards although it may take the victim sometime to die. In a confined space they are efficient, if messy, killers. The explosion bulged the door and the smell of cordite seeped through the gaps.

He pushed into the bunker. Two officers lay on the floor motionless. The radio operator, still in his seat, was pushed up against his radio set. Blood oozed from wounds to his back. Stepping over the bodies he made for Tongogara's bunker. He slipped the safety catch off his AK as he pushed his way through. Empty. No guards, no Makonzo. Only the body of Silas on the floor, left where it had fallen.

"No Makonzo!"

The Radio Operator groaned. He was not yet dead.

Tyoni laid the man on the ground.

"Comrade", he said, "Can you hear me? Can you hear me? Try it is very important."

The Radio Operator blinked his eyes. "Give me a drink, some water," he croaked.

"Yes, I will. But first tell me what has happened to the prisoner. Where is Makonzo?"

"Water… please."

Tyoni picked up a water bottle from the floor and removed the screw top. He took a deep swig. The air in the bunker was acrid after the explosion and irritated his throat.

"First tell me. Where is the prisoner?"

The radio operator looked at the canvass covered bottle, unable to reach it for himself. "They took him. Less than one hour ago."

"Where did they take him?"

"To the Mozambique Authorities in Chifumba town," he croaked. "They are taking him by staff car."

"Did Tongogara order that?" asked Tyoni. "Quickly tell me."

"No I could not get hold of Tongogara on the radio. Nobody outside the command bunker knows what has happened."

Tyoni thought for a moment.

"Now. Give me the water," pleaded the radio operator.

Tyoni was not listening. He dropped the water bottle to the floor and moved towards the bunker door. There was still hope.

"Please," pleaded the radio operator. "Just some water."

Tyoni stopped. He turned and looked at the outstretched hand of the radio operator. He could not risk a witness. He pulled the pistol from its holster and ratcheted a round into the chamber. One muffled shot and the radio operator had no more need for water.

"I must go quickly," thought Tyoni. "I must catch up." He ran down the communication trench and heard the crackle of small arms fire. And then there was the bark of a heavy machine gun. "The Rhodesians soldiers are coming. It would be difficult enough" He thought.

"Clear!" shouted Duncan. "3…2…. . The others never heard the "1". Duncan pushed the button that sparked the detonators. The charges had been well placed on the pivotal points of the bridge. The whole structure lifted a few inches before twisting and slipping off the supporting buttresses. The central span buckled and the main span crumpled into the gorge.

"Perfect" said Duncan, "Nothing's crossing that for a while. But no time to admire our work. Let's move out and get to the rendezvous point." The four men spread out and made their way up the road.

The driver stopped the green Moskovitch staff car in the middle of the jungle track, concealed in the shade of a giant tree. He left the engine running. Two of the occupants in the back argued, the prisoner in the middle listened.

"We should go back", said the one to Makonzo's right. "We must join the fight and help our Comrades."

"We have orders," said the one to his left. "We must go on."

The driver looked in the rear view mirror and watched. Makonzo was hunched, his handcuffed hands resting on his lap. They'd been out of the camp for only minutes when the bombers had come. Soon the explosions had been replaced by the sound of gunfire.

Makonzo had no wish to return to the camp. He knew the enemy would be ruthless. He joined in the argument.

"It's your duty to go and fetch help", he said. "You must obey orders and take me to Chifumba. It is your duty."

Even as a prisoner he spoke with authority. "Drive on," he commanded not waiting for the discussion to rekindle itself. The driver obeyed, thankful of a decision. Three klicks and they had left the track and joined the old Bira road, the once busy but now almost derelict highway that joined Rhodesia to the Indian Ocean. Years of war and neglect brought with it deterioration. Potholes and land slips made the route hazardous. They went slowly. Makonzo warned his guards. "Watch out that the Rhodesians do not follow us down the road. We do not know their objective. They may have vehicles. If they catch us they will kill us."

It was warning enough to keep the guards peering out of the rear window and the reason why the first thing they knew about the ambush was when the driver braked hard as they exited a bend. The car careered out of control.

"Don't stop", shouted Makonzo. He knew their best chance was to crash through the ambush. But it was too late, the windscreen shattered and the driver was shot.

They moved quickly up the road. Duncan brought up the rear. He knew their vulnerability and cursed the Sealous Scouts for abandoning their orders. Nothing stood between Duncan's squad and Chimoio Camp. Time was pressing. They had no choice but to use the road, the same road that escapees would use to get away. Vigilance was their only defence.

The noisy engine of the Moskovitch gave warning but not enough for the troop to hide in the vegetation. The car rounded the bend and was on them as they levelled their weapons. The four men fired simultaneously. Bullets pinged on the body work of the car. Out of control the vehicle ran on a few yards before veering into a low embankment.

Duncan ran forward, weapon raised. The vehicle was awash with blood. For a moment all was still, then a slumped head lifted and hands moved. Duncan aimed through the shattered window, his finger began to squeeze on the trigger. Suddenly he was back in Aden, twenty years ago.

The moment he fired the fateful shots that had changed his life flashed before his eyes. Clearly he saw the face of the innocent hostage in that split second before he pulled the trigger. Two decades of regret clouded his mind.

In an instant Duncan was back in Mozambique. He looked at the black face as it lifted. The two men made eye contact. The man's shirt was ripped revealing the scar on his chest, a scar too perfectly formed to be accidental. Duncan saw the cuffed hands of the prisoner.

He relaxed his trigger finger and lowered his gun. From behind one of his men spoke.

"Lieutenant, aren't you going to kill him?"

"No. Leave him," said Duncan.

"Do you want me to do it?" asked the Corporal.

"No. Just leave him to his chances. I have my reasons."

As the Rhodesian soldiers moved on Makonzo sat back in the seat, the only survivor of the ambush. He waited.

Tyoni lay still in the undergrowth. He'd heard the gunshots of the ambush. There was no time for him to do anything but hide. Now the soldiers passed him, unseeing in the euphoria of their success, heading towards Chimoio. When the soldiers were out of sight Tyoni rushed around the bend and ran toward the crashed car. Already Makonzo, struggling with cuffed hands, was searching the bodies for keys. He saw Tyoni coming toward him.

"Ha! Tyoni. Come quickly. Get me out of these things. We must make our escape. Now I am a fugitive even from my own people."

"No'" said Tyoni. "You do not need to run. You must only wait. Nobody outside of Chimoio Camp knows you were arrested. We must only wait till the Rhodesians have killed the witnesses. Then we can return the heroes once more. You are saved."

Makonzo laughed. "Let us see what the next month brings. Once again I am saved by my faithful friend Tyoni!"

Moscow 15th December 1979

"How old do you think I am?" asked Comrade Molenski.

Sergi Andropov was once again alone with his chief. He'd sat in the same chair many times before but he'd never felt as exposed as now.

"It is hard for me to say." Sergi's mind danced wondering what the Chief was leading up to. "You do not look old, yet I know you were a fearsome leader in the Patriotic War. I would not like to answer such a difficult question."

"You have changed. It is a shame," said Molenski. "When we first met you were bold, not scared to speak your mind. Now you become like the rest. Too scared to speak the truth, you only offer weak platitudes."

Molenski stood and walked around the desk. "I will tell you how old I am. I am old enough to escape the mess you have created – but you my friend, are not."

"What do you mean Comrade?" Sergi turned in his chair trying to keep Molenski in sight.

Molenski spoke as he paced the carpet. "For more years than I can remember I have sanctioned the funding of the war against Rhodesia, supporting your plan and accepting your assurances. Now the war is nearly over and power will go to this man called Mugabe and his Chinese sponsors. Our man, the one you have always assured me will lead Zimbabwe, Nkomo, will only eat the crumbs thrown to him. Our investment is wasted. When the Politburo realise this, heads will roll. That is why I am leaving now. I am retiring with my pension and privileges intact, to a Dacha in the country. You will have to do something very quickly to deliver on your promises or face the consequences of failure."

Umtali Road, Mozambique. 26th December 1979

Nearly four months has passed since the Rhodesians had raided Chimoio. In the weeks following the attack Ian Smith had conceded. Victory had come to the Liberation movement, only the formalities were to follow. The Whites were spent, Nkomo and the Matable would be sidelined. But new forces came into play. Who from the Shona would reap the ultimate reward?

Tyoni walked around the back of the lorry to make sure the rear lights weren't working. He could have left them switched off but he wanted to leave the switch in the 'on' position so that after the accident the investigator would think the truck had faulty lights which were a contributory cause of the accident. He returned to the cab and waited, listening to the cumbersome American walkie-talkie for the message that the target car was on its way. When the message did come all he had to do was let go the hand brake and the truck would roll down the shallow embankment on to the road, blocking the blind bend.

It was the day after Christmas, the height of the Southern African summer but it still got dark at 6pm. The car did not slow for the failing light. The driver was in a hurry, for him the last few days had been halcyon, he was on a high. The celebrations in Maputo had not been for Christmas, they'd been for something far more important. Now he drove at speed to be with his men. He drove too quickly for the unlit road that ran from Maputo to the Rhodesian border. It was the first time he'd risked this journey alone, without bodyguards for protection. Only now was he confident that Rhodesian forces were not hiding somewhere in the Mozambique countryside, waiting in ambush. His new-found sense of freedom was exhilarating. He opened the window and bathed in the rush of warm evening air and smiled. In a couple of days 1980 would dawn and a few months later the whole world would witness the birth of Zimbabwe. At last the Rhodesians had conceded defeat. They'd signed away their future in the Lancaster House Agreement on the 21st December. He, Tongogara, the second most important man in

ZANU, had countersigned the document for the Shona people, following his leader Robert Gabriel Mugabe.

But Tongogara's political skills were not as well honed as his military ones. He'd not appreciated that the Lancaster House Conference only determined who'd lost the war. Who'd won was a different question that would be settled in a different type of struggle. Nor did he appreciate his important position.

Tongogara recalled how as a child he'd played on the white man's farm where his parents were paid labourers. He remembered watching his father and mother toil in the tobacco fields under the blazing sun. He'd watched the farmer's son grow up. They'd spoken, even laughed together but never played as friends. The farmer and his son had not been bad but even in his innocent tender years Tongogara saw something wrong in a system that gave so much to whites and so little to blacks.

There was an irony. The same white boy he'd watch grow up alongside him on the farm had also signed the Lancaster House Agreement because Tongogara had been brought up on the farm owned by the parents of Ian Smith the last white Rhodesian Prime Minister. The irony of the situation was not lost on Ian Smith either.

Deep in thought Tongogara never noticed the absence of other traffic on the road, nothing following, nothing oncoming. He'd never know that road blocks had been set up both ahead and behind him. He was unaware that his was the only car on that sector of remote road. He was oblivious to the fact that his progress was being reported over the radio network.

The hand-set crackled to life. Tyoni heard the code word. The car was close. He released the hand brake and the truck rolled down the shallow embankment onto the narrowest part of the road, stopping three-quarters way around the sweeping bend in the middle of the carriageway. He made sure the hand brake was pulled up hard and first gear engaged. He didn't want the truck rolling forward, lessening the impact.

From his position, hidden in the bush Makonzo, or the man formally known as Makonzo, watched and waited. The car engine could be heard. In the distance flashes of headlight could be seen as the vehicle wove up the incline at speed. The driver worked the gears hard and the sense of speed was palpable. Stars twinkled and the sky was crystal clear. Just for a moment the sound of the car died away as the last outcrop shielded it from his listening ears, then almost unexpectedly it was close. The driver had no time to brake before hitting the solid rear of the truck. The car's engine immediately stalled. Momentarily the sound was of crunching metal and breaking glass. Then there was only the hiss of steam coming from a fractured radiator hose.

Tyoni stepped from the shadows, behind him came Makonzo. But he was no longer called Makonzo. He'd reverted to his birth name, now he was Joshua Sovimbo again, son of the martyred patriarch of the Party and war hero.

Tyoni shone a torch on to the wreck of the car. Tongogara was half way through the windscreen; no seat belt had restrained his sudden forward motion. His legs, trapped under the dashboard, had stopped his total ejection from the vehicle. Blood ran down the bonnet, it looked black in torchlight.

Tongogara was still conscious. He tried to push himself upwards but only slid back into the vehicle, slumping onto the broken seat. His head lolled to one side. He didn't have the strength to support it, but his mind was active.

"Who was so stupid, leaving a truck on the bend? It must have broken down," he thought. Then the flashlight registered.

"He's not dead?"

Tongogara recognised the voice. He tried to place it.

"Look at the wound on his chest and the bleeding from his head. He will not last long. We must only wait a short time."

Tongogara did not recognise the second voice but he wanted to shout. "No I am not gone, just help me I will survive this." But his voice would not work.

"We cannot wait for long, and it is too dangerous to leave him alive. We must finish the job ourselves."

Tongogara placed the voice. Joshua, Joshua Sovimbo. But what was he saying?

Joshua leaned in through the broken passenger window and lifted Tongogara's head by the hair. A spark of life lingered in Tongogara's eyes.

"Sovimbo!" said Tongogara. "You must help me. I have been in an accident."

Joshua Sovimbo laughed at the pathetic words. He saw the chest wound and placed the mussel of his pistol into the flesh, angled so the bullet would pass through the heart. He looked Tongogara in the eye and squeezed the trigger and spoke. "Here is a final message for you."

The shot was muffled by blood and flesh. Tongogara did not slump. Instead he stiffened as if with new strength. He lifted his arms and gripped his assailant. Panic overcame Joshua. He pulled the trigger again. It was too much this time. Tongogara's body gave up the fight. Five days after winning the war he had been killed at the hands of Comrades.

"It is done," said Joshua.

"So it is," replied Tyoni.

Joshua laughed. "We now take our instructions from the highest place. We have a guardian angel. You do not need to know more, we are safe."

The Washington Post
Friday 28th December 1979
As we go to press reports are coming through of the death in a motor vehicle accident of General J.M. Tongogara just five days after he co-signed the peace document ending the Zimbabwe / Rhodesian war.

Tongogara is widely attributed with masterminding the military defeat of the White Colonial Army. A popular folk figure in his native country he was tipped to become the first black President of Zimbabwe, a position second only to that of Prime Minister which will in all probability go to the political head of ZANU, Robert Gabriel Mugabe.

In a statement a spokesman from the US State Department said the reported accident was being treated as highly suspicious. The Spokesman went on to say, 'Tongogara had many enemies. He may have been murdered by renegade elements of the White Rhodesian forces seeking revenge for their defeat, or more probably by elements within his own Shona tribe that wanted the popular figure out of the way. A whole new dynamic is emerging for fledgling Zimbabwe as a result of this incident.'

'The fact that no post-mortem was carried out before burial and only an undertakers certificate stating that the injuries were consistent with a car crash is a totally unsatisfactory state of affairs.'

The Kraal, Shabini, February 14ᵗʰ 1980

For a long day and into the night Chief Dingisgani sat alone with his Nanga in the sacred grounds. The Witch studied the Oracle. He waited patiently for her interpretation. Hours passed mostly in silence but sometimes the Spirits came near. If it was a good Spirit the Witch added a faggot to the fire, if it was a bad one she drove it away with a handful of saltpetre thrown on to the glowing embers. Dingisgani reared when he felt the rush of heat as the saltpetre erupted in a giant flame, the flash of light would cast eerie shadows in the darkness.

A cloud still hung over Dingisgani. He did not share the joy of victory. He pined for Elizabeth. He would prefer servitude under the white man to freedom without Elizabeth, each passing day without news of her added to his despair.

Tembo and Morgan had received their last orders. They had reported to the international assembly camp, under the guard and protection of British and Australian soldiers. There would be no more fighting, they only waited for repatriation to their village as victors.

In his mind Dingisgani had been ready to lose a son. It was the way of the Matable. Warriors expected death, but he did not accept the loss of Elizabeth.

Not till the cockerel crowed did the Nanga speak in human tongue.

"It is possible she will return. But she is changed and can only come back if you are prepared to accept her as she is now." The Nanga did not look at Dingisgani as she spoke.

The Chief sat forward and replied without hesitation. "I will accept her without question, in any way."

"If she comes she will not be alone and her heart will be divided. Are you able to accept this?"

"To know she is safe and to see her is enough for me. Make her come to me under any circumstances."

The Nanga spoke. "Elizabeth will definitely come," she said assuredly, though not in possession of divine knowledge. It was the World Service of the BBC that had said the refugee camps in Botswana were closing.

The sky blue flag fluttered in the breeze over the camp on the outskirts of Francistown, Botswana. The protection and care the piece of cloth had given was about to be taken away. The young tall American was not much more than a college boy. He'd confidently stood on the tail board of the white pick up truck, the one with the emblem and markings UNHCR. He used a megaphone to address the whole camp. The war was over he said. Rhodesia no longer existed. They were no longer refugees. They could return home to a free and happy country where there would be plenty for all and danger had passed. Elizabeth and two thousand others listened with silent cynicism as the naive representative of the United Nations High Commissioner for Refugees patronised them.

Weeks passed. It seemed like an eternity before it was her turn but now the bus stopped at the border crossing point at Plumtree. It was escorted as far as the check point by a Toyota Land Cruiser flying the UN pennant. It was one of the last buses to leave the refugee camp. One had gone every day for the past twenty-five days. Now the camp was almost empty. They had organised it that way so as not to overwhelm the Receiving Centre at Bulawayo. Elizabeth had been kept back for one of the last buses. She wanted it that way. She lived in trepidation of her homecoming and revealing her secret.

Looking out of the window, she watched the huddle of men and the papers being passed back and forth. Eventually a straight faced European boarded the bus and walked the aisle looking at each passenger in turn. He wore no expression and made no comment. He was dressed in white, shorts, open neck shirt, knee length socks. He wore a brass badge above the flap of his shirt's breast pocket. It stated *'Rhodesian Immigration Department'*. Returning to the front of the bus he turned to face the occupants. All eyes were fixed on him. There was silent tension. His face relaxed and he drew a breath. He spoke loud enough for all to hear. His words were simple. "Welcome home!" he said.

For a moment there was silence. Then someone clapped. Others slowly joined in. The ripple turned to applause. The Immigration Officer smiled revealing brilliant white teeth. Someone at the back dared a cheer. The bus erupted into shouts and whistles. It was the first spontaneous celebration Elizabeth witnessed. For a second she thought perhaps it would be different now, perhaps white and black could get along together.

The bus pulled away, trundling the 60 miles to Bulawayo. Her mind wandered back.

It was only two days ago. Elizabeth had been called to the Administration Office at the Camp. They made her leave her child playing outside in the dusty yard. The Austrian nun wore a black habit and spoke with an unfamiliar German accent. Her words had a harshness about them, so different to the warm brogue of the Irish Sisters that she was used to. She ordered Elizabeth to sit on the chair that stood lonely in the centre of the room.

A strange man sat beside the nun, unkempt in his safari suit. The crumpled cream linen was impractical. He'd rested his Panama hat on the bare table. He began to speak.

"People have told me about you and I have read your file. I understand your problem and I am happy to say I can help you." He smiled.

Elizabeth felt discomfort. "What problem is it that I have?" asked Elizabeth.

"Oh, I think you understand Elizabeth. There is no need to be secretive. We are here to help you. At this time there are opportunities for all and you cannot selfishly think of yourself. You know that don't you?" he said. "You are a good woman."

The man got up and walked to the window. He looked at the child playing in the yard. "It is clear for all to see. The child is not African. Look at his hair, his nose, his complexion. He is of mixed race and more white than black if anything. It is a shame. When you return to your village what can you offer him? I think you can only offer him bad things. He is destined to an impossibly hard life with you. Even his name, James, is against him."

"But he has no problem here," responded Elizabeth. "No child he plays with sees he is different. Only older people are blinded by colour."

"That will change as the child grows," said the man. "Besides, there are other considerations. You are also tarnished. What African man will want a wife that already has a baby with a white man? Elizabeth, I think you already know, logic says you must give up your child."

The words cut into her. Elizabeth sat, alone and isolated on the spindly chair in the stark office. As panic grew her deep brown eyes glistened. Tears overflowed and trickled down her cheeks.

The nun spoke. "In America there are people who will take such a young child and give it a life that you could only dream of. It will bring you eternal happiness to know what good has been done by the sacrifice you have made by giving up your child at this time."

The man withdrew papers from a floppy briefcase that was propped up by the leg of the table. He spread them on the table top.

"Now Elizabeth this is a once only offer. I won't be here again. Think. If you miss this opportunity what will be the future of the child?"

He placed a pen on the table next to the papers. "I just need you to walk to the table and sign here. Then everything will be alright."

He sensed she was close, hesitating.

"Elizabeth," he said in a quiet voice, "I understand how hard it is. What mother would not have difficulty in such a situation? So if it helps you decide what I'm going to do is this. I'm going to give you fifty British pounds. Just for you to do with what you want. Just think of the start that will give you back in the village. All you have to do is sign the papers. Now."

Elizabeth was back on the rolling bus. She stopped looking out of the window at the passing bush and lowered her gaze to the child beside her. She squeezed James closer. He looked at his mother with unquestioning eyes and she knew she could never have betrayed him, they had been mistaken, the thought of giving James up had never crossed her mind. If she had given up James she would have lost the thing most precious to her and eradicated any chance of ever seeing Duncan again.

Three days later she returned to her Kraal. Dingisgani, the Chief, thanked the Spirits for the reunion. James came to know his grandfather and uncles. For now Elizabeth would wait.

Chevron Hotel, Fort Victoria, 1st April 1980

"Sat here a few times old chap but bet you never thought you'd be witnessing this spectacle?" Patrick Walker's voice could hardly be heard as the military convoy thundered through the main street of Fort Victoria headed south on April Fool's day 1980.

Duncan Murdoch sat with Walker on the patio at the Chevron Hotel, their old meeting place, the rumbles of the heavily laden trucks causing the ground to tremble. Vibrations travelled through the table and into their beers. Little peaks danced on the flat surface of the amber liquid.

'Look like a rum bunch don't they? Wouldn't like to try and stop them. They're not exactly famous for taking prisoners or entering protracted discussions," said Walker.

Duncan didn't answer.

"Of course you know this is not really happening, not officially," continued Walker. "Everybody is just turning a blind eye and letting them go with all their kit."

Duncan turned to Walker. "Is this the only unit going to South Africa en masse?"

"That's our information. It appears the SAS were just hanging on for the results of the election. They sort of had a secret pact between themselves. As soon as they found Mugabe had won they assembled at 1st Commando barracks in Salisbury. That was yesterday. Mugabe is their worst nightmare. They obviously had a plan. All the regimental records were burnt overnight. Apparently wives and children are long gone. Black and white! The Troopies took everything they could out of the armoury and motor pool and set off for South Africa first thing this morning."

"Nobody tried to stop them?"

"Not us or the Aussies. In fact our boys thought it was rather touching that they didn't surrender. They left the battle field as a unit, undefeated. Hats off to them sort of thing I suppose."

"Couldn't have the rest of the army doing it though. Definitely a one off. Of course the SAS were guilty of horrific war crimes, particularly close to the end. Couldn't deny it. The whole of bloody Salisbury saw their helicopters coming in with cargo nets stuffed full of bodies as they returned from contacts. They just went ape shit. You know in their mess room they changed the motto that was written on the wall *from 'Who Dares Wins'* to *'Who Cares Who Wins'*. Some of the whites were facing war crimes charges but the blacks wouldn't have the dignity of a trial. They'd just disappear."

"In the end, fair do's, they took all the blacks with them. Did you know more than half the SAS unit was made up of blacks? And bloody good they were too. No discrimination in that unit!"

The final vehicle was an Eland armoured car. On the back hung a sign. 'Last one out turns off the lights'. Patrick half saluted as it passed. The oversize Trooper manning the 50 calibre on the back grinned and returned the complement with a big 'V' sign and it wasn't 'V' for victory.

The noise died away and it was strangely quiet.

"You know I feel a bit empty with those guys out of the game," said Duncan. He drank his now flat beer making out the dust had made him thirsty. There was more than the hint of a tear as he gulped.

He put the glass down and for the first time noticed the man across the patio. There was a familiarity about the stranger. Duncan could not place him at first. He looked to Patrick for help. Patrick was smiling. The stranger rose and walked towards them. It was a military gait. The stranger offered his hand. Duncan stood.

"Mr Murdoch, or should I now say Captain Murdoch?"

The voice was unmistakable. "Major Cameron? What are you doing here?"

"Actually it's Colonel Stuart Cameron now but perhaps we better keep that a bit quiet."

"You keep doing that rank thing on me." Duncan laughed and shook Cameron's hand for slightly longer than necessary.

Cameron smiled. "Do you think I can join you?"

"Sit down. Beer?"

"Never seen you so befuddled before Duncan," said Walker grinning.

Hours later they finished eating in the hotel restaurant. Patrick Walker made his excuses and left.

Stuart spoke seriously for the first time. "Much as it gives me great pleasure to see you socially there is a business element to this meeting. I suppose you'd guessed that?"

"I did," said Duncan.

"We need to discuss your future. What's going to happen to you now the war is over?"

"I got a letter yesterday," volunteered Duncan. "It said I would not be required by the new Zimbabwean Army. They thanked me for my services and told me to return my kit to the Quartermaster. That's it. Not much of a send off."

"I can do a little better than that," said Cameron pulling an envelope out of his pocket and handing it to Duncan. "Go on. Open it."

Inside the envelope was a plastic covered booklet. Duncan examined it. *'National Savings Deposit Account'* Duncan's name was printed on the inside page. He flicked through the pages and noted the regular deposits. One every three months for years. The last entry gave a balance of £6 876 with interest.

"What's this?" asked Duncan.

"Your wages. It's the best I could do. I suppose it's more than you would have got inside the Glass House. It's tax free of course. And by the way I made sure you got all your NI contributions. Good for a pension later on you know."

"Thanks. I didn't expect anything. But is that it? Does this mean I'm sacked by you as well?"

"Not necessarily," said Stuart. "You can of course up sticks and go home at this point, that's true. I'm sure there would be no difficulty in getting your parole made permanent."

"I've got no home to go to. Only the Glass House."

"I think even our inept lot would have difficulty in sending you there," said Stuart. "Seriously, do you have any ideas?"

Duncan shook his head. "This is the only home I have. At least here I have a job and somewhere to live. I hear things are pretty grim back in the UK. Thatcher is doing nothing for the working man. I don't want to go back to the cold, rain and dole."

"Don't blame you for that and you're right about the PM. It's going to get worse before it gets better."

Duncan didn't mention the hope that lingered in his mind about Elizabeth. That was too intimate. He knew if he left this place there would be no hope and there must always be hope. "I'll be staying."

"From a selfish point of view that's good for me. I might have a use for you if you're interested?"

"Go on," said Duncan.

"The UK will have an ongoing interest in this country. It's

definitely not a clean break. I'll tell you why. There are still about two hundred thousand whites living here. Most of them British Citizens, nearly all of them have the right of entry into the UK. It would be difficult if they started to turn up at Heathrow in numbers. We'd like them to stay here and be happy. Added to that is this Mugabe fellow. He's saying all the right words but in truth he's a bit of an unknown quantity in practice."

"What's that go to do with me?" asked Duncan. "Me staying out won't help that much."

Stuart continued. "As part of the Lancaster House Agreement Britain is providing a generous aid package at Independence, more than £650 million in fact. Little of it is in cash and the details are complex but the crux of the matter is we want to keep an eye on things here for a while. Firstly we want to make sure the new Government is performing properly. For us that means not scaring the whites. Secondly we want to keep an eye out for other parties that might want to destabilise the status quo, if you get my drift."

"We've gone a long way to make the best of a bad situation. The incoming Government have agreed that the Minister for Agriculture will be a white man from Ian Smith's old cabinet. General Peter Walls, a Rhodesian sympathetic to Britain as you know, will head the new army. We've even got them to accept a permanent British Army presence in the country in exchange for some modern weaponry which includes a few Hawk Jet Aircraft."

"Hawk Jets? What are they going to do with them?"

"Yeah I know. Not the best thing to pass on to them. Ironically they didn't actually ask for them either. It was an idea from our side. Keep the British Aerospace lads in work is the idea I suppose. They're only being configured as trainers so it should be alright."

Stuart concluded. "With all that going on I wouldn't mind hanging on to your phone number. What do you think? No pay of course."

Duncan thought for only a moment. "Sure, why not."

"I should mention that should you get caught they might consider you a spy and you know what can happen to spies? So we'll be keeping it low key. Okay?"

"Nothing's changed then," said Duncan.

Salisbury, Zimbabwe, 18th April 1980

The streets were unusually quiet as dawn broke on Friday, the first day of independence. Few people wandered about. Most of those that ventured out were bleary eyed and had an air of dishevelment following a long night of celebration. Without exception they were black. Apart from a few journalists no white person dared show their faces on the morning of April 18th 1980, Independence Day for Zimbabwe.

The previous night Prince Charles and Lord Carrington had witnessed the Union Jack being lowered for the last time in a ceremony at Rufaro football stadium. Political power was transferred to the sound of Bob Marley singing *'Zimbabwe'* for the first time in public. Now, even as the sun rose on the world's youngest country, forces were manoeuvring and planning.

Joshua Sovimbo walked along Jameson Avenue. He didn't drive and had no car. His instructions had been clear but still he was filled with concealed trepidation as he approached his destination. Too soon he came to the junction of Jameson Avenue and Park Street. On his left was the ten story ESC building, HQ of the Electricity Supply Commission, its entrance just around the corner on Park Street. He stopped and looked around. Park Street was wide, wide enough for cars to park nose to nose on the painted central reservation. Most of the parking spaces were empty and he took little notice of the black Nissan Bluebird as it discharged its three occupants opposite. He didn't notice them walk towards the Jameson Hotel on the other side of the street. He was too preoccupied with his own thoughts.

Joshua walked through the glass doors into the open foyer. He looked around nervously. A uniformed commissioner came over to him.

"What can I do for you?"

"Second floor," said Joshua.

The commissioner's demeanour changed instantly. "Sir, follow me."

The commissioner led Joshua around into an alcove towards

an innocuous wooden door. There was a chrome plated speaker and button. Above the door a small sign read *'Export Packaging Group. No Admittance except by appointment'*.

The commissioner pointed to the button. Joshua pressed it. Instantly a curt female European voice answered.

"Yes."

"Mr Joshua Sovimbo," he replied.

The door clicked and opened. "Walk up the stairs. Somebody will be waiting."

At the top of the stairs was a windowless landing. A young white man waited. "I need to take your fingerprints before you can proceed," he said.

The procedure was quick and practised. The man rolled Joshua's index finger on the inked pad and then transferred the pattern to a blank form. He gave Joshua a tissue. "Wipe your hands with this and wait."

He tapped an electronic keypad on a double door and disappeared into the adjacent room. Joshua stood around looking, unaware he was being observed through the two way mirror. Five minutes later the door opened and a short slightly built white man appeared with an ingratiating smile.

"Mr Sovimbo. Please excuse our security measures. I am Ken Flower and I am in charge here. Welcome to this office of the Central Intelligence Organisation. This is where you will be based for the time being. You have the honour of being the first member of the ruling party to join our establishment. Prime Minister Mugabe has spoken highly of you. I understand you have a particular interest in our Matable colleagues?"

Joshua rubbed the scar that lay hidden beneath his shirt. "I do," he said.

"Good. It will take a few months before you become effective. So the quicker we get your familiarisation started the better."

Less than a hundred yards away, across Park Street, in the lobby of the Jameson Hotel the three that had got out of the Nissan Bluebird sat on leather arm chairs. They waited patiently without speaking. Eventually a lift door opened and an unsmiling shirt sleeved European came into the lobby. He took off his horn rimmed spectacles and looked around before approaching the men in the chairs. "Come with me," he said in a commanding Russian accent.

The Leander Suite was on the sixth floor. A solid mahogany dining table dominated the living room. Two Russians sat at the table waiting as the Africans entered the room. They did not stand. Three chairs were ready for the visitors.

"Sit." Sergi Andropov was in no mood for chit chat. His job was on the line and in the USSR that meant more than just employment.

"It is not good," said Sergi. "The elections were a disaster. Let us take stock. Mugabe has 57 out of the 80 available seats. Your leader, Nkomo 27. The cabinet is mainly Shona. There are a few whites but virtually no Matable in a position of power. Even Nkomo only has a 'without portfolio' cabinet appointment. The army remains in the hands of Peter Walls, security with Ken Flower. In other words you have won nothing. Today, the first day of Independence the American and Chinese ambassadors are presenting their credentials at State House whilst we, the USSR, are informed we cannot be seen by the President till Tuesday next. All this after fifteen years of continous support and investment for your cause. Do you have any good news for me at all, something for me to take back to Moscow?"

Herbert Wakunzi spoke for the three. His words were chosen and deliberate. "We are sorry that your investment, as you saw it, failed but we are grateful for the fraternal efforts of your great nation. I am sorry that you are not satisfied with having contributed to the removal of the great yolk of colonialism from all the black people of this country, for indeed that was a great achievement. I personally would like to help in the shaping of the future of my country and am disappointed that I may not have the opportunity but my mind goes back to my Comrades, my brothers and sisters that have fallen to make this great day possible."

"Bullshit! Fucking bullshit!" Sergi exploded. "Do you think I am a fool? Do you believe this war was funded out of good will? This was never less than a war of power and influence. It was one part in the jigsaw of international politics, the titanic struggle between competing ideologies. And at this point we are losing."

"We have lost," said Herbert Wakunzi. "We may have won the war but we lost the election. What more is to be done?"

Sergi shook his head in disbelief. "Do you think we in the Soviet Union were put off by elections? When the East Germans revolted in 1953, or the Hungarians in 1966 or even the Czechs in 1968 did we sit still? No! Elections and the ballot box are only weapons to beat the democracies over the head with." Sergi thumped the table. "If we win an election all is well and good. If we lose then we revert to traditional methods. Methods well known in Africa. We will take power, by force if necessary. And you will be the instruments that bring this about - and you will reap the rewards too."

The room became quiet. Sergi well knew the power of silence. Eventually Herbert spoke. "What is it you want of us?"

Now Sergi was measured and quiet in his response. "You will have to cut the head off the serpent. This will create a vacuum at the top. Then you must be ready to fill the vacuum. It will take some time to prepare but I will show you how it is done. We will seize power."The Kraal, Shabani, 10th June 1980

It was both a sign of veneration and acceptance. The Twins sat crossed legged in front of Elizabeth, careful to keep their head below hers and not make eye contact. Although no word had yet been spoken it was clearly a formal meeting, a meeting where advice was being sought. Protocol demanded she open the dialogue.

"So little brothers why do you honour me?"

Tembo spoke. "In the past days a call to arms has once more come."

"This is not a question for me," said Elizabeth. "Questions of war are for our father and chief."

"Look," said Morgan pointing to the middle of the compound. "You have been back for more than one year. In that time we have never seen our father so happy. See how he plays with James. It is all he thinks about. Can you see the comfort and joy the child brings him? Our father has nothing greater on his mind, nor should he have. He is happy and we will not break this happiness with worry. His mind has reverted to youth and we will let it dwell there"

No further argument was needed. She had seen with her own eyes her that it was the truth. She had seen how he was abdicating his tribal responsibilities.

"You are his rightful heirs. So you must answer your own question," she said.

"There can be only one leader in our tradition and our father has failed to decide which one of us it should be. That is why we have decided together that we will entrust you with our decisions. That is our final word on the matter." The Twins laughed like naughty children.

"That is an easy way out for you," Elizabeth smiled. "But come. Tell me your problem and let us see if there is an answer we can find together. Then we will not have to disturb our father in his twilight."

"The war is long finished," said Morgan. "I say finished because for us it is finished but not won. Things for our people are unchanged. The village and people are the same. We still pray for the rain in October and dance when it arrives. This is the main event of our lives. We have not received the houses or the cars that were promised, nor shall we ever receive them. We have not seen the school or clinic that was assured us before the election. In total we have gained nothing. Yet the word is that the Shona have benefited greatly. They have the good jobs, they have received new land and they get pensions. Some say that it is time we too received our reward and if it is not given we should take it."

"These are strong words," said Elizabeth. "But are they just the words of the beer hall?"

"In the last days things have been happening," said Tembo. "Our cache of arms in the Matopas has been moved, secreted away in the dead of night. We went to see this with our own eyes."

"So what decision do you have to make now?" asked Elizabeth.

"We must decide should we join them. Those that would see us eat from the table of victors."

Elizabeth thought for a while. She watched as James ran around and her father laughed.

"It is true that we have seen nothing improve for us. But we can also say that nothing has got worse. It is true that the Shona rule the country but so far they have not been bad. It is a shame we have no gain for the sacrifice we have made but I can tell you I have spoken with many people when I was in the refugee camp. They told me it is common for bad things to happen when the mantle of colonialism is first shrugged off. We must hope that doesn't happen to us. So I say that so long as the Shona do not harm us we must think carefully before raising our voice in anger. Look around, at least at this time we are happy. Let us do nothing to spoil this time. What do you think my brothers?"

The twins looked at each other. "Your words are good," said Tembo.

"Worthy of King Solomon," said Morgan. "We will take heed."

"Now you make fun of me!" she scolded with a false frown.

Joshua Sovimbo settled down on the back seat of the Peugeot 404. It was going to be a long journey. Now at least he had a car and driver. Joshua looked up and caught the driver staring at him in the rear view mirror.

"Look at the road you idiot, not me," he shouted.

"Yis Bas," said Tyoni in his most subservient voice, mimicking a colonial servant speaking to his white boss. Both men laughed. Joshua Sovimbo was in good mood. Tyoni had been taught to drive and was now both driver and bodyguard for Joshua Sovimbo. But it was not that, that made him happy today. It was the scent of retribution that hung in the air. He knew of nothing better.

In less than two hours they had passed through the town of Kadoma. Now there was nothing but cotton fields on either side of the road with their little bolls bursting out of pods, ready for harvesting. Tyoni slowed as they approached the Munyati River Bridge. They crossed the concrete structure in low gear.

On the left, slightly set back, was a ramshackle corrugated iron hut requiring paint and not quite achieving the vertical. An African woman sat on the dusty ground outside the hut. A baby hung onto a breast hungrily feeding. On a coloured cloth there were small pyramids of ripe tomatoes. The woman rocked back and forth, oblivious to the hot sun, cradling the child, waiting for customers.

Tyoni saw the inconspicuous unmarked turning and swung the car right on to the narrow well maintained road. At first the road followed the river bank but then it gently veered to the left and rose over the sparsely vegetated undulating ground. Without warning they broke the brow of a hill and looked down into the river valley.

Before them stood the giant Munyati Power Station, a colossal structure of red brick and rusty steel that scarred the landscape and was so out of place in the remote African bush.

It was a complex structure, built immediately after the Second World War. There were two five megawatt and ten ten megawatt Mitchell chain grate boilers each connected by a complex arrangement of giant steam pipes and valves to a hotch potch of GEC turbine generators built in Trafford Park Manchester. The whole thing should have been torn down a decade ago but international sanctions against Rhodesia had stopped new investment in the electricity supply system and so this industrial antique was duty bound to keep chewing up coal and pushing out electricity into the foreseeable future. Geography had dictated the improbable location. A year round supply of water and access to coal form the Wankie coal mines was key in the decision making process.

As a by-product an isolated strategic target had been created. Throughout the liberation struggle a substantial garrison protected the installation from attack. Now that hostilities were over the garrison facilities provided a hidden location to secrete away bits of the most ruthless elements of the new Zimbabwean Army – the North Korean trained 5th Brigade.

Lieutenant Colonel Sadi was a thick set man. His neck strained the button on the collar of his shirt and his cheeks were puffed out giving his face a bloated appearance, which coincidentally matched his stomach that threatened to pop the brass buttons off his dress tunic. It was said that Sadi had spent many years running around the bush during the Struggle. Most would question if he was capable of a decent walk nowadays.

"Do you come as part of the COI or as a Comrade from The Struggle?" asked Sadi.

"I come as a Comrade," replied Joshua.

"Good. Then I know what must be done."

"There are people that own me a debt of blood. I come to ask you to help me take what is due to me," said Joshua

"That is as I understood it. Say what you want of me. Tell me of the people we must visit.

When Joshua stopped talking Sadi replied. "I know the people of whom you speak. I am sure they are the same ones. I cannot believe that the Matable had more than one set of twins in their command structure."

"What do you know of them?" asked Joshua.

Sadi leaned back in his chair. "There is not so much to say. They were trained by the Russians and fought well for the Matable during the struggle. They gave themselves up to the Matable South Collection Point as instructed at the end of the war. They were one of the first to be sent home to their Kraal near Shabini. Their father is

Chief Dingisgani. He is reported to be senile so it is expected that one of the twins will take his place soon. The only thing out of the ordinary is that it is said they have a sister who has a bastard coloured child. A souvenir of the war. That she keeps the child and did not have it put to death says to me that the child is not the consequence of rape!"

"Will the Twins be there if I go?" asked Joshua.

"That is our information."

"Then I will go," said Joshua. "You can provide the men you promised?"

"For you I can do this."

RAF Valley, Anglesey, UK. 1ˢᵗ September 1980

The HS125 Executive jet followed the North Wales coastline. To the left were the snow capped Snowdonia Mountains, to the right the island of Anglesey. As the pilot passed over an unseen radio beacon he banked and headed due north until he picked up the ILS signal. He flicked a switch and locked on to the glide slope that would take him to the edge of the runway. The four passengers inside the jet tightened their belts in preparation for a bumpy landing. Already they knew that military transport pilots paid less attention to passenger comforts than their civilian counterparts.

The briefing room was more like a sixth form classroom. A blackboard hung on the wall behind the raised 'teacher's' dais. Twenty desks were arranged in neat lines. Old blackout curtains hung from the windows and a 16mm cine-projector pointed at an erected screen. A spool of film was threaded through the projector mechanism, ready to go. The four young Africans were still in their flying suits.

"You'll be the first Zimbabweans to pass through here," said the Wing Commander from the dais. "Let me tell you about the new Hawk 60's that your country has acquired. It is the first of a new generation of planes that many pilots in the UK would dearly love to get their hands on. And let me be clear from the beginning, by the time you leave this establishment you will be able to handle your aircraft as well as anybody. We will not compromise on standards. If you're not ready we will not let you pass the course."

"Now before I show you a short film from BAe about the Hawk are there any questions?"

One of the student pilots raised a hand. "I thought the Hawk was just a trainer. What makes it so special that so many people would want it?"

"Good question," said the wing commander. "The Hawk was introduced as a trainer a few years ago but it quickly proved itself to be very versatile. Early on the RAF gave it a defence roll and fitted slides to accept Sidewinder air to air missiles. Following that success it was felt that there was even more scope for development. As a result the latest aircraft have a strengthened fuselage and up-rated engines. This means the plane's take off weight is increased by over thirty percent. Five weapons pods have also been fitted. The centre line pod will take a 30mm cannon. Additionally the two pods on each wing are capable of carrying an external bomb load! The Hawk 60 now has serious ground attack capabilities." The Wing Commander smiled. "Of course I would stress that we will only be training you as pilots. You will receive no combat training in this establishment. Still I suppose it's nice to know what your planes are capable of. "

The Kraal, Shabani, 14th May 1981

The collective wealth of a Matable village is measured by the number of cattle it possesses and it is the collective responsibility of the village men to care for the cattle. Even Dingisgani's fading mind knew the dry season would soon be upon them and the lush grazing would be replaced by yellow tufts of dry stalks that yielded to the breeze. It was important to keep the cattle on what remained of the good grazing so that their bellies would be full and they would be strong enough to get over the coming period of scarcity.

Chief Dingisgani ordered the men to move the herd to the last of the good pastures, a place distant from the Kraal. He instructed them to stand guard, protecting their bovine charges from prides of roaming lions and scavenging hyenas. It was the traditional time when men sat around open fires, eating maize cake and biltong while reminiscing; a time when they slept under the distant stars of an African night and felt the closeness of their ancestors but were away from the Kraal. The men prepared to go.

Elizabeth rose with the cockerel each morning, James her companion. In the stillness, when the air was fresh, it was the time of mother and child. Today the Kraal was active and James was distracted by the men that gathered and moved towards the gate.

James now walked, the skin of his bare feet already hardened by sand and stone and although words were imperfectly formed by his young lips his ability to communicate was unhindered. By the hand he dragged his mother after the men. No amount of persuasion would deter him from the task of following the herders as they began their long march.

"Alright child," she gently spoke yielding to his demand; "we will follow the men until your young legs are tired. Then we will collect berries for your grandfather on the way back."

It was some time before his childish enthusiasm and gritty determination had been defeated by the long strides of the men. Eventually he sank to the floor, refusing to walk anymore.

"We will rest here," said Elizabeth. "But you will walk back by your own feet. I will not carry you. It is important that you understand the consequences of your own actions. This will be your lesson of the day."

Although the Leyland chassis was never designed for the purpose it fulfilled the function well. Sure the Crocodile anti-mine, personnel carrier was a bit top heavy and had a tendency to lurch around a bit on rough roads, but nobody would dispute it's strangely angled sides had deflected many landmine detonations and saved countless lives. So effective was the design, originally scribbled on the back of a cigarette packet, that it had been adopted in many guerrilla wars.

The sun was still low in the skies, it would be many hours before it reached its peak. The two ungainly Crocodiles made their way slowly down the dirt road towards the Kraal of Dingisgani. Sandwiched between the two vehicles was the olive green Peugeot of Joshua Sovimbo. Tyoni, the dark talisman, drove in silent anticipation.

The Kraal was a defensive concept, the equivalent of a castle, designed to keep danger out. Unfortunately once the entrance was compromised it became more like a trap for the inhabitants. That is why it was important to have the gates closed before the enemy arrived. But since the end of the liberation struggle the lookout had been removed. Nobody was watching as the trucks approached.

The North Korean instructors had been as thorough as they had been ruthless. They had taught their students to take the initiative and demonstrate commitment early in an operation. Shock was a weapon for quashing resistance. Twenty men disembarked from the Crocodiles and ran into the Kraal. Villagers were pulled from huts and driven from their fires. They were forced to the centre of the compound. Reluctance was countered by the butt of the rifle. Age or youth earned no leniency. Only when all were gathered and the village subdued did Joshua Sovimbo appear, slowly coming forward. His pistol remained holstered, he carried a panga. Menacingly, in time with his footsteps, he slapped the flat of the blade into his bare palm. The effect brought silence to the herded crowd. Alone, atop the mound, outside his Chief's hut, Dingisgani stood looking down on the scene his muddled mind fighting for comprehension. In his hand he held the tiny ceremonial asagi and shield, the symbols of his authority which he proposed to use to repel the hostile visitors.

Joshua walked towards the Chief, slowly climbing the mound. Dingiskani raised his right hand and pointed the asagi at Joshua in a symbolic threat. Joshua raised his hands and fell to his knees in mock submission.

"Oh great Chief, do not harm me!" he shouted.

The soldiers laughed at the performance. The villagers stood in stony silence. Joshua rose and turned to face the crowd.

"You do not like my joke?" he shouted.

They remained mute.

"None of you have a tongue? None will join me in some fun?" Joshua turned back to face the Chief and walked toward him. "Very well we will get to business. Where are your sons old man? I have a score to settle with them."

Never had a person walked to his hut uninvited. Dingisgani once again raised his spear. "Get down on your knees. Do not speak to me unless I tell you to do so."

Without warning the old man's legs collapsed and he fell to his knees. Behind him stood Tyoni. He'd only had to push the back of the old man's frail legs with the butt of his rifle.

"You will do well to answer my questions," said Joshua resting the flat of his panga on the Chief's shoulder. "Where are your sons, the Twins?"

From the herded crowd a youth stepped forward, one nearly a man, one waiting for his initiation. A soldier moved to push him back. Joshua saw.

"No let him come. Let me hear what he has to say."

The youth walked forward. "The men are away, they tend the cattle. There is no one here for you. We will tell the sons of the Chief that you came."

"You speak for the Chief?" asked Joshua.

"With your own eyes you can see he is an old man. He is not always sure of the truth. He can do no harm to you. Leave him alone."

"If I cannot have the Chief's son then I will have his daughter and his grandson. Bring them to me," demanded Joshua. "Then you will save others."

The youth took one more step forward. "They are also not here but even if they were we would not give them up."

"Brave words of defiance," shouted Joshua. He nodded to the nearest guard.

A burst of automatic fire riddled the youth's back. A flock of crows rose from a nearby tree as he fell forward. Blood soaked into the sand. He didn't move. The crowd stood silent. Joshua walked forward.

"Who else has words of defiance for me? I want the daughter. Give her to me. If you do not give her to me I will pick the next to die myself."

It was as if the gunfire had awoken the old spirit within. Dingisgani rose to his feet and stood erect, a long absent clarity filled his eyes and his voice was strong.

"By the Spirits of our ancestors you will pay for what you have done and unless you leave this place now I prophesise your end to be deserving of the serpent you are. Go." He walked towards his tormentor.

"You threaten me with your ancestors? Then perhaps you should join them." Joshua raised the panga and brought it down, in a sweeping stroke. The Chief lifted a protecting arm. The blade found no resistance in the scrawny flesh and easily shattered the brittle bone. The arm fell limply to his side, attached only by a scrag of skin and flesh. There was no protection from the second stroke. The keen blade sliced into his rib cage. The wound opened wide but blood only trickled. Inside the damage was great. The old mans knees crumpled. Never again would the descendent of the great Zulu warrior stand proud.

Joshua turned to face the silent crowd. His face flushed with anger, eyes bulging. "If you think this act of retribution is sufficient for me then you are mistaken. I have only just begun. This place is cursed. When I have finished all that will remain is charred ashes and you will all disappear in a conflagration of fire that falls from the sky that will be as great as that found in hell. Even the Devil himself will shun this place. As I speak your fate is being sealed. And if perchance any of you should escape I will hunt you down one at a time till the tribe of Dingisgani is no longer."

He signalled the soldiers to withdraw.

Tyoni walked alongside his master. "What did you mean about the fire? I did not understand."

Joshua spoke, "I am ready but my collaborators are not so strong. They require a pretext for action. It will not be long before the Matable provide me with the right excuse. Then I will be swift. Then you will see fire from the sky consume all of my enemies."

The gunfire had alerted her. She picked up her child and ran back toward the Kraal. Careful not to come into the open she circled the compound, hidden by the bush, until she had a view of the entrance. She saw men in uniform climbing on to trucks. They laughed and joked but still Elizabeth harboured foreboding and sensed danger. Gently she held her hand over the mouth of James lest he give them away. The engines barked to life and the lorries left the way they come spewing clouds of black diesel smoke out of their exhausts. She dashed forward.

The body of the youth was lying alone, surrounded by blood stained sand. On the mound villagers formed a silent ring. She pushed her way through. Her farther lay on the floor. Hands gently removed James from her. Elizabeth sank and cradled her father's head in her lap.

He responded to her gentle touch. The wisp of a smile appeared on his blue lips.

"Daughter my wish has been granted. I pass content from this world with your image clear in my mind."

"Do not speak," she soothed in the forlorn hope that his silence would extend the thread of life.

"I have little time, so you must listen. I will not say which of my sons shall inherit my mantle for I love them both equally and cannot choose one above the other. They are both good and will decide themselves what is best for our people. Until that time you will lead us through the coming danger. I see people who try to bring darkness upon us. You must resist. I will stand guardian over you. When the troubles are past I will send a signal."

He gulped for air and his voice sank to a whisper. With his last strength he pulled her closer. "You too will have a decision to make, a decision for your own life. I tell you be true to your heart, seek happiness and you have my blessing. I love you my daughter."

His final gentle breath felt warm on her cheek.

Salisbury, Zimbabwe, 8th December 1981

Sergi Andropov lit another Madison and slid the half red, half white 30 pack into his shirt pocket. The box reminded him of the Polish flag and by association the austerity of the vassal state to his mother country. He drew deeply on the heavily toasted tobacco. The kick was palpable, far superior to the crap Aeroflot tobacco he was used to in Moscow. The lights turned to green, he slipped the gear lever into first and accelerated away. The responsive Nissan pulled crisply, a far cry from the Moskovitch in which he'd learnt to drive. Either side of the road were pristine acre sized plots, each like a mini botanical garden surrounding an immaculate single storied colonial house. This was the northern suburbs of Salisbury, the former white enclave.

"No wonder the bastards fought so hard to keep it," he thought to himself.

The Socialist Workers paradise didn't compare well to this. He knew bemoaning his plight was not helping. He forced his mind back to the task. He'd taken a left from 2nd Street Extension onto The Chase. He followed the road past the University. Pick and Pay went-by on the left and then the petrol station. He missed the first left, turning after the garage, then indicated for the second turn. Pendennis Road was exclusive and secluded. He drove more slowly now, looking for the half concealed drive on the right. If he'd been concentrating on the job a little more he might have noticed the yellow VW Beetle that had been following him since he'd left the Russian Embassy.

The narrow drive twisted through some mature pines before breaking out into a clearing of manicured lawns. In the centre of the clearing stood the house. Sergi noticed the two black gardeners raking pine needles and cones into neat piles. The bulges that concealed pistols in their new blue overalls were barely visible to the casual observer but his eye picked them up.

Inside the house Nkomo waited. He was fat. So much so his walk had been reduced to a waddle. Sweat continuously ran down his jowls soaking the collar of his shirt. It was almost an effort for him to stand. The man that had almost won a place at the top table of international politics and had dined with the Queen of England was reduced to clandestine meetings as he desperately clung to the hope of political rehabilitation.

"You came alone?" asked Nkomo.

"I did not want to draw attention to myself," replied Sergi Andropov. "We jeopardise the project every time we meet."

"It is more dangerous for me than for you," replied Nkomo. "You are a diplomat and will merely be expelled from the country, whereas I could be branded a traitor and hung. Why was the meeting so important and urgent?"

"I would not be so sure of my fate it is a perilous as your own. To the business. Read this," said Sergi handing Nkomo a newspaper cutting.

Nkomo examined the cutting. Somebody had scribbled in the margin, 'Daily Telegraph, London, yesterday!' Nkomo read.

It has just been reported that General Peter Walls, Chief of the Zimbabwean Defence Forces and former leader of the rebel Rhodesian Army has been sacked from his post and will shortly be stripped of his Zimbabwean citizenship. It is expected he and his family will be exiled to apartheid South Africa.

Reliable reports claim the surprise move follows a confrontation between General Walls and Robert Mugabe when Mugabe asked Walls why his men were trying to kill him. Walls is said to have replied, 'If it were my men that were trying to kill you, you would now be dead!'

The confrontation follows a number of recent attempts on Robert Mugabe's life, the latest being a shoot out at the Prime Minister's private residence.

Nkomo put down the cutting. "So what is the problem with this? Do we not want Mugabe dead and is it not good they are fighting amongst themselves?"

"No, it is not good," said Sergi. "Despite his getting rid of General Walls, Mugabe will believe the General's candid words. So Mugabe will ask who is trying to kill him and he will come to the same logical conclusion as I have. It is you!"

Nkomo smiled and shrugged his massive shoulders. "It could be that some dissident former members of my forces may have tried to do us a favour."

Sergi shook his head. "All they have done is alert Mugabe.

And if they had succeeded in killing him it would have been worse. When Mugabe dies there will be a power vacuum. If we are not ready to fill that vacuum then anybody could take control."

Sergi continued, "We have given you money to buy properties around the capital. There are arms caches in each of the properties. These will be our bases. When Mugabe dies we will have people ready to capture or eliminate the rest of the Cabinet. We will have men trained to seize key installations. Parliament, the radio and TV stations, the airport and transport routes will be under our control within hours. Believe me organising a successful coup is not a simple matter! You must control your men until we are ready. Is this clear?"

Nkomo was not used to such harsh and direct words but pragmatism stilled his tongue. He knew without Sergi and the Russians he was destined to receiving nothing but crumbs from Mugabe's table and he craved better fare.

Sergi lit another cigarette as he pulled out of Pendennis Drive. It had gone as well as he could have hoped for. He drove for a while before signalling and pulling into the car park of the Hunters Lodge restaurant on The Chase. Time for a steak he thought. Again he failed to notice the yellow VW Beetle.

The lunch buffet at the Monopotapa Hotel on Park Lane was famous; the best in Harare as Salisbury was now known. Stuart Cameron stood in line ready to fill his plate, Duncan Murdoch behind him.

"Can't knock the meat," said Stuart, "shame about the scarcity of seafood though."

"Land locked country," replied Duncan. "No foreign exchange. Not seen a prawn or cockle for years. Can't say I miss them although I sometimes crave an old Scottish Smokee."

Plates full, the men selected a remote table on the balcony overlooking the pool. A waiter rushed over and raised the parasol for shade before taking the drinks order.

"How long you planning on staying in Zimbabwe?" asked Duncan.

"How long is a piece of string?" replied Stuart. "There's a lot going down at the moment. Could be in and out of here for quite a while really."

"Anything in particular you want to tell me about?" asked Duncan.

"Bits you know. Zimbabwe is a Front Line State now. Border is potentially very hot. Then there's the civil war in Mozambique. That's really rough. Worse than most people appreciate."

"I was in Mozambique," said Duncan.

"Of course, I forgot."

"Then there's our guys in BMATT. They pick up quite a lot.

"BMATT?"

"British Military Advisory and Training Team. Sorry. Bit of a mouthful," said Stuart. You'd be surprised what they are privy to. Got the run of KG5 Barracks and all the Intel that comes out of there."

Duncan changed the subject. "Why did you ask me to come up from the mine?"

"It's personal and I thought you would like to hear it directly. Besides you said you had something for me. Also the phones are terribly leaky nowadays. Take my word don't trust an open phone line. We'll have to organise ourselves something a bit more secure."

"What about Patrick Walker, don't you use him anymore?" asked Duncan. 'Where's he?"

"Gone," replied Stuart. "Back in Blighty, tending roses somewhere in Kent I expect. Be dead in two years though. Liver's buggered; cirrhosis. Still I'll come back to him. Give me your story first."

"I don't know if it's something or nothing," started Duncan. "I help with the training of the young mine lads. The young black ones coming through. Not a bad bunch really. Keen as mustard. As part of their training they spend time in the workshops of the Sabi munitions factory.

It's not unusual for individuals to come to me with odd questions but one day a chap came and told be he was working on a special project. He asked about different types of detonators and fuses. He was particularly interested in white phosphorus as an ignition agent. Now that's very specialist and we don't have any need for anything like that in the asbestos mine. The only applications are in the military field. In any event I give him a chat around the subject and that's it as far as I'm concerned. But a couple of weeks later he come back and to show me his project papers and to ask me what did I think. What I saw was the design for a fairly sophisticated fused white phosphorous igniter. Not the type of thing your everyday chap comes across."

"So what does that mean in English?" asked Stuart.

"Simple. Napalm-B is made up of a cocktail of benzene, gasoline and polystyrene. It is really easy to make, it is very stable and, above all, one of the nastiest substances known to man. A real terror weapon. It really puts the shit up people on the receiving end. The saving grace is that because of its stability it is hard to ignite when and where you want it. The best ignition system known for Napalm is white phosphorus because it burns at such a high temperature: 4532 degrees F to be precise."

"So," said Stuart, "you're saying somebody is making Napalm bombs?"

"Almost certainly," replied Duncan. "Or at least thinking about it. The good thing is you can't deliver the stuff by cannon. You really need to drop it from an aeroplane and as the Zimbabwe Airforce is entirely composed of white ex-Rhodesian pilots I doubt if they would find anybody willing to drop the stuff on civilians. I think I'm right on that. But I still think you need to know that they are going down that route."

Stuart thought for a while.

"Not quite without a delivery system," said Stuart. "Not quite."

For a while they sat in silence, sipping their beers.

Eventually Duncan spoke. "You had something to tell me?"

"Stop me at any time and that's the end of it, won't go any further," said Stuart.

"When Patrick went he left a pile of papers. Very naughty really. At least I got hold of them. I had a rummage and found a note about you – and your servant girl at Mashava. Do you want me to go on?"

Duncan's heart missed a beat. He said nothing.

"I'll take that as a yes. Patrick felt that there might have been some kind of feeling, possibly even a relationship between the two of you."

Duncan opened his mouth to speak.

Stuart raised a hand. "You owe me no explanation. I have no judgement to make. But from your reaction I think you might want to listen a little more."

"Patrick thought you compromised yourself at one time during some disturbances, even risking your life for this girl. It appears she disappeared shortly after that and there is nothing more in Patrick's notes. However, that is not the end of it. As a matter of course the United Nations High Commission for Refugees submits its lists of people being housed in refugee camps. We want to know if there are criminals or other undesirables tucked away in some camp or other. Just by chance I was looking at a list a few weeks ago and a name jumped out at me. For ages I couldn't think why. It only came back to me much later. Elizabeth Mashlonga was the name. Could it be the same person I asked? Truly I'm not sure but the dates tally up with Patrick's notes. At the end of the war I believe she was in a Botswana refugee camp."

"Where is she now?" asked Duncan not quite shocked into silence.

"That I don't know but I have put in a request to the UNHCR for further information. I will let you know as soon as I find something out if you want."

"I'd like that," said Duncan. "I did have a relationship with her. I didn't know if she survived the conflict. I've waited for her but never dared to search. If I found her in a native village it would not be the same and she would face rejection from her own people. I thought it better if I waited for her to contact me. It has been a difficult wait."

"By the way I'm not sure how to say this," continued Cameron, "but in the camp she had a child of mixed race with her. He was born in the camp and his name is recorded as James."

Mashava Mine, 13th March 1982

Duncan sat on his front stoop, beer in hand, gazing into nothing. His mind fixed on the conversation he'd had with Cameron months earlier in Salisbury. He could have worked an extra shift at the mine that day but couldn't be bothered, settling for another blank Saturday afternoon. At first he chose not to notice the African standing at the gate, preferring to leave his mind elsewhere.

Stewart Cameron had promised to find out more about Elizabeth and James. True to his word a letter had come a few weeks ago. Duncan's hopes lifted when he collected the brown envelope from his mail box at the mine Post Office. He'd fought the desire to rip it open there and then. Instead he took it home. With trembling hands he began to read the words, barely able to contain himself. Cameron wrote that he'd received an initial response from the UNHCR. The refugee camp in Botswana was now closed and all the inhabitants had been moved on, most going back to Zimbabwe. Elizabeth Mashlonga was among the last to leave. Cameron went on to say efforts would be made to find Elizabeth's final destination and another letter would follow as soon as there was news. The final paragraph struck fear into Duncan's heart. Cameron said that as Elizabeth had an illegitimate mixed race child she'd been approached by a US church group that specialised in settling unwanted children in the United States. The results of the approach were unrecorded. It was normal for the adopting organisation to offer money for children by way of compensation.

Duncan sank into a morose mood, unable to draw his thoughts from the lamentable position. His mother died leaving only an estranged and distant father. The only man that he ever felt close to, Jimmy Scobie, had died violently in front of his eyes. Then when he'd tantalisingly brushed with love the fruit was not only forbidden but also taken away when he'd barely tasted its sweet nectar.

On Cameron's advice he'd decided not to look for Elizabeth for the present time. He knew that despite his deep desire he'd not be able to face her if it turned out she'd given his child away. Not for the first time he thought about returning to cold grey Glasgow, to disappear anonymously into the murk that reflected his mood. He

shook himself from his depressing thoughts and looked at the
African still standing at the gate.

There was something different about him. His erect stance
and square shoulders separated him from the stream of grovelling
hawkers and traders that normally came to the house. His failure to
persistently whistle for attention was not normal. The stranger just
stood there waiting till Duncan was ready.

Duncan took a swig of his beer. The liquid had warmed in the
sun and tasted badly. It was flat. He put the bottle on the table and
walked down to the gate. The African did not speak at first, simply
offering a white envelope. It was sealed but not addressed. Duncan
opened it and withdrew a new $20 Zimbabwe bill. There was a note.
Duncan recognised the neat hand. It was the same as on the note that
he kept beside his bed. He read the few words that were formal and
lacked warmth. "Thank you for the loan. This is my brother. Please
listen to him". It was simply signed Elizabeth. Duncan looked at the
man. He didn't flinch under Duncan's gaze, only nodding his head
slightly in acknowledgement.

"What's your name?" asked Duncan.

"I am Morgan. I was your enemy. Now I come to ask for your
help on behalf of my people."

"How can I help you? Have you come to ask for money?"
Duncan saw from the man's expression that he was insulted.

"I return money to you not ask for it," he said pointing to the
$20 note still in Duncan's hand. "The help I ask for is much more
difficult but my sister Elizabeth says you are a good man and will
know the people to go to."

Duncan opened the gate and let Morgan in.

The Air Zimbabwe Boeing 720 had left London Gatwick
twelve and a half hours earlier. Now it taxied to its stand on the
apron at Harare Airport. Seven am, exactly on time. The stairs were
ready to roll up as soon as the engines were cut. Joshua Sovimbo
stood on the public observation balcony watching and drinking
coffee, failing to appreciate the low humidity and freshness of the
morning.

The doors of the plane opened and passengers started to
disembark. Joshua finished his coffee and slowly made his way down

the stairs to the arrivals hall. By the time he got there Tyoni had gathered the four men who had just disembarked from the 720, the ones Joshua was waiting for, the ones that had not long ago graduated from RAF Valley as pilots of Hawk Jets. The group moved off to a room, seconded for the meeting from the Immigration Department.

"Sit", ordered Joshua. He produced a letter from his pocket and spread it on the table in front of the men.

"Read this!"

One man picked up the single sheet. He red it and passed it the next. Each man in turn raised eyebrows in surprise at the content.

"Do you understand what is written and recognise the signature?" asked Joshua Sovimbo.

The first man answered. "I understand what is written but I cannot be sure of the signature."

Joshua nodded. I will leave the room. There is a phone. You may use it to call State House to verify that the letter is indeed signed by our leader, Robert Mugabe."

"No," said one of the others, "It is enough for me." The first man recanted his reservation.

"Good," said Sovimbo, "We in the Central Intelligence Organisation are charged with protecting the State from threats. After independence the Army was found to be corrupt and infiltrated by enemies of the State. To counter this we trained a special unit that is separate from the Army and reports to the Prime Minister. You will know this as the 5th Brigade.

We also know that the Air Force is corrupted and not loyal. So we must now place people into the Air Force who are unquestionably loyal to our leader. You four men are the first black African pilots to have completed their training. This is why you have been chosen to be the vanguard of truth. In a few weeks time your planes will arrive, new Hawks from England. The best planes that the Airforce will possess. We do not want you to be corrupted by the old guard you must stay separate and strong. This is why we are sending you to our Comrades in North Korea. They will give you further training, training in combat flying, particularly ground attack. When you return you will be the 5th Brigade of the skies." Joshua Sovimbo smiled. "And you will lead an operation that will eradicate the latest threat to our democracy. You will become heroes."

"Are you ready to help your leader? What shall I tell him?" asked Sovimbo.

"We are ready," they answered.

Tyoni drove the car away from the airport. Joshua sat in the back. They passed under the welcome arch as they left the Airport precincts.

"Are you not worried that their minds will have already been corrupted by the English?" asked Tyoni. "They have been in that country a long time."

"I have no worry of that," replied Joshua. "Maybe now they only pay lip service but by the time the North Koreans have finished with their minds they will be willing to kill their own mothers at my command! And when they return I will have everything else ready for them. All I will then need is an excuse. But why do you ask me about such things? Such issues are not the concerns of my chauffeur."

The journey continued in silence.

Stuart Cameron had paid cash for the room at the George Hotel. It was a double room and he'd had extra chairs sent up. Now the three of them sat together.

"This really needs to be special," said Cameron. "What we are doing is very dangerous. I could not risk a public meeting."

"It was enough for me to make the six hour drive. You listen to Morgan and be the judge for yourself," said Duncan Murdoch.

Cameron turned to Morgan. "From you own lips. Tell me the full story. We are here now so take your time, do not miss out any of the details."

Morgan the ex-combatant was sure and clear with his words. He told of the 5th Brigade's visit to his village and the killing of the youth and his father. He spoke of Joshua Sovimbo and his former life as Makonzo and the threats of fire from the sky that would come in the near future. He spoke in depth about the funeral of his father.

"After the funeral I sat down with my brother and sister to discuss the future," said Morgan.

"Go on", said Cameron.

"We discussed the murder of my father and the need for revenge. But Elizabeth my sister advised against action. She said the time was not ready.

"We told her we had already been asked to fight. Fight to redress the injustice of the elections. The word was about that the old organisation was coming back to life. My brother and I thought it would be raids on Government depots for food and equipment, maybe taking money or just chasing away Shona that had come to steal our jobs. We liked the idea and so rejected the advice of my sister. We joined the dissidents.

"Elizabeth's advice was not to fight?" asked Duncan.

"It was. But we did not listen."

"And what happened when you joined the dissidents?"

"Ah! We were surprised. We were not just bandits. The orders still came from the Russians. We had to go to a remote farm to the south of Harare. We went there by truck in the dark so as not to be seen. Everyday it was hard work. It was clear there was a plan. We were going to take over the country. Always we trained. When the time came it would be my job to take Government members from their beds. We had photographs of the people and the addresses of the houses where they live. Our instructions are to kill our targets and anybody that tried to stop us. Others groups were training, some were going to take the airport or other key buildings."

"Repeat what you told me yesterday, about who was doing the training," said Duncan.

"The special training was done by white people. They wore masks when they were with us. We never saw their faces. But I know the accent. They were Russians. Sometimes they came in diplomatic cars. Cars from the Russian Embassy. They brought maps and weapons. "

"So why do you come to us now?" asked Stuart, "Don't you want the Matable to rule the country? That is what you fought the war for wasn't it?"

"The people in the camp, the people who are plotting, are only a few who work for the Russians. They do not represent the Matable nation. If it goes wrong the Russians will disappear and the ordinary people will pay the price. Our country has already been at war for more than fifteen years. I cannot see it plunged into a civil war that will go on for another fifteen. Besides the next war will not be a European conflict where people at least pretend to follow the rules. No, the way of revenge will be an African conflict with African rules. My sister says the only hope is to stop it before it starts and she is correct. She knows that our village and people are already under threat from Makonzo, the one that now calls himself Joshua Sovimbo. He would only use any action we take as an excuse to destroy our people."

"Alright," said Cameron shrugging his shoulders, "can you tell me when you think this coup will take place?"

Morgan smiled. "You will do something then?"

"I will report it to my superiors. They will decide."

From the back of his pants Morgan pulled a folded map pouch. He handed it to Cameron.

"The plan; the start points, objectives and timings. It is set to happen in three days time," said Morgan.

"WHEN!" exclaimed Cameron. "What do you expect me to do in that short time?"

"You can do something. I know that," said Morgan. "I have taken a risk to bring this plan to your Duncan Murdoch. I must now go back to the training camp before I am discovered.

"Right," said Cameron, "I've heard and seen enough. You have given me the possibility of an almost genocidel attack on your people and a coup against a sovereign government. That's enough for a Sunday afternoon. Let's end this meeting before you think of anything else! Morgan, you must make your plan to get away from the training camp. It will be dangerous for you to stay. "

"This I know."

Duncan and Morgan stayed in the hotel room for a while, giving Cameron a head start. They watched from the hotel window as he got into his yellow VW Beetle and drove up St George Road, headed in the direction of the Northern Suburbs and the diplomatic residential area.

State House, Harare, Zimbabwe. 17th March 1982

Stuart Cameron wore full dress uniform out of respect for the person he was visiting. He was relaxed and confident. He had the approval of the British Government to hold this conversation.

"This is highly irregular," said Robert Mugabe, Prime Minister of Zimbabwe. "There are proper procedures that should be followed."

"I fully understand that Prime Minister but I assure you that what I have to say is of the utmost importance. I am sure you will appreciate that by the time I have finished."

"You may sit," said Mugabe pointing to a Louis XVI carved chair that was in the style of the rest of Mugabe's office furniture.

"As you know Prime Minister I head the British Military Advisory Team attached to your country. In this capacity I have received information from outside of Zimbabwe." He lied. "The information is of such significance that my superiors felt it could only be passed to you directly. It is hoped that you will accept the information as a sign of the special relationship that we feel exists between our two countries."

"Yes. Go on Colonel Cameron."

"It is our understanding that certain parties will attempt to assassinate you and take over the Government of Zimbabwe in the very near future."

Mugabe tipped his head back and looked down his nose at Cameron. "For the last fifteen years of the liberation struggle I lived a precarious existence in a world where many wanted me dead and since becoming Prime Minister the situation has not improved. There have been no less then eight attempts on my life in the past year! Why should I take your warning any more seriously than the rest?"

"I do have proof Prime Minister. But before I divulge my evidence I would like to mention that my Government have some concerns with which they feel you would be able to assist. I hope, that in return for the information I am about to divulge, you will give me the opportunity to discuss the matters and that you will treat the requests in a favourable manner."

"I am conversant with the capitalist and especially British

ways. Give nothing without receiving something in return, Mugabe sighed. "Go on."

Cameron withdrew a buff folder from his briefcase. From the folder he pulled a black and white eight by four inch photograph. "This is one Sergi Andropov, a senior KGB operative with special interests in Southern Africa. It is understood his connections go directly to the Politburo. Currently he is assigned to the Soviet Embassy here in Harare, accredited as a Trade attaché. He is orchestrating a coup d'état."

Mugabe nodded. "A man of your own ilk by the sound of it?"

"Two differences Sir. I am not concealing my position and secondly I am not conspiring to overthrow your Government."

Cameron withdrew more papers from the buff folder. They had been carefully transcribed by hand from the originals that Cameron had received yesterday in the George Hotel. He pushed them over the desk toward the Prime Minister. "These Sir are copies of the actual plans and include locations of bases and arms caches. We believe them to be authentic. You have less than three days to act!"

Mugabe looked at the papers and turned the pages, quickly scanning the contents. After a few moments he picked up his head. "If this is accurate it is of significance," he admitted. "Now what is it you want in return?"

Cameron was ready. "There are two things Sir. Firstly we do not believe that a coup would have been attempted if it were not for the Soviets provoking the situation. Therefore we would ask that you act with restraint towards your own countrymen when dealing with this situation."

"Ha. You don't want me to create panic in Zimbabwe in case I start a stampede of whites. You don't want too many turning up on your shores unannounced do you? What else?"

"As part of the independence aid arrangements we are supplying your country with a number of advanced training aircraft. It is technically possible that these aircraft could be converted to other less acceptable roles. HM Government would not like this. I am sure you understand that there is a certain sensitivity attached to arms exports and misuse of weapons can have rather unpleasant political repercussions. It can be embarrassing for the British Government at home. An assurance from you that both the letter and sentiment of the original agreement will be adhered to would be greatly appreciated."

"I have made notes of your concerns. If there is nothing else you can leave now."

Cameron, disappointed by the response, was escorted to the door of Government House by a footman. Before the massive front door shut behind him Cameron was almost certain he could hear shouts echoing down the corridors.

The two women knew what to expect and how to behave. Grace, the young secretary, stood back against the wall giving Mugabe plenty of room to stomp across the rich Persian carpet. Sally, his wife, sat on a chair, half leaning on the arm for support. Her face was strained and complexion ashen.

Mugabe raged. "The arrogance of those bloody English bastards. They send some junior along to tell me I am about to be killed and he then has the affront to tell me how to run my own country. They still think they are the colonial masters don't they?"

Mugabe looked to his wife. Little bits of foamy spittle had accumulated at the corners of his mouth.

Sally slowly got to her feet. "Robert you are so right but I have to go. It is time for my dialysis. I'm sorry I cannot wait. Grace will stay with you."

Sally limped to the door unaided. Mugabe looked on in silence till she had left the room. Then he resumed his ranting for the remaining audience. "Do you think if I sent a junior to knock on the door of Buckingham Palace the Queen would let him into her drawing room to give advice on bringing up children?"

Grace knew the question was rhetorical. She looked at her boss and smiled. For a moment their eyes locked. She did not look away.

Gradually his voice became calmer and more deliberate. "I will end this rebellion. No longer will I tolerate dissidents in my country. I will use the 5th Brigade to crush each one of them and if every white person leaves the country then so much the better. As for the aeroplanes, we did not want them in the first place. Now that somebody appears to have found a use for them the British squeal like pigs. Well let them squeal some more! That is what I say."

The guard stood some distance from the locked chain link gates that protected the old farm compound. He'd noticed nothing until his attention was grabbed by the truck coming up the long drive. He thought it was a delivery. Deliveries often came at dawn. Too late he recognised the unique profile of the Crocodile APC. He turned and ran towards the alarm bell that hung from the branch of a tree. He was stopped short by the thump in his chest of the 7.62 mm bullet. He took a couple more steps forward before slumping to the ground. From behind the tree came a soldier. He holstered his pistol and placed a red beret on his head so as not to be mistaken by the approaching troops. The 5th Brigade always wore red berets.

The Crocodile did not stop at the gates. It drove straight through, the bull bars making short work of the flimsy construction. Two more trucks followed into the compound. Men dismounted and fanned out entering huts and dragging bleary eyed occupants from their cots. Resistance came from one hut alone. Two separate shots were followed by a burst of automatic fire. Suddenly the Red Berets were crouching to make smaller targets of themselves as they ran around with rejuvenated urgency.

Men surrounded the resisting hut. The Crocodile APC moved forward until its mounted Browning M19 machine gun had a clear traverse. The gun operator cocked the weapon and slowly raked the length of the wooden clinker built walls with a continuous hail of bullets. The wood offered little protection to the hut's occupants. As soon as the machine gun stopped, two Red Berets ran forward and threw grenades through shattered windows. Return fire from the hut had long stopped. An officer, next to the APC, shouted, ordering the huts survivors to come out with their hands raised. The door opened, five men came out, two bleeding and limping. The officer ordered them to kneel on the ground. They obeyed. He walked behind them, going from one to the next firing a single shot into the nape of the neck. The action marked the end of resistance at Hope Farm.

The remaining prisoners were forced to carry the cache of arms into the open. Guns, explosives, RPG's and ammunition were logged and the information, together with a preliminary contact report, was radioed back to HQ in Harare. The report was collated with reports from the other four farm raids that had taken place simultaneously. Half an hour later, before 8am, the information lay on the Prime Minister's desk.

Sergi Andropov left the Embassy of the Union of Soviet Socialist Republics shortly before 9am and drove his Nissan towards the Northern Suburbs. He knew the route well and did not have to think. He correctly believed this would be his last trip to Pendennis Road. It was going to be his final briefing before the coup. According to his schedule in forty-eight hours there would be a new Government and his next journey out of the Embassy grounds would be the short drive to State House to congratulate the new occupants.

He stopped in the outside lane at the red lights on the junction of 2nd and King Edward Streets. The shunt from behind was unexpected. The back of his head hit the rest and prevented a whiplash injury. In the rear view mirror he saw the woman with her head in her hands. He got out of his car and stepped towards her vehicle. A police car came up the inside lane and halted. Two large uniformed officers got out.

The woman opened her window, now looking composed. The first policeman spoke to her. "What has happened here?"

"This man he is crazy," she said, "he drove too far through the red lights. Realising his mistake he quickly reversed and hit my car. I think I am injured."

"That is ridiculous", said Sergi. "She ran into the back of me."

"Be quiet," said the second officer. "You will get your chance to speak."

The first policeman spoke to the woman again. "Do you wish to press charges against this man?"

"I do," she said.

The police man turned to Sergi. "I have no option but to arrest you and take you to the police station."

"That is not possible.....," protested Sergi reaching for his inside pocket. He never finished the sentence and was prevented from pulling his diplomatic passport from his inside pocket. The policemen bundled him to the ground, the handcuffs were ready.

"I am a diplomat and have immunity," shouted Sergi. "I was only reaching for my diplomatic passport. You cannot do this. My Government will protest."

The policemen were not listening. They bundled him into the back seat of the patrol car and drove off, sirens howling.

Fifty yards up King Edward Avenue, under the shade of Jacaranda trees a black Toyota was parked. As the police car disappeared a man got out and walked to the scene of the accident. He got into Sergi's Nissan and drove off. The woman followed, and the scene was clear.

"Drive on," said Joshua to Tyoni. Tyoni put the black Toyota into gear and eased the car back onto the road. He followed in the direction of the police car, on the McIlwaine Road, out of town heading in the opposite direction to the police station.

Thornhill Airbase, Gwelo, 18th May 1982

Thornhill, the main airbase of the Zimbabwe Air Force, was packed with visitors. The signal had come from the control tower. Air Marshall Norman Walsh, in the full dress uniform of commander of the Zimbabwe Air Force, marched to the temporary podium. He waited to take the salute. It was not long coming. The four Hawks approached in a diamond shape, two hundred miles an hour at five hundred feet, a formation the pilots had practised in Wales. Windows in nearby buildings rattled at the combined roar of the up-rated Rolls Royce Adour Turbofan engines. All eyes were fixed on the planes.

The mass of spectators were kept behind a rope cordon. The crowd was made up of invited servicemen, their families and for the first time ordinary workers from the area. In the VIP stand politicians and Party Officials gathered to greet the arrival of the latest addition to the Airforce's complement of aircraft. In the rear tier of the stand sat Robert Mugabe's cousin and commander of the 5th Brigade, Colonel Perence Donga. Next to him sat Joshua Sovimbo.

Joshua leaned close to Donga. "It is innocuous that our Airforce should still be led by the man who was our enemy such a short time ago," he said.

"It is expedient," replied Donga, careful not to be overheard. "I have spoken with my cousin the Prime Minister. For the time being it is necessary to keep up appearances, but soon that will not be so. I tell you that it will not be long before I have that job for myself. But first there are important things to do."

After a second pass the planes landed and taxied to the apron, coming to a halt in front of the dais. The canopies opened and the pilots climbed down ladders that had been brought up to the side of their planes. On the ground they removed their helmets and stiffly saluted their commander. Air Marshall Walsh returned the compliment.

"It must be difficult for the pilots to salute such a man after their training in North Korea," said Joshua.

"That is true. The reports from our friends in Korea were good. They say the first black African pilots will do what is expected of them when the order is given. And now that the planes have arrived it will only be a matter of days before we will be ready. The timing could not be more fortuitous. Tonight my cousin will address the nation on television. It will be the beginning."

"That is clear," replied Joshua. "But before that I have some unfinished business to take care of with our guest."

Donga smiled.

"You bastard, you never said you were going to spill the beans to Mugabe and his henchmen," Duncan made no attempt to conceal his rage.

"I didn't know what I was going to do the last time I saw you," replied Cameron. "I don't operate off my own bat, I take instructions and those were the instructions I received."

"Oh! The 'orders are orders' defence. I thought more of you than that. Do you know Morgan and his brother might be dead now because of you?"

"I warned him to get the hell out of it and take his brother with him. Hopefully he took the advice. And if it comes to that, what the hell are you doing back in Harare?" demanded Cameron.

For a while there was a stony silence between the men. Cameron broke first.

"I'm sorry. But some things are just beyond my control. Please, tell me why you came."

Duncan spoke slowly and without warmth. "I came to tell you about my chap at the mine, the one that asked about detonators for napalm. He was seconded to the Airforce yesterday. That probably means one thing. They're still working on the project. I couldn't phone, it was too dangerous. I had to come to tell you personally," said Duncan his rage subsiding.

"Okay. Thank you. I'm sorry you had such a long journey but that tit-bit is important," replied Cameron. "I'll arrange for some accommodation. You can't go back for a few days."

"Don't need any place to stay here, I'm going to Shabani, the Matable village, to see if the Twins made it."

"You mean that you're going to find that girl Elizabeth."

Duncan did not reply.

"You can't go. The balloon is up. The Prime Minister is about to make a statement, there will be a curfew and roadblocks and all kinds of crazy people on the road. If you turn up in a Matable village it is just going to draw attention. You need to give it a bit of time. Besides I might need you here."

"If anything happens to Elizabeth and ......"

"Your son?" prompted Cameron. "I know how anxious you must be about that."

"I will hold you responsible if anything happens to them," said Duncan."

The TV lounge was situated at the rear of the lobby in the George Hotel. Duncan sat in an overstuffed armchair. A small group of white guests watched in silence. The ZBC caption card disappeared to reveal the Right Honourable Robert Gabriel Mugabe, Prime Minister of Zimbabwe, sitting at his desk. The continuity announcer spoke. "The Prime Minister will now make an emergency address to the Nation."

There was an uncharacteristic quiver in Mugabe's voice. Duncan was not sure if it was nerves or rage.

"It is my duty to report to you that in the last days our vigilant security services have uncovered a dastardly plot to destroy our infant democracy. Raids on a number of farms around the capital, owned by Joshua Nkomo and his cohorts, have unearthed hidden caches of arms and dissidents in training for a violent uprising. In desperate fighting many of the enemy within have been killed and a number of our loyal soldiers have earned a resting place in 'Hero's Acre'."

"It is obvious that there are dissident elements within the Matable, unwilling to accept the rule of democracy. I promise the fair people of Zimbabwe that I will crush the rebels with all the power at my disposal. As a result of the threat to our Nation, with immediate effect, a State of Emergency will exist throughout the country and a curfew from 6pm to 6am will be enforced in all areas of Matabeleland."

"I also announce that all Matable members of my Government are removed from office and warn that any Matable MP that shows his face in parliament will be immediately arrested. An arrest warrant for the Matable leader Joshua Nkomo has been prepared but our information is that he has already fled the country disguised as an old woman. Should he reappear he will be arrested for treason, receive a fair trial and then be hung like the traitor he is."

"I will leave no stone unturned. All dissidents and those who assist

them will be eradicated from free Zimbabwe."

Sergi struggled to sit upright in the police car. He cursed himself for being so stupid and shouted at the policemen to stop. They ignored his protests and drove at high speed. They passed the Polytechnic on the right. It was the last building that Sergi recognised. The car sped past the suburb of Marlborough and cleared city limits. Now there was only country. After half an hour, without warning, the car swerved off the tarmac onto a dirt track. Sergi looked behind at the billowing dust cloud they were creating. It wasn't far, possibly half a mile. He couldn't judge. The car shuddered to a halt, its tyres finding little traction on the dusty surface. An enclosed van was parked facing them. The police men pulled Sergi from the car. Two other Africans in civilian clothing approached. Sergi struggled to free his hands but the unyielding metal of the cuffs cut into his wrists. His protests and threats of the dire diplomatic repercussions went unheard. From behind somebody slipped a black hood over his head. Light disappeared and the feeling of desperation grew. Then he was being pushed, forced into the back of the van, the doors slammed shut. He lay on the metal floor. It was hot. The van's metal skin magnified the heat and the inside felt like an oven. They travelled for a long time, they drove mostly on tarmac but near the end on dirt track. Finally the vehicle came to a halt and the doors opened.

A heavily accented African voice spoke. "Welcome to Goromonzi where you are a guest of the Zimbabwe secret police. We are sure that our facilities are not as good as those of the KGB but we will do our best to make your stay comfortable."

Sergi heard men laugh and felt rough hands pull at him. He stumbled down unseen steps. He fell, nothing broke his fall. The wind was knocked from his stomach, he twisted to protect his face and his elbow struck the concrete floor. The pain was excruciating, he thought he'd broken the joint. There was more laughter. He was yanked back to his feet. He descended more wooden stairs. Sergi imagined a cellar.

He no longer demanded release, his ambitions had been reduced. "Give me some water," he asked.

The response to his request was a fist to his back. It knocked the wind from his lungs. He dropped to his knees. A heavy door shut behind him. He heard the key in the lock. Silence. Despite the pain in his elbow, or maybe because of it, his mind drifted. Consciousness slipped away.

Joshua and Tyoni reached Goromonzi before darkness. They had gone directly to the underground detention centre, one of the few facilities that were not a legacy of the Rhodesian period. It was purposely built in Mugabe's home area by the North Koreans who considered such a facility an essential part of the State's apparatus.

"It is not often we have a Russian spy in our hands. I will carry out the interrogation myself. You will be a witness so long as you can keep your mouth shut," said Joshua to Tyoni. "It should be interesting, although I have to admit we require no information from him."

"Then why do we do we question him?" asked Tyoni.

"Because we can, and it is fun," laughed Sovimbo. He turned to the two guards. Bring him. I am ready."

The interrogation hall had everything that was necessary. Joshua had considered using the medical chair but decided on the tilting table. It was a large wooden board, big enough for a man to lie on. In each corner straps were fixed to restrain the four limbs. A leather neck strap stopped the victim from lifting his head. The table was balanced on a central pivot, like a sea-saw, so it could be tilted. The subject could be held in an almost upright position, horizontal, or by taking the table to its full extent backward, almost upside down. It provided a good working platform.

Sergi was regaining consciousness as they fastened him to the table. The pain in his elbow was acute. It distracted him. Slowly he become aware of his nakedness. Then came a bucket of ice water. The shiver ran through his body. It was deep and uncontrollable. Joshua noted how he clenched his teeth to stop them chattering.

"You did not shout with the shock," said Joshua. "Let us try something else to relax your tongue." He turned to the guards, "Put the table flat."

The soles of Sergi's feet were exposed.

Joshua picked up a wooden baton from a table. Without warning he swung and hit Sergi on the ball of his left foot. It was a practised technique. The pain was intense, Sergi could not conceal the grimace but with all his effort he stifled a cry. Sergi in his own mind knew he had to find a way to beat his oppressor. He had to pick a battle ground for the test of wills. He would not let his tormentor have the pleasure of hearing him squeal. As long as he resisted he would be winning.

Again the baton was swung. This time on the right foot. Again and again Joshua swung the baton. Still his victim refused to capitulate. Bones were broken, skin ruptured and blood flowed. Both feet became a swollen bloody mass. It seemed the worse the injury the easier Sergi found it to resist.

Joshua's control ebbed as his anger rose at the stubbiness of his victim. He would make Sergi cry out before he escaped into unconsciousness.

"We will enjoy something else."

Joshua turned to Tyoni who had stepped back and looked on stony-faced.

"What is wrong with you? Have you lost your sense of fun? Tell me."

"I thought when the war was finished it would no longer be necessary to behave like this. There in no longer any reason. You said yourself he has nothing to tell us."

"Of all people I did not expect you to falter."

Joshua went to the wall and lifted the prod off the wall.

"You know what this is?" he asked Sergi who did not respond.

"You soon will. It's a cattle prod. Very popular with farmers for controlling cattle. When I switch it on and prod, you will get a shock large enough to make a cow jump. Shall we see how you like it?"

Joshua held the trigger and let the tips of the electrodes touch Sergi's naked thigh. It was impossible to stop the electrical current putting the muscles into spasm but still there was no scream of pain. Joshua prodded his victim once more. Again there was only a silent convulsion.

Joshua turned around. Without warning he pushed the prod at Tyoni. The pointed electrodes penetrated the thin material of his shirt and entered the skin just below the left nipple. The unexpected pain was intense, Tyoni screamed involuntarily and his legs gave way.

Joshua looked at his faithful talisman with surprise. "I thought the thing was not working properly. I wanted to test it. But in any case it was a just punishment for your wavering attitude," he laughed.

Tyoni struggled to his feet. "You should not have done that to me. I am not the victim." he shouted at his master.

"You shout at me?" said Joshua. "That is not allowed. I am the master here."

He pushed the prod forward once more and the electrodes went in to Tyoni's ribs. Again Tyoni fell to the floor and screamed with the pain. This time rage boiled over. He rose pulling his pistol from his belt and pointed it at Joshua. Joshua stepped backward.

"I told you not to do that again. Why did you do it?"

Both men became still, each waiting for the other to make a movement. Then Tyoni felt the gun pressed in to the small of his back. One of the guards had come from behind. The second guard stepped forward and removed the pistol from Tyoni's hand. He passed it to Joshua.

"I should kill you for that," said Joshua. "You cannot threaten me. But first I have other business. I will deal with you later."

Joshua now held the prod in one hand and the pistol in the other. He turned to Sergi. The Russian was conscious, straining his head to see his tormentors fight. Joshua rammed the prod hard into Sergi's exposed testicles. This time he was unable to suppress the cry. His involuntary scream was piercing.

"I knew you would not be able to resist in the end," said Joshua. He put the pistol square on to Sergi's head and pulled the trigger. With little more than a kick against his restraining straps Sergi died.

Joshua felt a surge of relief pass thorough his body, an indescribable emotional euphoria and his great anger subsided. Slowly he turned to Tyoni who still faced the guard's gun.

Joshua's anger had been satisfied and he spoke calmly.

"We have been together a long time Tyoni. Till now you have been a faithful servant. Because of this I will not kill you for this lapse. But from now on I will be watching. You will never carry a gun in my presence again."

Thirty Miles North East of Moscow 23rd May 1982

The spring thaw was late in coming. Snow still blanketed the ground although it had lost some of its pristine whiteness. Comrade Molenski had never liked the Russian winters; they reminded him of his time on the Stalingrad front in 1943. They had of course won the battle but the cost was too high for the experience to be tempered with romanticism, no matter how much time passed.

Now, almost forty years later, retired from the Politburo and Army, he sat in his country Dacha north east of Moscow looking out of the window. But he was still not free of the intrigue and duplicity that was Soviet politics. Again he looked at the papers that had arrived anonymously that morning. Were they sent by a friend or an enemy? It was impossible to know.

The first piece of paper was a transcript of an article from the Harare Daily Herald. It described how the body of a diplomat, a trade attaché attached to the Russian Embassy named Sergi Andropov, had been found dead in the 'Avenues District' of the capital. The area was notorious for its red light activities and the article speculated that the diplomat had resisted when approached by a gang of armed robbers and suggested that drink may have been involved.

Molenski picked up the second piece of paper, the draft of a communiqué to be issued simultaneously by the Soviet Foreign Ministry in Moscow and the Russian Embassy in Harare.

'Due to recent events the Russian Government feels that the deteriorating security situation in Zimbabwe, with reference to street crime in the Capital, makes normal activities excessively hazardous. It has therefore decided, with great reluctance, to temporally curtail its operations in Zimbabwe. All non essential embassy staff, particularly those associated with trade and cultural activities will be withdrawn immediately. Only a minimum presence for basic consular activities will be maintained. The Russian Government sincerely looks forward to a time in the near future when normal relations can be re-established.'

The last piece of paper was headed 'comments from the last meeting of the Politburo of the Union of Soviet Socialist Republics'. The comments were un-attributed.

'.....the adventure into Rhodesian and Zimbabwean politics has

been the most unsuccessful African initiative in Soviet history. The operation consumed vast amounts of precious foreign currency over many years and produced no positive results whatsoever. In fact we are so discredited in the region we have left the area wide open for our Chinese rivals.'

'.... It is appreciated that the head of the operation perished in the operation. However such failure cannot be left unaddressed. Consideration should be given to exiling Sergi Andropov's family to Siberia. This will serve as an example to other adventures. Additionally, Andropov had a sponsor who once sat on this committee. He must also bear responsibility for the debacle. The individual cannot be allowed to hide behind an heroic background in the Great Patriotic War, nor can he escape responsibility by quietly slipping into luxurious retirement. He must be brought to book and punished for his catastrophic negligence.'

Molenski put the papers down and wondered who'd sent them. Was it a warning from a friend or a threat from an enemy? He decided either way it didn't matter very much. He was just tired, tired of the system.

Across the field, in the distance, he saw a black car draw up at the gates of the Dacha. The guard came from his tiny hut and spoke to the occupants. Even a retired member of the Politburo got a guard, but was it to protect or inform? The guard opened the gates and let the vehicle through.

Comrade Molenski locked the door of his study. He took the old Nagant pistol from a drawer. It was the one he'd carried during the siege of Stalingrad. He'd kept a single bullet in the chamber. He'd have used it on himself to avoid capture by the enemy. The bullet was still there.

When the two officers from the NKVD kicked open the door to Molenski's study they found him slumped over his desk, a pool of blood around his head. They both agreed that it was most probably for the best.

The Valley of the Shadow

KGVI Barracks Harare, Zimbabwe 23rd July 1982

The journey to KGVI took place in silence. The entrance was flooded with lights. Guards at the barrack gate recognised the car and raised the barrier without question. Tyoni drove straight to the building reserved for the 5th brigade. Only one other car was in the parking area.

"Come with me," ordered Joshua Sovimbo.

Tyoni followed his master into the familiar building. They went down the corridor to the office reserved for the Commander. There was no secretary or adjutant in the anti-room. The door to the main office was slightly open and the light inside on.

Joshua raised his voice and knocked on the door. "Colonel Donga. It is Joshua. I have come."

From inside a voice replied. "Ah, Joshua, you are here, come in, shut the door. I have important news, good news."

"Wait here," Joshua ordered Tyoni as he disappeared into Donga's office.

The only available seat was the secretary's chair in the anti room. Tyoni walked around the desk and sat down.

Before the Goromonzi incident Joshua would have told him all that was happening, but now it was silence and closed doors. Tyoni cursed Joshua for using the cattle prod. At first it was as much for the humiliation as the pain. Now exclusion increased his feeling of estrangement.

He swivelled the chair around to look out the window. Nothing was to be seen in the dark apart from a few distant lights across the parade ground. Then the box on the desk, the little speaker, clicked and he heard clear metallic voices, the unmistakable sounds of Joshua and Colonel Donga talking. He was not to know that inside Donga had tossed a file onto his desk. The edge of the file came to rest on the tiny Bakelite lever of the intercom. The line would remain open until the pressure was taken from the spring loaded switch. Tyoni wondered if he should tell them. But no, he waited – and listened.

"..this is why he has given his permission. All dissidents and those that support them can be dealt with. You will have the pleasure of choosing and striking the first blow."

"You do not want to choose for yourself?" asked Joshua.

Donga replied. "I can be honest with you because we both desire different things. It is of no relevance to me where the attack on the Matable begins so long as it is vicious and without mercy. My only objective is to scare the white farmers, to make them want to leave our country of their own accord. The world is watching our new country. If we were to attack the white farmers directly there would be an outcry. But the people who protect them care little for Africans. Their high morals do not apply when black people kill black people. So by creating terror in the country, civil war, we will depress land prices and I will then take their land cheaply and without protest. But you, you are different, you have a different motive."

"This is true," replied Joshua.

Tyoni could imagine but not see Joshua gently feeling the scar under his shirt.

"I have a score to settle. I will destroy Shabani and all the people who live there. It will be sweet retribution for me. Already I have killed the Chief. Now I will kill his children and grandchild. I will destroy the blood line. On the 26th of July it will be the end. It has been a long time coming. As I promised them, fire will fall from the sky and destroy everything."

"That is good."

Joshua lowered his voice, almost to a whisper. He spoke of the incident with Tyoni, how his servant had raised a gun to his master. "I have decided that he too must go. It is like having a dog. Once they have bitten they get the taste and will only bite again. It is better to get rid of them immediately and not wait for the second attack. I can no longer trust Tyoni. His fate is sealed."

"It would be a kindness," said Donga. "Now let us drink a whisky to the success of our plans."

Before the glasses had been emptied and laid on the desk Tyoni had left the barracks and was driving towards the southern suburbs.

BETA Bottle Store, Shabani, 24th July 1982

Duncan's car was parked under the shade of the only tree, a spreading Acacia, a few yards from the ramshackle bottle store that stood on the main road at the Shabani turn off. He paced to and fro kicking the dusty ground. Two ancient toothless Africans sat on the bare planks of the stoop. They played draughts on a home made board using bottle tops for checkers. Curiosity got the better of one who would occasionally raise his head and look toward the stranger. Strangers, particularly white ones, were unwelcome in uncertain times.

Duncan took a swig of his Coke, draining the bottle. He wondered how long it would be before she came. It felt like he'd been there an age. Maybe she would not come at all! Since the day she'd left he'd wished and waited for this moment and now his heart was pounding. He didn't know what he was going to say – he didn't know what she would say. The last time had been in his culture, now he would intrude on hers. He knew he would also have to tell her about Morgan and the danger he was in. How he and his twin might have perished or been captured. It would be a harsh first message, one of little hope. Time passed slowly.

The drive from Harare had taken more than six hours. He'd driven slowly. He'd convinced himself it was to conserve fuel but really it was because he was nervous. He'd decided not to drive into her village. He came to the turn and the bottle store. There was a waiting decrepit taxi. He stopped and scribbled a note. The taxi driver struggled to understand at first but then he'd gone, gone to give Elizabeth the message and bring her back. Now Duncan just waited. He saw the cloud of dust before he saw the vehicle. There had been no rain for a long time, the dirt road was dry. He recognised the white Peugeot. The taxi was returning. His heart pounded as it pulled up a few yards away. The driver got out, his face expressionless. Before he turned to walk away he opened the back door. Elizabeth got out. She was exactly as he remembered her. The image in his mind had indeed proved to be indelible.

Duncan took a few steps forward but stopped short.

"You took my keys!" he said.

She raised her right hand and opened her clenched hand to reveal the keys for Duncan's house.

"I kept them," she said. "Here, take them back."

"I don't want then. You keep them," he replied.

For a while they faced each other in silence. Duncan looked at the child that hung to his mother's leg, trying to hide in her skirts. He kneeled to look at the boy. Even to his unobservant masculine mind the resemblance was striking. "My child," he said. It was a statement not a question.

"Yes. He's called James, after your friend. Just like you wanted," Elizabeth said softly.

Duncan stood motionless, unable to check the tears that rolled down his cheeks. Elizabeth moved toward him. Duncan picked up his son and for the first time the family embraced.

Alone Tyoni drove through the night. Insects splattered onto the windscreen; wipers smudged their blood and the washers smeared the mess even more. Every few miles he stopped to scrape and rub the glass clean. Then there was the game. Twice he'd had to break hard to avoid giant Kudu in the middle of the road, frozen by the glare of his headlights. It was a dangerous journey soured even more by bitter thoughts of treachery and recrimination.

Que Que, still not half way. Another roadblock. The fifth so far. He slowed. The uniforms were different now. The last time they'd worn the blue of the police. The new ones were camouflage fatigues and the red berries of the 5th Brigade.

Tyoni wound down the window. Bright lights shone in his face, they were intended to blind him and they worked. A body came up to the side of the car. Tyoni passed out his CIO identity card. The guard looked at the unfamiliar document, unsure if he should accept it. Tyoni then offered his party card, ZANU membership. It was marked ex-combatant. The guard smiled, handed back the documents and waved Tyoni through. "Pamberi!" he shouted.

"Pamberi," Tyoni replied without enthusiasm. 'Forward', the old battle mantra had become a sign of solidarity which was an irony as he'd never felt so alone and detached.

Through the night he thought how he'd transgressed the norms of civilisation just to please his master. He saw the faces of those he'd dispatched to another place. He knew he could not bring them back but somehow he would thwart the treacherous dog's desire for more blood. He'd left the main road and hidden the car in the bush. The last mile would be walked, in the open, unarmed.

The guard on the kopje overlooking the kraal had been re-instated but now he did not look for the white soldiers, he watched for men of his own colour. Through the night he'd struggled to stay warm without fire. He'd huddled under a tanned cow hide and silently looked into the darkness as the village slept. Matable guards did not fall asleep. The penalty was death, an effective sanction adopted by the British Army in times of crisis.

In the new daylight he saw the lone figure walk along the worn track being deliberately conspicuous. The guard cupped his hands and howled into the sky imitating the piercing cry of a roaming hyena. The sound carried over the still air. In the village people quickly scurried. Nobody would be allowed to just walk in and kill indiscriminately again. A group of panga carrying men assembled at the entrance. The gate of the Kraal was closed. Other men were concealed in huts with more forbidden lethal weapons. Others hurried around the perimeter watchful for a sneak attack from the rear when everybody's attention was distracted. Away from the entrance women ushered children together into a distant hut. Only dogs and chickens roamed freely.

The stranger stopped ten yards short of the gate and waited according to custom. Inside Morgan prepared to approach the stranger. A youth came up to Morgan and spoke.

"I have looked. The one outside came with the 5th Brigade. He helped to kill Dingiskani," said the youth. "Of this I am sure."

"I am tempted to kill him now without further word." Morgan's words were deliberate and not in temper.

Tembo came to his brother's side. "We should find out what he wants first. Killing him will bring trouble down on us. We should hear what he has to say"

Morgan nodded and stepped forward. A youth opened the gate and Morgan stepped out and stood in front of the stranger.

"The last time you were here my father died and you played a part in his death. Tell me why I should not kill you now?"

"Because if you kill me now all the people of the village will die," said Tyoni.

"So your comrades will come to take revenge if we harm you?"

"No. I no longer have any Comrades. But I do have information, information that will save your lives," replied Tyoni.

"Why would a Shona who has only done us harm in the past want to help the Matable? And why should I believe you? In the past there has been nothing but treachery," said Morgan.

"In that you are correct. We have done things that are wrong and I have been part of those things but they will look small compared to what is about to happen."

"What weapons do you have?" asked Morgan.

"None," he replied.

"I will search you then you can come into the Kraal if you dare, but be warned, I do not guarantee that you will walk out."

Tyoni followed. On Morgan's signal strong hands grabbed him and searched for hidden weapons. Tembo and Morgan led the procession to the big hut.

"Not the food I used to cook for you," said Elizabeth handing Duncan an enamel bowl of maize porridge.

"No," said Duncan, prodding the thick glutinous mass. "Not quite bacon and eggs."

He looked at Elizabeth sheepishly. She responded with a smile that was rather more sincere. The child sat next to his father, cross legged, using fingers to scrape his own breakfast bowl clean.

"You use the name James," said Elizabeth. "I thought when you saw him you would call him Jimmy. I only called him James at birth because the nurses told me it was correct in your way."

"So, you thought I would see him? That's good. For me James is a good name. It suits him."

"Is it strange for you to be here, in my village? You are the first white man that has slept in the Kraal."

"Sleeping on the floor was not new to me, but in the same hut as your brothers was nerve racking. Not long ago we were trying to kill each other."

"I would never have let them kill you. We knew you were not the same as the others for a long time," said Elizabeth.

"How long do we have to stay in here?" asked Duncan, "It would be good to go outside."

"We should wait. My brothers will call us when it is time."

The three men sat in the dark hut, cross legged, facing each other. For twenty minutes Tyoni had spoken uninterruptedly, telling his story to Morgan and Tembo, before finally giving his stark warning of the air attack.

Tembo got to his feet and walked around the hut. "What you say may be a trap, something to make us act foolishly and give the Shona another reason to attack us," said Tembo. "We need more than what you have given before we act."

Tyoni spoke again. "What I have told you is true but you do not have much time to think about it. If you do not act now it will be too late. I know of no other way of proving it to you."

Tembo came to his feet and spoke. "You will wait here. We will talk in private. There will be guards. Do not try to leave." Morgan followed his twin out of the hut.

They passed out of earshot. "We must talk with our sister," said Morgan.

"This is clear," replied Tembo.

Even in the hut's dim light Tyoni recognised the new faces that returned to the hut with the Twins.

Duncan saw the captive's eyes quickly drop, but too late to hide the glint of recognition. They sat. Duncan broke the silence. "Tell me how you know me."

"Once I saw you fight bravely, even killing one of my comrades," answered Tyoni.

Tyoni spoke of the night in Mashava when he had waited to ambush the people fleeing from the hostel and how Duncan had foiled the trap by taking everybody away on a bus. He told how, too late, they realised what was happening and how he'd arrived at the front of the building just to see Duncan kill Wilfred and make his escape.

"I do not remember you," said Duncan.

"There were many of us," said Tyoni.

"And what else do you know of me?" asked Duncan.

Tyoni shook his head. "Ah, I know you can be indecisive. If you had more resolution then we would not be sitting here now and many more people would be alive."

"What do you mean?" said Duncan. "Nobody has said that of me before."

Tyoni continued. "Joshua Sovimbo, the one that causes us trouble now, had the war name of Makonzo. He was not just feared by the white's and the Matable. Even some of our own knew he was too much to let live. It was decided by his own father he was to be tried and punished for his excesses. Because of this he killed his father. He was being taken to be handed to the Mozambican authorities when the whites attacked. The car taking him away escaped but was ambushed, ambushed by you. I came later and found all the people dead except Sovimbo. He told me it was you that led the attack, the same one that had driven the bus at Mashava, and it was you that had failed to pull the trigger on him. He'd laughed and said it was proof that the White man was in the end too weak and because of this they would lose the war. Now the man that you let free has killed the Chief of this village and has vowed to come back and kill everybody else. You must take some responsibility for this. "

For a while there was silence, then Morgan spoke. "Is it true what this man says?"

Duncan remembered the raid and the ambush. He spoke. "There was such an incident. I did not kill the man in the back of the car because he was tied up and defenceless. Once, a long time ago I had been in such a situation. Then I was young. That time I made the wrong decision and killed an innocent man. I paid a heavy price for my mistake."

Tembo spoke this time. "You again have made a mistake. Your misplaced compassion had resulted in the death of your child's grandfather and may even now end in the death of your child. You have no choice but to help correct the situation. It is clear that the only way that the people of this village can be saved is if Joshua Sovimbo is eliminated."

"It must be done," said Duncan, "and I must try and stop the planes. There is somebody who might be able to help. Tyoni will be kept, a prisoner here till the arrangements are made. But I must know how long do we have and where will we find Sovimbo?"

"You have no more than two days including this one. I know Sovimbo will be at Thornhill Airbase, ready, anticipating. I will stay here as you wish, if that is your decision. But really you should let me come with you. I can help get you close and I also have good reason to see the end of him."

"Duncan I know it's public phone to public phone but we really should not be having this conversation."

"Well stop using my fucking name then, and I won't use yours," replied Duncan.

"Okay. Point taken. But be careful," said Stuart Cameron speaking from a phone booth in the lobby of Meikles Hotel, Harare.

Duncan had quickly cobbled together the bones of a plan. It was simple and lacking detail but it was the best that could be done. There'd be virtually no preparations and definitely no dummy run. And he had to warn Stuart as well. He left the village and drove to Bulawayo. There'd been road blocks. Tension was high but his white face had got him through. Whites were no longer the enemy. Only blacks with the wrong Party card had to worry. Duncan saw that at each road block guards had rows of African civilians hunched down at the road side under armed guard. The trouble had started.

"What you feared was going to happen to the villages is going to happen," said Duncan.

"When? How reliable is your information, what's the source?"

"As soon as tomorrow morning," replied Duncan. "My source was close to the person organising the operation but he's turned. The first villages will see Napalm tomorrow morning."

"How can you be sure he's not setting this up?"

"I can't," replied Duncan, "I just believe him. Listen I've told you. I'm off. Do what you can with London. I've got my own plan to implement. This is something I have to do."

"Frankly given the timescale nothing is going to happen from the London end," said Stuart. "It's too late for that."

"Then a lot of innocent people are going to die at the wrong end of attacks by planes supplied by the British Government. The Prime Minister can carry her share of the blame for the catastrophe that is going to happen then."

"Where are you going now? I might need you."

"I'm not standing idle by. I have half a plan," said Duncan. "I'm going to try and clip the wings of some Hawks and put the gamekeeper in his place."

"You can't do that alone," replied Cameron.

"I'm not alone but I could do with help. Are you in?" asked Duncan.

"I don't know yet, I need time to think."

"If you decide yes bring what you can to the party. We'll meet at the Golden Mile Motel, Que Que. Tomorrow. Four PM.

Hanger 6, Thornhill Airbase, Gwelo. 25th July 1982

The olive green Peugeot 406 staff car led the convoy that left Harare's Inkomo barracks at 3am. Behind the staff car were twelve Hino lorries and a splattering of Chinese made jeeps. Racing ahead were the Brigades motorbike outriders on 500cc singly pot Yamaha trial bikes. Because of the predominance of Chinese and Japanese vehicles the column was nicknamed the 'Orient Express'. The vehicles drove through the northern suburbs of Salisbury in the dead of night. Dogs barked disturbing the silence, but few people stirred. Police were positioned at every set of traffic lights and waved the column through. Clear of the city the convoy built up speed to forty miles per hour. They travelled faster than a standard unit of the Zimbabwean Army, but this was not a standard unit, it was the 'flying column' of the 5th Brigade. The convoy passed through the sleeping towns of Norton, Kadoma and finally Que Que. After Que Que the main body slowed allowing two jeeps and a lorry to go ahead. It was exactly 6am that the advance vehicles arrived at Thornhill's main entrance. A red and white pole blocked access to the Airbase. All was not quiet. They were expected. Even so the activity was disorganised and frenzied. Telephones rang and bleary eyed Zimbabwe Air Force guards, not used to early hour's duty, milled around.

A quarter of an hour earlier unprecedented 'Flash' orders had arrived at the base. They came directly form the Defence Ministry. The codes were correct. There was no mistake. Confirmation had been requested and had been received. The Duty Officer had no choice but to obey and let the convoy pass onto his base. He'd immediately called the Base Commander, Dickey Evans. That was the limit of his resistance.

Once the red and white pole had been lifted the vehicles moved forward and stayed close together, moving towards the final destination of hanger 6, the only bombproof shelter on the airbase, the hanger chosen to house the pride of the Zimbabwe Airforce, the four new Hawk jets freshly painted and ready to go. Within twenty minutes, well before the Base Commander's Land Rover came into view, the 5th Brigade troops had de-trucked and established a defensive perimeter. The Base Commander, himself a pilot who'd flown combat sorties for years, was shaking with rage. He'd been on the Green Leader raid over Zambia and was not easily unnerved, but now he was annoyed, very annoyed. He drove the Land Rover himself, straight for the hanger, screeching to a halt on the concrete hard standing close to the rear personnel door where the 5th Brigade vehicles had clustered.

"Get out of my way," he'd said to a guard that blocked his passage.

The soldier didn't speak but stood his ground.

"Move," ordered Evans.

The guard cocked his gun and pointed it towards the Base Commander. Tense moments passed. From the personnel door came a 5th brigade officer. He nodded to the Base Commander and led him into the hanger, to see the one who'd lead the intrusion.

"Who are you?" demanded Dickey Evans. He didn't wait for an answer. "This situation is diabolical. I am the Base Commander of Thornhill and I have both responsibility and authority for the facilities, equipment and personnel at this establishment. I will be speaking to Air Marshall Walsh immediately. What is the reason for this intrusion?"

The response was calm. "I am General Albert Donga. I command the 5th Brigade. I am the ranking officer here and I have my orders. You are at liberty to contact your Commanding Officer but I think you will find that Air Marshall Walsh is powerless to intervene. My mission is one of national importance, you must understand this. Your unquestioning co-operation is demanded."

"I want to know what is going on," demanded Dickey Evans "That is just common courtesy. But more, I am informed that you are bringing prohibited ordnance onto this base. Will you confirm this?"

"Prohibited ordnance?" asked General Donga with raised eyebrows. "What is prohibited ordnance?"

"Napalm bombs, General. Napalm. Is that correct?"

"Your men are quick and observant over matters that are of no concern to them. As of now this hanger, the attached armoury, the Hawk Jets and the pilots that fly them are no longer under your command. I have my own support staff. You need not concern yourself over the niceties of war. Although I point out that you did not appear to be so fussy during the war of liberation when you dropped cluster bombs on innocent Shona villages on a daily basis."

"I protest. Never did the Rhodesian Airforce contravene the

rules of war."

"Bullshit," said Donga. "Get out of this hanger before I have you arrested. But take this with you." He handed the Base Commander a typewritten sheet of paper.

"What is this?" he said.

"It is my requirements in terms of refuelling and practice sorties for the Hawks this afternoon. May I suggest you cancel whatever plans you had for the day? Mine take precedence. You will receive our requirements for tomorrow in due course."

"Perhaps it has escaped your attention," retorted Evans, "This is a dual base. What about the civilian operators? We share the runway with private airlines."

"Not anymore," replied Donga, "Tell them to go. I will be coming to the Operations building shortly, you will make space. I will also require accommodation in the Officer's Mess for my representative and you will provide billets for the Company of men that accompany me, together with the usual messing facilities! Do not attempt to enter this hanger without the permission of my senior officer. An armed guard will be left on the building overnight."

The Base Commander knew he'd lost. He marched out of the hanger, struggling to contain himself. General Donga turned to face Joshua Sovimbo who had been standing silently behind.

"Not as difficult as I thought," said the General with a smile. "The way is clear now. The pilots and armours can get to work. Everybody knows their duty. I leave you, Joshua Sovimbo, to control the mission which after all is your inspiration. Tomorrow you will rain fire on the Matable Sell-outs. It will be your day of glory."

Joshua Sovimbo smiled. The hidden scar on his chest prickled as it always did when he thought of the Matable.

Golden Mile Motel, Que Que, Zimbabwe. 1300 hrs.

The Golden Mile Motel stood back off the main highway. Its bright yellow and white colour scheme promised casualness. Duncan picked the Golden Mile because it was only fifteen miles north of Thornhill Airbase. The Motel was an American inspiration, single story chalet accommodation with parking in front of each unit. It was always busy, a place where a few men staying for a day or so would go unnoticed.

Four men, Duncan, Tyoni, Morgan and Tembo, gathered in one of the rooms. Morgan and Tembo sat silently on a bed whilst Duncan huddled with Tyoni at the dressing table, sketching a layout of Thornhill. The silence was suddenly broken by a loud rap on the door. Without word three men picked up the weapons that were scattered around and packed themselves into the bathroom. Duncan, unarmed, answered the door and was relieved to see Stuart Cameron.

"This goes against all my instincts and training," said Cameron when he'd settled into the room. "It has the makings of a fool's mission. The risks are too high for the probability of success."

The silence was eventually broken by Duncan.

"Do you have an alternative? I don't think so. You would not be here otherwise. None of us would. Morgan and Tembo are trying to save their people, Tyoni seeks to redeem himself. I want to protect what has become important to me. And you Stuart have a duty to save people from the result of your Government's actions and to save that Government of yours in London embarrassment. We are all here because there is no alternative."

Cameron ignored the outburst, changing the subject. "I brought what I could lay my hands on. It's mostly borrowed from KG5. C5 a few satchel charges, detonators and timers. I doubt if they will ever miss the stuff. What other contributions are there?"

"We've got enough hand weapons and ammunition," replied Duncan. "Tyoni brought the latest 5th Brigade Intelligence Reports."

"What about a plan? Is there a plan? Does anybody have an idea of how we're going to achieve our objective? asked Cameron.

"We're working on something. It's simple really. We break into the camp, drive up to the hanger, blow up the planes and then leave."

"Glad you've got that organised then," said Cameron laughing. "Shall we try and join the dots?"

Joshua Sovimbo emerged from the shower avoiding looking at himself in the mirror. He never looked at himself in the mirror unless he had to, his eyes would only focus on his scars. Te first day had gone well at Thornhill. Now he was dressed in a commandeered officer's uniform, a uniform he was not entitled to wear. He looked out of the window across the expanse of the airfield and could make out the lights around Hanger 6. All appeared quiet. He'd left a guard of half a dozen men to keep watch overnight.

Sovimbo went through the plan in his mind. Everything was ready. The bomb racks had been fitted to the Hawks and the release mechanism tested. The pilots had flown test sorties. In the morning the Napalm would be fetched from the adjacent armoury. The bombs would be fixed to the planes. After fuelling, the planes would go. That was it. But tonight he would join the white officers in their Mess. He would eat their food and drink their whiskey. Not that he craved their company, in fact quite the opposite. He knew how much his presence made them feel uncomfortable and that gave him pleasure.

Exactly on schedule the car pulled up at the base's main barrier. Tyoni drove, Tembo sat next to him. The guards at the main gate were nervous. Tyoni wound down the car window. It was the same car he'd taken from KG5 barracks three nights previously, the night he'd heard Sovimbo plan his death. Without question the guard lifted the barrier. Suspicious Tyoni leaned out of the window.

"Don't you check passes any more?"

"You're 5th Brigade. I can see from the car. The orders are not to hinder you. Your Commanding Officer is in the Mess and the troops are billeted in the main barracks building. What else do you want to know?"

"It's the Hawks we've come for," said Tyoni with ironic truthfulness.

"There in hanger 6. Shall I phone ahead?"

"No, definitely not. We want to check the guards alertness."

Tyoni put the car into first gear and drove forward, following signs for the workshops, manoeuvring through the maze of buildings that had sprouted up over the years. He turned to look at Tembo with a grin on his face.

"I never thought it would be that easy to get in," he said. "They never even wanted to check us out."

"I saw," said Tembo,"It was too easy, the sentry was nervous and did you hear him say about the guards in the barracks. He thinks we're the 5th Brigade. There must be a lot of them here, guarding the planes."

"We'll worry about that later. Let's get to the workshops as planned."

A rough track ran outside and parallel to the perimeter fence. It was intended to give emergency vehicles access to the fire break in the event of a bush fire. Morgan had spotted it on the large scale ordnance survey map. The start of the track had been difficult to find in the dark and when they had found it they'd gone onto side lights. Morgan walked in front of the pick up, directing. Progress had been slow, but now they were in position. The truck was turned, facing the right direction for a quick get away. The three bergans were unloaded. Twenty yards to their left, through thin scrub, was the chain link fence that marked the boundary of the airfield. Morgan had gone ahead and waited for the signal. Duncan and Cameron prepared to join him.

Tyoni drove slowly, obeying the 10mph speed limit. He knew where he was going. On the left they passed the engineering admin block then came the electrical and mechanical workshops after that the garage and finally what they wanted, the motor pool. Dousing the lights he steered the car into the yard and tucked it up behind a three tonner that was standing there, engine removed for maintenance. Tyoni passed wire cutters and an empty fertiliser bag to Tembo.

"What's the bag for?" asked Tembo

"To mark the hole in case we need to find it fast in the dark. Old trick the Chinese taught us."

"Russians told us not to bother," replied Tembo. "If it's seen somebody can set an ambush. Or worse still move the bag a few yards and then we're fucked. That really helps in an emergency."

"Never thought of that," said Tyoni. "Maybe the Chinese aren't so smart after all. I'll meet you back here in ten minutes." Tyoni disappeared into the darkness. Tembo made his way to the perimeter fence. The links yielded easily to the cutters. Soon he had cut a flap, large enough to take a grown man. He cupped his hands and blew. The sound was of a bullfrog to anybody but his twin. The call was returned and in a moment he saw Morgan running towards him, crouched slowed by the weight of the bergan in his arms.

"Pass the bag to me brother. Come quickly. It is now we are most vulnerable."

Morgan passed the bergan through the hole and followed. Next came Cameron and then Duncan. Soon all four waited between the vehicles.

"Why is Tyoni so long?" asked Morgan.

"Maybe we were wrong to trust him," said Tembo.

"It is too late for you to think of that now," said Duncan. "If he is a traitor we will all soon be dead. But I don't think you have to worry about that."

Cameron broke in. "I have seen the intelligence reports. Tyoni truly takes a risk tonight. If caught he will suffer a slow death, the same death that his family suffered in last couple of days on the instruction of Sovimbo. He's lost everything and is as motivated as the rest of us this night."

From the dark came a voice. "It is true," Tyoni stepped from the shadows. "Not only do I carry the guilt of having committed evil actions for my mentor, but my punishment for those deeds has come from the same person. I will thwart him and have my revenge"

"I did not mean to doubt you," said Tembo.

"Here I stole these from the workshops."

He threw some dirty overalls on the ground in front of the others. Quickly they pulled on the one piece air force coveralls, the ones used by the maintenance engineers at Thornhill. Cameron was the first to finish. He grabbed the bergan with the weapons and withdrew the AK's from inside.

"Made in China. Folding wire stock. Useful for our needs." He passed the weapons around.

"We have only eight grenades between us. Use them sparingly. There are four magazines for each gun. If you need more bullets you will have to take them from the enemy! Now let's pick our transport. See if any of the long wheel base Land Rover's have keys in the ignition."

Joshua Sovimbo had drunk two large whiskeys in the bar as he waited for the Hawk pilots to join him. He surveyed the white's in the room. Those whom he gazed at quickly looked away. He felt their fear. This was the feeling of victory he'd longed for. At eight o'clock they appeared at the door, his guests the pilots, exactly on time. Sovimbo walked away from the bar towards the lobby. The waiter followed and intercepted him.

"Could you sign the chit Sir, two whiskeys, it's for your account."

Sovimbo looked at the waiter with disdain and walked on without word, reserving a broad smile for his guests. He put his large arms around the shoulders of the nearest two pilots and led them across the hall to the matre'd at the door of the dining room. The others followed.

"I will sit with my pilot guests in a private room," said Sovimbo.

"I'm afraid that's not possible," replied the Maitre d' "It is necessary to book private dining rooms twenty-four hours in advance. It's the staff you see sir. We don't have anybody available to serve. I can give you a very nice table inside the main dining room however."

Sovimbo leaned forwards and grabbed the Maitre d' by the lapels of his dinner jacket. "A private dining room, it is not a request."

"Sir." The man was unable to control his shaking. "I will arrange it."

The silence that overcame the hall quickly spread to the bar and dining room. The matre'd returned.

"Follow me please Sir." He led them to a panelled room off the main hall way. "Your table will be set immediately. Can I get you drinks in the mean time?"

"I will have a large malt whiskey. No bring the bottle. My guests are not drinking. They have work to do tomorrow. Apart from the waiters I do not want to be disturbed. More than your job depends on it. Do you understand?"

"It is perfectly clear Sir."

Tyoni drove. Duncan sat next to him. The other three were in the back of the canvas topped Land Rover. They travelled the pristine roadways slowly.

"Go left," said Duncan.

"It is not the way," replied Tyoni.

"Just go left. Go towards the fuel tanks over there." Duncan pointed to two cylindrical tanks that stood at least thirty feet high.

"Stop away from the security lights," he said. "Stuart, pass me a block of C5 and a timed detonator. I have an idea. The tanks are diesel and petrol for the trucks. I'll place a charge to go off at 2pm. We'll either be long gone by then or in the shit. Either way we'll be thankful for the distraction." Duncan slipped out of the stationary Land Rover and, unseen, disappeared over the bund wall surrounding the tanks. Five minutes later he returned.

"Right let's get back on track, head straight for the hangers."

Tyoni started to pull away driving back between service buildings. As they neared the junction, a lone figure stepped out of the shadows. A European in airforce fatigues. He stepped into the road and held up his hand. Tyoni's only choices were to stop or run him over. He chose the first.

"Hey, you guys going over the accommodation block? Can you give me a lift? I've been stuck, working late on urgent maintenance lists for the morning. I'll jump in the back."

Without waiting for an answer the airman walked around the back lifted the canvas flap and began to climb into the Land Rover. His eyes had not adjusted to the dark. He was half way in before he realised others were already there, strangers with guns. Too late he started to withdraw. The strong arms of Tembo and Morgan pulled the airman inside.

"What the fuck......."

Morgan punched the man in the rib cage. He was winded and collapsed in a heap, gasping for breath.

"Best be quiet if I were you," said Cameron to the airman before turning his attention to Tyoni. "Find a quiet corner so we can have a word with our new friend."

Tyoni drove between two buildings, around the back, parking behind a pile of fifty gallon oil drums stacked two high. He doused the vehicle lights. They were in almost total darkness, Duncan shone a flashlight in their prisoner's face.

"We need a few words,' he said. "You can do it the easy way, tell us what we want to know and I'll leave you tied up till morning, or I can pass you over to my friends here who might not be so friendly." Duncan nodded towards Tembo and Morgan. Morgan unsheathed a bayonet and made a motion, as if slitting his own throat.

"I'm only a mechanic," said the prisoner, fear clearly in his voice. "I don't know anything?"

"That's okay. Lets start with your name and we'll go on from there shall we," said Duncan.

"My name's Nigel."

Twenty minutes later Nigel was trussed up and gagged. They'd dumped him behind some oil drums with a warning about trying to escape before daylight.

"That was not the worst piece of luck," said Duncan as they drove. Tyoni slowed as they came close to the end of the cluster of service buildings. Morgan and Tembo jumped from the back of the moving Land Rover with their weapons and disappeared into the dark.

Only the isolated hangers lay ahead now. The hangers were not in a row but not because of poor design. The buildings had been purposely placed haphazardly. Any potential enemy trying to bomb the hangers was not going to be presented with a neat row. The lessons of neat rows had been learnt by all air forces during the Battle of Britain and Pearl Harbour. Random was good.

Tyoni drove straight at the hanger, stopping directly in front of the improvised sandbag structure thrown up by the guards of the 5th Brigade. Getting out of the Land Rover Duncan could see 5th Brigade guards pointing their weapons at him.

"Maintenance!" shouted Duncan. "We've come to do repairs."

"No repairs!" A shout came back out of the darkness. "You must go away now."

"Fine," replied Duncan straining his voice. "We'll go now. But can I get your name so I can say we tried to do the job. I don't want to get into trouble when tomorrow's mission gets called off."

There was silence for a moment. "What do you mean?"

"There's a fault with the hanger doors. It was reported last night. They won't open unless we fix them."

"What do you mean," the voice shouted back.

"Hey listen I'm unarmed," Duncan raised his hands. "Can I come forward? It's hard shouting like this."

"Just you. Come forward slowly. Keep your hands in the air."

Duncan walked towards the voice, stopping in front of the sandbags. The guard rose to his feet. Duncan could just make out, in the gloom, the insignia of sergeant.

"Listen," said Duncan, "yesterday when they closed the main hanger doors something went wrong. They put in a maintenance request. The say the doors won't open now. I was told to come over and get them going because there's an important mission going down early in the morning. But, hey guys, if you want me to go away, who am I to argue? Just cover my arse. What's your name?" Duncan produced a maintenance request form from his breast pocket and waved it under the sergeant's nose.

"Wait," said the sergeant, "I will check with my commanding officer."

The sergeant walked to the side of the hanger. Next to the reinforced personnel door was a wall mounted steel box. He lifted the flap to reveal a field telephone. After five minutes the sergeant returned. My CO is eating and cannot be disturbed. You must come back later."

"Fine," said Duncan, "so long as we understand that if there isn't time to fix the problem it's down to you. Personally I think you should at least let me have a look at it. Take care now." Duncan turned to walk away.

"No, wait," said the sergeant. "Show me the problem. "Just you, not your friends."

Duncan led. The sergeant followed gripping his AK tightly. Duncan pulled on the steel personnel door. It was heavy and needed effort to open it. A single 100 watt bulb did nothing but light the immediate area, allowing Duncan to see the giant MEM wall mounted electrical breaker. He hoped he was right as he twisted the lever ninety degrees to the 'on' position. The spring loaded contacts snapped into the closed position. Lights, high up, flickered. Not brightly at first. But as the mercury vapour filaments warmed, the intensity of the light grew and grew until the luminosity matched daylight. Duncan's eyes hurt as his pupils failed to contract quickly enough to block out some of the light. The hanger looked big from the outside but, perhaps because it stood isolated in an open space, the true scale could not be appreciated. Inside the hanger was truly cavernous, big enough to hold two 707's according to Nigel. Duncan looked around what was mainly empty space. The cream walls and red painted floor were spotless. Along the sides were racks and cabinets containing the tools and equipment necessary to maintain aircraft. To the rear of the hanger stood something Duncan had not seen close up since his days in Aden, a lone Hawker Hunter aircraft, its canopy raised and a ladder fixed to the side for the pilot. He could not help but admire the sleek classical lines of the plane that had captured his imagination as a youth. But most important, to the front of the hanger stood the object of his attention, four pristine, state of the art Hawk Jets, their canopies also raised, as if waiting for their pilots to enter.

Duncan turned his attention to the building. He'd learnt about bomb-proof hangers in his training as a combat engineer. He knew about the concrete roof, reinforced with thousands of bars of criss-crossed steel. A hit might crack the concrete but the steel would provide that little bit of give and still hold the structure together. But it was not just the roof that offered protection. The walls and doors were strong enough to resist the impact of a strike from most air to ground missiles. The problem was that the doors became so big and heavy they could only be opened and closed by huge electrical motors driving rack and pinion gearing mechanisms. There were two basic designs of door configuration; the concertina type, which allowed a bigger opening or the overlapping design that was heavier and stronger. This hanger had the latter type.

Duncan walked across the vast floor, past the Hawks and to the side. Bolted to the concrete side wall was a Drysdale electrical circuit breaker box. A Bakelite plaque was attached displaying 'Door Opening/Closing Instructions'.

"Let's try," said Duncan to the sergeant. He read the instruction out loud as he tried to open the doors.

"Twist red stop button till it clicks free. Set open/close toggle lever to open. Continuously press green push button while pulling side ratchet lever till it runs freely."

Nothing happened. Duncan looked to the sergeant. "Buggered. You want to try?"

The sergeant shook his head.

"I have an idea," said Duncan. "I'm just going up top."

The sergeant said nothing as Duncan started to climb the steel ladder that was bolted to the wall, between the switch and doors. The ladder led to a gantry and walkway, high up, alongside the giant rail and hanger brackets that supported the doors. Duncan waited on the platform for a while, out of the sergeant's sight, recalling what Nigel had told him.

"The micro switch that signals that the door is fully closed is buggered. Every time the door gets to the closed position the electrical motor keeps going till it trips the overload on the high level electrical panel. We're waiting for parts to come in. For now the lads that work in the hanger just pop up the ladder and press the reset button. Then the door opens normally. The problem only occurs when you close the door. The crowd that turned up yesterday don't know about the problem!'

Duncan found the high level control panel, pressed the reset switch and made his way back down the ladder.

"Give it another go shall we?" he said to the sergeant.

Duncan went through the instructions. As he ratcheted the side lever, somewhere high up an electrical motor came to life and the giant doors began to move, sliding one over the other, opening. Duncan pressed the 'stop' button after a few seconds and the motor stopped.

"Lets try and close it shall we?"

The sergeant was smiling now.

"You want to do it?" asked Duncan. "Come on I'll show you."

The sergeant laid his AK on a nearby workbench.

"Twist the red button till it pops out. Turn this lever to close," said Duncan. "Good. Now hold that green button and just keep pulling that side lever." The high motor started again and the doors began to close.

"Great," said Duncan. "I'll just give it a final try now. Then I can go."

"I'll do it," said the sergeant.

The sergeant went through the sequence, but when he pushed the green button and ratcheted the lever there was only silence. He turned to look at Duncan with a puzzled expression.

"Don't know what you did there," said Duncan. "Better let me have a go."

After a few abortive attempts Duncan turned to the sergeant. "Nope it's no good. I got to test it some more, maybe strip it down. It will take a couple of hours and I need my assistants."

Joshua Sovimbo sat at the head of the table, steadily working his way through the whiskey bottle. He droned on about his courageous contribution to the War of Liberation. A combination of alcohol immunity and a strong constitution kept him *compos mentis* whilst his guests flagged under the deluge of words and self congratulation. Eventually one dared to say what all wanted to say.

"May I be excused? I need to rest so I can do my best for our cause tomorrow?"

Sovimbo studied the young man. "When I trained to be a fighter I studied day and night. As a young man, like you, I would not let fatigue hinder my efforts. I fought and overcame my tiredness." His seriousness eventually broke into a broad smile.

"But you have not endured what I have endured. It is not fair to make comparisons. I came to my position because I have special powers. It is wrong of me to expect others to be like me. You may go now, but do not fail me tomorrow. Tomorrow will be the most important day of your life."

It was fifteen minutes before midnight when the pilots left the private dining room. Joshua rose and carried the bottle and his glass towards the lounge bar. The Maitre d' stood at the door.

"Is there anything else I can get you Sir?" he asked in a tone of trepidation. He made no attempt to get his client to sign a docket. Sovimbo walked on.

"Just one thing Sir," continued the Maitre d', "I know you ordered me not to disturb you and I followed your instructions. However there was a phone call for you. Apparently one of your men wanted to report ongoing maintenance of some kind in hanger six. He thought you would like to know."

Sovimbo barely nodded an acknowledgement as he passed. The lounge was emptying early, in no small part due to the presence of Sovimbo. With nobody else to address he turned his attention to the barman.

"What is wrong with the people here? Are they scared of their new masters? Does the colour of my skin worry them? What do you say?"

The barman was stiff with fear. Never in his six years had any officer entered into a social conversation with him. It had not happened when the country was Rhodesia and it had not changed since Zimbabwe was born. He did not know what to do or say.

Sovimbo waited for a reply but none came. "Ah! You have been too long with them, the whites. You are brainwashed. Perhaps you will never be liberated in your mind."

Sovimbo became aware of a presence behind him. He turned to find the Duty Officer standing to attention. "Sir."

"What?" said Sovimbo.

"Sir. One of our men is missing. A maintenance engineer. Before I initiate a search, may I ask if his disappearance is connected with the activities of your men?"

Any dullness that was present in Sovimbo's mind soon dissipated. "What maintenance do you carry out at night?"

"None, unless it is of an urgent nature," replied the Duty Officer.

"Get my car and driver and rouse my men from the barracks. Now!"

Cameron sat with Duncan, concealed from view on the high gantry, their only weapons a pistol each stuffed in the back of their pants. Below two guards walked around the hanger, following no particular pattern. They were just there, disinterested and tired.

"We're stuck with those two wandering around," said Cameron referring to the guards. "We need a distraction."

"Not quite stuck," replied Duncan removing two packs of C5 from inside his coveralls. "Make a trip to the Land Rover. Bring me another two packs. Tell Tyoni to bring some more a bit later. Carry some cable back in your hands for them to see. I've got detonators and timers in my pocket."

"Fat lot of good the C5 will do up here," said Cameron.

"Trust me," replied Duncan. "I'll get to work whilst you're away."

Cameron left his pistol behind. "Just in case," he said before he climbed down the ladder and crossed the hanger, heading for the Land Rover that was parked at the rear.

Tyoni was standing at the vehicle. The tail gate was down, held horizontal by its retaining chains. The bergans were pushed back inside. An old jacket that Tyoni had found in the cab lay on the tailgate.

"Anything happening?" asked Cameron in a voice low enough not to be overheard.

"Two by the sandbags," said Tyoni, "The sergeant and another have gone for a walk around the hanger. And there's the two inside of course. But there's some activity just starting over there, around the main administration buildings." Tyoni looked across the open ground. "Just started seeing headlights flashing about. Maybe they found the mechanic?"

They saw them coming, the headlights of several vehicles heading towards them. Suddenly the calmness of the night was broken by the rattle of machine gun fire. The vehicle lights in the distance seemed to dart in all directions as the drivers took evasive action.

"Tembo and Morgan are at work," said Cameron. "Be ready!"

The sergeant came running back, his companion close behind. "What is happening? Is there an attack?"

The two at the sandbags were straining to look into the distance as the two guards from inside came to the door alerted by the gunfire. The wall phone began to ring. The sergeant was some distance away, distracted. Cameron nodded to Tyoni. Each grabbed a bergan. Tyoni pulled the jacket away from the tailgate, exposing two AK's. "They're ready to fire," he whispered as he passed one to Cameron. They got halfway to the doorway before anybody noticed.

"Stop," shouted one of the guards.

Tyoni fired one handed on the turn, the muzzle flash bright and clear in the darkness. The bullets were wholly inaccurate but the effect was enough, the guards dived for cover. It bought precious seconds. They had enough time to duck inside the door. Cameron was first through and was already pushing the heavy steel door shut, even before Tyoni was in. The metal slammed with a thud and Cameron yanked home the security bar into its receiver. Tyoni fumbled pushing the other bolts home as bullets bounced off the outside of the door causing sparks to jump from the inside of the metal.

Duncan leaning over the rails of the gantry shouted, "What's happening?"

"They rumbled us," shouted Cameron in reply. "There's a column coming over. Tembo and Morgan intercepted them. We're locked in. We should be okay for a while. I don't think even an RPG will bring the side door down and they have got no chance with the big doors."

"Bring me the C5, I'll finish this," said Duncan.

Tyoni went up the ladder with the bergan containing the explosives and handed them to Duncan. He worked quickly, running backwards and forward along the gantry.

Tyoni rejoined Cameron on the ground. Duncan leaned over the rail again. "See if you can find a way into the armoury," he shouted. "I'll be down now."

Tyoni was the first to the steel door that was marked *'Danger Explosives'*. He grabbed the giant padlock that held the hasp closed fast. "You got grenades?" he asked Cameron.

"Yes, two."

"Fragmentation or high explosive?"

"One of each. You're getting fussy aren't you?"

"Give me the high explosive one and pass me the insulation tape off that bench. Then leave me alone."

"That's a bit dangerous don't you think," said Cameron.

Tyoni turned and looked at Cameron. "Bullet or bomb, it doesn't make much difference. We'll be dead either way if we don't find a way out."

Tyoni wrapped insulation tape around the grenade, fixing it to the padlock, making sure he could still remove the pin and clip. "Get clear he shouted as he pulled the pin and the clip flew clear under the power of the retaining spring. He dived for cover behind a tool locker. The explosion echoed through the building. Tyoni dashed forward. The padlock was shattered, Tyoni grabbed hold of the remnants that hung limply from the hasp. "Fuck," he shouted.

"Hot?" said Cameron with a smile. "You do need to be careful." Cameron removed the bits of lock with the aid of a rag. He raised the hasp and slid back the bolt. "There you are."

Duncan was back on the ground. The balance of the C5 was on the floor. He moulded two neat balls, bigger than the palm of his hand, out of the plasticine like material. He inserted an aluminium tube detonator into each ball and connected the wires to digital timers. "Fifteen minutes," he shouted as he ran to one of the two rear Hawks. He pushed the C5 balls as far as he could down the engine air intake, deep, as close to the wing root as he could reach. The explosion would not only destroy the engine but also irrevocably damage the plane at its most vulnerable point, where the wing connects to the fuselage. He did the same to the next plane. Cameron and Tyoni joined him.

"What about the front two planes? asked Tyoni.

"Taken care of," replied Duncan. "We just have to worry about ourselves now.

Sovimbo's car arrived in minutes, before he'd even got to the door of the Officer's Mess. The driver must have been sleeping at the wheel.

"Drive past the barracks," he ordered.

The scene was chaotic. In the dull light cast by a few security lights men ran, pulling on clothes, carrying weapons, piling onto their trucks. Major Dota, a calm young officer with childlike features came towards Sovimbo.

"Do you have orders for us?" he asked.

"I believe that somebody is attacking the hanger that houses the Hawks. They may already be inside, posing as maintenance people. You must stop them before they do damage."

The Major spoke quiet words to his lieutenants. Five trucks spluttered to life and moved away as the last of the Company's troops were clambering on board. Sovimbo told his driver to follow closely.

The vehicles ran along the service roads, between the buildings, before bursting out into the open, heading along the taxi ways towards the hangers. The bursts of automatic fire were short lived and unexpected. They came out of the dark and riddled the cab of the first truck. The driver, wounded, lost control of his vehicle and veered off the road onto the rough grass. The truck rolled on until its front wheels suddenly disappeared into an unseen drainage channel bringing it to an abrupt halt. Injured men scrambled out of the rear. Major Dota, himself uninjured, emerged from the cab, clutching his rifle. He shouted orders to his NCO's.

"This attack was only to delay our progress to the hanger. You will organise the remaining fit men from this truck. Chase and find the people who have tried to delay us. I will carry on to our objective." Dota ran towards the undamaged, stationary second truck and climbed onto the driver's side running board.

"Carry on. To the hanger," he shouted.

From a distance Dota saw the guard detail assigned to Hanger six running around as if in panic. One man fired a burst of automatic fire at the personnel door, another fumbled with an RPG launcher. The sergeant ran and pulled the man clear of the door and the one with the grenade launcher fired his missile. It exploded on impact. The smoke cleared. The door was damaged but still intact.

Dota dismounted the truck before it had come to a halt and shouted to his men. "Surround the building, see if you can find a way in. Kill the intruders. Do not wait for orders.

Sovimbo's car arrived, his mind now crystal clear. "Bring me the man who was in charge here, and the rest of the guard detail as well."

The sergeant and his men were paraded before Sovimbo.

"Tell me what happened?" demanded Sovimbo.

The sergeant's words were hardly coherent, his words garbled. Panic ran through his voice. All that was clear was that three men had barricaded themselves inside the hanger and the sergeant thought it was good that he had not let them escape.

Sovimbo listened. As the words penetrated a metamorphosis took place. His neck bulged, veins stood proud on temples and his eyes appeared to glaze. Sovimbo looked to Dota and spoke.

"Shoot him," he said. "Shoot him now."

Major Dota looked directly at Sovimbo with his youthful eyes. He did not understand the gravity of the situation. He spoke to Sovimbo, hoping to bring calm.

"You are not a serving officer of the 5th Brigade. I do not think I can obey this order. I cannot shoot my own man like this."

Sovimbo remained silently dangerous. He upholstered his pistol and released the safety catch. He raised the gun to the sergeant's head, then suddenly changing his mind, turned and shot the major between the eyes. The major dropped to the floor in a heap.

"Who else will disobey me?"

There was only silence.

He pointed the gun at the sergeant's head and pulled the trigger.

"That is the price for stupidity," said Sovimbo, pointing to the prostrate sergeant's body with his pistol. He pulled the trigger once more and the torso jerked in a final spasm. "Now find a way into the hanger before the intruders have time to do damage."

Duncan ran towards the armoury with the last of the explosives. The others followed carrying the weapons.

"What are you going to do?" asked Tyoni, "Blow this place

up?"

"That is exactly what I am going to do."

"But you will kill us too."

"No, I won't," said Duncan as he prepared the explosive charge. "Armoires and magazines are constructed in a special way. Explosions are most dangerous when contained. So stores for explosives are always constructed with a weak point in the building. A part of the construction is designed to give way easily, directing and releasing the energy in a safe way. Sometimes upwards or sometimes out of a side wall. If we lock ourselves in the hanger we will be safe as the armoury blows up. Only those outside are in danger. We will make our escape in the confusion that follows."

"I hope you're right," said Cameron.

"There will be a severe shock wave," said Duncan. "You must press your hands hard against your ears and keep your mouth open. This should save your ear drums. Even so you will most probably not be able to hear for a few minutes. There will be loud ringing in your ears." The three had gone back to the personnel door and crouched in a corner behind packing crates.

"The explosion will immediately draw people. We count to twenty after the explosion and then open this door and run for our Land Rover or the nearest available transport and go. We pick up Tembo and Morgan on the way. Clear?"

"Cameron and Tyoni," nodded.

Duncan looked at his watch. "Thirty seconds. Good luck."

The hanger was surrounded. Sovimbo sat in his car waiting, his heart pounding with rage. There was no easy way to get into the hanger when it was locked down. He looked across the field and watched as an old Willis jeep raced towards the hanger, bringing the explosives that would blow off the personnel door. The jeep arrived bringing with it all four Hawk pilots.

"We came," said one. "We are ready to fight to protect our planes."

Sovimbo nodded. "You cannot help now and I do not want you injured. You will be needed later Go to the side of the building, where it is safe, wait till I call for you."

"Sir." The pilots obeyed. They trotted to the end of the

building and disappeared around the corner.

The C5 itself had been wedged between a bundle of 250llb bombs that were strapped to a wooden pallet. The brittle, high explosive bomb casings shattered and the explosives inside became part of the conflagration that was, once started beyond control.

The armoury was about to be tested. Whilst everything looked strong, the gable end wall was different. Instead of being constructed of solid concrete, reinforced with iron rods, it was built of lightweight cinder blocks and fixed together with a weak mix of mortar. It gave way to the explosion, just as it was supposed to. The whole process, from detonation to the wall disintegrating, took seconds. The four pilots and half a dozen 5th Brigade soldiers that were at the end of the building never knew what happened. They just disappeared into oblivion. Bits of body would be collected in daylight, but it would be impossible to piece them together.

Sovimbo struggled to regain his balance. It reminded him of childhood when he would spin around to get dizzy. He tried to move towards the side of the building but found he couldn't walk in a straight line.

Inside the building, protected and forewarned the effects were less dramatic. Duncan counted to twenty and stood. He slid back the bolts and locks of the armoured personnel door which had become bowed with the effects of the attacks made on it in the last hour. It took the combined strength of the three of them to prise it open, just far enough for them to squeeze through. Duncan was first out, Cameron second. The Land Rover stood alone, twenty yards away, where they had left it. Duncan pointed and began to run.

They were more than halfway to the vehicle before a lone soldier noticed the men running. He shouted, but too many others were shouting too. The panic had not yet abated and his words were lost, the soldier lifted his gun and fired. Loss of equilibrium in his ear drum ensured his aim was hopelessly off target but the rattle of the AK alerted others.

Duncan arrived at the Land Rover first and got into the drivers seat. Cameron jumped on the back. Only then did he notice.

"Tyoni's not with us," shouted Cameron.

Others had seen the two men running and were bringing their guns to bear with increasing accuracy.

"We can't wait," shouted Duncan, firing the engine, "We have to go."

As the Land Rover pulled away Cameron emptied a magazine in the general direction of the soldiers. It had the desired effect, men dived for cover. An extra few seconds had been won.

Sovimbo was looking at the carnage at the side of the building when he heard the first shots. He turned and ran back only to see the Land Rover driving away.

"Follow them," he shouted. "Bring them to me. I want them. They will pay for this."

Men mounted the trucks and followed but already the Land Rover was in the distance. There was a moment of hope for the pursuers when the brake lights came on and it looked like the vehicle was stopping. But it was soon on its way again. They could not have known that Duncan had only slowed to allow Tembo and Morgan to clamber on board.

Sovimbo watched, his knuckles squeezed and white, blood trickling from his palms where he had dug into the flesh with his own nails. From inside the hanger, almost simultaneously, came two muffled explosions. They were much quieter than the first explosion but Sovimbo knew they signified the end of his dream. He walked towards the door. Soldiers followed.

"No, wait here," he said. "I will go alone." He wanted nobody to see his anger and despair. The smell in the hanger was of sweet almonds. C5 had virtually no detectable odour in storage but after ignition the smell was unmistakable. Thin curls of smoke hung in the air but the haze was clearing, the brightness of the mercury vapour lamps forcing its way through. He walked forward and came to the first Hawk. One leg of the undercarriage had collapsed and the plane rested on a single wheel and one wing tip, the wing itself was twisted, evidence of the damage to the air frame. He walked to the next plane. It stood on both undercarriage struts but its back was clearly broken as both wings tips rested on the ground. It did not take an engineer to know that these two planes would never fly again. Sovimbo walked forward to the front two planes near the hanger doors. He saw but did not dare believe his eyes. He walked around them and saw no visible damage. They stood, as he had seen them yesterday, except for a few scratches and dust, pristine and proud. For a moment hope dawned, the situation might be retrieved. Two planes would be enough. He would get pilots from North Korea. It would not be difficult to make more Napalm bombs. The curl of a smile appeared on his face.

"I will still do it!" he said aloud.

Sovimbo never noticed the movement. He was once again locked in his own thoughts. He didn't see Tyoni descend the ladder from the cockpit of the Hawker Hunter, the plane tucked away in the corner of the hanger.

Tyoni knew this moment would come, he just knew it because nobody knew Joshua Sovimbo like Tyoni did. He walked slowly towards his former master, a Browning pistol in his hand, the gun that had been left by Duncan.

Sensing danger Sovimbo turned.

"Ah! It is you, my little hedge-hog. I have missed you. Have you returned to your master?"

Tyoni shook his head. "No. I will never return to you. You are the epitome of evil. You stole my mind; you corrupted me and made me as bad as you. I did things for you that no man should ever do. I cannot live with the things I have done for you. No I have not come back to be with you, I have only come back because I wanted to see your end, nothing more than that."

"So you want the pleasure of killing me with your own hand? If so you are no better than me.

"It matters not if you die by my hand, it only matters that you die," replied Tyoni.

"You have missed your chance. You are too late." Sovimbo looked past Tyoni.

Tyoni unnerved turned, he saw too late, he had no time to dodge, the soldier that stood behind him. He saw the flash from the gun and felt the thuds in his body as the bullets ripped into his flesh. He fell to the ground, twisting to face Sovimbo. Momentarily he felt the emptiness of defeat. Then from high up came crisp cracks. They were hardly explosions. The charges were small. It was precision work, the nearest a combat engineer could come to artistry. The six sliding brackets that held the great hanger doors to the supporting rail were made from cast iron. Cast iron, incredibly strong in compression, has a weakness. It is not resistant to sudden shocks. The small charges that Duncan had fixed to the brackets went off simultaneously and were enough to shatter the brittle metal. Sovimbo turned and saw the doors drop two inches. The bottom of the sixty tonne doors now rested on the ground. Sovimbo did not realise the implication, that nothing secured the top of the doors to the rail any more. He sensed no danger.

Then the last charges exploded the ones between the door

and the vertical stanchions, the door uprights. They explosions provided just enough lateral energy to push the doors away from the vertical. Once moving gravity quickly took over and the doors gained momentum. Too late Sovimbo realised what was happening.

The last reflection in Tyoni's dying eyes was that of the terror stricken face of his tormentor, a moment before sixty tonnes of steel door crushed him and the two remaining Hawks. When all movement had ceased and only dust swirled around the hanger Tyoni allowed his eyes to close. Now he was ready to rest in peace.

Botswana, 23rd March 1983.

The Okavango River begins its journey in Angola and ends in the Kalahari Desert of Botswana. Its year round waters never get to reach the sea. Instead they feed the desert sands, creating one of the most beautiful and remote natural wonders of the world, a lush area of lagoons, islands and floodplains. The fertile land is shared by cattle farmers and magnificent wildlife. The natural wealth of Botswana, the sparse population and gentle people make this land one of Africa's great secret wonders.

"Never could I have imagined this day," said Stuart Cameron settling back in one of the wicker chairs that stood on the stoop, coffee cup in hand. He watched a group of Springbok getting their breakfast drink in the natural pool a couple of hundred yards away from Duncan's house. "It's good of you to share the moment with me."

"I like this part of the day, the early morning," said Duncan. "I always like the African dawn, it is clean and fresh, full of optimism. More than that, today is special, it will be the best day of my life. And as you've been so embroiled with almost every aspect of my life so far how could I not share it with you? It is good that you made the trip from London to be here. I hope you're not too tired to enjoy the moment."

"I can't believe I only got here last night and I feel so rested. Go on, tell me your news," replied Cameron.

"I think you know most of it," Duncan said. "After the do at Thornhill I had to get out of Zimbabwe pretty quickly. The border crossing at Plumbtree was closest. That's how I ended up in Botswana. I know your lot were helpful getting me a resident's permit and all that. It's nice to know the Brits still have some friends in Africa."

"I scraped what money I could together. It was more than I thought. I had bits on deposit from when I worked in Scotland. It was frozen during the Rhodesian war. I couldn't spend it then, sort of enforced savings. Then there was my cash from Mashava. Managed to black market that lot out of Zimbabwe. Then of course there was the chunk you got me from the Army. It was more than enough to put a deposit down and set up this place."

Stuart interrupted. "What made you want to go into cattle ranching though? Bit of a deviation from blowing things up!"

"It seemed like a good idea at the time. I thought there was a bit of potential."

"I don't think that's the whole truth," laughed Stuart.

"It isn't," Elizabeth's soft voice came from behind. "I think I'll join you to make sure he does tell you the truth." Elizabeth sat down next to her husband and held his hand.

"Go on," said Stuart.

"Well I felt a bit bad taking Elizabeth from her brothers and the village and all that. And it wasn't going to be good for Morgan and Tembo. So I thought the Matable are good cattle farmers, I'll get a cattle ranch."

"You mean Tembo and Morgan are here?" said Stuart, barely able to contain his delight.

"Yes. You'll see them later on. They are looking forward to seeing you too," replied Duncan.

"That's great. So you three run the ranch?"

Duncan smiled. "Us and a couple of others."

"You have help?"

"Tell him," Elizabeth pretended to scold her husband.

"It's a bit embarrassing really."

"Go on. You can't stop now."

"Well I reckoned Mugabe wouldn't be able to stop and the village was likely to be a bit of a target so I brought them with me."

"What, the whole village!"

"Well those who wanted to come."

"How many Duncan?"

"Well, if you include the kids, about 150 all in all."

"How do you manage?"

"I've enough for a year or so. They don't want much. We're building huts and growing our own maize. The cattle are doing well. We'll be self sufficient by next year."

"Well I'm buggered," said Cameron laughing aloud. "I just don't believe it."

"It's not really that dramatic," said Duncan. "You have to keep in mind that Africans traditionally moved around. It's only us white chaps that tried to nail them down to a specific place. Borders and even land ownership are recent concepts here and don't carry much weight in tradition. Nobody forced them to come, I promise."

A cry came from the crib.

"Oh! I've woken the baby now."

Elizabeth picked up and cradled her new baby. "Don't worry. She should be awake, it's her special day too, her Christening day."

"Look," said Duncan. He pointed down the path to the left of the house. Young James was leading his charge gently by the hand. It was her first day in Africa, her first day out of Britain in fact. Every so often James stopped to pick a flower from the border and give it to her.

"That was such a nice thing that you did," said Stuart.

"What calling the baby Mary?"

"No. You know what I mean, bringing Mary Scobie from Scotland to be Godmother."

"And to meet James," said Elizabeth.

Printed in Great Britain
by Amazon.co.uk, Ltd.,
Marston Gate.